*Sophie Hannah*

# Little Face

HODDER

First published in Great Britain in 2006 by Hodder & Stoughton
A division of Hodder Headline
This Hodder paperbacks edition 2006

A Hodder paperback

8

A CIP catalogue record for this title
is available from the British Library

ISBN 978 0 340 84032 0


Typeset in Sabon by Hewer Text UK Ltd, Edinburgh
Printed and bound by Clays Ltd, St Ives plc.

Hodder Headline's policy is to use papers that are natural, renewable
and recyclable products and made from wood grown in sustainable
forests. The logging and manufacturing processes are expected to
conform to the environmental regulations of the country of origin.

Hodder & Stoughton Ltd
A division of Hodder Headline
338 Euston Road
London NW1 3BH

*About the author*

Sophie Hannah is a bestselling, award-winning poet. Her latest collection, *First of the Last Chances*, was chosen for the Poetry Book Society's Next Generation promotion in June 2004. She regularly performs her poetry to live audiences nationwide and abroad, and recently won first prize in the Daphne Du Maurier Festival Short Story Competition for her psychological suspense story *The Octopus Nest*. *Little Face* is her first psychological crime novel. Sophie lives in West Yorkshire with her husband and two children. Her website is www.sophiehannah.com.

For my grandmother, Beryl, with love

# I

## *Friday September 26, 2003*

I am outside. Not far from the front door, not yet, but I am out and I am alone. When I woke up this morning, I didn't think today would be the day. It didn't feel right, or rather, I didn't. Vivienne's phone call persuaded me. 'Believe me, you'll never be ready,' she said. 'You have to take the plunge.' And she's right, I do. I have to do this.

I walk across the cobbled yard and down the mud and gravel path, carrying only my handbag. I feel light and strange. The trees look as if they are knitted from bright wools: reds and browns and the occasional green. The sky is the colour of wet slate. This is not the same ordinary world that I used to walk around in. Everything is more vivid, as if the physical backdrop I once took for granted is clamouring for my attention.

My car is parked at the far end of the path, in front of the gate that separates The Elms from the main road. I am not supposed to drive. 'Nonsense.' Vivienne dismissed this piece of medical advice with a loud tut. 'It's not far. If you followed all the silly rules these days, you'd be terrified to do anything!'

I do feel ready to drive, though only just. I have recovered reasonably well from the operation. This could be thanks to the hypericum that I prescribed for myself, or maybe it's mind over matter: I need to be strong, therefore I am.

I turn the key in the ignition and press my right foot

down hard on the gas pedal. The car splutters awake. I turn on to the road and watch my speed rise steadily. 'Nought to sixty in half an hour,' my dad used to joke, when the Volvo was still his and Mum's. I will drive this car until it falls to pieces. It reminds me of my parents in a way that nothing else ever could. I feel as if it is an old, loyal member of my family, who remembers Mum and Dad as lovingly as I do.

I wind down the window, inhale some of the fresh air that hits me in the face, and think that it will take many more horror stories of gridlock before people stop associating cars with freedom. As I hurtle along the almost empty road past fields and farms, I feel more powerful than I am. It is a welcome illusion.

I do not allow myself to think of Florence, of the growing distance between us.

After four miles or so of open countryside, the road on which I am driving becomes the main street of Spilling, the nearest small town. There is a market in the middle and long rows of squat Elizabethan buildings with pastel-coloured fronts on either side. Some of these are shops. Others, I imagine, are the homes of old, rich snobs, bi-focalled bores who witter on endlessly about Spilling's historical heritage. This is probably unfair of me. Vivienne very definitely does not live in Spilling, even though it is her nearest town. When asked where she lives, she says simply 'The Elms', as if her house is a well-known municipality.

Waiting at lights, I rummage in my bag for the directions she gave me. Left at the mini-roundabout, then first right, and look out for the sign. I see it eventually: 'Waterfront' – thick, white, italic letters on a navy blue background. I turn into the drive, follow it round the square domed building and park in the large car park at the back.

The lobby smells of lilies. I notice that there is a tall,

rectangular vase of them on almost every flat surface. The carpet – navy blue with pink roses – is expensive, the sort that will not look dirty even when it is. People with sports bags walk back and forth, some sweaty, some freshly showered.

At reception, I meet a young girl with blonde, spiky hair who is keen to help me. She wears a badge that says 'Kerilee'. I am glad that I chose the name Florence for my daughter, a real name with a history, rather than something that sounds as if it has been made up by a fifteen-year-old pop star's marketing team. I was worried that David or Vivienne would veto it, but luckily they both liked it too.

'My name is Alice Fancourt,' I say. 'I'm a new member.' I hand over the envelope that contains my details. It strikes me as funny that Kerilee has no idea of the significance of this day for me. The meaning of our encounter is completely different in our two minds.

'Oh! You're Vivienne's daughter-in-law. You've just had a baby! Couple of weeks ago, wasn't it?'

'That's right.' Membership of Waterfront is my present from Vivienne, or rather my reward for producing a grandchild. I think it costs about a thousand pounds a year. Vivienne is one of the few people who is as generous as she is rich.

'How is Florence?' asks Kerilee. 'Vivienne's absolutely besotted with her! It'll be lovely for Felix to have a little sister, won't it?'

It is odd to hear Florence referred to in this way. In my mind she is always first – my first, the first. But she is David's second child.

Felix is well known at Waterfront. He spends almost as much time here as at school, taking part in junior golf tournaments, swimming lessons and Cheeky Chimps play days while Vivienne divides her time between the gym, the pool, the beauty salon and the bar. The arrangement seems to suit them both.

'So, are you recovered?' Kerilee asks. 'Vivienne told us all about the birth. Sounds like you had quite a time of it!'

I am slightly taken aback. 'Yes, it was pretty horrendous. But Florence was fine, which is all that matters, really.' Suddenly I miss my daughter terribly. What am I doing at the reception desk of a health club when I could be getting to know my tiny, beautiful girl? 'This is the first time we've been apart,' I blurt out. 'It's the first time I've been out of the house since getting back from hospital. It feels really strange.' I wouldn't normally confide my feelings in a total stranger, but since Kerilee already knows the details of Florence's birth, I decide that it can do no harm.

'Big day, then,' she says. 'Vivienne said you might be a bit wobbly.'

'She did?' Vivienne thinks of everything.

'Yes. She said to take you to the bar before we do anything else, and give you a large cocktail.'

I laugh. 'I have to drive home, unfortunately. Though Vivienne . . .'

'. . . thinks the more tipsy you are, the more carefully you drive,' Kerilee completes my sentence and we both giggle. 'So, let's get you on to our system, shall we?' She turns to the computer screen in front of her, fingers poised above the keyboard. 'Alice Fancourt. Address? The Elms, right?' She looks impressed. Most local people know Vivienne's home by name even if they do not know its owner. The Elms was the last home of the Blantyres, a famous Spilling family with royal connections, until the last

Blantyre died and Vivienne's father bought the property in the nineteen forties.

'Yes,' I say. 'At the moment it's The Elms.' I picture my flat in Streatham Hill, where I lived until David and I got married. An objective observer would have called it dark and boxy, but I loved it. It was my cosy den, a hideaway where no-one could get to me, especially not my more threatening and obsessive patients. After my parents died, it was the one place where I felt I could be myself and express all my loneliness and grief without there being anyone around to judge me. My flat accepted me for the damaged person that I was in a way the outside world seemed unwilling to.

The Elms is too grand to be cosy. The bed David and I share resembles something you might see in a French palace with red rope around it. It is enormous. Four people would fit in it, or possibly five if they were all thin. Vivienne calls it God-size. 'Double beds are for gerbils,' she says. Florence has a spacious nursery with antique furniture, a window seat and a hand-carved rocking horse that was Vivienne's when she was a child. Felix has two rooms: his bedroom, and a long thin playroom in the attic, where his toys, books and cuddly bears live.

The views from the top floor of the house are breathtaking. On a clear day you can see as far as Culver Ridge on one side and the church tower at Silsford on the other. The garden is so big that it has been divided into several different gardens, some wild, some tamed, all ideal for pram walks on a warm day.

David cannot see any reason to move. When I suggest it, he points out how little we could afford to spend on a house. 'Do you really want to give up everything we've got at The Elms for a two-bedroom terrace with no garden?' he says. 'And you work in Spilling now. It's convenient for us to live with Mum. You don't want a longer commute, do you?'

I haven't told anyone, but gloom settles on me like a fog when I contemplate going back to work. I see the world in a different way now, and I can't pretend that I don't.

'I'll just get Ross, our membership advisor, to give you a tour of the facilities.' Kerilee's voice brings me back to the present. 'Then if you want to, you can have a swim, or use the gym . . .'

My insides clench. I imagine my stitches tearing, the still-pink wound gaping open. 'It's a bit soon for that,' I say, one hand on my stomach. 'I've only been out of hospital a week. But I'd love to look round and then maybe have that cocktail.'

Ross is a short South African man with dyed blond hair, muscly legs and an orange tan. He shows me a large gym with a polished wooden floor that contains every sort of machine imaginable. People in lycra sportswear are running, walking, cycling and even rowing, by the look of it, on these sleek black and silver contraptions. Many of them are wearing ear-plugs and staring up at the row of televisions suspended from the ceiling, watching daytime chat shows as their limbs pound the metal and rubber. I begin to realise why Vivienne looks so good for her age.

Ross shows me the twenty-five metre swimming pool and draws my attention to the underwater lighting. The water is a bright, sparkling turquoise, like an enormous aquamarine gemstone in liquid form, throwing and catching light as it moves. The pool has a stone surround and roman steps at both ends. Beside it, there is an area ringed by pink marble pillars that contains a round, bubbling jacuzzi. It is full to the brim, foam and froth seeping over the edge. On the other side of the pool there is a sauna with a sweet, piney smell, and a steam room, the glass door of which is cloudy with heat. A sudden drumming sound startles me and I look up to see rain hitting the domed glass ceiling.

I inspect the ladies' changing room while Ross waits outside. Like everything else at Waterfront, it transcends the merely functional. There is a thick plum-coloured carpet on the floor, and black slate tiles in the toilets and showers. On each surface there seems to be a pile of something tempting: fluffy white bath sheets, complementary bathrobes emblazoned with the Waterfront logo, hand creams, shampoos and conditioners, body lotions, even nail files. Three women are drying and dressing themselves. One rubs her stomach with a towel, making me feel faint. Another looks up from buttoning her shirt and smiles at me. She looks strong and healthy. The skin on her bare legs is pink with heat. Fully clothed, I feel fragile, awkward and self-conscious.

I turn my attention to the numbered wooden lockers. Some are open a fraction and have keys dangling from them; others, without keys, are shut. I circle the room until I find Vivienne's, number 131, chosen because Felix's birthday is the thirteenth of January and because it occupies an enviable position, close both to the showers and to the door marked 'Swimming Pool'. Vivienne is the only member of Waterfront who has her own dedicated locker that no-one else is allowed to use. They keep the key for her behind reception. 'It saves me carting all my possessions in and out every day like a refugee,' she says.

Ross is waiting for me in the corridor by the towel bin when I emerge from the changing room. 'All satisfactory?' he says.

'Very.' Everything is exactly as Vivienne described it.

'Any questions? Did you figure out how the lockers work? It's a pound coin in the slot to close them, which you get back, of course.'

I nod, waiting for Ross to tell me that I too will have my own locker, but he doesn't. I am slightly disappointed.

He marches me round Chalfont's, the health club's smart restaurant, and a cheerful, noisy, mock-American café bar called Chompers which I know Vivienne loathes. Then we go to the members' bar, where Ross hands me over to Tara. I decide to be bold and have a cocktail, in the hope that it will make me feel less on edge. I pick up the menu, but Tara tells me she has already prepared something for me, a fattening concoction of cream and Kahlua. Vivienne, it turns out, has ordered it in advance.

I am not allowed to pay for my drink, which is no surprise. 'You're a lucky girl,' says Tara. Presumably she means because I am Vivienne's daughter-in-law. I wonder if she knows about Laura, who was not quite so lucky.

I gulp down my cocktail quickly, trying to look calm and carefree. In actual fact, I am probably the least relaxed person in the building, so keen am I to get home, back to The Elms and Florence. I realise that, deep down, I have been itching to return from the second I left. Now that I have seen everything Waterfront has to offer, I am free to go. I have done what I set out to do.

Outside, the rain has stopped. I break the speed limit on the way home, alcohol buzzing through my veins. I feel brave and rebellious, briefly. Then I start to feel dizzy, and worry that I will drive past Cheryl, my midwife, who will gasp with disapproval to see me speeding along in a clapped-out Volvo only a fortnight after my daughter's birth. I could kill someone. I am still taking the pills they gave me when I left hospital. And I've just downed a strong cocktail . . . What am I trying to do, poison myself?

I know I should slow down but I don't. I can't. My eagerness to see Florence again is like a physical craving. I accelerate towards traffic lights that are on amber instead of braking as I normally would. I feel as if I have left behind one of my limbs or a vital organ.

I am almost panting with anticipation as I pull into the driveway. I park the car and run up the path to the house, ignoring the strained, bruised feeling in my lower abdomen. The front door is ajar. 'David?' I call out. There is no reply. I wonder if he has taken Florence out in her pram. No, he can't have done. David would always close the door.

I walk through the hall to the living room. 'David?' I shout again, louder this time. I hear a creaking of floor-boards above my head and a muffled groan, the sound of David waking from a nap. I hurry upstairs to our bed-room, where I find him upright in bed, yawning. 'I'm sleeping when the baby sleeps, like Miriam Stoppard said I should,' he jokes. He has been so happy since Florence was born, almost a different person. For years I have wished that David would talk to me more about how he's feeling. Now any such talk seems unnecessary. His joy is obvious from his sudden new energy, the eagerness in his eyes and voice.

David has been doing the night feeds. He has read in a book that one of the advantages of bottle-feeding is that it gives dads the opportunity to bond with their babies. This is a novelty for him. By the time Felix was born, David and Laura had already separated. Florence is David's second chance. He hasn't said so, but I know he is determined to make everything perfect this time. He has even taken a whole month off work. He needs to prove to himself that

9

being a bad father is not hereditary. 'How was Water-front?' he asks.

'Fine. Tell you in a sec.' I turn my back on him, leave the room and walk on tiptoes along the wide landing towards Florence's nursery.

'Alice, careful not to wake her up,' David whispers after me.

'I'll just have a little look. I'll be quiet, I promise.'

I hear her breathing through the door. It is a sound that I adore: high-pitched, fast, snuffly – a louder noise than you might think a tiny baby could make. I push open the door and see her funny cot that I am still not used to. It has wheels and cloth sides and is apparently French. David and Vivienne spotted it in a shop window in Silsford and bought it as a surprise for me.

The curtains are closed. I look down into the cot and at first all I see is a baby-shaped lump. After a few seconds, I can see a bit more clearly. Oh God. Time slows, unbear-ably. My heart pounds and I feel sick. I taste the creamy cocktail in my mouth again, mixed with bile. I stare and stare, feeling as if I am falling forward. I am floating, detached from my surroundings, with nothing firm to grip on to. This is no nightmare. Or rather, reality is the nightmare.

I promised David I would be quiet. My mouth is wide open and I am screaming.

# 2

## 3/10/03, 11.50 am (One week later)

Charlie was waiting for Simon on the steps of the police station when he arrived for the start of his shift at midday. He noticed that for the first time this year she was wearing her full-length black wool coat with fake fur collar and cuffs. Her bony ankles were no longer visible under thin transparent tights as they had been all summer. As one season succeeded another, Charlie's legs turned from transparent to opaque and back again. Today they were opaque. Yesterday they'd been transparent. It was a sure sign that winter was on the way.

At least it was October. Charlie was so skinny that she normally started to feel the cold when most people were still wearing sandals. Today her face was pale and, behind her gold-rimmed glasses, her eyes were anxious. In her right hand was a half-smoked cigarette. Charlie was addicted to holding them and allowing them to burn themselves out. Simon hardly ever saw her take a puff. He could see her red lipstick on the filter as he got closer. There was more colour on the fag end than there was on her mouth. She exhaled a small cloud which might have been either smoke or breath.

A flick of her other hand, waving him over impatiently. So she *was* waiting for him. It must be serious if she was meeting him on the bloody steps. Simon cursed quietly, sensing the imminent presence of trouble, angry with himself for being surprised. He should have known it was on the way. He wished he could say that he had been expecting, any day now, to turn a corner and see the ominous face of somebody who had bad news for him. Charlie, this time.

Simon would have liked to meet whatever fate intended to throw at him with the confidence of the entirely blameless. Ironically, he felt he would be better able to bear his punishment if it were undeserved. Something about the concept of martyrdom appealed to him.

He found he could hardly swallow. This time it would be more serious than a Reg 9. He'd been a fool to forget – however briefly, however understandably – that he was not the sort of person who got away with things. Those creepy bastards from the Internal Discipline Unit had probably already emptied his locker.

He felt a churning in his gut. Half of his mind was busy rehearsing his defence while the other half fought to suppress the urge to run, to take off. In Simon's fantasy it would not be a cowardly flight. It would be slow, dignified, disappointed. He pictured himself becoming smaller and smaller until he was a line, a dot, nothing. The allure of the grand gesture, the silent departure. Charlie would be left wondering how, precisely, she'd let him down and then, once she'd worked it out, wishing she'd listened to him.

Some hope. Simon's departures from all his previous jobs had been frenzied, chaotic, with a soundtrack of shouted threats, of fists and feet smashing against doors and desks. He wondered how many new starts a person was entitled to, how many times one could say it was the other person's fault and truly believe it.

'What? What is it?' he asked Charlie, skipping the pleasantries. He felt hollow, as if someone had taken a large scoop out of him.

'Have a fag.' She opened her packet of Marlboro Lights and thrust it at his face.

'Just tell me.'

'I will, if you'll keep calm.'

'For fuck's sake! What's happened?' Simon knew he couldn't hide his panic from Charlie, which made him even angrier.

'Would you care to amend your tone, detective?' She pulled rank whenever it suited her. One minute she was Simon's friend and confidante, the next she was reminding him of her superior status. Warmth and coldness were modes she could switch on or off at a second's notice. Simon felt like a creature squirming on a small glass slide. He was the matter upon which Charlie was conducting a long-term experiment, trying radically different approaches in quick succession: caring, flirty, distant. Result of experiment: subject permanently confused and uncomfortable.

It would be easier to work for a man. For two years, Simon had armed himself, privately, with the idea that he could request a transfer to another sergeant's team. He had never got as far as doing it, needing the thought that he could make the change at any time more than he needed the change itself. Charlie was an efficient skipper. She looked after his interests. Simon knew why, and was determined not to feel guilty; her reasons were her business and should be no concern of his. Was it superstitious to believe that the minute he no longer had her protection, he would urgently need it?

'I'm sorry,' he said. 'Sorry. Please, just tell me.'

'David Fancourt is in interview room 2 with Proust.'

'What? Why?' Simon's imagination wrestled with the jarring image of Inspector Giles Proust face to face with a civilian. An actual person, one who hadn't been reduced to a name in a sergeant's report, tidied into a typeface. In Simon's experience, unusual meant bad. It could mean very bad. Every nerve ending in his body was on full alert.

'You weren't here, I wasn't here – Proust was the only person in the CID room at the time, so Proust got him.'

'Why's he come in?'

Charlie took a deep breath. 'I wish you'd have a fag,' she said.

Simon took one to shut her up. 'Just tell me – am I in trouble?'

'Well, now . . .' Her eyes narrowed. 'Isn't that an interesting question? Why would *you* be in trouble?'

'Charlie, stop jerking me around. Why's Fancourt here?'

'He came in to report his wife and daughter missing.'

'What?' The words stunned Simon, like a brick wall in the face. Then the sense of what Charlie was telling him sunk in. Alice and the baby were missing. No. They couldn't be.

'That's all I know. We'll have to wait for Proust to tell us the rest. Fancourt's been here nearly an hour. Jack Zlosnik's on the desk. Fancourt told him that his wife and baby daughter disappeared last night. There was no note, and he's heard nothing since. He's phoned everyone he can think of – nothing.'

Simon couldn't see straight. Everything had become a blur. He tried to push past Charlie, but she grabbed his arm. 'Hey, slow down. Where are you going?'

'To find Fancourt, find out what the fuck's going on.' Rage bubbled inside him. What had that bastard done to Alice? He had to know, now. He would demand to know.

'So you're just going to storm in to Proust's interview, are you?'

'If I fucking have to!'

Charlie tightened her grip on him. 'One day your temper's going to lose you your job. I'm fed up of supervising your every move to make sure you don't fuck up.' She'd care more than I did if they kicked me out, Simon thought. It was one of his safety barriers. When Charlie wanted something it happened. Usually.

Three bobbies kept their eyes down on their way into the station. They couldn't get through the double doors fast enough. Simon shook his arm free, mumbling an apology. He disliked the idea that he was causing a scene. Charlie was right. It was about time he grew out of this sort of behaviour.

She took the cigarette from his hand, put it in his mouth, lit it. She doled out fags medicinally, the way other people did cups of tea. Even to non-smokers like Simon. He needed this one, though. The first drag was a relief. He held the nicotine in his lungs for as long as he could.

'Charlie, listen . . .'

'I will, but not here. Finish that, then we'll go and get a drink. And calm down, for God's sake.'

Simon gritted his teeth and tried to breathe evenly. If he could get through to anyone, Charlie was the one. At least she would give him a fair hearing before telling him he was talking bollocks.

He took a few more drags, then stubbed out the cigarette and followed her into the building. Spilling Police Station used to be the public swimming baths. It still smelled of chlorine, haunted by the memory of its former self. Aged eight, Simon had learned to swim here, tutored by a maniac in a red tracksuit with a long wooden pole. Everyone else in his class had already known how. Simon remembered how he'd felt when this became apparent to him. He felt it now, at thirty-eight, when he turned up for the beginning of each shift.

The weight of his anxiety pulled him down, dragging, sinking. Again he felt the urge to run, though he wasn't sure if his legs would take him further into the building or out of it. He had no plan, only a need to shake himself up, dislodge his fear. He forced himself to stand still behind Charlie while she had a trivial conversation with Jack Zlosnik, the rotund, grey fur-ball on the desk who leaned where grumpy Morris had leaned all those years ago, grimly handing out green paper tickets that said 'Admit One'.

There was no reason to assume the worst – to state, even to himself, what the worst might be. Alice couldn't have come to serious harm. There was still time for Simon to make a difference. He would have sensed it, somehow, if it were too late, would not be so aware of the present trickling into the past, grain by grain. Still, this was hardly scientific proof. He could imagine Charlie's reaction.

After an age, Zlosnik was behind them, and Simon forced his feet to mimic Charlie's, step by step, as they made their way to the canteen, a big echo-chamber full of glaring strip-lights, the clash of voices – mainly male – and bad smells. Simon's mood made everything appear grotesque, made him want to shield his eyes against the cheap wood laminate floor, the piss-yellow walls.

Three grey-haired middle-aged women in white aprons stood at the serving hatch, dispensing grey and brown slop to tired, hungry bobbies. One of them slid two cups of tea towards Charlie without moving her features. Simon stood back. His hands wouldn't have been steady enough to carry anything. A table had to be chosen, chairs pulled out, pulled back in: mundane tasks that made him impatient to the point of fury.

'You look like you're in shock.'

He shook his head, though he suspected Charlie was right. He couldn't shift the image of Alice's face from his mind. An abyss had opened in front of him and he struggled to stop himself falling in. 'I've got a bad feeling about this, Charlie. Really bad. Fancourt's behind it all, somehow. Whatever he's telling Proust, it's a fucking lie.'

'You're not exactly the most objective judge, are you? You've got a thing about Alice Fancourt. Don't bother to deny it. I saw how flustered you were when she came in last week, just from being in the same room as her. And you look secretive whenever you mention her name.'

Simon stared purposefully at his tea. Objective? No. Never. He distrusted David Fancourt in the same way he had two other men in recent weeks, both of whom had turned out to be guilty. When Simon proved as much, unequivocally, his fellow officers praised him loudly, bought him drinks and claimed they'd known he was right all along. Including Charlie. She'd had no complaints about his lack of objectivity then. Though, in both cases, when he'd first voiced his suspicions the rest of the team had laughed and called him a nutter.

Most people rewrote history when it suited them, even those whose job it was to stick to the facts, unearth the truth. Simon didn't know how they managed it; he wished he had the knack. He remembered, in precise detail, the convenient and the inconvenient, knew exactly who'd said what when. His mind would let go of nothing, not one single thing. It didn't make for an easy or comfortable life, but it was useful for work purposes. If Charlie couldn't see that Simon's occasional rages were a direct result of being constantly underestimated by everybody he worked with, even after he'd proved himself time and time again, how good a detective could she be, objective or otherwise?

'I hope I don't need to remind you how much trouble you'll be in if you've been seeing Alice Fancourt in your own time, after I told you to have nothing more to do with her,' said Charlie. That lectern voice again, that podium tone. Simon couldn't stand it. Couldn't she see the state he was in? Did she have any idea what it felt like to be so trapped in your own preoccupations that the disapproval of others rolled off you, like rain off the waxy bonnet of a car? 'Her case, such as it was, was closed.' Charlie watched him carefully. 'If she really is missing, you could be suspended, or worse, arrested. You'll be a suspect, you bloody idiot. Even I can't protect you from something as serious as this. So you'd better hope she turns up.' She laughed bitterly and muttered, 'Like you don't already.'

Simon's mouth was full of tea he couldn't swallow. The neon lights were giving him a headache. A smell of stewed meat wafted over from the next table, making him want to retch.

'You suspect David Fancourt of what, exactly?'

'I don't know.' Such an effort, to keep his voice steady, to stay in his seat and go through the ritual of a civilised conversation. He felt his right knee twitch, a sign that his whole body was aching to bolt. 'But this is too much of a coincidence, after what happened to his first wife.' Simon was unwilling to draw his long history of suspecting the right people to Charlie's attention. If she wanted to focus on his weaknesses, let her. It wasn't as if he could deny their existence. Yes, he was incapable of thinking clearly where Alice Fancourt was concerned. Yes, he sometimes steamed in and fucked things up, usually when the obtuseness of his colleagues made him so angry that he lost all sense of proportion.

'Forget about *me*,' he told Charlie sharply, placing a

heavy emphasis on the last word, 'and start looking at David Fancourt. Or rather at the picture that's taking shape around him. Then maybe you'll see what's staring you in the fucking face.'

Charlie's eyes slid away from him. She fiddled with her hair, picking at stray strands. When she next spoke, her voice was light and flippant, and Simon knew his point had struck home. 'Some famous bod, can't remember who, said "To lose one wife is unfortunate. To lose two looks a bit careless." Something like that, anyway.'

'Or a bit guilty,' said Simon. 'Laura Cryer's death . . .'

'Is a closed case.' Charlie's face hardened. 'Don't even think about going there.' Then, because she disliked ambiguity, she said, 'Why? Spit it out!'

'It's a lot to happen to one innocent man, that's all,' said Simon. 'I can't believe you need me to spell it out. What if Fancourt murdered his first wife and got away with it?' He crushed his fingers into fists. 'What if he's about to try his luck again? Are we going to do anything to stop him while he's actually in the building, or are we just going to let the bastard walk out of here as free as he walked in?'

# 3

*Friday September 26, 2003*

'What's wrong? What's the matter with you?' David is in the nursery, out of breath. I am still screaming. A loud roar, like a siren, is coming from my mouth. I don't think I could stop it even if I wanted to. A shriller, high-pitched wail blares from the cot. David slaps me across the face. 'Alice, what's got into you? What is it?'

'Where's Florence? Where is she?' I demand. Our ordinary day has mutated into something terrible.

'Are you out of your mind? She's right here. You woke her up. Ssh. Ssh, darling, it's okay. Mummy didn't mean to scare you. Here, you come for a cuddle with Daddy. It's okay.'

'That's not Florence. I've never seen that baby before. Where's Florence?'

'What the . . . what on earth are you talking about?' David never swears. Vivienne disapproves of foul language. 'Of course it's Florence. Look, she's wearing her Bear Hug suit. You put her in it before you went out, remember?'

The outfit is the first thing I bought for Florence, when I was six months pregnant. It is a pale yellow cotton all-in-one, with the words 'Bear Hug' sewn on to it, above a picture of a brown bear cub in its mother's arms. I saw it in Remmick's, Spilling's only department store, and loved it so much that I had to buy it, even though by that point Vivienne had filled the nursery wardrobe with enough clothes from the exclusive boutiques she favours to keep Florence going for the first three years.

'Of course I recognise the babygro, it's Florence's. David, who is this baby? Where's Florence? Just tell me! Have we got visitors? Is this some kind of practical joke? Because if it is, it's not funny.'

David's dark eyes are unreadable. He will only share his thoughts when he is happy. Misery or trouble of any kind makes him withdraw into himself. I can see from the shut-down look on his face that the retreat has already started. 'Alice, this is Florence.'

'It's not! You know it isn't! Where is she?'

'Is this some sort of sick joke, or have you gone mad?'

I begin to sob. 'Please, please, David, where is she? What have you done with her?'

'Look, I don't know what's got into you, but I suggest you pull yourself together. Florence and I will be down-stairs, awaiting your apology.' His tone is cold.

Suddenly, I am alone in the nursery. I sink to my knees, then curl into a foetal position on the floor. I cry and cry for what seems like hours but is probably only a few seconds. I can't fall apart. I have to go after them. Time is passing, precious minutes that I can't waste. I have to make David listen to me, although part of me wishes I could listen to him, apologise, pretend everything is okay even though it isn't.

I wipe my eyes and go downstairs. They are in the kitchen. David doesn't look up as I come in. 'That baby is not my daughter,' I blurt out, disintegrating into tears again. There is so much unhappiness and fear in me and it is all spilling out, here in Vivienne's kitchen.

He looks as if he is considering ignoring me, but then thinks better of it. He turns to face me. 'Alice, I think you ought to calm down so that we can discuss this rationally.'

'Just because I'm upset doesn't mean I'm not being rational. I'm as rational as you are!'

'Good,' says David patiently. 'In that case, we should be able to clear this up. If you're seriously suggesting this baby isn't our daughter, convince me.'

'What do you mean?' I am confused.

'Well, in what way is she different? Florence hasn't got any hair. She's got milk spots on her nose. She's got blue eyes. You'd agree with all that, presumably?'

'Look at her!' I scream. 'She's got a different face! It isn't Florence!'

David stares at me as if he has never seen me before. He thinks I am a lunatic. He doesn't recognise me as his wife. I can see him drawing a line, mentally. David is defensive, as emotionally immature as a teenage boy. I wonder if this is because his mother has always looked after him. He has never needed to think his way through a complex adult situation on his own. He would rather cut you out of his life, shut you out of his mind, than deal with the less-than-perfect reality that you represent. Problematic people such as his father and Laura are never mentioned. How long before I too am condemned?

'David, you must *know* it isn't her. That is not the baby I kissed goodbye a couple of hours ago. The one we brought home from the hospital. The one who wriggled and cried when I put that babygro on her. Take it off!' I yell suddenly, startling myself as much as David. 'It's Florence's! I don't want that baby wearing it. Take it off her!' I back away into the hall.

'You're acting as if you're scared of her.' I have never seen David look so disgusted. 'Alice, what's wrong with you? There's only one baby. Florence. This is her.'

'David, look at her!' I yell. I have become a creature, wild and uncivilised, some sort of beast. 'Look at her face. It's a different face, can't you see that? Yes, she's got blue eyes and milk spots, but so have hundreds of newborns. I'm calling Vivienne.' I run from the room. In the hall, my eyes dart from left to right. My vision blurs. Adrenaline makes me pant. I am so confused and upset, I momentarily forget what I am doing here, what I am looking for. Then I remember. The phone.

David follows me into the hall. I see that he is alone. 'What have you done with the baby?' I ask. I felt uneasy when I could see her. I feel even more so now that I can't. David pulls the phone out of my hand and slams it down. 'Don't dare to interrupt Mum and Felix's holiday with this rubbish! Mum'll think you've lost it. Alice, you've got to get a grip. Listen to yourself.'

Vivienne has taken Felix to Florida for a treat, to celebrate the new baby. I would have preferred him to stay, but Vivienne insisted that this was the best way of ensuring that he doesn't resent the arrival of Florence. It is apparently a successful tactic for avoiding jealousy. Vivienne is an only child and always hated the idea of siblings. She asked her parents not to have another child, as soon as she was old enough to understand the concept. What is perhaps more surprising is that they obeyed her.

David's father wanted a big family. He himself was one of six. 'I told him on no account,' said Vivienne. 'A child should grow up feeling special. How can you feel special if there are six of you?' She was careful to wait until David was out of the house to tell me this story. His father is never mentioned in front of him.

I am not accustomed to forcing my husband to confront unwelcome truths. I have always tried to protect him.

'The front door was open,' I say.

'What?'

'When I got back. The front door was open. You were asleep. Someone must have come in and taken Florence and . . . and left that baby instead! We've got to phone the police, David. Oh, God, Florence! Where is she? What if she's not all right? What if something awful's happened to her?' I am pulling at my hair, howling.

There are tears in David's eyes. When he speaks his voice is quiet. 'Alice, you're scaring me. Don't do this, please. You're really scaring me, okay. Please, calm down. I want you to walk into the kitchen, take a good look at the baby in the bouncy chair and I want you to realise that it is Florence. It *is*. Okay?' There is a flicker of hope in his eyes. He is softening, giving me a final chance. I know how significant an admission of fear is from David. He must really love me, I think. And now I have to crush his hopes.

'But it *isn't*!' I insist. 'Listen to her crying! Listen!' Poor, poor baby, confused, screaming for her mother. 'That's not Florence's cry. Give me the phone.'

'No! Alice, please, this is mad. Let me phone Dr Dhossajee. You need a sedative, or . . . some sort of help. I should phone the doctor.'

'David, give me the phone right now or I swear I will get a kitchen knife and stab you.'

He winces. I cannot believe I said that. Why couldn't I have threatened to strangle him instead? I didn't say it deliberately to hurt him, but he must think I did.

'David, someone's got our daughter! We've got to do something, quickly!'

He lets me pick up the phone. 'Who are you ringing?' he asks.

'The police. And then Vivienne. She'll believe me, even if you don't.'

'Ring the police if you insist, but not Mum, *please*.'

'Because you know she'll back me up. That's why, isn't it?'

'Alice, if it isn't Florence, who is it? Babies don't just drop out of the sky, you know. I was only asleep for ten minutes . . .'

'That's long enough.'

'There are tests we can do, DNA tests, to prove it's Florence. We can sort it all out before Mum gets back. Look, she's my mother, not yours. It's up to me whether we ring her or not, and we're not ringing her.' David is babbling desperately. He cannot bear the thought of being observed in a situation of personal difficulty. I think he regards any sort of unhappiness as a shameful and absolutely private matter. For Vivienne to see him like this, tangled up in this awful mess, would be his worst nightmare.

'Well, I haven't got a mother, have I?' My voice cracks. 'Vivienne's the closest I've got and I'm damn well phoning her. Police, please,' I say into the telephone. 'I should never have agreed to move in here. This house is jinxed!' I snap. 'If we lived somewhere else, this would never have happened.'

'That's rubbish!' David looks as if I've slapped him across the face. I have insulted his beloved family home. 'You can't expect me to leave my son.'

'Of course I don't! We'd take Felix with us.' This is the most direct exchange David and I have ever had on the matter of where we ought to live.

'Yes, great, we'll just take him away from Mum, who's been like a mother to him since Laura died! I can't believe you'd even suggest it!'

'Police, please. I need to report an . . . I've just *been* on hold!'

'This whole thing will blow over. It will blow over,' David mumbles to himself. He sits down on the stairs and puts his head in his hands. Despite his efforts at self-control, his misery and shock overtake him. He has never cried in front of me before. He must be wondering if he could be wrong, no matter how sure he feels. I realise he will not forgive me for having witnessed this display of emotion.

'Go and comfort the baby. David, listen to me. Please. The baby's scared.' The helpless, baffled cry pierces my heart. It is all I can do to remain upright.

Poor, poor Florence. I cannot bear to think about how badly she might be suffering. All I want is to be able to hug her close to me, feel her soft, squashy cheek against mine.

A moan rises from David's throat. 'What are you saying? Listen to yourself – "the baby". She's our daughter, our Florence. How can you do this? Put the phone down! *You* go and comfort her.' He is furious with me, but also angry with himself for believing so wholeheartedly in his second chance, his new life with me and Florence. He must feel shamed now, taunted by the elation that he has felt in the past two weeks. It makes me sad to think that I understand his pain better than he will ever understand mine.

'Help me, help me, need to report a . . . sorry, sorry.' A woman's voice is telling me to calm down. I am crying so hard that she cannot tell what I am saying. 'I need to report an abduction.' I have to repeat this twice. The misery of three people echoes around the house. 'My baby daughter, Florence. Yes. My name is Alice Fancourt.'

# 4

## 3/10/03, 12.10 pm

'Run that one by me again,' said Charlie. 'You're suggesting that David Fancourt killed Laura Cryer?'

'It's remedial fucking logic! Anyone with a brain would say the same, now that Alice and the kid have disappeared. And there's something about him. I thought so as soon as I met him.' Simon tried to put the reason for his mistrust into words. 'There's no real person behind his eyes. I looked at him and all I saw was a blank. Remember that Billy Idol song, 'Eyes Without a Face'?'

'Call me slow,' said Charlie, knowing Simon would never be foolish enough to do so, 'but I could have sworn I headed the team that worked on that case myself, and I could further have sworn that we got someone for it.'

'I know all that,' said Simon distractedly. He'd still been in uniform in those days. Charlie was the expert. Still, he couldn't silence the voice in his head, the one that was shouting Alice's name in the dark. And underneath that, the same question, over and over: would she have run away without telling him? Would she know that her disappearance would worry him personally as well as professionally? He hadn't really said anything. He hadn't said or done nearly enough.

Simon's parents were the only two people in the world whose behaviour he could predict with absolute accuracy: their tea at six o'clock, church on Sunday morning, straight to bed after the ten o'clock news. He came from a stable background, all right. Most people seemed to think stable equalled happy.

Behind Simon's back, a spotty bobby was playing Pokey. Every so often he hissed 'Yesss!' and banged into the back of Simon's chair. The one-armed bandit machine, the canteen's only asset. Simon hated it, regarded it as the mark of an uncivilised society. He disapproved of everything that he perceived as being in that category: noisy, beeping machine entertainment. If he ever had children – unlikely, yes, but not impossible – he would ban all computer games from the house. He'd make his kids read the classics, just as he had as a child. The lyrics of another eighties song, The Smiths this time, sprang to mind: *'There's more to life than books, you know, but not much more'*.

Morrissey had it right. Sport was pointless, socialising too stressful. Simon loved the careful, deliberate nature of books. They gave shape to things, trained you to look for a pattern. Like a man's second wife going missing after his first wife's been murdered. When an author took the time and trouble to choose exactly the right words and arrange them in the right order, there was a possibility of genuine communication taking place, the thoughtful writer reaching the thoughtful reader. The opposite of what happened when two people opened their mouths and simply let their half-formed, incoherent thoughts spill out. Speak for yourself, Charlie would have said.

'I assume it was the lovely Alice who put these suspicions about Fancourt into your mind. What's been going on between you and her, Simon? As soon as this becomes a misper, you'll have to tell me, so why not get it over with?'

Simon shook his head. When he had to, he'd tell her, not a moment before. As yet, no case file had been opened. He didn't want to hurt Charlie, less still to admit how badly he'd fucked up. *I hope I don't need to remind you how much trouble you'll be in if you've been seeing Alice Fancourt in your own time. You'll be a suspect, you bloody idiot.* How was he supposed to know that Alice and the baby would go missing? 'Tell me about Laura Cryer,' he said. Listening would be a distraction; speaking at any length would be an ordeal.

'What, over a cream tea? We've got a shitload of work to get on with. And you haven't answered my question.'

'Work?' He stared at her, outraged. 'You mean the paperwork I thoughtlessly created by coming up with the evidence we needed to secure convictions in two major cases?'

He felt the fierceness of his own stare, wielded it like a drill. Eventually Charlie looked away. Sometimes, when Simon least expected it, she backed down. 'This'll have to be quick,' she said gruffly. 'Darryl Beer, one of the many bloody scourges of our green and pleasant land, killed Laura Cryer. He pleaded guilty, he's banged up. End of story.'

'That was quick,' Simon agreed. 'I know Beer. I arrested him a couple of times.' Just another piece of Winstanley estate scum, streets cleaner without him. Once you'd met enough characters like Beer, you fell into using clichés, the ones you were sick of hearing other cops use, the ones you swore you'd never resort to.

'We've all arrested him a couple of times. Anyway, you wanted the story so here it is: December 2000. I can't remember the exact date, but it was a Friday night. Laura Cryer left work late – she was a scientist, worked at Rawndesley Science park for a company called BioDiverse. She went straight from the lab to her mother-in-law

Vivienne Fancourt's house, where her son Felix was. She parked just inside the gate, on that paved bit, you know?'

Simon nodded. He had set himself the task of sitting still for as long as it took Charlie to fill him in. He thought he could do it.

'When she walked back to her car ten minutes later, Beer tried to mug her. He stabbed her with a bog-standard kitchen knife – one clean slice – and left her to bleed to death. Ran off with her Gucci handbag, minus the strap, which we found by her body. Cut by the same knife. Vivienne Fancourt found the body the next morning. Anyway, we struck lucky on the DNA front. Beer left so much hair at the scene, we could have made a wig out of it. We ran the DNA profile and there was a match. Step forward, Darryl Beer.'

Charlie smiled, remembering the satisfaction she'd felt at the time. 'We were glad to be able to bang him up, useless junkie scrote that he is.' She noticed Simon's frown. 'Oh, come on! In the two weeks before Cryer's death, Vivienne Fancourt had phoned the station twice to report a young man loitering on her property. She gave us a description that was Darryl Beer to a tee – dyed pony-tail, tattoos. He was questioned at the time and denied it. Said it was her word against his, the cocky little shit.'

'What was he doing there?' asked Simon. 'The Elms is in the middle of nowhere. It's not as if there's a pub or even an all-night garage nearby.'

'How should I know?' Charlie shrugged.

'I'm not saying you should know. I'm saying it should bother you that you don't.' Simon was regularly amazed by the lack of curiosity displayed by other detectives. All too often there were aspects of cases about which Charlie and the others seemed happy to say, 'I guess that'll have to remain an open question.' Not Simon. He had to know, always, everything. Not knowing made him feel helpless, which made him lash out.

'Did Vivienne Fancourt see Darryl Beer on the night of the murder?' he asked Charlie.

She shook her head.

'The two times she saw him, where in the grounds . . .'

'Behind the house, on the river side.' She had seen that one coming. 'Nowhere near the scene of the murder. And most of the physical evidence we found was on the body itself, on Laura Cryer's clothes. Beer couldn't possibly have left it during a previous visit. Because, obviously, that possibility occurred to us just as it occurred to you.' There was a bitter edge to her voice. 'So you can stop thinking of yourself as the lone genius amid a cluster of morons.'

'What the fuck is that supposed to mean?' Simon wouldn't be told what to think, not by anybody.

'I would have thought it was unambiguous.' Charlie sighed. 'Simon, we all know how good you are, okay? Sometimes I think you'd actually prefer it if we didn't. You need to have something to grate against, don't you?'

'Why was there so much hair? Did Cryer pull it out? Did she struggle?' Fuck all that psychological bullshit. Simon was interested in Laura Cryer and Darryl Beer. Really interested now. He wasn't just asking in order to avoid an explosion. He still had that twitch in his right knee.

'Or else the fucker's got alopecia. No, he tried to snatch her handbag. She fought for it, probably more than he'd anticipated. She must have done, or it wouldn't have ended in a stabbing, would it?'

'You mentioned tattoos.'

'Love and hate on his knuckles.' Charlie mimed a yawn. 'Not very original.'

'So, you arrested him,' Simon prompted. As if by speeding up her account he could find Alice quicker.

'Sellers and Gibbs did. As soon as they heard about Vivienne Fancourt's intruder, they picked him up. The lab put a rush on the DNA, and let's just say we weren't exactly surprised to get the result we got.'

'You knew where you wanted the evidence to take you, and lo and behold . . .'

'Simon, I'm not in the mood for one man's struggle against the system today, I'm really not. This isn't a Greek tragedy, it's Spilling fucking nick, okay? Shut the fuck up and listen!' Charlie paused, to compose herself. 'Beer protested his innocence, predictably. Made up some shite alibi which didn't really stand up. Claimed he was in his flat, watching telly with his mate, who appeared to be marginally less trustworthy than Beer himself. He didn't have a brief, so he got the duty solicitor. We kept at him for a while, trying to trip him up. He didn't know we had a trump card up our sleeve, of course.'

'And you didn't tell him,' Simon guessed aloud.

'Phase disclosure, all above board,' said Charlie smugly. 'We did our best to twirl him and it didn't work. Once we were sure we weren't going to get anything out of him, we pulled the DNA match out of the hat. His solicitor went mental.'

'What did Beer say?'

'He still denied it. It didn't do him any good, though. We had the evidence we needed. Anyway, his brief must have talked some sense into him. After a few weeks as Her Majesty's guest at Earlmount, Beer suddenly changed his story. He confessed. Not to murder, to aggravated assault. He turned Queen's, shopped a couple of prominent local low-lifes, promised to go into rehab and counselling, and got himself a lighter sentence. Fucking disgrace, when you think about it. Twat'll probably be out before we know it.'

'Where is he now? Not still at Earlmount?'

Charlie pursed her lips and glared at Simon. After a few seconds she said, grudgingly, 'Brimley.' A category A/B prison, about ten miles from Culver Ridge in the direction of the very unlovely town of Combingham. An iron grey sprawling concrete offence, it stood neglected among drab fields that looked, whenever Simon drove past them, as if they had been shorn by a particularly savage piece of machinery and doused with noxious chemicals.

'Did Beer know the details of how Cryer was killed?' he asked. 'When he confessed, I mean.'

'Only a hazy version. He claimed he'd been off his head on drugs and barely remembered anything. That was how he got the charge dropped to aggravated assault.'

'He didn't tell you robbery was the motive?'

'What else could it have been?' Charlie frowned. A question, thought Simon; an important question, yet she presented it as an answer. 'Beer didn't know Cryer. They didn't exactly mix in the same circles. He'd obviously been hanging round The Elms in the weeks before, looking for opportunities to break in. It's a fairly obvious target, let's face it – biggest house in the area. He was probably having another scout round the place when he saw Cryer walking towards him with a Gucci handbag dangling from her shoulder. He ran off with the bag, he was a drug addict – yes, I'd say it's a pretty safe bet that robbery was the motive.'

Just occasionally, the expression on Charlie's face when she said certain words reminded Simon of the class difference between them. There was a way of saying 'drug addict' as if you'd never met one, as if the flawed and the weak belonged in a different universe. That was how Charlie said it. And she'd met hundreds. 'Did he give you the murder weapon? Or the bag?'

'He couldn't remember what he'd done with either, and we never found them. It happens, Simon,' she added, defensively. 'Doesn't mean the scrote's innocent.' All male offenders were scrotes. Women were splits. The police's secret language was a second uniform. It made everyone feel safe.

'A kitchen knife, you said?' That sounded wrong. 'Wouldn't Beer's type be more likely to have a shooter?'

'He might be more likely to, but he didn't,' Charlie said calmly. 'He had a kitchen knife. Focus on the known, Simon. The DNA match. The knife wound in Laura Cryer's chest.' She was as vigilant in defending her certainties as Simon was in examining his doubts. The combination wasn't always comfortable.

'Did you interview the family? The Fancourts?'

'God, if only we'd thought of that! Of course we bloody did. David Fancourt and Laura Cryer had been separated for several years by the time she was killed. They were in the process of getting a divorce and he was engaged to his second wife. He had no reason to want Cryer dead.'

'Alimony? Custody?' She'd avoided mentioning Alice by name. It could have been a coincidence.

'Fancourt's not exactly strapped for cash. You've seen the house. And why assume he'd have wanted full custody? He still got to see his son, and he had his new romance to think of. Having a kid around full-time might have been a bit of a passion-killer.'

She had the air of somebody answering these questions for the first time, which worried Simon. 'The family would have closed ranks,' he said. 'They always do, especially when there's a prime suspect like Beer in the frame. It's much easier to assume it's the outsider.'

' "The outsider!" ' Charlie sneered. 'Aw, you make him sound all sweet and lonely. He's a fucking drug addict piece of shit. Simon, come off it, for Christ's sake. You know as well as I do that drugs are always involved. There are three kinds of murders: domestics blown up out of control, sex attacks, and drug-dealing scrotes with shooters waging turf wars. But basically, most of them usually boil down to drugs at some level.'

'Usually that's true. But not always.' Simon's body and mind felt numb, anaesthetised. What did he know now that he hadn't before? There was a difference between facts and truth. Very fucking profound. It was too easy to hide behind words. Movement now seemed impossible. Talking to Charlie had trapped him in the cerebral, the theoretical. He was discussing a woman he had never met, either alive or dead. He might never get up out of his chair.

'Okay, then, I'm listening. Why would David Fancourt want to kill Laura Cryer? Why?' Charlie demanded.

'They were separated. Did anyone ask why? Maybe the reason they split up was relevant. There might have been some animosity between them.' Coward, said the voice in his head. Do something.

Charlie chewed the inside of her lip. 'True,' she said. 'And there equally might not. Plenty of people separate because they fall out of love, but they still like each other. Or so I'm told. Let's face it, you and I know sod all about marriage. I'm sure the way we imagine it is nothing like the real thing.' A knowing smile pulled at the corners of her mouth.

Simon cast about for a plausible change of subject. Being single was something Charlie thought they had in common, but Simon preferred to think of himself as not yet attached. Single sounded too defensive. If you felt defensive, you really didn't want to sound it.

Charlie slept with a lot of men and was vocal about it at all the wrong times. Like now, when Simon had no space in his head for her comic flippancy. If she hadn't mentioned sex yet, then she was about to. She made a point of turning her love life into entertainment for her team, which was enough to get Colin Sellers and Chris Gibbs in on time every day for the next instalment. Was there a new one, daily? It sometimes felt that way. And there was little love involved as far as Simon could tell.

He didn't like the thought of men mistreating Charlie. He couldn't understand why she allowed so many to use and discard her. She deserved better. He'd raised it once, tentatively, and she had pounced on him, insisting that she was the one who did the using and discarding, the one in control.

Simon shook his head. Charlie could distract him too easily. Alice was the one who was missing. She was still missing. Nobody had come to tell them it was a mistake.

'You're wasting your time and mine with all this, Simon. David Fancourt wasn't anywhere near Spilling the night Laura Cryer was killed.'

'He wasn't? Where was he, then?'

'In London, with his fiancée.'

'You mean . . . ?' Simon felt heat under his skin. Charlie had been sitting on Fancourt's alibi all this time, saving her trump card. Phase fucking disclosure.

'Yes. Alice was his alibi, although no-one really thought he needed one because – did I mention this? – the evidence against Darryl Beer was beyond doubt.' Charlie leaned her elbows on the table and rested her chin on her hands. 'So, if

Alice Fancourt told you her husband killed Laura Cryer, she's lying. Or else she was lying then. Either way, I'd say there's quite a lot pointing to her being untrustworthy. If you remember, I said she was unhinged right from the start.' Charlie's expression darkened. 'A mad bitch, I think was how I put it.'

Simon knew that if he spoke now, he'd say something that would be difficult, later, to take back. He grabbed his jacket and got the hell away from Charlie as quickly as he could.

# 5

*Friday September 26, 2003*

The worst things in life only strike once. I say this to my patients to help them move forward with their lives, to enable them to process the disasters that have befallen them. As soon as it is over, whatever it is, you can begin to console yourself with the thought that it will never happen again.

It worked for me when my parents died in a car crash eight years ago. I stood at their funeral, feeling as if the stitches that had held my soul together all these years were now slowly, painfully coming undone. I was a twenty-eight-year-old orphan. I didn't have any siblings to turn to. I had friends, but friendship felt thin and inadequate, like a summer jacket in winter. I needed, craved, family. I carried my lost, beloved parents around with me like a hole in my heart.

My friends and colleagues were surprised by how badly I was affected. People seemed to think that, having had twenty-eight years of love and security, I would be well-equipped to deal with my sudden loss. I quickly learned that I was expected to be somehow insulated against what might otherwise have been extreme pain by having had a secure, happy childhood. Everyone waited for me to bounce back, to start to focus on the good times, the fond memories. Their complacent assumptions were an insult to my grief and pushed me from a state of mourning into one of severe depression. I got the impression my friends were itching to say, 'Oh, well, they had a good innings, didn't they?' But my parents were only in their early fifties when they died.

I kept in touch with nobody when I left London. The company of my friends, when I'd really needed them, had made me feel lonelier than any amount of solitude ever could. It wasn't their fault, of course. They tried their best to jolly me along. They weren't to know that their forced and ever-so-slightly impatient cheerfulness was suffocating me like poison gas.

I survived in the only way I could – by allowing myself to feel the worst feelings for as long as they needed to be felt. At my lowest point, I had only one consolation. I was able to say to myself, plausibly, that at least this would never happen to me again. I could not lose my parents twice. Whatever else my future might contain, there would be no lorry that would skid on a patch of ice and plough on to the wrong side of the A1 near Newark, straight into my parents' car, the new Audi they'd bought when they passed the trusty old Volvo on to me. That had already happened. It was over.

But this nightmare, the one I'm living now, is not over. It is only just beginning. I see now that trouble doesn't always strike, in a clean, wham-bam-thank-you-Ma'am kind of way. Sometimes it drifts into your vicinity like bad weather, creeps up on you and lingers, deepening with every day that goes by. I cannot see any way out of this despair because I still do not know how much worse things are going to get.

I have locked myself in the bedroom. David has tried to reason with me through the door, to persuade me, feature by feature, that the baby in the house is so identical to

Florence in every particular that she can only be Florence. He has given up now. I didn't allow myself to hear him. I blocked out his words with a pair of foam earplugs. I keep these in the top drawer of my bedside cabinet at The Elms. Without them, David's snoring would keep me awake. He is always indignant when I mention this. He says I snored while I was pregnant and he didn't make a fuss about it, but then David could sleep through a rock concert. Nothing wakes him.

This is one of the details I know about my husband. What else do I know? That he is excellent with machines of all kinds, anything electronic or mechanical. That his favourite meal is roast beef with all the trimmings. That he buys me flowers for my birthday and our anniversary and treats me to long weekends in five star hotels to celebrate these and other special occasions. That he calls women ladies.

I have never opposed him before. I have always perceived him as being too fragile. When we first met, Laura had recently left him and he was dealing not only with the disintegration of his hopes for a happy family life but also with the agony of separation from Felix. Although he didn't like to talk about how much this hurt him, I could imagine it all too easily. I handled him with extreme care, not wanting to add to his unhappiness in any way.

When Laura died so suddenly and violently three years ago, David stopped confiding in me altogether. He became quiet and withdrawn, and I found myself being even more tactful and placatory around him. Felix came to live at The Elms, which must have made David happy, yet at the same time he is bound to have felt guilty and confused because the event that led to his reunion with his son was one which must have been terribly painful for him. I have learned from the counselling component of my homeopathy training that it is often much harder to deal with the death of somebody who is close to us if our feelings for that person are in any way unresolved or problematic.

I thought that by respecting David's emotional privacy and loving him as fiercely as I did, I would eventually convince him that it was safe to open up to me, but I was wrong. As he got used to life with Felix at The Elms, and as he came to terms with the idea that Laura was not around any more, David became, on the surface, his old, charming self, but the emotional distance between us remained, and he seemed so resistant to my attempts to close it that I began to wonder if he actively wanted a barrier in place. I was reluctant to force or rush him. I told myself that he probably still found the rawness deep down too painful to confront, that in order to believe in his façade of normality he might need to operate, for a while, on a more superficial level. Three years on, we have still not discussed Laura's death, and I have never managed to shake off the feeling that I must be careful not to say anything that will disturb his mental equilibrium.

Part of the reason I refused to open the door when he begged me to is that I cannot bear to confront the damage all this is doing to him. I worry that the nightmare we have embarked upon today will destroy him.

Vivienne is coming home. She is cutting short her and Felix's holiday, as I knew she would. How could she not? I don't know what she will say to Felix, what any of us will say. Nothing, if the past is any kind of indicator. Neither Vivienne nor David talks to Felix about Laura, at least not in front of me. Her name is never mentioned.

I wish I could spend more time alone with Felix. If things had been different, he and I might by now have become close. I might have been almost like a mum to him. I want to be a proper step-mother, but there is no room for such a figure in Felix's life. Vivienne is his mother substitute. He even calls her Mum, because he is used to hearing David call her that.

I'm not sure Felix realises that I am one of the grown-ups. He relates to me as if I am another child who happens to live in the same house as him.

David is a conscientious father. He and Vivienne make sure that he spends at least one whole day each weekend with Felix. He regards his son as a test that he must pass, and would vehemently deny, if I were to suggest it, that Felix reminds him of Laura in any way, even though, with his shiny black hair and pale blue eyes, he is the image of her.

David is good at denial. He will deny that he fell asleep and left the front door open. He is an exemplary father, he will insist. He wouldn't let anyone abduct his beloved daughter, the child of his happy second marriage.

I am impatient for Vivienne and the police to arrive. I sit here quietly, cross-legged on the bed, pressing my back, which still aches from the months of pregnancy, against the iron frame, and await these two very different authorities. I try to imagine the next hour, the next day or week, but my mind is one giant blank. I simply cannot envisage any future at all. I feel as if time stopped when I walked into Florence's nursery and started to scream.

I wish I had cuddled her more, breathed in more of her sweet, fresh baby smell while I could. Not to be able to hold her is torture, but worse than the pain, far worse, is the fear. There is a horribly uncertain future ahead, one that I'm not sure I can influence in any way.

David will tell everybody that I am deluded. Who will

the police believe? I have heard that they are, by and large, male chauvinists. What if they decide I'm an unfit mother and call in social services? I might not spend another night in this room, with its large sash windows and real fireplace, its view of the Silsford hills in the distance. David and I might never again sleep side by side, here or anywhere. When we first met, I was so full of hope for our life together. To think of that now makes me ache with sadness.

I will not speak to my husband again until there are witnesses present. How odd that only last night the two of us sat on Vivienne's sofa drinking wine and watching a silly romantic comedy together, laughing and yawning, David's arm round my shoulder. The speed of the way things have changed between us has left me dizzy with shock.

I hear his voice downstairs. 'Come on, Little Face,' he says. That's a new one. I make a mental note to mention this to the police when they arrive. David has called Florence 'Mrs Tiggywinkle' since the day she was born, apart from when he calls her 'Mrs Tiggy' for short. 'Ten tiggy fingers, ten tiggy toes, two tiggy ears and one tiggy nose,' he has sung to her every day, at least once. He did so this morning.

I know that David loves Florence as much as I do. The urge to comfort him is so firmly embedded in me that it will be a struggle to fight it. I must, though, if he continues to insist that the baby downstairs is our daughter. I will have to learn to regard his pain with total detachment. This is what danger and fear do to a person, to a marriage.

'Shall we lie you on your changing mat for a bit of a kickabout?' he says now. His voice floats up from the little lounge, directly underneath our bedroom. He sounds calm and efficient, for my benefit, I suspect. He is playing the role of the rational one.

A jolt of adrenaline shocks me into action. The camera. How could I have forgotten? I leap up off the bed, run to my wardrobe and throw open the door. There, on top of a pile of shoes, is my hospital bag, not yet unpacked. I rummage frantically and find my camera, a little black box with curved edges that contains the first photos of Florence. I open the back, stroke the smooth black cylinder of film with my thumb. Thank God, I murmur to myself. Now, surely, I have a chance of being believed.

# 6

## 3/10/03, 1.30 pm

There was no sign of Charlie in the CID room. Shit. Without her, Simon could hardly find out from Proust what David Fancourt had said. Colin Sellers and Chris Gibbs, two of the other Ds in Charlie's team, were working their way through a tower of files with what looked to Simon like slightly overdone urgency. For which there could only be one explanation.

Simon turned and saw Detective Inspector Proust in his office in the corner of the room. It was more of a glass box than an office, a bit like an exhibition case in an art gallery, one in which you might find the cross-section of a dead animal, except that the bottom half was made of cheap plasterboard which, for some reason, was carpeted – the same drab, ribbed grey as the CID room floor. The inspector's top half was visible through the glass as he orbited his desk, holding the phone in one hand and his 'World's Greatest Grandad' mug in the other.

David Fancourt must have left, then. Unless Proust had handed him over to Charlie. Perhaps that was where she was, in an interview room with that bastard. Simon sat down beside Gibbs and Sellers, drumming his fingers on the desk. The CID room closed in on him, with its peeling green paint and smell of stale sweat, its constant computerised hum. A person could suffocate in here. Pinned to one wall were photographs of victims, blood visible on

45

some of their faces and bodies. Simon couldn't bear to think of Alice in that condition. But she wasn't, she couldn't be. His imagination wouldn't allow it.

Something nagged at his subconscious, something to do with what Charlie had told him about the Laura Cryer case. He wasn't wise enough to stop fretting about it and allow it to come to him effortlessly later. Instead, he sat in his chair, shoulders hunched, and made his brain pound trying to dredge it up from the murky depths of his memory. Pointless.

Before he was aware he'd made a decision, Simon was on his feet again. He couldn't sit and twiddle his thumbs when he had no idea if Alice was okay. Where the fuck was Charlie? Free, for once, of her restraining influence, he marched over to Proust's office and knocked on the door, hard, beating out a rhythm of emergency. With Proust, you normally waited until you were summoned, even if you were a sergeant, like Charlie. Simon heard Gibbs and Sellers speculating in whispers about what his problem was.

Proust didn't look as surprised as he might have done. 'DC Waterhouse,' he said, emerging from his cubicle. 'Just the man I need to see.' His voice was stern, but that told Simon nothing. The inspector always sounded severe. According to his wife Lizzie, whom Simon had met at a couple of parties, Proust used the same tone when he spoke to his family that he used in court and at press conferences.

'Sir, I know David Fancourt's been in.' Simon got straight to the point. 'I know his wife and daughter are missing. Is he with Charlie?'

Proust sighed, flaying Simon with his glare. He was a small, thin, bald man in his mid-fifties, whose bad moods were able to travel beyond his skin and contaminate whole rooms full of people. Thus he ensured that everyone benefited from keeping him happy. The Snowman; Proust knew about the nickname and liked it.

'Listen very carefully, Waterhouse. I'm going to ask you a question, and I want you to tell me the truth, even if you know it means big trouble for you. If you lie to me . . .' He paused to stare portentously at Simon. 'If you lie to me, Waterhouse, you can consider your career in the police force to be at an end. You will rue this day. Do we understand each other?'

'Yes, sir.' Pointless to say that neither of the alternatives sounded particularly appealing.

'And don't think I won't find out if you lie, because I will.'

'Sir.' Frustration coursed through Simon's veins, but he tried to look calm. There was no short-cut when talking to Proust. You had to jump through the many hoops he set up. He started each conversation with a firm view about how it ought to be structured. He spoke in paragraphs.

'Where are Alice and Florence Fancourt?'

'Sir?' Simon looked up, startled.

'Is that the only word you know, Waterhouse? Because if it is, I'd be happy to lend you a Thesaurus. I'll ask you again: where are Alice and Florence Fancourt?'

'I've no idea. I know they've gone missing, sir. I know that's why Fancourt came in this morning, but I don't know where they are. Why would I?'

'Hmph.' Proust turned away, rubbing his nose. Deep in thought, perfecting his next line. 'So anyone who suggested that you and Mrs Fancourt are closer than you ought to be would be incorrect, would they?'

'Yes. They would, sir.' Simon feigned indignation. With some success, he thought. Proust's controlled pauses raised the stakes so high that he ended up watching everybody's finest performances. 'Who said that? Is that what Fancourt said?' Or perhaps it was Charlie, the traitor. Simon knew only one thing: he couldn't lose this job. He'd done it better than most, first as a bobby and then in CID, for seven years. He'd half-wanted to lose all his previous jobs, to go out in a blaze of misunderstood glory once things started to go wrong. The dental hospital, the tourist information bureau, the building society – he hadn't cared about any of them. They were full of dullards who droned on about 'the real world' every time they saw Simon with a book in his hand. As if books weren't as real as cash ISAs, for fuck's sake. No, he'd regarded getting the sack from those shit-holes as a tribute, proof of his worth.

His mother had disagreed. Simon could still picture the way her face had drooped when he'd told her that he'd been fired from his job as an art gallery security guard, his fourth in two years. 'What will I tell the priest?' she'd said.

No reply from the Snowman. Simon could feel beads of sweat forming on his forehead. 'Fancourt's a liar, sir,' he blurted out. 'I don't trust him.'

The inspector took a sip from his mug and waited. Alarmingly cool, like an ice cube down your back on a hot day.

Simon knew he probably ought to keep his mouth shut, but he found he couldn't. 'Sir, shouldn't we look at the Laura Cryer case again, in the circumstances?' Proust had nominally been in charge of the investigation three years ago, though it had been Charlie, Sellers, Gibbs and the rest of the team who'd done all the work. 'I've just told Char . . . Sergeant Zailer the same thing. Alice Fancourt didn't trust David Fancourt either. It was obvious she didn't. And women know their husbands, don't they? Sir, given that

Fancourt's first wife was killed and now Alice has gone missing as well, shouldn't Fancourt be our prime suspect? Shouldn't that be our first line of enquiry?' He wasn't normally so talkative. Proust would have to see the logic of what he was saying if he repeated himself enough.

' "Women know their husbands!" '

Simon jumped. The sudden increase in volume told him that his turn was over and he had used it unwisely. Proust was going to make him pay for trying to determine the direction of their dialogue. He shouldn't have said so much, so urgently. He'd introduced a new element; Proust hated that.

'Women know their husbands, do they? And on that basis, you suspect David Fancourt of murder?'

'Sir, if . . .'

'Let me tell you something, Waterhouse. Every Saturday night, my wife and I have dinner with some-tedious-body or other, and I have to sit there like a prat while she makes up stories about me. Giles this, Giles that, Giles doesn't like lemon meringue pie because he was forced to eat it at school, Giles prefers Spain to Italy, he thinks the people are more friendly. Seventy-five per cent of these stories are fiction, pure and simple. Oh, there's a grain of truth in some of them, but mostly they're made up. Women do not know their husbands, Waterhouse. You only say that because you're not married. Women talk drivel because it entertains them. They fill the air with random words, and they don't much care whether what they're saying has any basis in fact.' Proust was red in the face by the end of his speech. Simon knew better than to reply.

'A pretty, manipulative woman spins you a yarn and you fall for it! Darryl Beer killed Laura Cryer because she fought for her handbag. He left half the contents of his scalp all over her body. What are you playing at, Waterhouse? Hm? You could end up where I am if you play your cards right. You could be a seriously good detective. I was the first person to say so, when you were here on secondment. And you've struck lucky more than once recently, I'll grant you that. But I'm telling you now, you can't afford any more mistakes.'

Struck lucky? Simon's fists itched to fly through the air in the direction of Proust's smug face. The inspector made it sound as if anyone might have achieved what Simon had in the past month, when he must have known damn well no-one else could or would have, certainly not anyone presently working in CID. At least, no-one else *had*, and that was what fucking mattered.

And what was all this shit about 'any more mistakes'? Simon had had a couple of Reg 9s but never anything serious. Everyone had the odd Reg 9, minor disciplinary stuff. And, unless his memory was playing up, Proust had just described Alice as manipulative. That opinion must have come from Charlie, who was herself capable of being ruthlessly manipulative. Alice seemed to Simon to be an utterly straightforward person, entirely without guile. He clamped his mouth shut and started to count inside his head. By thirty-two, he still wanted to knock Proust to the ground. And Charlie, while he was at it.

'What is it with you and women, Waterhouse? Why don't you get yourself a girlfriend?'

Simon froze, eyes fixed on the floor. This was something he definitely didn't want to talk about. To anyone, ever. He kept his head down and waited for Proust to finish his rant.

'I don't know what's going on in your personal life, Waterhouse, and I don't care, but if it affects work then I care. You come in here, giving it "Charlie this" and "Alice that" – this is CID, not a tawdry soap opera. Sort yourself out!'

'Sorry, sir.' Now was a bad time to start shaking. It was probably the effort of suppressing all his anger and frustration. Simon hoped Proust hadn't noticed, Proust who noticed everything. Why had he said that, about girlfriends?

'Look at the state of you! You're a mess!'

'I'll . . . sorry, sir.'

'So let's be absolutely clear: apart from your official involvement with Alice Fancourt over the allegations she made about her baby, you've had no contact with her at all. Is that correct?'

'Yes, sir.'

'You aren't carrying on with her?'

'No.' This, at least, was true. 'She had a baby less than a month ago, sir.'

'What about while she was pregnant? *Before* she was pregnant?'

'I've only known her a week, sir.'

Was it really only last Friday? It felt like longer. Simon had been on his way to pick up some CCTV footage his team needed for an ongoing misper, when he'd heard PC Robbie Meakin's voice on his radio, asking for any car to go to a residence called The Elms, on the Rawndesley Road. 'Woman by the name of Alice Fancourt. Says her baby's been abducted.'

Simon had been struck by the coincidence. He'd passed that property only about twenty seconds earlier and noticed the open, wrought-iron gates that must have been specially made to incorporate the name of the house in two large circles: 'The' on the gate on the left, 'Elms' on the right. Classier than those painted wooden signs, Simon had thought. 'I'm there. I'll take it,' he'd told Meakin. Reluctant though he was to be saddled with another case when he already had more than enough in his crime cue, he would have felt guilty ignoring this one when he was on the spot. It was a baby, after all.

He pulled in, turned the car round and headed back in the direction of Spilling. He'd barely accelerated when he found himself in front of The Elms. He could see a long driveway, a slice of tall, white house at the end of it, cut off by trees on one side and what looked like a barn on the other. In front of the barn, on the side nearest to the road, there was a paved area on which two cars were parked under bent, overhanging trees – a metallic blue BMW and a maroon Volvo that looked four hundred years old.

Simon waited not so patiently for a gap in the oncoming traffic so that he could turn in to the driveway. As he drummed his fingers on the steering wheel, Meakin's voice emerged from the static again. 'Waterhouse?'

'Yep.'

'Are you confidential?'

'Yeah.'

'You're gonna love this. The woman's husband's just phoned. He reckons the baby hasn't been abducted.'

'Hey?'

'There is a baby in the house. They both seem to agree on that. Husband reckons it's the one they brought home from hospital, wife says it isn't.' Meakin chuckled.

Simon groaned. 'Fucking hell!'

'Too late. You said you were taking it.'

'You bastard, Meakin.' Finally the traffic stopped and Simon was able to get across the road. Not that he wanted to any more. Why hadn't he left this one for uniforms to deal with? He was too bloody conscientious for his own good. An abducted baby was one thing. That was serious.

A woman claiming her baby was the wrong baby, that was a whole different kettle of fish. Simon was sure he'd landed himself a real winder. Alice Fancourt, he had no doubt, would turn out to be a hormonal housewife who woke up on the wrong side of bed this morning and decided to waste everybody's time.

And so more paperwork was generated. It didn't matter how absurd the allegation was. In these days of ethical crime reporting, every load of nonsense had to be crimed, given a case number and assigned to a sergeant, who in turn would assign it to a detective. It was part of the police force's attempt to pretend that it took all members of the public seriously. Which of course it didn't.

It wasn't the paperwork that worried Simon. He'd been in his element, while on secondment to CID, as evidence officer. He was less comfortable with the messy and often horrific human pantomimes he encountered on a daily basis, the ferocity of feeling that his work sometimes brought him into contact with. He was embarrassed to be present at many of the scenes that required his presence, and did most of his best work alone with his thoughts, or with a stack of files in front of him. Away from other people, anyway, other people and their mediocre ideas.

'Oh, and one more thing,' said Meakin.

'Yes?' It was unlikely to be good news.

'The address, The Elms – it's got an information marker against it on the computer.'

'Saying?'

'Just says "See linked incident", and the incident number.'

Simon sighed and scribbled down the number Meakin gave him. He'd check it out later.

He parked next to the BMW and the knackered Volvo,

noticing that the former was covered in dead leaves from the trees above, while the Volvo had only two on its bonnet, one red and one brownish-yellow. Simon walked up the driveway and rang the bell. The front door was solid wood and looked absurdly thick, as if it might be as deep as it was wide. The house was palatial, with a perfectly square, symmetrical façade. Its blank tidiness made Simon think of an article he had once read in a newspaper about a hotel that was made of ice. There was something forbidding about the apparent perfection on display that made Simon look even harder for chips and cracks. He found none. The white paintwork on the outer walls and window frames was immaculate.

After a few seconds, a slim, clean-shaven man wearing a checked shirt and jeans opened the door. He was a few inches shorter than Simon, and the vastness of the house made him appear even smaller than he was. His hair was light brown and looked as if it had been expensively cut. Simon guessed that most women would find his regular, well-proportioned features attractive.

David Fancourt. He had looked guilty, or embarrassed, or furtive. Something, anyway. No, not guilty. Simon hadn't thought that at the time. That was hindsight, backwards projection, like when you watch a film you've already seen and you know what's going to happen in the end. 'At last,' Fancourt said impatiently as he opened the door. He was holding a very young baby in his arms and a bottle of milk in one hand. The baby had a rounder head than many Simon had seen. Some looked dented, squashed. This one had hardly any hair and a couple of tiny white spots on its nose. Its eyes were open and it seemed to peer with intense curiosity, although Simon was sure he'd imagined that part. More memory tricks.

54

Behind Fancourt, he saw a spacious hall and a curved staircase made of dark, polished wood. How the other half lives, he thought. 'I'm Detective Constable Waterhouse. You reported the abduction of a baby?'

'David Fancourt. My wife has gone mad.' His tone implied that this was, if not Simon's fault, then at the very least his sole responsibility now that he had turned up.

And then, at the top of the stairs, Simon had seen Alice.

# 7

## Friday September 26, 2003

There is only one policeman. I'm sure they send two when they think it's serious. That's what happens on television, at any rate. I could scream with frustration. I decide not to. David has just told Detective Constable Waterhouse that I am mad, utterly mad, and I must not behave in a way that will instantly prove him right.

The policeman spots me at the top of the stairs and smiles briefly. It is a worried smile, and he continues to look at me long after it has faded. I cannot tell if he is trying to assess my mental state or find clues somewhere on my person or clothing, but he certainly stares at me for a long time. He is not wearing a police uniform. He described himself as a detective. Maybe these are both good signs. I think I remember someone telling me that plain clothes policemen are more senior.

I am heartened by his appearance. He is not handsome, but looks solid and serious. Best of all, he seems alert. He does not have the air of someone who is coasting along on autopilot, doing the bare minimum to get through his working day.

His big grey eyes are still locked on me. He is well-built, broad-shouldered, heavy without being fat. Burly is the word that springs to mind. The bridge of his nose is slightly misshapen, as if it has been broken. Beside him, David looks slight. Also vain, with his expensive, Italian salon haircut. Detective Constable Waterhouse has short bristly brown hair that looks as if it has been cut by a barber for a few pounds.

He has a square, slightly rugged face. It's the sort of face you could imagine being carved into a rock. I have no difficulty believing that he is a man who protects and rescues people, delivers justice. I hope he will deliver some to me. I guess that he is about my age, maybe slightly older, and wonder what his first name is.

'I'm Alice Fancourt,' I tell him. On legs that feel as feeble and inadequate as pipe-cleaners, I make my way towards him. When I am near enough, I shake his hand. David is furious that I am not proving him right by gibbering neurotically.

'She's drunk,' he says. 'She came back stinking of booze. She shouldn't even have been out driving! It's only two weeks since she had major abdominal surgery. She threatened to stab me.'

I feel my throat constrict with shock and hurt. I know he's upset, but how can he be so quick to bad-mouth me in front of a stranger? I would find it hard to do the same to him. It isn't as if love has a switch that you can flick to 'on' or 'off' at will. Then it occurs to me that perhaps it is the strength of David's love for me that fuels his rage. I would prefer to think this.

When he last spoke to Vivienne on the phone, he agreed with her that it was safe for me to drive, despite what the midwife had said. Now, it seems, he has changed his mind. David is not accustomed to disagreeing with his mother. Faced with one of her strong opinions, he is usually quiet and acquiescent. In her absence he spouts her theories about life word for word, as if he is trying on a personality that is too big for him. I sometimes wonder if David really knows himself at all. Or perhaps it is just that I do not know him.

'Please, Mr Fancourt, there's no need to be unpleasant,' says Detective Constable Waterhouse. 'You'll both get a chance to have your say. Let's just try to sort out this mess, shall we?'

'It's more than a mess! Someone's kidnapped my daughter. You need to get out there and start looking for her.' The policeman looks uncomfortable when I say this. I suspect that he is embarrassed on my behalf. How can she stand there and say that, he wonders, when there is a clearly visible infant in her husband's arms? He will be tempted to draw the most obvious conclusion: there is a baby in the house, therefore that baby must be our daughter.

'Florence is right here,' David snaps.

'I think my husband feels guilty,' I explain frantically, feeling my composure begin to slip away. I realise what is wrong. There is a sense of urgency missing from the proceedings. Everything is happening too slowly. That means the policeman doesn't believe me. My words come rushing out in a torrent. 'His guilt is expressing itself as anger. He fell asleep when he should have been looking after the baby. When I came back, I found the front door open. It's never open! Someone must have come in and swapped our daughter Florence for . . .' I point, unable to say any more.

'No, that's all rubbish, actually, because this is Florence, right here! Notice who's the one holding her, Inspector, the one looking after her, giving her her milk, comforting her while her mother cracks up.' David turns to me. 'Guilt expressing itself as anger – what a load of rubbish. Do you know what she does for a living, Inspector? Go on, tell him.'

'I'm not an inspector, I'm a detective,' says Waterhouse. 'Mr Fancourt, you're not helping by being so aggressive.' He doesn't like David, but he believes him.

'He's being aggressive because he's frightened,' I say. I believe this is true. My theory (I have had to resort to developing theories about my husband over the years, since he never confides in me) is that a lot of David's behaviour is motivated by fear.

He appears to think my occupation is in itself enough to discredit me. I feel wounded and belittled. I have always craved David's good opinion. I thought I had it. I have been married to him for two years. Before today, we have never exchanged harsh words, never argued, sulked, rowed. I used to think this was because we were in love, but in retrospect, our politeness seems entirely unnatural. I once asked David which party he voted for. He dodged the question, and I could tell he was shocked I'd asked. I felt awful, like an oaf with no sense of decorum. Vivienne regards it as bad manners to talk about politics, even to one's own family.

David is a very handsome man. The mere sight of him used to make me feel as if my stomach was doing somersaults. Now, I can neither imagine nor recreate my former desire for him. It would seem absurd, like lusting after an illustration. I admit to myself for the first time that my husband is a stranger. The closeness I have yearned for since I met him has eluded me, eluded us.

David works for a company that makes computer games. He and his friend Russell set up the business together. Russell was an acquaintance of mine at university, and it was at his wedding that I met David for the first time. I had finally surfaced from my depression, but the aching loneliness was still there. I could just about dodge it during the day if I kept myself busy, but it always caught up with me in the evening, when I would cry for at least an hour, usually more.

I am ashamed to admit it, but I even invented an imaginary friend for myself. I gave him a name: Stephen Taylor. I chose a common, everyday name to make him seem more real, I think. I could only get to sleep at night if I pretended he was holding me in his arms and whispering that he would always be there for me.

Stephen disappeared on the day of Russell's wedding. Somebody wrote my name next to David's on the seating plan and saved my life, or at least that was how it felt.

Almost the first thing David told me was that his wife had left him before their son was born, that he only saw Felix occasionally, for a couple of hours at a time. Ironically, I remember admiring his openness. I didn't know then that he would never again confide in me in the way that he did on that day. Perhaps there was an element of calculation involved and the Felix story was David's equivalent of a chat-up line.

It worked. I told him about my parents, of course. Talking to David made me realise that death is only one way in which we can lose those we love. I wanted to console him in his misery, and for him to console me in mine. I felt as if I'd met him for a reason and was totally determined that we would rescue one another, that I would end up as his wife. I was desperate to be Mrs Fancourt, to belong to a family again and have children of my own. Fear of being alone, of remaining alone throughout my life, was an all-consuming obsession.

Despite his obvious sadness about Felix, David kept saying that he didn't want to ruin my day by being miserable, and spent the afternoon entertaining and flattering me. He told me his Welsh joke, having first asked, 'You aren't, by any chance, at all Welsh, are you?' The joke was about a man who went to the police station to report that his bicycle had been stolen. 'I came out of chapel, and there it was – gone!' David delivered the punchline in an appalling accent that made me giggle for days afterwards every time I thought about it. I couldn't get him out of my mind. He had the warmest smile and twinkliest eyes of everyone at the wedding, and looked as much like a caricature of a wonderful, dream-come-true, romantic hero as the baddies in the games he and Russell design look like caricatures of pure evil, with their red and black capes, their mouths full of fangs and fire.

David and Russell never seem to run out of ideas for how baddies might be killed. Thanks to my husband, young children all over the country are able to simulate murder, some of it semi-pornographic, in the safety and comfort of their own homes. And yet I have always been supportive of David's work, approving of something I might normally have had qualms about in order to be loyal to him. If David does it, it must be okay – that was my life's motto. I thought he felt the same about me.

'Is there a quiet room somewhere where I can take your statement?' Detective Constable Waterhouse asks.

'There isn't time!' I protest. 'What about Florence? We need to start searching for her.'

'Nothing can happen until I've got your statement,' he insists.

David points to the kitchen. 'Take her in there,' he tells Waterhouse, as if I am an unruly dog. 'I'll take Florence upstairs to the nursery.'

I begin to cry. 'That isn't Florence. Please, you've got to believe me.'

'This way, Mrs Fancourt.' Waterhouse steers me into the kitchen, his big, bear-like hand wrapped around my arm just above the elbow. 'Why don't you make us some tea while I ask you a few questions?'

'I can't – I'm in too much of a state,' I say honestly. 'Get your own tea if you want some. You don't believe me, do you? I can tell you don't. And now I'm crying and you'll think I'm just a hysterical . . .'

'Mrs Fancourt, the sooner we get this statement done, the sooner . . .'

'I'm not stupid! You're not out there looking for Florence because you think that baby David's holding is her, don't you?'

'I'm making no assumptions.'

'No, but if there was no baby in the house, if David and I were both saying our daughter was missing, it'd be a different story, wouldn't it? The search for Florence would already be under way.'

Waterhouse blushes. He doesn't deny it.

'Why would I lie? What could I possibly have to gain by making this up?' I try very hard to keep my voice level.

'Why would your husband? Or are you suggesting he genuinely believes it's his daughter when it isn't?'

'No.' I consider carefully what I will say next. It goes against years of love and habit to malign David, but I can't hold back anything that might help to influence the policeman. 'He fell asleep when he was in charge of Florence. The front door was open. If he admits that baby's not Florence, that means admitting he allowed her to be taken. Not that I would ever blame him for what's happened,' I add quickly. 'I mean, who could predict something like this? But I think that's it, I think David isn't allowing himself to see the truth, because he's scared of the guilt he'd feel. But eventually he'll have to admit it, when he realises that his pretence is getting in the way of you looking for Florence!' I feel as desperate as I sound. I must speak more slowly.

Detective Constable Waterhouse is starting to look jittery, flustered, as if all this might be too much for him. 'Why would anyone swap one baby for another?' he asks me.

It strikes me as a slightly cruel question, though I know he doesn't mean it to be. Cruel is a bit strong, perhaps. Insensitive. 'You can't ask a mother to try to get inside the mind of the person who's stolen her child,' I say sharply. 'I honestly can't think of a single reason why anyone would do it. But so what? Where does that get us?'

'What is the difference between the baby I've just seen and your daughter? Anything you can tell me about any difference of appearance will help.'

I groan, frustrated. David asked me the same thing. It is a male thing, this desire to tick off items on a list. 'There is no significant difference that I can point to, apart from the absolutely crucial one that they're different people! Different babies. My daughter has a different face, a different cry. How the hell am I supposed to describe the difference between two babies' cries?'

'All right, Mrs Fancourt, calm down. Don't get upset.' Detective Constable Waterhouse looks as if he is slightly afraid of me.

I adopt a more soothing tone. 'Look, I know you come into contact with a lot of unreliable people. My job's the same. I'm a homeopath. Do you know what that means?' I prepare to launch into my usual introductory speech about conventional medicine being allopathic whereas homeopathy is based on the idea of curing like with like. His eyes widen briefly. Then he nods and blushes again.

I once had a patient who was a policeman. He was younger than me but already married with three children and suffering from severe depression because he hated his job. He wanted to be a landscape gardener. I told him he ought to follow his heart. That was how I felt at the time, having recently left a tedious administrative job at the Inland Revenue to become a homeopath. When I met David, when he and Vivienne rescued me from my miserable isolation, I was so grateful that all I wanted to do was help people. Now I wonder if I helped or hindered that poor man with my idealistic, impulsive advice. What if he resigned from the police force and was plunged into poverty as a result? What if his wife left him?

'A lot of my patients have their own unique perception of reality,' I say. 'In layman's terms, a lot of them are nutters. But I'm not, okay? I am a sane, intelligent woman, and I'm telling you, that baby upstairs is not my daughter Florence!' I open my shirt pocket, pull out the camera film and put it down on the table in front of him. 'Here. Hard evidence. Get this developed and you'll see lots of photos of the real Florence. With me and David, at the hospital and at home.'

'Thank you.' He picks up the film, puts it in an envelope and writes something on it that I can't see. Slow, steady, methodical. 'Now, if I could take some details.' He produces a notebook and pen.

His lack of urgency infuriates me. 'You still don't believe me!' I snap. 'Fine, don't believe me, I don't care if you believe me or not, but, please, get a team of detectives out there looking for her. What if you're wrong? What if I'm telling the truth, and Florence is really missing? Every second we waste could be a second closer to disaster.' My voice shakes. 'Can you really afford to take that risk?'

'Do you have any other photos of your daughter, Mrs Fancourt? Ones that are already developed?'

'No. Call me Alice. What's your name? Your first name, I mean.'

He looks doubtful. 'Simon,' he says eventually, cornered. Simon. It was on David's and my shortlist for Florence, if she'd been a boy. I wince. For some reason the memory of the list is particularly painful. Oscar, Simon, Henry. Leonie, Florence, Francesca. ('Fanny Fancourt! Over my dead body,' said Vivienne.) Florence. Mrs Tiggywinkle. Little Face.

'The hospital photographer was supposed to come and take her picture while we were on the ward, but she didn't come. Her car broke down.' I begin to sob. My body convulses, as if an electrical charge is running through it. 'We never got a "Baby's First Photo". Oh, God. Where is she?'

'Alice, it's okay. Try to calm down. We'll find her, if . . . we'll do the best we can.'

'There are other photos, apart from mine. Vivienne took some when she came to see us in hospital. She'll be back soon, she'll tell you I'm not mad.'

'Vivienne?'

'David's mother. This is her house.'

'Who else lives here?'

'Me, David, Florence, and Felix. He's David's son from his first marriage. He's six. Vivienne and Felix are in Florida at the moment, but they're coming back as soon as Vivienne can get them on a flight. She'll back me up. She'll tell you that baby's not Florence.'

'Your mother-in-law's seen Florence, then?'

'Yes, she came to the hospital the day she was born.'

'Which was?'

'The twelfth of September.'

'Has Felix seen Florence?'

I flinch. It's a sore point. I wanted Felix to meet Florence before he went to Florida. He could have come to the hospital after school, before going to the airport, but he had a snorkelling lesson at Waterfront that Vivienne insisted he should attend. 'The last thing you need is for him to associate Florence with missing something he loves,' she said. 'There's no rush for him to meet her, there'll be plenty of time later.' David agreed with his mother out of habit, and I didn't challenge her because I knew she was afraid on Felix's behalf. You can't argue with fear.

She assumes he will be as reluctant to share his kingdom as she herself was as a child. I think she's wrong. Not many children are as territorial as Vivienne was. She even objected to sharing her parents' attention with the family dog, who had to be given away when she was three. I wanted to ask his name when she told me this story but didn't dare. Ridiculously, I'd have felt disloyal showing an interest in Vivienne's rival.

'No,' I say. 'Felix was at school when Vivienne came to the hospital, and then they went away later that same day.'

'He's been away for a fortnight? Isn't it term time?'

'Yes.' At first I don't see the relevance of the question. 'Oh, but the school Felix goes to is very accommodating,' I add when I do. They have little choice. Vivienne is one of their more generous board members. They wouldn't dare to tell her when she can and can't take her grandson on holiday. 'He's at Stanley Sidgwick.'

Simon raises his eyebrows a fraction. Everybody has heard of the Stanley Sidgwick Grammar School and Ladies' College, and most have strong views about them of one sort or another. They are unashamedly élitist, fee-paying, single sex, strong on discipline. Vivienne is a big fan. She sent David to Stanley Sidgwick, and now Felix. Florence's place at the ladies' college was reserved as soon as my twenty-week scan revealed I was having a girl; her name went down on the list as 'Baby Fancourt'. Vivienne paid the three-hundred-pound registration fee herself, and only mentioned it to me and David afterwards. 'There's no better school in the area, or, for that matter, in the country, whatever the league tables say,' she insisted. I probably nodded vaguely and looked bemused. All I wanted was to deliver my unborn child safely into the world. I hadn't given schools a thought.

'Felix doesn't live with his mother?' asks Simon.

I wasn't expecting him to ask this. I admire his thorough approach, the way he asks questions around the obvious point of focus. I do the same with my patients. Sometimes, by looking only where you're directed to look, you miss everything that's important. 'Felix's mother is dead.' I watch Simon carefully as I say this. He doesn't know, evidently. It is absurd to assume that every policeman will be familiar with the details of every case. Or maybe he knows, but hasn't yet made the connection. Laura's surname wasn't Fancourt. She didn't change it when she married David. That was the first thing that annoyed Vivienne about her, the first of many.

'So, apart from Vivienne Fancourt, who's seen Florence?'

'Nobody. Oh, Cheryl Dixon – she's my midwife. She's been round three times. And she was on duty at the hospital when Florence was born. Why didn't I think of that before?' I wonder aloud. 'Cheryl'll back me up, talk to Cheryl.'

'Don't worry, I'll be talking to everyone, Mrs . . .'

'Alice,' I insist.

'Alice,' he repeats awkwardly, trapped in a familiarity that he is clearly uncomfortable with.

'What about a search?' I ask. I still have not had a satisfactory answer to this question. 'Someone might have seen something. You need to appeal for witnesses. I can give you precise times. I went out at five to two . . .'

Simon shakes his head. 'I can't get a search started just like that,' he says. 'That's not the way it works. I'd need to get approval from my sergeant, but first I'll need to talk to everyone and anyone who could corroborate your story. I'll need to talk to your neighbours, for example, see if anyone saw anything unusual. Because your husband . . .'

'Isn't corroborating. I know. I've noticed,' I say bitterly. 'There aren't any neighbours.' Vivienne told me proudly, the first time David brought me to The Elms, that the only people with whom she shares a postcode are those she welcomes into her home. She smiled, to make it clear that I was included in this category. I felt privileged and protected. When my parents died and I realised there was no-one in the world who truly loved me, I lost a lot of my self-esteem. I couldn't shake off the conviction that my tragedy was a punishment of some kind. To be so warmly accepted by a woman like Vivienne, who took for granted her own value and importance and had absolute confidence in her every opinion, made me feel that I must be worth more than I'd imagined.

'I can't get a search started or do anything on your say-so alone,' says Simon apologetically.

I sink into a chair and rest my aching head on my arms. When I close my eyes, I see strange shifting spots of light. Nausea rocks my stomach. For the first time in my life, I understand the people who lose the will to fight. It is so hard to try and try to make yourself heard when the whole world seems to have its fingers in its ears, when what you have to say sounds so unlikely – impossible, almost.

I'm not a fighter, not by nature. I've never thought of myself as strong; at times I've been downright weak. But I am a mother now. I have Florence to think of as well of myself. Instead of myself. Giving up isn't an option.

# 8

## 3/10/03, 2pm

Ten minutes after the conclusion of his interview with Proust and Simon was back in the canteen. The one-armed bandit machine was mercifully, unusually silent, as if out of respect for the gravity of his mood. The inspector had treated his hypothesis with contempt, called him paranoid and ordered him to go and get his head together. 'I don't want you working in this state. You'll only make an irritation of yourself and ruin everything,' he'd said – Proust's equivalent of compassionate leave.

What was wrong with everybody today? Why couldn't they see what seemed to Simon to be glaringly obvious? Was it because Proust and Charlie had both been involved in putting Darryl Beer away? Was that why they were so keen to cast Simon as the unstable eccentric who let his personal agenda get in the way of the facts? Meanwhile, the possible personal agenda of David Fancourt was ignored by all. First wife dead, second wife missing. Fact.

Simon got himself a cup of tea and fantasised about beating the truth out of Fancourt. Some things were worth doing time for. What had the bastard done to Alice? What had he told Proust about Simon? It had to be him who'd said something, not Charlie. These questions were a torment that brought Simon no closer to any sort of answer. He heard a cough behind him and turned.

'Proust said I'd find you here. I've just spoken to him.

Correction: I've just listened to him. At length. He's not happy with you, not happy at all.'

'Charlie!' Seeing her made him feel that perhaps there was hope, perhaps doom could be warded off for a while longer. 'Did you manage to calm him down? You're the only one who can.'

'Don't put me in a foul mood again straight away,' she said grimly, sitting down opposite him. It was impossible for Simon to give Charlie a compliment without her getting cross. There was only one sort of compliment she wanted, one that Simon couldn't give her. She seemed determined to dismiss all lesser endorsements from him as pity or charity. Sometimes he wondered how she could even look at him. How could she see him as anything but pathetic after Sellers' fortieth birthday party last year? Simon pushed the horrific memory away, as he did whenever it rose to the surface.

'What did The Snowman say?' he asked.

'That you were babbling like a fool. He thinks you've got a thing about Alice Fancourt. Her husband thinks so too. Anyone with eyes and a brain can spot it a mile off. You get that slobbering idiot look on your face when you talk about her.'

Her words stung. Simon didn't bother to argue.

'He also says you denied that any inappropriate behaviour had taken place.'

'Does he believe me?'

'I very much doubt it. So you'd better make damn sure he never finds out, if you're lying. Anyway, my instructions are to treat mother and baby's disappearance as a misper if they don't turn up within twenty-four hours.'

Simon's eyes widened. 'You? Does that mean . . .'

'Proust's assigned it to me, yes. To our team. Because of

our extensive experience of the Fancourt family,' she added sarcastically.

'I thought there was no way he'd let me near this one. Thank you!' Simon cast his eyes towards the ceiling's buzzing strip-lights. He believed strongly in something unspecific. His mother had always hoped he would become a priest. Maybe she still did. Simon had inherited her need to cling to something, but not her conviction that God was that thing. He hated the idea that he had anything in common with his mother.

'Proust's full of surprises, I'll give him that,' said Charlie. 'He told me he thinks you might get a result simply because you care so much. He reckons you want to find Alice Fancourt a fuck of a lot more than anyone else round here does.' Her tone suggested she was part of the anyone else.

Simon put his head in his hands. 'If I get the chance to start looking.' He groaned. 'Charlie, this business could really fuck me up. I've met Alice twice, unofficially. She . . . she told me things that I'm going to have to come clean about, once the investigation starts. You *know* I don't deserve to lose my job, you know how good I am . . .'

'As do you,' she said flatly, raising an eyebrow. 'How could I forget? Without you, we'd all be scratching our ears and picking our teeth, incapable of closing a single case.'

'Yeah, well. When you're as shit as I am at most things, it's hard to miss when, surprise fucking surprise, you find you can actually do something well. And this – being a detective – is something I do well.'

'Oh, really? So how come you never mention it? You should have said.'

'Fuck off!'

Charlie laughed. 'Only you could boast outrageously and sound like a victim at the same time.'

And only you could patronise me in that particular fond, proprietorial, sneery way that makes me want to give you a good hard slap, thought Simon. He said, 'I know I've got no right to ask you but . . . any ideas about how I get myself out of this mess?'

Charlie looked unsurprised. She shook a set of car keys in front of his face. 'Come on.'

'Where?'

'Somewhere we can't be overheard.' The canteen was a breeding ground for gossip. They pushed their way through the tables, chairs and loud graphic jokes and headed out of the building.

Charlie drove like a man, steering with two fingers, or sometimes with her wrist, ignoring speed limits, swearing at other drivers. They left Spilling on the Silsford road, with Radio Two blaring. Simon only ever listened to Radio Four by choice, but had long ago given up trying to persuade Charlie to compromise. Radio One in the morning, Radio Two from one o'clock onwards, that was her rule. Which meant Steve Wright in the afternoon, factoids, songs that should only be played in lifts or hotel lobbies, everything bland that Simon hated.

He focused instead on the flat, orderly landscape that was passing too quickly. Normally he found it calming but today it looked empty. It was missing something. Simon realised with a rush of embarrassment that he was hoping to see Alice. Every face, every figure he saw that wasn't hers was a disappointment. Desperate panic had given way to a sort of mournful wallowing.

What was it that he had seen in Alice that seemed to speak to something similar in him? She was pretty, but Simon's feelings for her had nothing to do with the way she looked. It was something in her manner, a hint of unease, a sense that she was not in her element, that she was negotiating unseen obstacles. It was how Simon felt all the time. Some people knew how to glide effortlessly through life. He didn't, and he guessed Alice didn't either. She was too sensitive, too complicated. Though he'd only seen her in a state of extreme distress. He had no idea what she was like before last week.

Charlie would call him a fantasist, inventing Alice's character on the basis of so little evidence. But weren't all perceptions of other people based on such inventions? Wasn't it crazy to assume that one's family, friends and acquaintances added up to coherent wholes whose natures could be summarised and fixed? Most of the time Simon felt more like a collection of random behaviours, each driven by an insane, anarchic compulsion he didn't entirely understand.

He shook his head when he heard Sheryl Crow's mediocre voice. Typical. Charlie sang along: something about days being winding roads. Simon thought it was bollocks.

Charlie slammed on the brakes just before they got to the Red Lion pub, about five miles from town, and swan-necked into its car park. 'I'm not in the mood,' said Simon, his stomach protesting at the prospect of alcohol.

'Don't worry, we're not going in. I just didn't want to give you this anywhere near the station.' She rummaged in her large black suede handbag and produced a standard issue police pocket book, the sort that every officer carried. Every incident of every shift, significant or insignificant, had to be recorded, along with details of the weather and the conditions on the roads. Simon had his in his inside jacket pocket.

Charlie threw the book into his lap. It was brown, seven inches by five, and, like all pocket books, had an issue number on the cover next to a sergeant's signature, in this case Charlie's.

'Are you saying what I think you're saying?'

'It's your only option, isn't it? Make your unofficial meetings with Alice Fancourt official. Your chance to rewrite history.'

'You shouldn't have to lie for me.' He was pissed off that she'd had the book ready and waiting. She'd known he'd come running to her for help sooner or later. Embarrassingly predictable.

'Yeah, well.' Charlie grimaced. 'It's still a risk. If anyone looks too closely at the serial numbers . . . It goes without saying that if you get rumbled, you didn't get that book from me.'

'I'll have to write everything out again.' Simon closed his eyes, tired by the mere thought of the effort involved.

'You're not the first and you won't be the last. Look, I'm not thrilled about this, but I can't bear to stand back and watch you fuck up your entire life. I'm too much of a control freak. And . . . you're the cleverest, most inspired and inspiring person I've ever worked with – and don't agree with me or I'll bloody strangle you – and it'd be a tragedy if this one fuck-up ruined everything. If anyone asks, I'll say I knew about the meetings and gave you the go-ahead.'

Her careful deliberate compliments made Simon feel belittled. She was incapable of treating him as an equal, and he was pretty sure it wasn't just because she was a sergeant. He wondered what precisely it would take to satisfy him. 'That won't work, will it? Doesn't everyone know you were all for cuffing the swapped baby allegation? Why would you authorise me to conduct further interviews?'

Charlie shrugged. 'I pride myself on my thorough approach,' she said drily.

They sat in silence for a while, watching people enter and leave the pub.

'I'm sorry,' said Simon eventually. 'I shouldn't have lied to you. I hated it. But you never believed Alice's story. You thought she was wasting our time. That's why I didn't tell you. I was worried about her and . . . look, I'm not saying I believed her about the baby, but . . . well, I felt I couldn't just abandon her.'

Charlie's face twitched, tightened. Simon regretted his use of the word 'abandon'. They were talking about work, a clash of his professional judgement and hers, but that didn't change the fact that he'd lied to Charlie, that his lie had involved another woman.

'I take it that, in your eyes at least, I'm not a suspect.'

'A fool, yes. A suspect, no. They say it's blind, though, don't they?' Charlie looked out of the car window so that he couldn't see her face. 'We'd better shift our arses, much as I'm enjoying this romantic interlude,' she said. Again, Simon pushed the image of himself and Charlie at Sellers' fortieth birthday party out of his mind. He closed his eyes, craving unconsciousness. Today was proving to be more than he could handle. He tried to banish all thoughts from his head.

Immediately, something clicked inside his brain. He had it. He knew what it was that had been stuck like a piece of grit in his mind's eye. 'The night Laura Cryer was killed,' he began. 'When Beer tried to mug her . . . ?'

'Not that again.'

'She was alone, right? You said she went back to the car alone.'

Charlie turned to face him. 'Yes.' She frowned. 'Why?'

'She didn't have her son Felix with her?'

'No.'

'He was at The Elms that night with his grandmother, because Cryer was working late,' Simon persisted.

'Yeah? So?' Impatience crept into Charlie's voice.

'Why didn't she pick up her son and take him home? He lived with her, presumably?'

A flicker of uncertainty passed across Charlie's face. 'Well, because . . . because he was staying over at his gran's house, maybe.'

'In that case,' said Simon, 'why did Laura Cryer go to The Elms at all that night?'

# 9

## *Friday September 26, 2003*

My midwife, Cheryl Dixon, has arrived. She is in her late forties, a tall, buxom woman with strawberry blonde straight hair, cut in that short, feathery style that is fashionable at the moment, and pale, freckly skin. Today she is wearing trousers that are slightly too tight and a velour V-necked jumper that highlights her substantial cleavage. Cheryl's passion in life is amateur dramatics. She is currently appearing in a production of *The Mikado* at Spilling Little Theatre. The first night of the show's two-week run was two Saturdays ago. I had to apologise for missing it on account of having had a baby the day before. I got the impression that she didn't think it was a wholly satisfactory excuse.

Cheryl nicknamed Florence 'Flipper' when her position in my stomach changed from week to week. When I asked silly questions, she called me a 'funny onion'. Sometimes she got exasperated with me, when I became neurotic and requested unnecessary monitoring. 'Cheese on bread!' she would say, or 'Flipping Ada!'

She was on duty at Culver Valley Hospital the night Florence was born. It was she who told me to bring Florence into bed with me when she wouldn't stop crying. 'Nothing like a cuddle with Mummy in a nice warm bed to make baby feel better,' she'd said, swaddling Florence in a hospital blanket and tucking her under my arm.

Tears prick the backs of my eyelids. It will do me no good to think about that now.

'When did you last see Florence Fancourt?' Simon asks Cheryl. 'Before today, that is.' He glances apologetically in my direction. I refuse to meet his eye.

We are in the room that is known as the little lounge, although it is not little by anyone's standards. This is where evenings are spent at The Elms, watching television and talking. Vivienne will not allow any television until after Felix has gone to bed. Even then, she is only prepared to watch the news or documentaries. Occasionally she catches an accidental glimpse of a reality TV programme and mutters, 'How ghastly!' or 'How different from the home life of our own dear Queen.'

Sofas and chairs line the walls – too many, as if a party of twenty people is expected at any moment. A long, rect-angular, glass-topped coffee table is the room's centrepiece, a family heirloom. Its base is bronze, a thick S-shape on its side. I have always thought it hideous, the sort of thing an ostentatious Pharaoh might have in his palace. At the moment there is no coffee on the table, only a Moses basket that contains a baby in a Bear Hug babygro, sleeping under a yellow fleece blanket.

I sit in an armchair in the corner, knees pulled up to my chest, arms wrapped round my legs. This position hurts my Caesarian wound. The physical pain is almost comforting. I haven't taken my hypericum pill today. Soon they will run out and I'll have to go to my office to get more or switch to gelsemium. I felt sorry for a woman who was in the bed next to mine on the labour ward, and gave her most of my hypericum tablets. Mandy. She'd also had a Caesarian and her wound had developed a haematoma. She had bad acne scars and was tiny, tooth-pick thin. She looked too small to have ever contained a baby. Her boyfriend harangued her in front of the whole ward about when she'd be home and able to look after him again. They argued endlessly about what to call their child. Her voice sounded tired and hopeless as she suggested name after name. The boyfriend kept insisting on Chloe, swearing at her.

David and I eavesdropped through the plastic hospital curtain that separated our quarter of the ward from the other three, and could hardly believe our ears when we found out that the reason he was so set on Chloe was because he already had a daughter by that name from a previous relationship. Mandy kept trying and failing to convince him that this was a reason against, not in favour.

I decided that she needed the hypericum more than I did, and gave it to her after the horrible boyfriend had gone home one night. She said thank you abruptly, as if no-one had ever been kind to her before and she considered it almost rude.

David sits on the white sofa by the window, tapping his right foot on the floor. Every so often he inhales sharply and we all look at him, expecting him to speak. He doesn't, though. He just shakes his head and closes his mouth. He cannot believe what is happening. After I gave my statement, he gave his. Soon Cheryl will give hers. It is as if we are all taking part in a bizarre cult ceremony.

I would like to be able to say that, as Florence's mother, my statement is worth any number of other people's, but I fear that it isn't. Simon wouldn't let me say half of what I wanted to say. He kept telling me that it had to be a factual account. I was not allowed to use what he called flowery language. I was not allowed to begin any sentence with the words 'I felt', or to say that it was my suspicion that someone crept into the house and took Florence while

David was napping. Apparently you can only include an opinion in a statement if it is a 'Hobstaff', whatever that might be. Simon tells me that this situation is not one.

In the end, all I was permitted to say was that when I came home this afternoon after having been to Waterfront, I noticed that the front door was open, which was unusual, and then I went upstairs and observed that the baby in the cot was not my daughter, although superficially she looked like Florence.

I will not speak again for the time being. I will not contradict David, whatever he says. What's the point? It isn't as if Simon believes me, and nothing I say or do is going to change anybody's mind. I will save my next effort for when Vivienne arrives.

'Mrs Dixon? I asked you when you last saw Florence?'

Cheryl stands on the Persian rug in the middle of the room, peering into the Moses basket. Every few seconds she looks up at me anxiously. She is uncomfortable with my silence and wants me to say something to make her task easier. 'I saw her on Tuesday this week. Three days ago.'

'And is this the same baby that you saw then?'

She squirms, wrinkles her forehead. I have to look away. I feel utterly drained. My brain has grown fuzzy around the edges, as if someone is trying to rub it out. I hug my knees tighter and steel myself for Cheryl's response. 'I don't know,' she says. 'I'm really not sure. They change so much in the early days and I see so many babies, sometimes ten or twelve a day. I mean, if Alice is positive . . .' She tails off.

Shock, astonishment, surges through me. At last, somebody who is not one hundred per cent certain that I am wrong, someone who thinks I might actually be worth listening to. 'Now will you do something?' I beg.

'Not sure? What does that mean? You can't say that!'

'Mr Fancourt, please.' Simon's voice is low, authoritative. 'Mrs Dixon is here to help us. If you're going to intimidate her, I'll have to ask you to leave the room.'

'It's my house!' David snaps.

'No, it's not. It's Vivienne's house, and she's on her way back,' I remind him. Suddenly it seems worth speaking again.

'I'm really sorry I can't be more definite,' says Cheryl. 'I just don't have a clear memory of Florence's face. And, as I say, they change so much in the early days, don't they?'

'They don't change into different people,' David bellows. He leaps up off the sofa. 'This is preposterous. This is the most ludicrous thing that's ever happened to me in my whole life. It's Florence! It's definitely her!'

I feel sorry for him, but sorrier for myself, and, above all, for Florence. I used to think I had enough love and determination in me to help everyone who needed it equally. Not any more.

'You've checked it's a girl, then?' says Cheryl. We stare at each other, mute and paralysed. Silence spreads through the room like sticky, black syrup. 'You haven't checked the sex of the baby?' Cheryl asks Simon, who hardens his face at the perceived criticism.

'He hasn't checked because he doesn't think there's any need to,' I tell her. 'He doesn't believe me.'

'For God's sake.' David turns away in disgust. 'Go on, take her nappy off. She's due a change anyway. I can tell you exactly what nappy she's wearing too – it's a newborn size Pampers Baby Dry.' And she has blue eyes and milk spots on her nose, and no hair, I wait for him to add.

'All babies wear those,' I say quietly. 'David, that doesn't prove anything. You had plenty of time to change her while I was talking to Simon in the kitchen.'

'*Simon?*' David looks at him, then at me. 'So you two have got all pally, have you?'

'You're making this more unpleasant than it needs to be, Mr Fancourt.'

Cheryl begins to unbutton the Bear Hug babygro. She does not ask for anybody's permission.

'Can't you take her upstairs to change her?' I say shakily. 'She's a baby, not a piece of evidence.' My eyes and brain hurt, and the inside of my nose tingles with the constant effort of not crying. I cannot take much more.

'Her!' David pounces on the word.

'She's obviously a girl,' I say.

'See, you know it's Florence.' David jabs a finger at me. 'You've gone mad, but deep down you know it's Florence.'

'Do I?' I say vaguely. He sounds so certain. I look round the room, at each face in turn. Three big faces, one little face. 'No. No, I don't know that at all.'

I leave the room, unable to watch as Florence's Bear Hug babygro is removed. I wait outside the little lounge with my eyes closed for what feels like hours, pressing my forehead against the cool wallpaper in the hall. 'It's a girl,' I hear Cheryl say eventually, shouting to make herself heard above the noise of outraged crying. I remember the last time I heard those words, at my twenty-week scan, and my knees buckle. *It's a girl. You're going to have a daughter.* But for how long will she be mine? – I didn't think to ask. How long before someone takes her away from me, or me from her? Nobody said anything about that.

'In a Pampers Baby Dry nappy,' says David. 'Now do you believe me?'

'Put her clothes back on,' I plead from the hall.

'Alice, where's her red book?' Cheryl asks briskly. 'It's got all Florence's details in it – weight, height, any birthmarks. Every baby has one,' she tells Simon. 'That's one way to check the basics. I've got my scales in the car. I'll go and get them.'

'Her red book's in her room,' I say.

'I'll get it,' says David. 'This should settle it once and for all.'

I don't see how. Babies gain and lose weight all the time, especially when they are very young. There is always height, I suppose. That is an area in which one would expect only an upward curve.

David passes me in the hall and gives me a puzzled look, as if he's not sure, but he thinks I might be somebody he once knew. I want to reach out to him, but it is already too late. We have both set off on our separate paths.

'Right, little lady, you wait here,' I hear Cheryl say. 'There's no point dressing you just to undress you again, is there? We'll just wrap you in this nice blanket, keep you lovely and warm. No funny business, mind!' Funny business is Cheryl's cover-all term for bodily functions. Perhaps this is not the most difficult situation she has encountered in her professional life. She must have to deal with real tragedies sometimes. She knows how to be calm and practical even in the worst of circumstances. Please let this not be the start of a real tragedy, I pray, let it be only a temporary horror.

David comes downstairs with the red book. This time he looks at me with utter contempt. I follow him into the lounge. 'Florence was last weighed on Tuesday,' I say. 'She was eight pounds and thirteen ounces. That baby looks a bit heavier.'

' "That baby",' David mutters. He has his back to the room and is staring out of the window. His voice sounds as if it's coming from far away. When he turns, his face is pale with anger. 'All right, then. All right. I didn't want to have to do this, but you've asked for it. Are you going to tell *Simon* about your history of mental illness or shall I?'

'Don't be ridiculous,' I say. 'David, do you remember that woman from the hospital? Mandy?'

'Alice was on Prozac for depression for nearly a year after her parents died. Also, and Cheryl will back me up on this, the night after Florence was born she claimed another baby was Florence, some random baby in the hospital.'

I freeze. This is true, but I'd forgotten about it almost completely. It's so stupid and irrelevant. I didn't even know David knew about it. I certainly haven't told him. One of the midwives must have, when he came to visit the next day.

Cheryl appears in the doorway, carrying her scales. I can see from her face that she heard what David said. She looks at me unhappily. She doesn't want to betray me, but her common sense is telling her that perhaps the incident is relevant, perhaps her belief in my sanity and trustworthiness has been a little rash.

'I was exhausted,' I explain. 'I'd just had an emergency C-section after a three-day labour. I was so tired I was hallucinating, literally.'

'You still are,' says David. 'Look where your hallucinations have got us.'

'Cheryl offered to take Florence so that I could sleep, and I let her. Then I felt guilty. It should have been my first night with my little girl and I'd been only too glad to hand her over.' I cannot stop the flow of tears as I tell this story. Part of me feared, that night, that I was the worst mother in the world. A good mother would surely cling to her precious baby twenty-four hours a day and make sure no harm came to her. 'After ten minutes or so I was still awake, overtired and feeling guilty, missing Florence like mad, so I thought I might as well go and get her back. I buzzed for a midwife, and Cheryl came in a few seconds later holding a tiny baby. I . . . I thought it was Florence, but only because it was Cheryl who'd taken her away a few minutes earlier. I was almost out of my mind with tiredness. I hadn't slept at all for three days!'

'And as soon as I brought Florence into the room, she realised her mistake,' says Cheryl. Thank God. She is still on my side. Simon knows this too, and he is inclined to take me more seriously because I have the tacit support of my midwife. Thank God for Cheryl.

'Cheryl, do you remember Mandy?' I ask.

'Three days she was in agony,' David tells Simon. 'It wasn't even proper labour, that's what they said. They tried to induce her twice and failed. Even when they put her on a drip, it didn't work. Nothing did. In the end they did an emergency Caesarian but the anaesthetic didn't work properly. Did it?' His eyes challenge me to deny it.

I shake my head.

'The pain was so bad she passed out. She missed the best bit, when they lifted Florence out. By the time she came round, it was all over. And the breast-feeding was a total failure too, Alice was devastated about that. She'd really wanted to feed Florence herself. Don't you think all that'd be enough to traumatise anyone, Inspector? To bring on a sort of . . . I don't know, post-natal madness?'

I am too shocked by David's account of Florence's birth to say anything in my defence. He seems to know all the facts but none of the truth. Did he perceive it so negatively at the time? If so, he showed no sign of it.

For the first time, I visualise his mind as a dangerous country, one I am afraid to enter. All these years I have waited for him to let me in, assuming that I knew or could imagine how the land lay. I pictured the anguish and insecurity that were the legacy of having grown up without a father, been separated from his son, suffered the trauma of Laura's death. I attributed to him the thoughts and feelings that I would have had if I were him.

'This isn't getting us anywhere,' Simon sighs. 'Let's weigh the baby.'

In my head, I start to write an alternative statement, one that is far truer than the thing I signed for Simon:

*My name is Alice and I love my daughter Florence more than life, more than all the best things in the world put together. Her full name is Florence Imogen Fancourt. She has a perfectly round head, hardly any hair, dark blue eyes and a tiny, perfect mouth like a little pink flower. Her fingers, toes and eyelashes are all surprisingly long. She smells clean and fresh, powdery and new. She has my dad's ears. When I lean her over my hand to burp her, her round shoulders slump forward and she makes a funny throaty noise, as if she is trying to gargle. She has a way of tucking her hands and feet neatly together, daintily, like a ballet dancer, and she doesn't cry in the random, anarchic way that some babies do. She cries like an angry grown-up with a serious grievance.*

'Nine pounds exactly.'

'So? So? That proves nothing. She's put on weight, that's all. Babies do.'

*On Friday 12th September 2003, she was delivered by emergency Caesarian section at Culver Valley General Hospital. She weighed 7 pounds and 11 ounces. It was not a nightmare, as my husband says, but the happiest day of my life. As the doctors and midwives were wheeling me through from the delivery room to the operating theatre, I heard one of them shout to David, 'Bring some clothes for the baby'. That was when it hit me that all this was real.*

*I craned my neck and just managed to catch a glimpse of David ransacking my hospital bag. He pulled out a white bodysuit and a white babygro with little Pooh Bears and Tiggers all over it. 'Pooh likes his honey, but Tigger thinks it's funny'. Vivienne bought it. 'A baby's first outfit should be white,' she said. I remember thinking to myself, my daughter is going to wear those clothes. Soon.*

'Have you contacted the hospital?' says Cheryl. 'There's an outside chance they'll still have the placenta and the umbilical cord. You could test whether they come from this baby. We're supposed to dispose of them after two days, but, between you and me, it doesn't always happen. You'd better get on to them quick, mind.'

'Oh, for Pete's sake. This is a farce! Are you really going to . . .'

*As they pushed me into the operating theatre, a song by Cher was playing loudly, the one where her voice goes all wobbly. I instantly loved it, and knew that from now on it would remind me of my baby's birth. It would be my song, mine and my child's. The anaesthetist squirted blue gel on to my stomach. 'This shouldn't feel cold,' he said.*

'That wouldn't be too costly, I suppose, in terms of manpower and resources. Could take a while for the result to come through, though.'

'See! He doesn't want to get in trouble with his boss, for wasting public money on what's obviously sheer lunacy.'

'And the other women on the ward, this Mandy girl Alice mentioned.'

'None of those women so much as gave Florence a second glance!'

'Mr Fancourt, you're not helping. Excuse me a minute, everybody.'

*It felt cold.*

# IO

## Entries from DC Simon
## Waterhouse's Pocket Book

### (Written 3/10/03, 7 pm)

*27/9/03, 11 am*

*Area: Spilling Police Station. Received a phone call from Alice Fancourt (see index). She said she needed to talk to me urgently because she had some new information pertaining to the matter of her allegation that her baby has been abducted and swapped for another baby (case no. NS1035–03-Q). I suggested that she should accompany her mother-in-law Mrs Vivienne Fancourt (see index) to the police station later today (Vivienne Fancourt has arranged to come in and give us her statement) and I said I would talk to her then. Mrs Fancourt started to cry and said she needed to talk to me alone, in private, away from both her mother-in-law and her husband David Fancourt (see index). I consulted with my sergeant, DS 326 Charlotte Zailer, who authorised me to meet and talk to Mrs Fancourt. Mrs Fancourt suggested we meet at Chompers Café Bar in her health club, 'Waterfront' (Saltney Road, Spilling), at 1400 hours on Sunday 28 September. I told her that was impossible and suggested Monday 29th. Mrs Fancourt became agitated and said she didn't think she could wait that long, but I told her I couldn't see her sooner. I said the police station might be a more suitable venue than Chompers, but Mrs Fancourt insisted that she wanted to meet somewhere 'less official and intimidating'.*

*She then told me that Vivienne Fancourt was also a member of Waterfront, but that she never went to Chompers Café Bar* because she thought it was 'a hell-hole'. Just in case Vivienne Fancourt went to the health club on the same afternoon, Alice Fancourt said that I should not go in via the front door and the main lobby area, but rather I should enter the café bar through the door on Alder Street. That way, Mrs Fancourt was certain that, even if her mother-in-law was on the premises, she wouldn't see me. I said that this sounded too complicated and again asked her to come to the police station. She refused, became hysterical, and said that if I didn't meet her where she said, she wouldn't give me the new information she had. She said that Chompers was the one place Vivienne Fancourt could be guaranteed not to go to because she 'boycotts the place on principle'.

I told Mrs Fancourt that I would seek my sergeant's approval and that she should call me back in ten minutes. I then consulted DS Zailer and told her that I was worried about the unusual nature of Mrs Fancourt's demands, but she said we should agree to her terms in order to obtain whatever new information she had. Mrs Fancourt phoned back four minutes later and we agreed to meet at Chompers Café Bar in the Waterfront Health Club complex at 1400 hours on Monday 29th September. Mrs Fancourt then said that if she wasn't there by 1430 hours, I shouldn't wait any longer. She said that she feared she might not be able to leave the house. She sounded frightened when she told me this, and said goodbye and hung up immediately afterwards.

29/9/03, 2 pm

Area: Chompers Café Bar at Waterfront Health Club, 27 Saltney Road, Spilling. 1400 hours: when I arrived, Alice Fancourt (see index) was already there, sitting at a table in the non-smoking part of the room. The conditions in Chompers were as follows:

full, noisy, smoky, very warm. There was a lot of background noise of talking and laughing and loud pop music coming from speakers all round the room. On one side of the room, there was a children's zone, full of toys, a paddling pool containing plastic balls, a small plastic climbing frame and a Wendy house. There were ten or so children, between the ages of approximately two and seven, playing in this section of the room.

As I sat down, Mrs Fancourt said to me, 'Look at the parents. They don't even glance over to check they're okay. Clearly none of them has ever seriously feared for the safety of their children.' I pointed out that there was nothing to fear, and Mrs Fancourt replied, 'I know. I just wish I could tell them how lucky they are.' She seemed calm at first, but as she started to talk, she became more distressed. She said she had a favour to ask me. She wanted me to help her to track down her husband's father (name unknown), about whom she has been told almost nothing except that he left the family home when David Fancourt was six and has not been in touch with his son since. I explained that I couldn't do anything without the authorisation of my sergeant, and that Sergeant Zailer would definitely not allow me to track down David Fancourt's father because there was no good reason to do so in relation to any of our active investigations.

I asked her why she wanted to find her father-in-law and she said, 'I want to ask him why he left, why he just abandoned his son. What sort of a father would do that? Why does nobody ever mention him? What if . . . ?' She did not complete her question, even after I prompted her. She said, 'I think, if I could speak to David's father, it might help me to understand David better.' She told me that her husband used to 'idealise' her and that now he has 'demonised' her. 'Did you know that people who've had brutalised, abusive childhoods often do that? It's a typical response,' she said.

Mrs Fancourt then told me that there was a woman on the

labour ward at the same time as her whom she wished to contact. She said that the woman's name was Mandy, but that she didn't know any of her other details. She asked me if I could help her to find this woman. At first she appeared reluctant to tell me why she was interested in Mandy, but then she seemed to change her mind quite suddenly. She said that she had told Mandy where she lived, and that she had 'seen in Mandy's eyes' that Mandy had recognised her description of The Elms (see index). She claimed that it would put her mind at rest if she could pay Mandy a visit and reassure herself that the baby in Mandy's care was Mandy's daughter and not her own.

'Mandy had a horrible, aggressive boyfriend,' Mrs Fancourt told me. 'What if she was worried he'd harm their daughter, so she swapped her with Florence in order to protect her? I've been racking my brains and I can't think of any other reason why someone might swap one baby for another.' Mrs Fancourt became extremely panicky and tearful as she said this. 'It would be my fault,' she said. 'I told Mandy where we lived.'

I tried to calm Mrs Fancourt down, but she talked over me, telling me that, although she did not know the name of Mandy's boyfriend, she could describe him. She began to do so, but I interrupted her and told her that I very much doubted Sergeant Zailer would allow me to follow any of this up. Mrs Fancourt ignored this remark and continued with her description. She said that Mandy's boyfriend had brown hair but, she said, 'There's definitely a redhead somewhere in his family. Do you know what I mean? One of his parents is a redhead, I'm sure. He's got that sort of ivory skin, with a yellow undertone.'

Throughout the interview, Mrs Fancourt talked in this manic, determined and peculiar way. She seemed to have difficulty focusing on one issue at a time, and kept veering from the subject of her husband's father to the subject of Mandy's boyfriend. I had the impression that she was irrationally *preoccupied with both these men. At one point she realised she didn't have her mobile phone with her and got very upset, insisting that her husband had 'confiscated' it. I felt concerned about her emotional state and advised her to see a doctor.*

# II

## *Friday September 26, 2003*

I stand at the door of our bedroom. David is lying in bed. He doesn't look at me. Every so often the hard, icy reality of our situation strikes me afresh, as if for the first time: the unbearable fear, the possibility that everything might not be all right in the end. It does so now. My body quakes, and I have to struggle to keep still.

'Do you want me to sleep in another room?' I ask.

He shrugs. I wait. After ten seconds or so, when he sees that I am not going anywhere, he says, 'No. Let's not make things any more abnormal than they are already.' It's for Vivienne's benefit. He is still hoping to present what has happened as a minor problem: 'She's just being silly, Mum, honestly. She'll snap out of it.' Neither of us wants to confront the worry and misery our news has caused her. At one time, I believed that as long as Vivienne was happy, I, as a member of her inner circle, would come to no harm. The flip side of that – a fear that if Vivienne is displeased the world will end – has proved harder to dispel.

I am relieved that David does not want to banish me. Perhaps, when I get into bed, he will give me his usual goodnight kiss. I feel encouraged, enough to say, 'David, it's not too late. I know it's hard to back down after what you've said, but you must want the police to find Florence. You must! And the only way is to tell them you know I'm right – then they'll look for her.' I try to keep my voice level, rational. David is afraid of excessive displays of emotion. I don't want to push him further away.

'I could say the same to you,' he says tonelessly. 'It's not too late for you to abandon this ridiculous charade.'

'You know it isn't that. Please, David! What about the other mother, the mother of the baby in the nursery? What about her? She'll be missing her daughter as much as I miss Florence. Don't you care?'

'The other mother?' he says sarcastically. 'Oh, her. No, I don't give a shit about her. You know why? Because there is no other mother.'

I think about Mandy from the hospital. How would her boyfriend treat her, in this situation? I only talked to her properly once. She told me she lived in a one-bedroom flat and didn't know how they'd manage for space now that they had the baby. 'You know what men are like when their sleep's interrupted.' She sighed. I felt awful when she asked me how I was fixed for space. I didn't want to lie, and had to admit I lived in a big house, though I made it clear I wasn't the owner.

'David, do you remember Mandy, from the maternity ward?' I touch his arm but he pulls it away. 'I told her where we lived. She knew the house.' My voice begins to tremble. 'Well, she said she'd seen it, she knew what road it was on.'

'I don't know how you dare,' he says quietly. 'Yes, I remember Mandy. We felt sorry for her. What are you saying, that she's stolen Florence?' He shakes his head. 'I don't know how you have the nerve.'

I see that it is too late. He tried to reason with me earlier this afternoon, but I locked myself in the bedroom and ignored him. This is one trauma too far for him. I have introduced panic and uncertainty into his life. I am the source of all his troubles, the bogeyman.

David turns to face me. 'Earlier today I thought you were mad, sick,' he whispers, 'but you're not, are you? You're as sane as I am.'

'Yes!' Tears flood my eyes. My shoulders sag with relief.

'You're just evil, then.' He turns away, his face hard with animosity. 'You're a liar.'

My brain is in revolt, unwilling to accept what it has just heard. How can he apply the word evil to me? He loves me, I know he does. He must. Even now, after the terrible things he's said today, I cannot banish from my mind all the kind things he has done, all his smiles, kisses and endearments. How can it be so easy for him to turn against me?

'I'll go and get changed,' I say quietly, pulling out my nightie from under my pillow. David and I are not in the habit of undressing in front of one another. When we make love, it is always semi-clothed, in the darkness. I thought David's modesty was unusual when we first got together. Then I told myself that it was sweet that he was so old-fashioned, that perhaps it was a class thing. I had never had a relationship with a properly well-bred person before. I didn't know until David told me that milk had to go in a jug, butter in a special dish. In my parents' house it had been normal for milk bottles to sit on the big, battered pine kitchen table, which was where we ate all our meals.

David climbs out of bed. Before I have time to wonder what he is doing, he has slammed the door shut. He leans against it, saying nothing, staring at me blankly.

'I was just going to go to the bathroom, to get ready for bed,' I say again.

He shakes his head, doesn't move.

'David, I need to go to the toilet,' I am forced to say. I cannot physically remove him from my path. He is far stronger than I am.

He looks at me, then at the nightie in my hand, then back at me, making it clear what he wants me to do. I see no way out, not with my bladder as full as it is. Counting to ten in my head, I begin to undress. I turn slightly to one side to obscure his view of my body, feeling as violated as if I'd been made to undress in front of a hostile stranger, but David makes a point of moving, craning his neck to make sure he can see everything. He smirks.

I think I would have found a punch in the face preferable.

Once I am in my nightie, I look at him again. I see triumph in the set of his features. He nods and stands aside, allowing me to leave the room. I have just enough time to lock the bathroom door and get to the toilet before I am sick. It is not fear that turns my stomach so much as shock. Whoever that cold, cruel presence in the bedroom is, it isn't David. I do not recognise my own husband. This cannot be the same man who wrote, in the first birthday card he ever sent me, 'You're the measure of my dreams'. I later found out, by pure accident, that this line was a lyric from a song by The Pogues. David grinned when I told him I knew. 'What, you didn't expect me to write my own romantic lines, did you?' he said. 'I write computer software, Alice. I can sweep laptops off their feet, but not women. You're better off in the capable hands of Shane McGowan, believe me.' I laughed. He has always known how to make me laugh.

I cannot believe that forcing me to strip in front of him is rational behaviour on David's part. Something must have flipped in his brain, like when a fuse blows. He is terrible under pressure. People who don't know how to talk about their feelings usually are.

I can't risk provoking him again, so I return to the bedroom and slide silently under the duvet. David is facing away from me, at the furthest edge of the mattress. I fall quickly into the worst sort of sleep, an agitated, jolting progress through unsettling dreams, like driving through hell at a hundred miles an hour. I see Florence, alone and crying, and I can't go to her because I don't know where she is. I see Laura, lying on the path between The Elms and the road, not yet dead, trying to pull the knife out of her chest.

I hear rhythmic beating. Ticking. I sit up, confused, not sure if I'm awake or asleep. David's side of the bed is empty. For a second I am frozen, terrified. I am the one who is alone, the one who has been stabbed, the one lying in the pitch black. Then realisation, appalling knowledge, floods my brain with a cold, choking dread. Florence. I want Florence. My lungs are full of something heavy, my breath squeezed into my throat. I am too miserable to cry.

I look at the clock. Nearly five. I creep to the bedroom door and open it as quietly as I can. The nursery door is ajar, and a sliver of warm, yellow light has spilled on to the landing carpet. I can hear David's voice, whispering, though I can't make out what he's saying. Resentment writhes inside me, threatening to burst out of my mouth and give me away. I should be in that room, not shivering on the landing like an intruder.

But that's wrong too. Nobody should be in the nursery, not yet. Florence should be asleep in her Moses basket by the side of my bed. That was what I wanted, but Vivienne objected, as usual, to 'these modern ideas'. 'A child should be in its own room in its own cot from the day it's born,' she said firmly. David agreed, so I gave in.

I spent my whole pregnancy giving in. Every time David supported Vivienne, I swallowed my pride and hid the hurt I felt at being excluded from yet another important decision that involved my child. I told myself it was difficult for him to stand up to Vivienne; he's such a devoted son. I have always thought this is a good thing. On the outside I must have looked like a model of obedience, while inside I burned with unspoken defiance. And in a strange sort of way, my passivity didn't bother me because I knew it was only a temporary state. It always felt as if I was just resting, gathering my strength. Florence was my daughter, not Vivienne's, and I would have my say when the time was right.

Sometimes I catch myself feeling sorry for Vivienne, as if I've let her down by developing a mind of my own. Her interfering, controlling nature is precisely what I loved about her at first. I wanted her as a mother-in-law as much as I wanted David as a husband.

Feeling as if my breath and my heartbeat are, between them, louder than a brass band, I tiptoe towards Florence's room, stopping as soon as David's words become audible. 'Good girl,' he says. 'A whole four ounces. Just what a growing girl needs. Well done, little girl. Well done, Little Face.' That name again. I hear a soft pock-ing noise, a goodnight kiss. 'Now, a new nappy, I think.' I note the 'I'. Not 'Daddy', 'I'. I must tell Simon Waterhouse all of this. I know it won't count as evidence, but it might help to shape his opinion. David has been referring to himself in the third person as Daddy for the past two weeks. I run back along the landing, not caring if he hears me, and throw myself into bed. From some reservoir of despair deep inside me, I find more tears. The sound of that kiss has finished me.

I want to kiss my daughter. I want to be able to hug and kiss my parents, but I never will again. I can't stand it. I want them to tuck me up in bed and tell me that it was just a silly nightmare and everything will be okay in the morning.

When I was a child, I had an elaborate bedtime ritual. First my dad would read me a story, then my mum would come upstairs and sing me some songs, usually three or four. However many she sang, I always asked for another one and she always gave in. 'Bye-Bye Blackbird', 'Second-Hand Rose', 'The Sunny Side of the Street' – I still know the words to all of them. After the songs, my dad would come back upstairs for the finale, a bedtime chat. This was my favourite part. He always let me choose what I wanted to chat about, and, once the topic for the evening was decided, I asked as many questions as I could think of, to keep him there for as long as possible.

I must have been about four or five at the time. David was six when his dad left home. I don't even know my father-in-law's name, and I don't know why I feel I can't ask. All those nights I delayed my bedtime as a child, interrogating my dad. All the things I ask my patients, to try to work out the best way to treat them. It is in my nature to ask questions. Only David makes me feel I can't. He reacts as if I am being rude or intrusive if he suspects me of trying to get to the bottom of some aspect of his character. 'What is this, the third degree?' he says. Or 'Objection, Your Honour. Counsel is badgering the witness.' Then he laughs and leaves the room, to make it clear that the conversation is over. I have attributed his defensiveness to past hurt and made allowances accordingly.

This is a hard habit to break. Even tonight, I cannot help blaming myself for his behaviour. I have always led him to believe that I would do anything for him, and now he sees that is not true. I will not say that the baby in this house is Florence, even for him. I didn't mean to let him down, but I have. Some situations are impossible to foresee.

I hear a low, rumbling sound. A car engine. Vivienne and

Felix. Was that what woke me? I climb out of bed and go over to the window. My hands search for the gold chain. None of the curtains in Vivienne's house are ones that you can pull open easily. After some unsuccessful fumbling, I manage to tug the chain in the right direction and the curtains slide gracefully open. The headlights of Vivienne's Mercedes stretch up the driveway, two long, white-gold bars of shining dust. There is a softer light on the wall of the old barn that casts a dim, orange glow over most of the area between the house and the road. This has been installed since Laura was killed. Before that you wouldn't have been able to see a thing at this time of night.

I wonder if the police know the exact hour – minute, even – that Laura was killed, whether they ever narrowed it down. When they interviewed me and David immediately after her murder, all they could tell us was that she'd been stabbed at some point between nine in the evening and the early hours of the following morning. I do not like to think of her dying in the pitch black. I only met Laura once. She disliked me. She died believing that I was a shallow, spineless fool.

I reach for the chain that will close the curtains, not wanting Vivienne to see that I am awake. My heart pounds. Quick, quick. I am not ready for her yet. The curtains slide shut, leaving just a small gap. Peering through it, I see her. She does not look happy. She is wearing dark trousers with a crease in them and her black wool coat. She stares at the house dispassionately for several seconds, like a woman planning an onslaught of some kind, before extending a hand in Felix's direction. He takes it, and together they march up the driveway, stiff-backed and purposeful, Vivienne pulling a large suitcase on wheels behind her. They do not speak as they walk. No two people have ever looked less like holiday-makers, returning from a fun time in Florida.

I feel David's breath on my neck. 'You're right to be scared,' he whispers. I gasp and nearly lose my balance. I was so focused on Vivienne, I didn't hear him come in. 'She'll see through your act straight away.' How he must have hoped, right up until this moment, that I would back down, apologise unreservedly for my madness, enable him to greet Vivienne with a reassuring, 'Don't worry! It's all blown over!' He is trying to frighten me because he is frightened.

He succeeds. I want to phone Simon Waterhouse, scream at him to come and save me. I want to hide in his embrace and hear him say that Florence and I are going to be safe thanks to him. I have turned into every therapist's text-book patient. Needy, unable to cope with the expectation that I will behave like a responsible adult, I have created what is known in the trade as a drama triangle, casting myself in the role of victim. David is my persecutor and Simon my rescuer.

The front door opens with a click, closes with a wooden thud. Vivienne is back.

# 12

## *3/10/03, 9 pm*

'I'm not saying definitely not. I don't know yet. I'll do my best.' Simon bit back the urge to say, 'Didn't we speak earlier today? And has anything important happened since then?' It had been easier when his mother had worked full-time. There hadn't been so many phone calls.

'But when will you know?'

'I don't know. It depends on work. You know what my job's like.' Did she fuck. She didn't have a clue. She thought Sunday dinner was more important.

'So, what's your news?' asked Kathleen Waterhouse. Simon could see her even though he couldn't, knew she was pressing the phone hard against her ear, as if trying to embed it in the side of her head. She feared the connection with her son might be lost if she didn't exert maximum force. Her ear would be red and sore afterwards.

'No news.' He'd have said this even if he'd won the lottery that morning, or been invited to man the next space shuttle. In theory, he wanted his chats with his mother to be relaxed, enjoyable. He often imagined the things he would say to her, jokes or anecdotes he would tell her when they next spoke, but they all died on his tongue the instant he heard that timid 'Hello, dear. It's Mum.' That was when he remembered there was a script he could never abandon, no matter how much he might wish to. That was when he said, 'Hi, Mum. How are you?' and resigned himself to another wrangle over his availability for Sunday lunch this week, next week, every fucking week.

'Have you got any news?' His next line, on cue. She would tell him one item; she always did.

'I met Beryl Peach today, in the launderette.'

'Oh, right.'

'Kevin's staying at home for a while. You could see if he wanted to meet up.'

'I'm probably going to be too busy.' Kevin Peach had been Simon's friend at school. Briefly. Until Simon had got fed up of being the mascot, the token 'mad bastard' of Peach's little coterie. They enjoyed watching him start fights for no reason, egged him on to approach girls who were way out of his league. They copied out his carefully written notes and still blamed him when they didn't get the As he got in exams. No thanks. He had a new social life now, The Brown Cow after work with Charlie, Sellers, Gibbs and a few others. Police friendships were easier to keep at a surface level, work-related banter. Except Charlie. She was always trying to go beyond that, to take more and go deeper. To know more.

'So when will I see you, if not on Sunday?' Kathleen Waterhouse asked.

'I don't know, Mum.' Not until Alice had been found. Simon couldn't stand seeing his parents when he was feeling at all shaky. Their company, the stifling atmosphere of the house he grew up in that hadn't changed in over thirty years, could turn a mild bad mood into the most deadening misery. Poor sods; it wasn't their fault. They were always so pleased to see him. 'Why don't we wait and see about Sunday?'

The doorbell rang. Simon's whole body stiffened. He prayed his mum hadn't heard it. He'd get the full list of questions: who is it? Well, who might it be? Wasn't it rude to call round unexpectedly at nine o'clock? Did Simon know anybody who would do that? Kathleen Waterhouse was afraid of spontaneity. Simon had spent most of his life trying hard not to be. He ignored the doorbell, hoping that whoever it was would give up and leave.

'How's the house?' asked his mother. She asked after it every time she phoned, as if it were a pet or a child.

'Mum, I've got to go. The house is fine. It's great.'

'Why have you got to go?'

'I just have, okay? I'll ring you tomorrow.'

'All right, dear. Goodbye. God bless. Speak to you later.'

Later? Simon gritted his teeth. He hoped it was a figure of speech, that she didn't mean later tonight. He hated himself for being unwilling, unable, to ask her to phone less often. It was a reasonable request. Why couldn't he do it?

The bloody house was fine. It was a two-up, two-down terraced cottage in a quiet cul-de-sac next to the park, five minutes walk from his parents' place. It had a lot of charm but not much space, and was probably the wrong choice for someone as tall as he was, but that hadn't occurred to him at the time. Now he'd got attached to it, and it wasn't too much of a hardship to duck as he moved from one room to another.

Property prices had been on the verge of becoming ridiculous when he'd bought it three years ago, and he still struggled, every month, to pay the mortgage. His mother had neither wanted him to leave home nor understood why he felt the need to. She would have been unhappy if he'd moved much further away than he had. This way he'd been able to say, 'I'm just round the corner, nothing will change'. Change: a thing to be dreaded.

The bell rang again. As he made his way down the hall,

he heard Charlie's voice. 'Let me in, you fucking hermit!' she called out amiably. Simon looked at his watch, wondering how long she was planning to stay. He opened the door.

'For God's sake, relax.' Charlie pushed past him, a brown packet in her hand. She made her way through to the lounge without being invited, took off her coat and sat down. 'I just came to give you this.' She thrust the padded envelope towards Simon.

'What is it?'

'Anthrax.' She made a face at him. 'Simon, it's a fucking book, all right? Just a book. No need to panic. I'm sorry I didn't ring, but I was just in the pub with Olivia and she gave me this. She had to go early so I thought I'd pop round and give it to you, for your mum.'

Simon opened the envelope and saw a plain white paperback called 'To Risk it All' by Shelagh Montgomery, his mother's favourite author. Under the author's name, in black capital letters, were the words, 'UNCORRECTED BOUND PROOF'. Charlie's sister Olivia was a journalist and did a lot of book reviews. The few Simon had read had been unnecessarily savage. 'Does this mean it's not published yet?'

'That's right.'

'Mum'll be really pleased. Thanks.'

'Don't thank me. Read the first paragraph and you'll see it's one of the worst books ever written.' Charlie looked embarrassed, as she always did when caught in the act of being considerate. She often gave him books she'd got from Olivia, either for him or for his mother to read, depending on whether they were serious or trashy. Every time, she mocked the book mercilessly, determined to hide her thoughtfulness under a veneer of sarcasm. It was almost as if she were ashamed of having virtues.

'So, you've still not decorated.' She looked around disapprovingly. 'Anyone'd think a ninety-year-old widow lived here. Why don't you paint over that hideous wallpaper? And those ornaments! Simon, you're a young man. You aren't supposed to have china dogs on the mantelpiece. It's not natural.'

The dogs had been a house-warming present from his parents. Simon was grateful for the book, so he tried to suppress his irritation. He and Charlie were so different, it was a wonder they managed to speak to one another at all. Simon would never have dreamed of passing comment on somebody else's home, yet Charlie seemed to inhabit a world in which rudeness was a sign of affection. Sometimes she brought Olivia to The Brown Cow, and Simon was amazed by the way they hurled insults back and forth. 'Fucking mentalist', 'psycho bitch from hell', 'freak-show', 'gormless mong' – the two of them regularly exchanged these and other slurs as if they were the warmest of compliments. They ridiculed each other's clothes, behaviour, attitudes. Every time Simon saw them together, he felt relieved that he was an only child.

In Charlie's world it was acceptable to drop in on someone at nine in the evening, without warning, to give them a book that could easily have waited until the next day at work. 'You asked why Laura Cryer left The Elms alone,' she said, picking up *Moby Dick* from the arm of a chair and flicking through it as she spoke. 'I checked the files. She was dropping off her son's comfort blanket. She'd forgotten to pack it. Vivienne Fancourt was having him for the night, babysitting. Laura was supposed to be going out to a club.'

'A club?' Simon wasn't in work mode, and found it difficult to switch so quickly. His mind was still on how to get rid of Charlie so that he could get on with his book. He noticed that she'd just closed it without bothering to replace his bookmark. Again, he stifled his irritation.

'Yes, you know, one of those places young people go to have fun. Cryer was single, just waiting for her divorce to come through.'

'Maybe she'd found someone new and Fancourt was jealous.'

'She hadn't. Friends said she was actively looking. She was lonely,' said Charlie, somewhat aggressively.

Simon felt thwarted, as if circumstances were deliberately conspiring to protect David Fancourt. He had to be guilty of something, if not murder. Probably murder, though. Alice's disappearance and Laura's death were connected somehow, Simon would have bet his life. 'Would you mind if I paid Darryl Beer a visit in Brimley?'

Charlie groaned. 'Yes, I bloody well would. Why would you want to do that? Simon, you've got to try to resist these . . . strange tangents you like to go off on.'

'Except for when they turn out to be bang on, you mean?'

'Yes. Except for then. But now isn't one of those times. Now is the time for you to admit you're wrong and move on.'

'Yeah? And when have you ever done that? You're just as stubborn as I am, and you know it. Just because you say something doesn't make it true. You always do this!'

'Do what?'

'Try to turn your personal opinion into some kind of universal moral law!'

Charlie recoiled. A few seconds later she said, 'Don't you ever wonder why you're so shitty to me when most of the time I'm actually quite nice to you?'

Simon stared down at his hands. Yeah, he wondered.

'It isn't my personal opinion,' she went on quietly. 'It's Beer's confession. It's the DNA evidence. The only person around here with a spurious, groundless opinion is you! Darryl Beer killed Laura Cryer, all right? Take my word for it. And that case has got nothing to do with this one, with Alice and Florence Fancourt.'

Simon nodded. 'I didn't mean to offend you,' he said.

'So, have you fallen for her? Alice?' Charlie asked. She looked almost frightened. As soon as she'd said it, Simon knew that this was the true purpose of her visit. She had wanted – needed, perhaps – to ask him this question.

He resented it. Who did she think she was, to ask him that? It was only his residual guilt that prevented him from asking her to leave, guilt because he couldn't feel the way she wanted him to feel.

Charlie was the only woman who had ever pursued Simon. The flirting had started on the day he was seconded to CID. At first he'd assumed she was taking the piss, until Sellers and Gibbs convinced him otherwise.

If Simon could only develop a romantic interest in Charlie, it might make them both happy. It'd certainly make his life a damn sight easier. Unlike most men – certainly most policemen – Simon didn't care all that much about looks. So what if Charlie had large breasts and long, skinny legs? Her trim figure, combined with her obvious keenness and availability, was part of what he found off-putting. She was way out of his league, like the girls he'd fixated on at school, before countless humiliations had taught him to know his place. And she had been successful in two careers. She was the sort of person who could do well at anything she set her mind to.

She'd got a first in ASNAC – Anglo-Saxon, Norse and Celtic – from Cambridge. Before joining the police, she'd been a promising young academic for four years. After she was denied a promotion she knew she deserved by a head of department who was resentful of Charlie's superior intellect and publication record, she started from scratch in the police and became a detective sergeant in record time. Her achievements both impressed and intimidated Simon. Mostly, she made him feel inadequate.

Looking back, Simon could see what a fool he'd been. Charlie had made it clear she wanted him, and there was an undeniable vacancy; convention dictated that he ought to have a girlfriend, and she was the only volunteer. A voice in his head had screamed its dissent from that first day, but he'd ignored it and kept telling himself, instead, how great Charlie was, how lucky he should feel.

She had finally made her move at Sellers' fortieth birthday party last year. Simon, stunned and zombie-like, needed to make no effort at all. She was all over him, taking the lead in everything. She'd even reserved Sellers' spare room for them, she told him. 'If anyone else gets in there before us, Sellers'll be looking for a new job!' she joked.

This alarmed Simon, but still he said nothing. He feared she'd be the same in bed as she was out of it, that she'd spend the whole time issuing instructions about what she wanted done, when and where, in a tone that brooked no argument. Simon knew some men didn't mind that sort of thing, but he personally found the prospect repellent. He knew he'd get it all wrong anyway, make a pig's ear of everything.

Still, he allowed himself to be drawn further in. As the kissing went on, Charlie seemed to be becoming more enthusiastic, so Simon behaved as if he was too. He imitated her fast breathing, said a few nice things that he hoped were romantic, things it would never have occurred to him to say if he hadn't heard them in films.

Charlie eventually led him into Sellers' tiny spare room and pushed him down on to the single bed. I'm lucky, Simon repeated to himself again. Most men would give their World Cup final tickets to be in this position. He watched in horror and fascination as Charlie undressed in front of him. Logically, with the rational part of his brain, he admired her for being liberated, for refusing to go along with that sexist nonsense about men having to make the first move. Yet, ashamed though he was to admit it, all Simon's instincts mutinied against the idea of a sexually aggressive woman.

It's too late, he told himself as Charlie climbed on top of him and started to unbutton his shirt. The best thing to do was get it over with. He ran his hands over her body, doing what he assumed was expected of him.

At this point in the narrative, Simon's memory always lurched violently away from the specific details, which were far too awful to dwell on. It was sufficient to recall that he had known at a certain point that he couldn't go through with it. He'd pushed Charlie off his knees, mumbled an apology and run from the room without looking back. What a coward and a loser she must have thought he was. He expected news of his humiliating failure to be all over the police station the next day, but no-one said anything. When Simon tried to apologise to Charlie, she cut him off, saying, 'I was pissed anyway. I don't remember much.' Trying to spare him further embarrassment, no doubt.

'Well?' she said now. 'Answer came there none, as Proust would say. What is it with Alice Fancourt? Do you just fancy her because she's got long, blonde hair?'

'Of course not.' Simon felt as if the Spanish inquisition had landed in his living room. He was offended to have such shallowness imputed to him. Long blonde hair had nothing to do with it. It was the openness in Alice's face, her vulnerability, the way he could see what she was feeling just by looking at her. She had a gravity about her that touched him. He wanted to help her, and she believed that he could. He wasn't a joke to her. Alice had seemed to see Simon exactly as he wanted to be seen. And now that she had vanished, he saw her in his mind constantly, went over everything she'd ever said to him, buzzed with the need to tell her he believed her, finally, wholeheartedly, about everything. Now that it might be too late she consumed his thoughts; it was as if somehow by disappearing she had transcended reality, become legend.

'You have fallen for her,' said Charlie glumly. 'Be careful, okay? Make sure you don't explode. The Snowman's got his beady eye on you. If you fuck up again . . .'

'Proust said that to me this morning. I didn't know what he was talking about. Okay, I've had a few Reg 9s, but no more than most people.'

Charlie sighed heavily. 'A few more than most, actually. I haven't had any. Gibbs and Sellers haven't either.'

'I didn't say I was perfect,' Simon muttered, feeling instantly defensive. He was a better cop than Gibbs or Sellers would ever be, and Charlie knew it. Proust knew it. 'I take risks. I know it sometimes gets out of hand, but . . .'

'Simon, those Reg 9s were only Reg 9s because I begged Proust on bended knees to go easy on you. You can't go round flattening everyone who questions your judgement!'

'You know it wasn't as simple as that!'

'The Snowman was all for throwing you out. I had to lick his arse until my tongue nearly fell off, and he had to lick a fair few higher-up arses himself. Which didn't go down at all well.'

This was all news to Simon. He'd lost his temper only with those who deserved it. 'So . . . what are you saying?' he asked, feeling like an idiot. He should know more about this than Charlie. 'Why didn't you tell me?'

'I don't know!' she snapped. 'I didn't want you to feel everyone had it in for you, though you seem to feel that way whatever happens. Look, I hoped I could get you to . . . moderate your behaviour. And you've been a lot better recently, which is why I don't want this Alice Fancourt business to fuck that up. I promised Proust I'd keep you under control, so . . .'

'So you're going to start trying to control how I feel about people too?' Simon was incensed. Charlie had got him out of trouble and kept it from him at the same time. He couldn't think of anything more patronising. As if he were a child who couldn't handle the harsh truth.

'Don't be ridiculous. I'm only trying to help, okay? If I was about to fuck up, I'd want you to advise me not to. That's what friends do.' There was a tremor in her voice.

Simon saw her hurt expression, panicked at the prospect of tears. 'I'm sorry.' He decided as he said it that perhaps he ought to be, perhaps he was. Charlie could appear thick-skinned, but Simon knew she often felt wounded and betrayed. As did he. Another thing they had in common, she'd have said.

She stood up. 'I'd better go. I might go to a club,' she said pointedly.

'Thanks for the book. I'll see you tomorrow.'

'Yeah, yeah.'

Once she had gone, Simon sank into a chair, feeling dislocated, as if he had lost an important part of himself. He needed to think, to rewrite his life story in accordance with the new information Charlie had given him. Lies were lethal, however honourable the intentions of the liar. They deprived people of the opportunity to know the basic facts of their own lives.

The impulse to flee, to start afresh somewhere far away, returned with all the allure of a new idea. It would be too easy not to turn up for work tomorrow. If only he trusted Charlie, anyone, to find Alice. But without him, the team wouldn't do a thorough enough job, not by his standards. Not that Simon trusted himself particularly at the moment. Maybe he wasn't as good at his job as he imagined. Maybe obedience and placidity counted for more than passion and intelligence in this shallow, superficial world.

To find out, retrospectively, that most of his superior officers had been eager to get rid of him made Simon feel as if all his efforts were in vain. Might as well go and start kicking heads in right now. So what if the chronology was all wrong? It didn't change how he felt. Tonight he would sleep badly.

# 13

## *Saturday September 27, 2003*

Vivienne and I are at the police station, in an interview room. It is one of the most unpleasant spaces I have ever been in, small and airless, about three metres square, with sickly green walls. As we walked in, our feet stuck to the grey linoleum. We had to peel them off after every step. The only window has bars on it, and all the chairs are screwed to the floor. The table in front of us is covered in cigarette burns. I breathe through my mouth to avoid inhaling the unpleasant smell, a mixture of urine, cigarettes and sweat.

'What sort of awful place is this?' says Vivienne. 'This is a room for criminals. You'd have thought they'd know from looking at us that we aren't criminals.'

Vivienne certainly does not look like one. She is wearing a grey wool suit and grey suede court shoes. Her short silver hair is immaculate and her nails are trimmed and varnished, colourless as always. Anyone who didn't know her would not be able to tell that she is in a state of extreme distress.

Vivienne does not rant and sob and make a fuss. The more despondent she feels, the quieter and more composed she is. She sits and broods. She stares at the wall, and out of windows, her face revealing nothing, sinister in its stillness. Even for the benefit of her beloved Felix, she cannot pretend to be her usual animated self. She holds him tightly in her arms, as if afraid he too might vanish. I told her this morning that I thought Felix ought to go and stay with friends, but she said firmly, 'Nobody is leaving this house.'

She has always issued orders in this way, like a ruling force, confident of her absolute power. When David first took me home to meet her, I loved the way she laid down the law about which train I was to take back to London, what I must eat at the restaurant she took us to. It seemed to me then that friends offered polite suggestions before abandoning you to plough through your life alone, carrying the full weight of responsibility. They didn't try too hard to meddle or force their views on you because, at some fundamental level, they didn't care.

When Vivienne dogmatically seized control of my life, I thought that she was treating me as she would a daughter. I mattered to her, a lot, otherwise why would she have bothered? And she was right about the train, right about the food. Vivienne is no fool. She made decisions for me that were better than the ones I would have made for myself. Within two months of meeting David, I had a more flattering hairstyle and clothes I loved and looked fantastic in but would never have dared to choose for myself.

We have arrived at the police station in good time for Vivienne's appointment. Vivienne explained who we were, and the man behind the front desk, a middle-aged officer in uniform, ushered us in here and told us to wait while he went to get the OIC for our case. Neither of us knew what he meant, whether to expect a person, a document or a committee.

Vivienne is here to give her statement. I begged her to let me come with her. I find it too upsetting and frightening to be around David. But I am more nervous than I thought I would be. I have never been inside a police station before and I am not enjoying the experience. I feel as if, at any moment, I might be found guilty of something.

The door opens and Simon comes in, followed by a tall, thin woman with a large bosom that looks as if it would fit better on somebody more buxom. Her lipstick is bright red and doesn't suit her. She has short, dark brown hair and is wearing oval-shaped glasses with gold frames, a red jumper and a black skirt. She glances fleetingly at Vivienne, then leans against the wall and stares coldly at me. I feel frumpy in my cream, empire-waisted maternity dress. My stomach is still too big for normal clothes. The woman has a hard, mean look on her face and I instantly fear and dislike her. Simon blushes when his eyes meet mine. I am sure he hasn't told his unfriendly colleague about the meeting the two of us have arranged for Monday afternoon. When I suggested that I should come to the police station, he very quickly said that was impossible. I have not told Vivienne either.

Simon turns to Vivienne. 'I'm Detective Constable Waterhouse,' he says. 'This is Detective Sergeant Zailer.'

'Sergeant Zailer and I have met before,' says Vivienne briskly. The speed with which she moves on tells me that this prior meeting must have been connected to Laura's murder. 'Now that you're here, could you take us to a nicer room? This one leaves rather a lot to be desired.'

'We don't have any nicer rooms,' says Sergeant Zailer, sitting down opposite us. There is only one chair on her side of the table, so Simon has to stand. 'We have four interview rooms and they're all like this. It's a police station, not a hotel.'

Vivienne purses her lips and sits up straighter in her chair.

'DC Waterhouse? Would you care to give the two Mrs

Fancourts an update on the case?' Sergeant Zailer empha-
sizes this last word sarcastically.

Simon clears his throat and shifts his weight from one
foot to the other. He seems ill at ease. 'No babies have been
reported missing yesterday or today, or in the past two
weeks,' he says. 'Also, we, er, we had a disappointing
response from Culver Valley General Hospital. They didn't
have the, er, placenta or the umbilical cord. They only keep
them for a couple of days. Unfortunately that means we're
unable to do a DNA comparison between the placenta and
the baby . . .'

'There was a woman in the hospital at the same time as
me . . .' I begin, but Vivienne has started to speak as well,
and it is her voice that everybody hears. I wonder if I ought
to try again to tell them about Mandy. Vivienne's presence
stops me. I know what she would say: that Mandy was too
stupid to plan anything as imaginative as a substitution of
one baby for another. I have a little Vivienne in my head all
the time, as if she's fitted a representative of herself in my
brain, one that reacts exactly as she would, even when she
isn't there.

'You could take DNA samples from Alice and David and
see if they're the biological parents of the baby.' I notice
Vivienne's wording. The baby, not Florence.

'We could.' Sergeant Zailer flashes us a cold-eyed smile.
'But we're not going to. If you want to pay for that, you're
welcome to arrange it yourself. It'd probably be a good deal
quicker to do it that way, in fact. There is no case here, Mrs
Fancourt. No baby is missing. We've spoken to your
nearest neighbours and nobody saw anything suspicious.
There's no evidence that anything at all is amiss, apart from
in the mind of your daughter-in-law. My detective here
. . .' – she pauses and looks pointedly at Simon – '. . . has

been extremely thorough. He has contacted the hospital in pursuit of physical evidence in the form of a placenta or umbilical cord, but since neither is available . . . well, I'm afraid there's not a lot more we can do. Even if they had been available . . . our lab is very busy with DNA analysis relating to serious crimes. It's a question of resources, Mrs Fancourt, as I'm sure you'll appreciate.'

I wonder how Simon feels about being described as *her* detective. She didn't even look at me when she suggested to Vivienne that I was mentally impaired. I can feel the beams of her hostility as they radiate across the table. She is busy and regards me and my ludicrous baby-swap story as a waste of her time, but I sense that it is more than that. She dislikes me personally.

I tell my patients, or I used to, that the best way to deal with someone who is aggressive towards you is to follow the DESC script: describe, explain, strategies, consequences. You describe the unacceptable aspects of their behaviour and explain how they make you feel. Then you suggest strategies for change – normally, that they stop doing whatever it is that they are doing – and point out the positive consequences of such a change for all concerned.

I do not think I will try the DESC script now.

'Thank you for your suggestion,' says Vivienne. 'I certainly will organise a DNA test, to put my family's minds at rest.' There is no gratitude whatsoever in her voice.

'Do I take it, then, that you also think the infant in your house is not Florence Fancourt?' asks Sergeant Zailer.

Since she returned from Florida, Vivienne has not said what she believes. She is observing me and David very closely. We both find it unsettling. She prefers asking questions to answering them. She always has. She fires them at you, one after another, and listens attentively to your replies. When I first met her, I was amazed and profoundly grateful to discover that no detail of my daily life, no thought or feeling I had, was too small to hold her interest. One doesn't normally expect that sort of attention from anyone but a parent. Vivienne seemed determined to know everything there was to know about me. It was as if she were collecting facts for a future test. I was only too keen to help her in her mission. The more firmly the data of my existence was lodged in Vivienne's sharp mind, the more real and substantial I felt. I have felt less concrete since I started to hide aspects of myself from her.

'I only saw Florence once, on the day she was born,' says Vivienne. 'I then went to Florida with my grandson. When I got back yesterday, I had already spoken to Alice. I know that she believes the baby at The Elms is not her daughter, and I am inclined to take her seriously. The memory plays tricks, Sergeant Zailer, as I'm sure you know. A DNA test is the only way to resolve this.' She appears calm, but inside she must feel the same churning, restless agitation that I feel, as if the contents of my head have been repeatedly stabbed at, mashed to a pulp. Yet here I sit, here Vivienne sits: polite, demure. We are both in disguise.

'Does the baby at The Elms resemble the baby you saw in the hospital?' Simon asks. His gentle tone provides a welcome contrast to his colleague's brusqueness.

'That's irrelevant, detective,' Sergeant Zailer snaps at him. 'There's no evidence of a crime having been committed here.' She turns to him and mutters something that sounds like '. . . cuff it.'

'She resembles her very closely, yes,' Vivienne replies.

'Of course she does!' I blurt out. 'I've never denied that.'

'Would you like to deliver the other bad news, DC Waterhouse?' Sergeant Zailer prompts. Simon doesn't want to say it, whatever it is. She is forcing him to be horrible to us. 'My detective is tongue-tied, so I'll tell you myself. You gave us a camera film, Mrs Fancourt.'

'Yes!' I sit forward in my chair. Vivienne puts her hand on my arm.

'It was damaged. Light contamination, we were told. None of the photos came out. Sorry.' She doesn't sound it.

'What? No!' I am on my feet. I want to slap Sergeant Zailer's smug, snide, gloating face. She has no idea what it feels like to be me, doesn't even try to put herself in my place. Somebody with so little empathy should not be allowed to do the job she does. 'But . . . those were the first ever photos of Florence. Now I haven't got . . . oh, God.' I sit back down and squeeze my hands together in my lap, determined not to cry in front of this woman.

It is almost unbearable to think that I will never see those pictures, not even once. The one David took of me with my cheek pressed against Florence's. Me kissing the top of her head. David with Florence's fingers curled round his thumb. Florence bent over the midwife's knee with a comical yawn on her face, during a burping session. A close-up of the sign that dangled from her glass cot in the hospital: a pink elephant holding a bottle of champagne, with the words 'female infant of Alice Fancourt' written in blue biro on its stomach.

I shut these things out of my mind before they destroy me.

'This is very peculiar.' Vivienne frowns. 'I took some photographs of Florence myself, with my new digital camera, on the day she was born.'

'And?' asks Simon quickly. Sergeant Zailer looks resolutely uninterested.

'The same thing. While I was in Florida, I noticed that all

of them had been deleted. They simply weren't there any more. I couldn't understand it – all my other photographs were still there. It was only the ones of Florence that had vanished.'

'*What?*' She is telling me this for the first time now, in front of two police officers. Why didn't she mention it as soon as I told her Florence was missing? Was it because David was also there?

I bought Vivienne the digital camera for her birthday. She is usually resistant to anything she regards as modern, but she wanted to take the best possible photographs of her new grandchild. I still have a vivid picture in my mind of her frowning at the manual, too proud to admit she was daunted by its many instructions, determined not to be defeated by new technology. She refused to accept help from David, even though he could have saved her a lot of time.

When Vivienne was a child, her parents used to tell her that there was nothing she couldn't do. She believed them. 'That is how you instil confidence in a person,' she told me.

'This is impossible,' she mutters now, lost for a moment in her own thoughts.

'Now will you admit something funny is going on?' I demand. 'Come on, what are the odds of two sets of photos being wrecked accidentally? This is evidence!' I plead with the sergeant. 'Two films, both ruined, and they just happen to be the only photos of Florence ever taken!'

The sergeant sighs. 'It appears that way to you. But I'm afraid it's not what any police officer or court of law would regard as proof.'

'Cheryl Dixon, my midwife, believes me,' I say tearfully.

'I've read her statement. She said she wasn't sure, couldn't say either way. She sees dozens of babies every day. If I were you, Mrs Fancourt, I'd make an appointment with your GP and see what he can do for you. We know about your history of depression . . .'

'Don't make out that's got anything to do with this! My parents had just died. That was grief, not depression!'

'You were prescribed prozac,' says Sergeant Zailer with exaggerated patience. 'Maybe you need some sort of medication now. Post-natal depression is a very common complaint and it's nothing to be ashamed of. In fact, it affects . . .'

'One moment, please, Sergeant.' Vivienne's interruptions are so polite, they make the original speaker appear rude for not having stopped in time. 'Alice is right about the photographs. It is simply impossible that the same thing should happen to both of our cameras. It has never happened to any camera of mine before.'

'Nor mine,' I say. I feel like a coward, hiding behind the swagger of a braver, more powerful protector.

Sergeant Zailer's nostrils flare and her lips move slightly as she stifles a yawn. 'Coincidences happen.' She shrugs. 'It's not enough for us to use as the basis for an investigation, I'm afraid.'

'Is that also your opinion, Detective Constable Waterhouse?' asks Vivienne.

A good question. Simon is trying not to let his expression give anything away.

'Mrs Fancourt, I'm the senior officer here, and I say there's no case. Now, you can give DC Waterhouse your statement, if it'll make you happy, but I'm afraid that'll have to be the end of it. I'm sure you'll agree, we've been more than patient with this whole matter . . .'

'I do not agree, Sergeant Zailer.' Vivienne stands up. She reminds me of a cabinet minister, about to demolish her opposition. I am glad to have her on my side. 'On the contrary. I've never seen anyone in more of a hurry. You were in a hurry the last time we met, as I recall. You are a woman who would rather do lots of things badly, in order to be able to tick off more items on your list, than do fewer things properly. I'm sorry that you are Detective Constable Waterhouse's boss. We would all be better off if it were the other way round. Now, I'd like the name of *your* boss, so that I can write a letter of complaint.'

'By all means: Detective Inspector Giles Proust. Make sure to mention, when you drop him a line, that you have a solid case based on two knackered cameras and the wild paranoia of a woman who's just had a baby.' The sergeant's face is stony.

'Shall I get on with taking Mrs Fancourt's statement, then?' Simon interrupts, before any more ill-will has a chance to seep into the air between us. He scowls at Sergeant Zailer. He is angry with her for ratcheting up the animosity. Her manner strikes him as unnecessarily nasty, but he cannot criticise her because she is his superior officer, which frustrates him. I wonder if Simon is really an ally, or if I am simply making it all up, putting into his head the thoughts I want to be there. I have had imaginary friends before.

'I'm going to get to the bottom of this, with or without your help,' says Vivienne. 'My grandchildren are everything to me, Sergeant, do you understand that? I live for my family.'

This is true. Vivienne could have risen to the top of any profession she chose, but she was not interested in being prime minister, chief constable, QC. She once told me that mother and grandmother were the only titles she ever wanted. 'If you have a career, you will, if you're lucky, spend five days a week with people who admire and respect you,' she said. 'But if you make your family your life's work, you get to spend all your time with people who admire, respect *and* love you. I can't see that there's any comparison. My mother never worked,' she added. 'I wouldn't have liked it at all if she had.'

But a family is not a single entity with a single character. A family, Vivienne's in particular, comprises different people, each with his or her own needs. Sometimes the many demands for trust and loyalty cannot be reconciled. Sometimes you have to choose: child or grandchild, husband or daughter, son or daughter-in-law.

Vivienne agrees that the damage to the photographs cannot be a coincidence, but I wonder if she has pursued her hunch to its logical conclusion. She has been too busy resenting Sergeant Zailer's abandonment of us. How long before it occurs to her that, if it wasn't an accident, that means someone sabotaged the pictures of Florence deliberately, someone who must have had both motive and opportunity? Somebody like David.

# 14

## *4/10/03, 3.15 pm*

Simon sat in the waiting room at the Spilling Centre for Alternative Medicine. He'd spoken to a reflexologist, an acupuncturist, a Reiki healer, and now stared at the books in the glass-fronted wooden cabinet by the door. Nothing tempted him to cross the room and take a closer look. *How to Heal Your Self. The Spiritual Road to Enlightenment.* Simon didn't want to be healed or enlightened by a battered paperback with yellowing pages. He didn't subscribe to the view peddled by most of these alternative quacks, that spirituality was a fast track to happiness. He believed the opposite was true: spiritual people suffered more than most.

The centre occupied a battered white three-storey town-house in the pedestrianised part of Spilling, with peeling black paint around the windows. The only side of the building that was visible was covered in deep cracks and rust-coloured stains. Inside, there was evidence of money having been spent, money made from people's maladies and inadequacies. The grey-green carpet was thick, so soft that Simon could feel the spring and bounce of its fibres through his shoes. The walls were ivory and the furniture minim-alist: light wood, cream cushions. Somebody had had the thought of a harmonious soul firmly in mind.

Not Simon's soul, that was for sure. It occurred to him that Alice's clothes, whenever he had seen her, had followed roughly the same colour scheme: beiges, greeny-greys, creams. He was inside a building that was dressed like Alice. The thought made his chest feel heavy. Now that she was nowhere to be found, she had become all-pervasive. She was everywhere.

Embarrassing, but Simon felt lonely without her. How was that possible when he hardly knew her? He'd seen her a total of four times. It was his idea of her that had kept him company since he met her, not Alice herself. He should have reached out to her more. He'd wanted to, but feared he would have ended up having to push her away.

More than twenty-four hours had passed since David Fancourt had reported his wife and daughter missing. A case file had been opened, and Simon had spent the morning chasing CCTV footage. For the afternoon Charlie had assigned him the task of interviewing Alice's colleagues. A ruse, to keep him away from The Elms and David Fancourt. He couldn't say he blamed her. She was bound to think that one of the other Ds, someone who was less convinced of Fancourt's unsavouriness, would stand a better chance of getting him to talk. All the same, Simon felt slighted, at a distance from the real action.

He'd spoken to everyone apart from the emotional freedom therapist. Her name was Briony Morris. She was with a client, keeping Simon waiting. At least he'd heard of acupuncture and reflexology, and that degree of familiarity made them seem almost respectable. Emotional freedom therapy sounded unpromising. Its name made Simon scornful and impatient, even a little nervous. He had spent his life trying to keep his emotions under control. He wasn't looking forward to meeting a woman whose life's work was to encourage the opposite policy.

Alice's office had yielded no clues as to her whereabouts, only a lot of books and leaflets about homeopathy, two flat black suitcases full of homeopathic remedies with peculiar names like 'pulsatilla' and 'cimicifuga', and a box full of empty brown glass bottles. In one of the desk drawers there was a Stanley Sidgwick Grammar School and Ladies' College brochure with a glossy maroon cover, the school's crest and motto in the centre. Simon didn't understand the motto, which was in Latin. Perhaps it meant 'if you haven't got lots of cash, you're fucked'. A yellow Post-it note was stuck to the front cover. Alice had written, 'Find out about F – when name down? How long waiting list?'

Poor bloody Florence, Simon thought. Not even a month old and they're already planning her fucking Classics degree at Oxford. The sight of Alice's handwriting made him feel wobbly. He touched it with his index finger. Then he gritted his teeth and peeled off the post-it to reveal a colour photograph of three grinning children in turquoise uniforms – two girls and a boy – who were manifestly as well-fed as they were diligent.

In the next drawer down, Simon had found a framed photograph of Alice, David, Vivienne and, he assumed, Felix that looked as if it had been taken in the garden at The Elms. Vivienne was sitting on the grass with Felix on her lap, her arms around him, and David and Alice stood on either side of them. Vivienne and David were smiling, Felix and Alice were not. The river was behind them, and Alice was visibly pregnant.

The only other picture occupied a prime position on the desk. It had a large, wooden frame and was of a man and a woman in their fifties or sixties. They were both open-mouthed and smiling, as if they were joking with whoever was taking the picture. Alice's late parents. Her mother had the same big, clear eyes. Again, Simon felt an oppressive tightening in his chest.

He'd seen Alice in person only a few days ago, and he hadn't felt then the way he did today, as if there were some strange force blazing inside him, scorching him. What had changed, apart from her having disappeared?

He became aware that he was no longer alone in the waiting room. A tall woman with an athletic, wiry body and shoulder-length ginger hair stood beside him, staring down. She wore square, frameless glasses and a stretchy black dress. Something about the way she looked at him felt intrusive. 'DC Waterhouse? I'm Briony Morris. Sorry I've been so long. Shall we talk in my office?'

As he followed her along the corridor and up two flights of stairs, she turned twice to check he was still behind her. She gave off an air of being in charge, like a teacher supervising children on a school trip. Too much self-esteem, thought Simon: the real curse of our age.

'Here we are.' Briony's office was the only one on the attic floor. She opened the door and waved Simon in. 'Have a seat on the sofa over there.'

The room smelled of a perfume that brought to mind fruit salad, mainly grapefruit. There were two large, framed pictures on the wall that Simon didn't like – colourful, swirling collections of buildings, flowers, horses and apparently boneless people floating together in space. Most of their limbs pointed in the wrong direction.

Simon lowered himself awkwardly on to the sagging beige sofa, which offered little in the way of support or resistance. Each of the seat cushions was concave, designed to swallow whole anyone who landed on it. Briony sat at a desk identical to Alice's, on a straight-backed wooden chair. She was several inches higher than Simon; he felt confined, claustrophobic.

'So, you're here about Alice and Florence. Paula told me.' Paula was the reflexologist.

'Yes. They disappeared in the early hours of yesterday morning,' said Simon. He'd told nobody he'd interviewed that the baby who disappeared from The Elms was not, according to Alice, her daughter. After her original allegation that her baby had been swapped, Simon had been strongly in favour of interviewing Alice's friends and colleagues to find out whether they thought she was trustworthy, whether they knew of anything in her past that might shed light on her present baffling behaviour. But Charlie had insisted on cuffing it. 'I'm not wasting any more resources on this,' she'd said. 'Alice Fancourt's got a history of depression, she's been on prozac, she's just had a baby in about the most traumatic way possible. It's a shame for her, I agree, but post-natal depression is not a police matter, Simon.' When he'd looked doubtful, she'd said, 'Okay, then, you tell me. Why would anyone want to swap one baby for another? What could possibly be the motive? I mean, people steal babies, yes, but that's usually when they haven't got one themselves and are desperate.' Simon knew it would have been pointless to mention Mandy, the woman in the hospital that Alice had told him about, the one whose boyfriend had wanted to call their baby Chloe, after the daughter he already had. There was no proof of anything, as Charlie would have been quick to point out. And she'd have demanded to know when, precisely, Alice had told him all this.

Now, he heard himself tell Briony Morris that Alice and Florence had gone missing in the early hours of yesterday morning, and it sounded like a lie. Did that mean that, deep down, he believed Alice? Two people had disappeared, yet there was a prior, more fundamental mystery that remained unsolved.

Simon's confidence in his own judgement had been badly shaken by what Charlie had told him last night. He'd always trusted his instincts; they let him down less frequently than other people did. Yet he'd been in serious trouble and hadn't even known about it. What else might he have missed?

'So, how can I help?' said Briony Morris. 'Do you want to know when I last saw Alice? I can tell you exactly. September the ninth. I think I saw her more recently than anyone else here.'

'You did.' Simon consulted his notebook. 'No-one else has seen her since she started her maternity leave.'

'I had a day off, and she came round. To my house, in Combingham. Yes, I live in hideous Combingham, for my sins!' She looked embarrassed suddenly, as if she wished she hadn't told him. Simon didn't care where she lived. 'But you try buying a decent sized house in Spilling or Silsford, or even Rawndesley these days, on a single woman's salary. It's bloody impossible. I've got a detached house with four double bedrooms in Combingham. Mind you, I'm probably surrounded on all sides by crack dens . . .'

'What was the purpose of Alice's visit?' Simon cut through her nervous chattering. Perhaps Briony Morris wasn't as self-assured as he had first thought.

'You know what I do? Emotional freedom therapy?'

Simon nodded, feeling a sudden uncomfortable warmth beneath his skin.

'Alice was a bit tense. She was due to go into hospital at nine the next morning to be induced. Do you know what that means? It's when . . .'

'I know what it means.' Another interruption. Tough. 'So she came to see you as a patient? At home?'

'She wanted a session with me, yes. To boost her confidence. It was a sort of last minute thing. I mean, we're friends as well, of course. Well, friendly, anyway. Alice doesn't really have close friends.' Briony leaned forward, tucking her hair behind her ear. 'Look, you're probably not allowed to tell me, but . . . do you have any leads yet, about Florence? I mean, she's only two weeks old. I know it's early days . . .'

'It is,' said Simon. He wondered why Alice hadn't simply prescribed herself a homeopathic remedy if she was nervous about giving birth. A perk of the job, he'd have thought, being able to cure oneself relatively easily, and for no charge.

Eight years ago, Simon had been to see a homeopath. Not in Spilling; he'd made sure to pick a place in Rawndesley, at a safe remove from home and anyone his parents were likely to know. He'd heard a programme about homeopathy on Radio Four, heard people talking about how they had been cured of psychological hang-ups as well as physical conditions, and decided it might be good for him to do something so entirely out of character. A kind of escape from the confines of his usual self.

An hour in the hot-seat was all he'd been able to manage; he'd stormed out halfway through what his homeopath had called the introductory session. When it came to the crucial moment, Simon had been unable to tell the man – a kind, bearded ex-GP named Dennis – what the problem was. He talked about his subsidiary concerns easily enough: his inability to hold down a job, his fear that he was a disappointment to his mother, his anger about the amoral, vacuous state of the world, anger he hadn't known he possessed until Dennis asked him that particular combination of questions.

But when their conversation strayed on to the subject of women and relationships, Simon got up and headed for the door without a word of explanation. He regretted that now – his rudeness, not his departure. Dennis seemed like a good bloke. He'd been a bit too good at getting things out of Simon, who was afraid that if he stayed, he'd talk. He couldn't imagine what his life would be like once someone else knew.

'You say Alice doesn't have any close friends?'

'Don't get me wrong, she's very friendly,' Briony went on. 'We all like her, I certainly do. And I'm sure everyone else does. Haven't they said so?' She spoke frenetically, like someone on speed. But what did Simon know? Perhaps all emotionally free people talked like this.

'Yes,' he said. Harmless, to share this information. All Alice's colleagues had said she was lovely, kind, considerate, sensitive. Sane, too, was the unanimous verdict.

'But she didn't have time for proper friendships. She was so caught up in family stuff. We invited her to social things, you know – drinks out, meals, birthday parties, but she could never come. Every minute of her spare time seemed to be taken up with ridiculous . . .' Briony stopped and covered her mouth with her hand. 'Sorry,' she said. 'I shouldn't really stick my oar in.'

'You should. Without oars stuck in, we're unlikely to find Alice and the baby. Anything you can tell us might help.'

'Surely no-one would harm a two-week-old baby.' Briony frowned. 'I mean, obviously I know there *are* people who would, I'm not naïve. But, I mean, most people . . .'

Simon talked over her, desperate to stop the frantic flow

of words. 'Every minute of Alice's spare time seemed to be taken up with . . . what?'

'Well . . .' Briony rubbed her collarbone with the fingers of her left hand, leaving pink marks on her pale skin. 'Okay, well, I might as well tell you, then. It was her mother-in-law.' She exhaled, relieved to have spoken the unspeakable.

'Vivienne Fancourt.'

'Yes, that old bat. I can't stand the woman. She was always popping in here, to tell Alice some stupid trivial thing that could easily have waited till Alice got home, some pointless crap – sorry! – when Alice was busy working. And if ever Alice had arranged a night out with any of us, she'd end up cancelling because Vivienne had reminded her that they were going here or there, or Vivienne had arranged a surprise do, or Vivienne had got tickets for this show or that in London. It drove me mad. And Alice seemed to worship the old witch. You know what Alice is like, so tolerant and patient and kind. I think she was looking for a surrogate mother, with her own parents dead, but Jesus Christ on a bicycle! Sorry, you're not a Christian, are you? I'd rather belong to the bloody Plymouth Brethren than to Vivienne Fancourt – you'd get more freedom, that's for sure.'

'So Alice and Vivienne were close?' Simon tried not to be offended by the Christian remark.

'I don't know if that's the word for it. Alice was in awe of Vivienne. When she first came to work here, she quoted her almost non-stop. Vivienne had a saying or a rule for just about everything. It was a bit like a religion, actually. I think Alice liked the certainty it provided.'

'What sort of rules?'

'Oh, I don't know. Yes, I do. Never buy a carpet that isn't a hundred per cent wool, that was one of them. Alice told me when I was buying my house. Oh, and never own a white car. Two important mottos for life, I'm sure you'll agree,' said Briony sarcastically.

'Why not? A white car, I mean?'

'Lord only knows,' Briony said wearily. 'Thankfully the quoting died down after a while, otherwise I think we'd have had to strangle her. What are – if you don't mind my asking – what are the chances of Florence and Alice being found safe and sound?'

'I'll do my best,' said Simon. 'My best is better than most people's. That's all I can say.'

Briony smiled, seemed to relax a little. 'And is your worst worse? Or also better?'

A therapist question if ever Simon had heard one. He was damned if he was going to answer, or even think about it. 'Would you have liked to have a closer friendship with Alice?' he asked, wondering whether Briony's jealousy could have affected her view of the situation. Did she resent Vivienne's influence because she wanted to dominate Alice herself? Perhaps Alice had had plenty of time on her hands, but had used Vivienne as an excuse. She too might have found Briony's company exhausting.

'No, I was quite happy with mine and Alice's relationship. But it annoys me to watch people being stupid, especially intelligent people. Alice should have stood up to Vivienne and insisted on having a life of her own.' Her tone challenged Simon to disagree.

'Did you tell her that?' He wondered what it would be like to receive therapy from somebody so opinionated.

'No. She's not the sort of person you can be overly familiar with, you know? She has . . . boundaries.' That's what I like about her, thought Simon. Though 'like' was such a weak word, one step up from 'tolerate'.

'She's quite a private person in many ways. Like, in the couple of months before she went on her maternity leave, something was definitely bothering her. Unless it was just nerves about impending parenthood. But, somehow . . .'

'What?' Simon scribbled in his notebook.

'I don't think it was only that. In fact, I'm sure not. The last time I saw her, I could tell she was considering confiding in me about something.' Briony Morris grinned suddenly. 'I can be quite a mind-reader. For example, I know you're thinking, how come a harridan like her can be a touchy-feely therapist by profession. Right?'

'I was under the impression that people in your sort of job were supposed to be non-judgemental,' said Simon, scorn underlining the last word. How could you be a force for good in the world unless you used your judgement? Simon hated the sort of flabby-minded empathy peddled by most of these quacks, the assumption that everyone was equally deserving of compassion and consideration. Bollocks. Nothing would ever shake Simon's conviction that life – every day, every hour – was a battle between moral salvation and the abyss.

Briony surprised him by saying, 'All the emphasis on positive, calm feelings in the world of alternative health and therapy is just nonsense. We all have negative feelings, we all have people we hate as well as people we love. You can't achieve true emotional freedom unless you recognise that the world consists of bad as well as good things. I love westerns, me. I like it when John Wayne shoots the bad guys.'

Simon smiled. 'So do I,' he said.

'You see, Alice would hate that,' said Briony. 'Actually, if I had to criticise her, I'd say she's a bit naïve. She's so kind and generous, she sees good in people even when it's not there.'

'Like Vivienne?'

'I was thinking of David, actually. Her husband. Alice is always trying to make out he's deep and sensitive, but quite frankly, I think the lights are on but there's nobody home.'

'What do you mean?'

'He's one of those people who, no matter how many times you meet him, no matter how long you talk to him, you never feel you're getting to know him any better. I've met people like that before, personally and professionally. Sometimes it can be a defence mechanism – they're scared of anyone getting too close, so they hide behind a shield that no-one can penetrate. And then some people are just plain shallow,' she concluded. 'I'm not sure which David is, but put it this way, I saw no similarity between the man I met several times and the man Alice used to talk about. None whatsoever.' Briony shrugged. 'I sometimes wondered if there were two Davids that swapped back and forth without anyone knowing.'

Simon looked up, startled.

'What? Did I say something wrong?'

He shook his head.

Briony played with her hair. 'Will you let me know as soon as there's any news?' she asked.

'Of course.'

'I can't stop thinking about Florence, poor little mite. Do you think . . . ?' Her words ran out. It was as if the mere act of asking a question reassured her, even when she couldn't think of anything new to ask.

Simon thanked her for her time and left. Two David Fancourts. And two babies. No matter what Charlie said, he knew that nothing would now stop him from looking at the Laura Cryer case files as soon as he had the opportunity.

# 15

## *Sunday September 28, 2003*

The phone rings while we are eating dinner. We are all desperately grateful. Suddenly we can breathe again, and move. Vivienne marches into the hall. David and I lean in the same direction, wanting the news faster than we can get it.

'Yes. Yes,' says Vivienne briskly. 'Friday? But . . . I was hoping you might be able to fit us in sooner than that. It's an urgent matter, as I thought I made clear. I'm willing to pay more if you can see us immediately. Today, or tomorrow.' She has spent the whole morning making calls to private hospitals. I could have insisted on arranging the DNA test myself, but I need Vivienne's support, and I will only get it if I don't challenge her authority. I wonder if she senses how desperate I am to have her as an ally.

'All right. It doesn't look as if I have much choice,' she says coldly. I press my eyelids tightly shut. Friday. Nearly a week. I don't know if I can stand it. When I open my eyes, my uneaten lemon meringue pie spins in front of me, garish yellow goo and stiff white foam. I managed to swallow about a quarter of my shepherd's pie before a twitching in my throat told me I couldn't risk another mouthful.

David finished all his food. I could tell Vivienne was surprised. He ate more quickly than usual, making a big show of scraping the food off his plate and into his mouth, to demonstrate that he wanted this family meal-time to be over as quickly as possible. He and I haven't looked at one another since we sat down at the table.

Vivienne appears in the doorway, her arms folded. 'Friday morning. Nine o'clock,' she says, her voice deadened with disappointment. 'And then another two days before they can give us the results.'

'Where?' I ask.

'The Duffield Hospital in Rawndesley.'

'I don't need any results,' David mutters angrily.

'One of you is going to have a lot of explaining to do,' says Vivienne. 'Why not admit you're lying now, save us all the agony of a week's wait?' She looks at David, then at me. 'Well? You can't both be telling the truth.'

Silence.

'My photographs of Florence were deleted from my camera before I went to Florida. Which means it must have happened in the hospital, on the day Florence was born, because I went straight from the hospital to the airport. Whoever did it knew what was going to happen.'

Mandy was in the hospital. And her boyfriend. And Vivienne didn't go straight from the hospital to the airport. She went to Waterfront in between, to take Felix to his snorkelling lesson. I do not dare to remind her of this. There is no point. It proves she is wrong about a minor detail, not that I am telling the truth, not that I'm as sane as she is.

I wonder what she did with her camera while she was at Waterfront. Was it with her all the time, in her handbag? Did she put it in her locker, for safe-keeping? I know the key lives behind the reception desk most of the time, and in any case, there must be a master key. In theory, any of the Waterfront staff could have broken into the locker and tampered with the camera. But I know what Vivienne would say: the health club staff worship her, and would never dream of violating her privacy. Besides, how could they possibly have anything to do with any of this? It is inconceivable.

'Well? Alice? David? Is anybody going to say anything?' Vivienne wants one of us to own up. I want David to tell her that I'm right, that the baby in the house is not our daughter. Little Face. I wonder if I can call her that. I have to call her something. The phrase 'the baby', with all the distance it suggests, breaks my heart.

Felix's puzzled stare burns into me across Vivienne's enormous mahogany dining table. The four of us always sit in this precise formation: Vivienne and David at either end, metres apart, me and Felix in the middle, facing one another. The dining room is my least favourite at The Elms. It has dark purple flock wallpaper on all four walls, navy curtains and a dark, polished wooden floor that can't have been sealed properly, because in the winter cold air blows around your legs while you eat.

On the walls there are framed black and white photographs of Vivienne's adored parents and Vivienne herself as a child. Her mother is a small, plump woman with sloping shoulders and her father is tall and athletic-looking, with bulbous eyes and a moustache that conceals his upper lip. Neither of them is smiling in any of the photographs. I have always found it difficult to believe that these are the same loving, indulgent people Vivienne talks about so warmly. 'They bought me two of everything,' I remember her telling me. This was so that her friends, when they came to the house, could play with one set of toys and it wouldn't matter if they ruined them; Vivienne had her duplicates, her 'real toys', safely stashed away.

'Have it your own way,' she says icily. 'I'll find out the truth soon enough.'

Never mind you, I think impatiently. It's the bloody police who need to find out the truth.

'What is the baby's usual routine?' Vivienne asks. 'Is she likely to stay asleep now?'

Routine. The word makes me want to weep. She's a baby, I scream inside my head. Vivienne expects everyone to operate according to a strict timetable, even newborns.

'Which baby are you talking about?' says David. 'Oh, sorry, do you mean Florence? She has a name, you know.' I have never heard him speak to Vivienne like this before. I spent most of my pregnancy wishing that he were able and inclined to stand up to her. I know he was as taken aback as I was when Vivienne showed us the letter from Stanley Sidgwick Ladies' College, confirming that a place had been reserved for Florence in their lower kindergarten year for the January after her second birthday. I willed David to say thank you but no, to tell Vivienne that we didn't want Florence to attend any school or nursery full-time until she was quite a lot older. He said nothing. Nor did he object when Vivienne insisted on paying all Florence's school fees herself.

'I won't tolerate unpleasantness,' she says now. 'I want to make that clear to both of you. Until this matter is resolved, we will all behave like civilised people. Is that understood? David, answer my question. What is the child's routine?'

'She'll sleep all night, but she'll wake up twice for bottles.' He is the obedient little boy again.

'I want to feed Little Face tonight,' I blurt out. 'David always does the night feeds and . . . I want to . . .' I can't say it because it's too painful. I am desperate to do all the things mothers do, to freeze small blocks of puréed vegetables in ice-cube trays, brush each new tooth as it appears, sing lullabies, hear myself called 'Mummy' for the first time. I clear my throat and continue, looking at Vivienne. 'I hope that, wherever Florence is, some woman is looking after her and will keep her safe until I find her. I want to do the same for the baby upstairs. If I can't be a mother to my own daughter, I want to at least do the best I can to take care of the baby I've got.' My eyes fill with tears. 'The way you looked after me when my mother died.'

Because that is Vivienne's appeal. When you are under her wing, she makes you feel that the harsh blows of life cannot touch you. When David and I were engaged, my car was photographed by a speed camera. It was going at eight miles an hour over the legal limit, and I received a notice of intended prosecution from the police. With a carefully worded letter, Vivienne made the whole unpleasant business disappear, just as she did when my credit card company froze my account after a misunderstanding about a payment. 'Leave it to me,' she says, and the next thing you know, your troubles have vanished as if by magic.

I can see from her face that mine have not. She is not on my side, not yet, or not entirely. Certainly not in the way I need her to be. I feel exiled, desolate. This would be hard even with Vivienne's support. Without it the next few days will be agony.

'No way,' David snarls. 'You've chosen to disown Florence. You're not going anywhere near her.' His words jar. I can't understand why I am shocked anew every time he is cruel to me, every time he attributes the worst possible motives to me and refuses to give me the benefit of the doubt. I realise what a sheltered life I have led. Like many people who grow up taking their happiness and safety for granted, I find it hard to believe in destructiveness, unkindness, horror, unless I see them on the news or read about them in the papers. Faced with such things in my own life, my first instinct is to assume it must be a misunderstanding, that there must be a more innocent explanation.

'Mum, is Alice being naughty at the moment?' Felix continues to inspect me, as if I am the most mysterious and fascinating object he has ever seen.

'Finish your dessert, Felix, and go and get into your pyjamas. You can read in bed for ten minutes, and then I'll come up and tuck you in.' I despise myself, momentarily, for the rush of grateful relief I feel when Vivienne doesn't say, 'Yes, Alice is being very naughty.'

'Mummy Laura was naughty, wasn't she, Dad?' Felix turns to David, as if hoping he will be more forthcoming. I freeze. Felix has never mentioned Laura before, not in my presence.

David looks at Vivienne, as surprised by the question as I am.

'Mummy Laura was naughty and she died. Will Alice die too?'

'No!' I blurt out. 'Felix, your mother didn't . . . she wasn't . . .' I stop. Too many eyes are on me.

I wait for Vivienne or David to say 'Of course Alice isn't going to die,' but they don't. Instead, Vivienne smiles at Felix and says, 'Everybody dies eventually, darling. You know that.' Felix nods, his upper lip trembling.

Vivienne believes that children grow up to be stronger adults if they are told the truth about the harsh realities of life. Her parents brought her up in the same way. They were not religious, and instilled in Vivienne the idea that heaven and hell were fictions invented by weak, flawed humans in an attempt to dodge responsibility. There is no afterlife in which people are punished or rewarded; one must strive for justice in this world, while one is still alive. When Vivienne first told me this, I couldn't help but admire her philosophy, even though my own beliefs about what happens after we die are a lot more ambiguous.

'But you aren't going to die for a very, very long time, not until you're very old,' she tells Felix. I realise I am waiting for a similar reassurance. She says nothing about me.

'Now, come on, young man – it's bedtime for little imps . . .'

Felix smiles at the familiar phrase. 'And bedtime for little chimps!' he joins in.

As soon as he has left the room, before my courage has a chance to fail me, I say, 'What have you told Felix about Laura's death? Why does he think she was naughty? Have you told him that she died *because* she did something wrong? Don't you see how terrible that is, even to let him think it? Whatever she did, whatever you thought of her, she's still his mother.'

Vivienne purses her lips and leans her chin on her hands, saying nothing. She won't talk about Laura's death any more, I've noticed. She refuses to engage with the subject if I ever bring it up. I have a theory about this. I actually think Vivienne resents Laura for being dead. They were adversaries, on an equal footing, and then suddenly Laura was murdered and the whole country felt sorry for her. She was elevated to a higher realm, fixed for ever as a victim, a wronged woman. To Vivienne, this would have seemed like cheating, as if being fatally stabbed were a cheap, easy way to gain sympathy.

And Laura was out of reach for ever. Vivienne couldn't battle against her any more, which meant she couldn't win in the way she'd always wanted and needed to. She knew she'd never hear Laura say, 'I'm sorry, Vivienne. I can see that you've been right all along.' Not that Laura would ever, in a million years, have uttered those words.

'Laura's dead,' says David. 'And you're a lying bitch,' he snaps at me. He sounds like Mandy's boyfriend. Worse. I wonder what would happen if I phoned the hospital and asked about Mandy. Would they give me her full name, her address?

'Stop it, both of you,' says Vivienne. 'Didn't you hear me before? You're to behave courteously while you're in this house. There will be no slanging matches over the dining table. This isn't a council estate.'

I push back my chair and stand up, shaking. 'How can you care about manners at a time like this? Florence might be dead! And the test isn't until Friday, which means the police won't start looking for her until then – doesn't either of you care? Yes, I will bloody well shout if I want to. I want my daughter, and time's slipping away and there's nothing I can do about it! Every day, every hour . . . can't you both *see*?'

There is a glint of triumph in Vivienne's eyes. She enjoys the sight of other people losing control. She believes it proves that they are wrong and she is right, their need to resort to emotional hyperbole. 'I'm sorry,' I say quickly. 'I'm not shouting at you. I'm just . . . I can't bottle it up any more or I really will go mad.'

'I'd better go and see to Felix,' says Vivienne, her voice hoarse. 'I shan't come back downstairs. Good night.'

I listen to her footsteps as she crosses the hall. I know that the words 'Florence might be dead' are ringing in her ears. Good. I want her to be as full of dread and terror as I am.

David leaves the room without a word. Bedtime is much earlier for all of us now that we are so miserable. I clear away the dinner things slowly, allowing him plenty of time to fall asleep before I go upstairs. As I walk along the landing, I try the handles of all the spare bedrooms and find them locked. I cannot sleep downstairs. Vivienne wouldn't allow it. It is one of her house rules, and I have no doubt that David would alert her to my absence from our bedroom. I can picture her shaking me awake in the middle of the night, telling me that The Elms is not a youth hostel. I do not want to antagonise her.

I pray that David will be asleep. He is awake, flat on his back in bed. There is a bottle of formula milk on his bedside table. I am exhausted, but if I force myself to stay awake, I might hear Little Face before he does. I might be able to give her her night-time bottle and see the shadow of her small, round head cast by the barn wall light against the fabric of her cot. Imagining the experience, I ache for it to be real.

'Is there no limit to what you're prepared to do?' says David bitterly. 'First you try to drive me mad, make me believe that Florence isn't Florence, and now you want to try and stop me feeding her! What have I ever done to you, to deserve this?'

'I don't want to stop you feeding the baby.' I begin to cry. 'I just want to feed her too. Not all the time, just sometimes.'

'Even though, according to you, she's not your daughter.'

'A mother's maternal feelings don't disappear just because her baby does,' I sob.

'Oh, very good, very convincing. How long did it take you to come up with that line?'

'David, please . . .'

'Who were you talking to on your mobile yesterday? That call that ended abruptly as soon as I came in?'

I stare at the floor, cursing myself for my recklessness. I must be more careful in future.

'No-one,' I whisper. He doesn't ask again. I pull my nightie out from under my top pillow and lay it on the bed in front of me. I decide, on the spot, not to try to leave the room to get changed. I have no doubt that David would stop me if I tried, so I will not give him the satisfaction. As I start to wriggle uncomfortably out of my clothes, David makes a point of averting his eyes, as if he can't bear the sight of me. I thought nothing could be worse than the way he ogled me last night, but this is. The disgust on his face hurts me so much that I cannot accept it. I thought I had given up trying to argue with him, but I find myself saying, 'David, please will you think about what you're doing? I don't believe that deep down you want to be cruel to me. Do you?'

'I'm not doing anything,' he says. 'I'm just minding my own business.'

'I know this is difficult, I know it's horrible, but . . . this isn't you. You don't want to be like this. I *know* you. You're not an unkind person. It's well-known that in extreme situations, in moments of crisis, people are scared and disorientated and they lash out, they persecute people and do all sorts of awful things because they're scared.'

'Shut up!' His ferocity startles me. He sits up in bed. 'I'm not interested in anything you've got to say. You're a liar. All that therapy language is just your way of obscuring the truth! You're happy to talk feelings, but you won't talk facts, will you?'

'David, I'll talk about anything you want. What facts?'

'Facts! If Florence wasn't Florence, why would I say she was? Don't you think I'd want her found as much as you? Or are you suggesting I'm some kind of imbecile who can't tell the difference between his own daughter and another baby? I mean, you need to get your story straight because, frankly, it doesn't hold water. What exactly are you saying has happened here? That some intruder came into our house and swapped Florence for another baby? Why would they? Why? Or do you think it was me that did it? Again, why would I? I want my own daughter, not some random child.'

I put my hands up to stop him. 'I don't know! I don't know who's taken Florence, or why, or who the other baby is, okay? I don't know! And I don't even know what you know, or what you think, or why you're saying what you're saying. You're right! I haven't got the story straight, because I've no idea what's happened. I feel as if I don't know anything any more and it's terrifying. *That's* what you can't understand. And all I can do is cling on to the one thing I do know without the slightest shadow of a doubt: the baby in this house is not Florence!'

David turns away. 'Well, then,' he says. 'There's nothing more we can say to each other.'

'Don't turn away!' I beg him. 'I could ask you the same question you asked me. Are you suggesting *I'm* an imbecile, that *I* can't recognise my own daughter?'

He says nothing. I want to wail with frustration. I want to scream *I haven't finished yet. I'm still talking to you.* I cannot believe he is as certain as he claims he is. I must be getting through to him on some subliminal level; I have to cling to that belief.

One by one, I drop my clothes on the bed. I reach for my nightie but David is too quick. He pulls it away, scrunching it into a ball in his hand. The sudden movement startles me and I cry out in shock. He laughs. Before I have a chance to anticipate his next move, he grabs the pile of my discarded clothes and gets out of bed. He opens the door of my wardrobe, throws my clothes and nightie inside, then closes and locks the door.

Now he looks at my body. I feel his gaze as it crawls over my cold skin. 'I doubt you'll be going anywhere tonight,' he sneers. 'I wouldn't, looking like that.'

I consider my choices. I could call Vivienne, but by the time she got here, David would have given me back my nightie. He would pretend I made up the whole story. He is waiting for me to say that I need to use the bathroom, but I will not. Nor will I walk along the landing naked. I know exactly what would happen if I did. David would unlock my cupboard, put my nightie back on the bed and summon Vivienne, who would be out of her room in seconds. He wants to call my judgement and behaviour into question. I am not going to make it easy for him. I would rather be kept awake all night by the discomfort of a full bladder. I climb into bed and pull the duvet up to my chin.

David does the same. I stiffen, but he doesn't touch me. I wait for him to turn out his bedside light so that I can cry in private, about Florence, about the person my husband is turning into, and, yes, even now, about the pain I know he is in. David's viciousness is aimed at himself as well as me. He has an all-or-nothing attitude: if things cannot be made to be all right, he might as well make them as bad as they can possibly be, as quickly as he can. At least then there will be nothing more to fear.

My mother used to say that I was able to imagine and empathise with the suffering of others in a way that most people were not. She thought this was why I had so many unsuitable boyfriends as a teenager – 'some right lulus' was how she put it. It is true that once you try hard to see any situation through another person's eyes, it becomes impossible to write that person off. That is the way in which I have always approached the world, with compassion. Evidently I was foolish to assume the world would reciprocate.

I cannot keep making excuses for David, hoping he'll change. I need to learn to respond to him as I would to an enemy if he continues to behave like one. I, who have told countless patients not to think in terms of good and evil, of allies and enemies. I should give them all their money back.

I don't know how early David will wake up tomorrow morning, how soon he will give me my clothes. Will he make me beg? The thought of what might happen is too awful to contemplate. Whatever it is, I must survive it. I have to hold on until tomorrow afternoon, until my meeting with Simon.

# 16

## 5/10/03, 11.10 am

'What?' demanded David Fancourt. 'What do you want from me? Mum's already told you everything. Alice and Florence were here on Thursday evening. They both went to bed as normal. By Friday morning, they'd gone. It's your job to find them and you won't find them here. If they were here, I'd never have reported them missing in the first place. So why don't you go out and look for them?' He perched, stiffly upright, on the edge of the least comfortable chair in the room, the narrow wooden one with a navy velvet seat and a cushionless back. Charlie could feel his anger almost as tangibly as if he'd punched her in the face. She felt sorry for him, didn't blame him for being in a rage. Vivienne sat across the room, on a white sofa. She belonged to the old school: one did not show one's feelings in public.

'We fully intend to find Alice and Florence,' said Charlie. David Fancourt was guilty only of rudeness; that was her gut feeling, based on the first half minute of the interview. Simon's paranoid theories were ridiculous. Fancourt had a rock solid alibi. He and Alice were in London in a crowded theatre when Laura was killed. 'We always start in the missing person's home, even though obviously that's the one place we know the person isn't. I know it must seem confusing.'

'I don't care where you start as long as you find my daughter.'

151

Charlie noticed that he didn't mention Alice. 'Try to calm down,' she said. 'I know this must be very upsetting for you, especially after what happened to Laura . . .'

'No!' David's cheeks were flushed. 'I'm perfectly all right, or I will be as soon as you've found Florence. I'm actually furious. First I nearly lost Felix, and now Alice has stolen Florence from me. Except that no-one believes me that it *is* Florence. Even . . .' He mumbled something, glancing at his mother.

'I've never said that I don't believe you,' said Vivienne coolly, raising her chin. Charlie wondered if this was how the Queen would behave in a similar situation. She vaguely remembered having been told, at the time of the Laura Cryer murder, where Vivienne's father's wealth had come from, but she couldn't bring to mind the details. He had founded a big company of some sort, plastics or packaging. Vivienne was not old money, no matter how aristocratic her bearing.

The sitting room looked smaller than it was because of all the furniture that was crammed into it. There were three sofas, seven chairs, a monstrosity of a coffee table, two large bookcases in alcoves on either side of a real fire, and a small television on a stand that was oddly positioned behind an armchair in one corner as if to make the point that in this house television was not an important part of daily life. Almost all the books on the shelves were hard-backs, Charlie noticed.

Today she was here alone. Yesterday, there had been a team of officers at The Elms, turning the place upside down, methodically going through Alice Fancourt's pos-sessions. They'd found her handbag and keys in the kitchen and her Volvo outside. No clothes belonging to either Alice or Florence appeared to be missing, apart from the ones they were wearing. Vivienne had provided this information and seemed fairly sure. Charlie had to admit that this was a very bad sign. The most worrying thing of all was that Vivienne insisted Alice only owned three pairs of shoes, and they were all still in her wardrobe.

On Thursday night, Vivienne had locked both front and back doors, as she always did before going to bed. By the morning, Alice and Florence had gone and the doors were still locked. There was no sign that anybody had broken in. Vivienne, David and Felix had slept soundly; no loud noises or scuffles had woken them, no baby cries. Charlie found these facts, viewed as a whole, extremely puzzling.

Could someone have persuaded Alice to let them in and then abducted her and the baby? If so, they must have exited via the back door. The window beside it had a narrow top panel, about fifteen centimetres by forty, that had been left open, and Alice's keys were on the kitchen work-surface beneath. The kidnapper would have had to get Alice and Florence outside in virtual silence, lock the back door again and drop the keys in through the window.

Or else Alice herself had done this. Charlie wondered if she could possibly have been deranged enough, even in an advanced state of post-natal depression, to leave with none of her own or Florence's possessions. Simon, when she had spoken to him this morning, had reiterated his certainty that Alice was alive and unharmed. 'I'll find her,' he'd said, with a passionate determination in his voice and eyes that had made Charlie turn away.

'Sergeant Zailer, David and I will help you in any way we can,' said Vivienne Fancourt. 'But that baby must be found. Do you understand? Florence is . . .' She broke off, apparently to examine her skirt. When she looked up, her eyes were bright and piercing. 'Excuse me,' she muttered. 'You have no idea how distressing this is for me. Not only is my darling granddaughter missing, but I don't even know if she went missing last Friday or the Friday before. I don't know whether I've only met her once, or . . .' She pressed her lips together.

'You hear of women who flip and murder their babies,' David interrupted angrily. 'Don't you? Women with post-natal depression. They smother them, or throw them out of windows. What's Alice likely to do? How often do these women bring back the babies unharmed? You must know.' He covered his face with his hands. 'Alice was unbalanced before she disappeared. She had an obsession with this woman from the hospital who she hardly even spoke to . . .'

'Mr Fancourt, it's not clear that your wife has abducted your daughter. She took nothing with her. We have to consider the possibility that Alice left here against her will.'

David shook his head. 'She ran away and took Florence,' he said.

'What did you mean when you said you nearly lost Felix?'

There was an awkward pause. Then Vivienne said, 'He meant that Laura did everything she could to keep Felix away from us. She allowed us to see him once a fortnight – can you imagine? – for two or three hours, and she made sure she was there to supervise every time. It was impossible to build a proper relationship under her awful scrutiny. And she'd never let Felix come here, or allow David and me into her house. We always had to meet in a neutral place.' She paused to catch her breath. Two pink spots had appeared on her cheeks.

Charlie frowned. 'But on the night Laura was killed, Felix was here, alone with you. You were babysitting.'

'Yes.' Vivienne smiled sadly. 'That was the one and only

time it happened. Because she was desperate for a sitter, so that she could go off to some party in a nightclub.' It was clear from Vivienne's tone that she had never been inside such a place and had no wish to. Simon had said 'a club?' in the same way, yet his police work regularly took him to Spilling and Rawndesley's dingy, strobe-lit night spots.

'David and I put up with Laura's rules for nearly three years,' Vivienne went on. 'We hoped that if we went along with her . . . monstrous regime, she'd relax and allow us to have a bit more contact with Felix. But we were deluding ourselves, I'm afraid. She showed no sign of changing her mind, or the rules. We were getting so desperate that we were on the point of consulting my lawyer about the problem, when . . . when she was killed.'

'Leaving David as the sole parent,' said Charlie. She felt a few grains of her certainty slipping away. She pictured Darryl Beer standing in the grounds of The Elms with a kitchen knife concealed somewhere in his clothing. For the first time, the image struck her as an unlikely one. Why come armed with a kitchen knife if the purpose of his visit was to see how the land lay for a future burglary?

Once Laura was out of the way, David could marry his new girlfriend and have sole custody of Felix, with his mother conveniently on hand to do most of the child care. Convenient for David and Vivienne, convenient for Alice, thought Charlie. Mad Alice. What if it had taken the shine off her engagement, having a miserable fiancé who was preoccupied by his absent son?

Behind David's chair, on one of the shelves, there was a photograph of his second wedding. Alice wore a cream dress and a tiara, and beamed at her husband. Her blonde hair was shorter, chin-length, and had been curled for the occasion. It had been lank and straight last week when

Charlie met her. David, a couple of inches taller than Alice, was smiling proudly down at his new wife. They were an attractive couple, thought Charlie, trying to ignore the jab of envy she felt. Why did this woman who was already married, already loved, deserve Simon's attention more than she did? It wasn't fair.

Ever since Simon had rejected her so brutally at Sellers' fortieth birthday party, Charlie had become almost pathologically frightened of indignity of any sort, which often made her needlessly brittle and aggressive. She was intelligent enough to recognise this, but not, sadly, to know how to begin to tackle the problem. A year after the hideous event, she still wasn't anywhere near over it. Nothing in her life, before or since, had injured her psyche and ego as much as what Simon had done to her. The awful thing was, she knew he felt terrible about it and was genuinely sorry. That there was nothing planned or malicious about his actions made her pain worse. Charlie still thought as highly of Simon as she ever had. She was still in love with him, for Christ's sake. And if there was nothing wrong with him, that had to mean there was something wrong with her.

She'd gone over and over it in her mind. Simon had been enthusiastic at first. 'This isn't going to be just a fling,' he whispered to her, as they made their way to Sellers' spare bedroom. 'This relationship is going to last a long time.' No, there was no doubt he had wanted her at that stage. Charlie was able to identify only too easily the point at which Simon's attitude changed, changed radically enough to make him push her off his lap so that she landed on the floor, and run from the room as if from a plague. He probably didn't realise at the time, probably hadn't since, that in his haste he had left the door wide open. Several faces, including that of Sellers' wife Stacey, had appeared in the doorway while Charlie was frantically scrambling for her clothes.

She had not told anyone afterwards, not even her sister Olivia. She doubted she ever would. The details were such agony to recall, even in the privacy of her own mind. The worst thing of all about the disaster (Charlie didn't think it was over the top to call it this – it felt like an accurate description) was that it allowed no possibility of corrective action. It had happened. It would always have happened. It could never be undone, though she tried as hard as she could to erase it. In the past year, she'd had casual sex with, on average, a man a month. None of them had run away, but Charlie could see it wasn't doing her any good. She still felt undesirable, and now she also felt cheap and easy. The behaviour had a compulsive element to it, though. Next time it would work. The next man would rub Simon out.

Of all the inconvenient people to love, I had to bloody go and choose him, she thought. Though it hadn't been a choice, not really. Simon was nothing like anybody Charlie had ever met before. She would have found it impossible to lie to herself, to pretend that he was one of many similar fish in the sea. Who else would be nostalgic, as Simon had once told Charlie he was, for a time when there was a danger that, as a Catholic, he might be burned at the stake?

'You want to be burnt?' she'd asked, thinking he had to be taking the piss.

'No, of course not,' he'd said. 'But in those days, beliefs meant something. They were seen as dangerous. Thoughts and ideas should matter, that's all I'm saying. It's right that people should be scared of them, that men should be willing to die for things. Nothing seems to matter to anyone any more.' And Charlie had fought the urge to tell him how much he mattered to her.

'I was relieved when Laura died,' Vivienne broke the silence. That got Charlie's attention. 'Not happy, you understand, but relieved. It was a dream come true when Felix came to live with us. I don't care if that sounds heartless. Although . . .'

'What?'

'Some time after Laura's death, I realised I had never asked her, directly, *why* she was so determined to keep me away from Felix. Now I'll never know. She can't have thought I'd harm him. I adore him.' Vivienne frowned at her hands. Her mouth twitched, as if she were trying to stop herself from saying something. But it came out in spite of her efforts. 'I wish, every day of my life, that I'd asked her. You know, in a funny sort of way, losing an enemy is as hard to bear as losing a loved one. You're left with the same strong feelings you always had, but no-one to attach them to. It makes one feel . . . cheated, I suppose.'

'I know this might not seem immediately relevant,' Charlie began gently, 'but there is one line of enquiry that might prove worthwhile . . .'

'Yes?' For the first time since the interview began there was hope in David Fancourt's eyes.

'Alice talked to DC Waterhouse about your father. I know you're not in touch with him, but . . .'

'What?' Creases of disgust appeared all over his face. 'She talked to *him* about . . . ?'

Vivienne's mouth pulled in tightly at the sides. She looked angry. 'Why on earth would she be interested in Richard?'

'I don't know. Any ideas?'

'None. She didn't say anything about it to me.' There was irritation in her voice. Charlie had the impression that Vivienne was not a woman who took kindly to being left out of the loop.

'Do you know how we could contact Richard Fancourt?'

'No. I'm sorry. I don't remember him with much fond-ness, and I'd rather not talk about him.'

Charlie nodded. A proud woman like Vivienne would not wish to be reminded of her life's failures. Charlie felt that way about most of the men she'd been involved with: Dave Beadman, a sergeant from Child Protection, who, when the condom split, said, 'Don't worry, I know where the abortion clinic is. Been there before!' Before him, an accountant, Kevin Mackie, who was, as he put it, 'not into kissing'.

Charlie had always mistrusted people who stayed chum-my with their exes. It was unnatural, sick even, to tolerate the tepid, watered-down presence in your life of what was once love or lust, to save the detritus washed up after the wreckage of a romance and call it friendship. Simon was different. He was not Charlie's ex. He's my never-to-be, she thought sadly, and therefore much harder to get over.

Failed relationships. They affected everything that came after them, like radioactive accidents. They poisoned the future. Which reminded her of something she had not yet covered, something that might explain, directly or indir-ectly, why Alice had vanished. 'Why did you and Laura Cryer separate?' she asked David Fancourt.

# 17

## *Monday September 29, 2003*

'He's called her Mrs Tiggywinkle since the first moment he saw her. It's more than a nickname. She *was* – is – Mrs Tiggywinkle. But this other baby, he calls her Little Face. He *knows* she isn't Florence. And I heard him call himself "I" when he was talking to her in the night, when he didn't know I was listening. If he was talking to Florence, he would have said "Daddy".' I know I should speak more slowly, that a less manic delivery would make me sound more rational, but I have waited so long to say all this. I can't stop the words pouring out.

Simon and I are in Chompers. As I rant, he eyes me awkwardly across a polished wooden table. He is nervous. He traces the grain of the wood with his index finger. Noise blasts out all around us – music, laughter, conversation – but I hear only the silence after I have spoken, Simon's silence. His hair is clean, freshly combed. His denim shirt and black trousers look brand new, even if they do not go particularly well with each other or with his brown shoes. I don't know why the ensemble doesn't work, but the first thing I thought when he walked in was, 'David wouldn't be seen dead in that outfit.' I find Simon's bad dress sense endearing, almost reassuring.

'I'm afraid that doesn't prove anything,' he says after a long pause. His voice is apologetic. 'Plenty of parents give their children more than one nickname, or one replaces another. And for your husband to describe himself as "I" is normal as well. He might refer to himself as "Daddy" most of the time but "I" occasionally.'

'I don't know what I can say to convince you, then. If my word isn't enough.' I am numb with misery. He is not on my side. I can't rely on him. I consider telling him what happened to me this morning, after my long, uncomfortable sleepless night. I had to beg for my clothes, to be allowed to use the bathroom. Eventually David unlocked my wardrobe and selected a dress he knew was too small for me, a horrible fitted green thing I haven't worn for years. 'You shouldn't have let yourself get so fat while you were pregnant,' he said.

I was desperate to use the toilet. I did not have time to argue with him, so I squeezed awkwardly into the dress. Once I was in it, I felt an even greater pressure on my bladder. I might have lost control at any moment, and David knew it. He laughed at my helplessness. 'It's lucky you didn't have a natural birth,' he said. 'Your pelvic floor muscles wouldn't have been up to the task, would they?' Eventually, he moved aside and let me leave the room. I ran to the bathroom, got there just in time.

I cannot bring myself to tell Simon about David's little tortures. I am not prepared to share my humiliation with him, only to hear him say that David's cruelty does not prove Little Face isn't Florence. I am still wearing the horrible green dress. David wouldn't give me the key to my wardrobe, so I couldn't get changed. Vivienne wouldn't have believed me if I'd told her. She'd have believed David, when he said, as he would have, that I'd locked the wardrobe myself and lost the key, that I was going mad.

Looking so awful in public makes me feel ashamed. I am sure Simon would pay more attention to what I'm saying if

I were wearing clothes that fitted properly. But I am not, and Simon also believes David.

'I find it hard knowing what to think,' he says. 'I've never met anyone like you before.' His face is not exactly as I remembered it. I forgot, for example, how wide his lower jaw is, and that his bottom teeth are wonky, with some jutting out in front of others. I'd memorised his uneven nose, but forgotten the texture of his skin, the wide pores and slightly bumpy, roughened area around his mouth that makes him look weathered and tough.

I ask him what he means.

'Everything tells me I shouldn't believe you . . .'

'Sergeant Zailer, you mean,' I said bitterly. I still have not forgiven her for the compassionless way she dealt with me at the police station.

'Not just her. Everything. You're asking us to believe that a stranger or strangers entered your house while your husband and daughter were sleeping, and swapped your daughter for another baby without your husband hearing anything. Why would anyone do that?'

'I never said it was a stranger!'

'Or else your husband was involved somehow, and then deliberately destroyed all the pictures of Florence so that no-one could prove anything. But again, why?'

I told him I had no idea, that just because an explanation was not immediately accessible, that didn't mean there wasn't one. Stating the obvious to someone who is supposed to be intelligent, who should know better, makes me want to scream with frustration.

'No babies have been reported missing, and you've got a history of depression.' Hearing my indignant gasp, he said, 'I'm sorry. I know your parents had just died, but still, from our point of view, you count as someone with a history.

The simplest explanation for all this is that you're suffering from some sort of . . .'

'Trauma-induced delusion?' I finished his sentence for him. 'But that's not what you think, is it? However hard you try to believe that, you don't. Which is why you're here now.' Perhaps if I tell him what he thinks, he will start to think it. I am desperate enough to try anything.

'Normally, in any other case like this, I *wouldn't* be here.' Simon's expression was pained, as if he was disappointed in himself.

'So what's different?' I demand, impatient. He is more interested in his own motivation than in Florence's or my safety.

'My instincts tell me to trust you,' he says quietly, looking away. 'But what does that mean? It's a contradiction, isn't it? It's doing my head in, to be honest.' He looked at me then, as if wanting encouragement of some kind.

Finally, a sliver of hope. Maybe I can talk him round, persuade him to help me, no matter what sneery Sergeant Zailer says. 'It's like me and homeopathy,' I tell him, forcing myself to sound calm. 'I know the theories behind it and they sound like nonsense – you'd have to be a fool to believe that anything so outlandish could work. And yet it does. I've seen it work, time and time again. I trust it completely, even though logically it sounds like something I could never believe in.'

'I went to see a homeopath once. Never went back.' Simon studied the fingernails on his left hand.

*I don't care* I yell inside my head. *This isn't about you!* Instead I say, 'It's not everyone's cup of tea. The remedies can sometimes make your symptoms worse at first, which confuses a lot of people. And then there are bad homeopaths, who prescribe the wrong thing or don't listen to you properly.'

'Oh, Dennis was a good listener. It wasn't him that was the problem, it was me. I got cold feet about talking to him. In the end I chickened out and never even told him why I'd come.' Simon brings his story to an abrupt conclusion, saying, 'It was a waste of time and it cost me forty quid.'

I understand that I am not to ask any further questions. In his own stilted way he is trying to confide in me, but he will only go so far. Good. The sooner he shuts up, the sooner we can get back to Florence. I am about to ask if he will do something to help me, finally, when he says, 'Do you like your job?'

*Who cares about my stupid, stupid job?* 'I used to. A lot.'

'What's changed?'

'Going through this.' I make an all-encompassing gesture with my hands. 'Losing Florence. I don't have the same unwaveringly positive view of people that I used to have. I'm afraid I might be too cynical now.'

'I don't think you're cynical at all,' said Simon. 'I think you could help a lot of people.' This, like a lot of what he has said, strikes me, suddenly, as peculiar. He talks as if he knows me well, when in fact this is only the third time we've met.

I don't want to help strangers, not any more. I want Simon to help me and Florence. Maybe cynical is the wrong word. Maybe selfish is what I have become. And my last thread of patience has just snapped. 'Are you going to look for my daughter or not?' The words slip out, sounding more accusatory than I want them to.

'I've explained . . .'

'I wanted to bring Little Face with me today. Did I tell you that? I wasn't allowed.' I am too exhausted to stop my resentments pouring out. My nerves feel as if they are rattling under my skin.

'Alice, calm down . . .'

'If David and Vivienne really believe Little Face is Florence, you'd think they'd want me to spend time with her, wouldn't you? You'd think they'd see it as a good sign, that I wanted to take her out with me. Well, they didn't! I was forbidden.'

My disappointment was so acute, so piercing, I couldn't contain it. I had so looked forward to being alone with Little Face. I had imagined myself slotting her car seat into the Volvo and setting off with her changing bag in the boot, packed full of nappies, wipes, milk and a spare babygro. She would probably fall asleep in the car. Tiny babies usually do. Every so often I would adjust the rearview mirror to try to catch a glimpse of her features – her thin, shell-coloured eyelids, her half-open mouth.

'Vivienne said I was trying to substitute Little Face for Florence,' I tell Simon, weeping. 'She says it's not a good idea for me to get too attached to her. She said letting me take her out was a risk. As if I'd hurt a defenceless baby!'

'Alice, you've got to try to calm down, get some perspective on this,' says Simon, patting my arm. Vivienne's words were almost identical. Everyone is so good at sounding perfectly reasonable. Everyone except me.

'Put yourself in my position,' Vivienne said. 'You're saying one thing, David's saying another. I *have* to consider the possibility that you're lying, Alice. Or that you're . . . not well. Don't look so hurt – you must be able to see that it's a hypothesis that's difficult for me to avoid. How can I allow you to take the baby out on your own? You must know from your own experience that even the tiniest of fears can grow and become all-consuming. I'd be sick with worry if I let that baby out of my sight.'

'If she's my baby, I should be able to take her wherever I want!' I yell at Simon. I am aware of heads turning at other tables, but I don't care. 'Well? Shouldn't I?'

'When you're a bit calmer, I'm sure . . .'

'They'll let me? No, they won't! And I can't take her anywhere unless they let me. They'd easily overpower me. Even Vivienne on her own is stronger than I am, thanks to the machines in this bloody, bloody . . . place!' I wave my arms around. I hate everyone and everything. 'She has to make all the decisions, every single one. The cot, nearly all of Florence's clothes. She reserved a place for Florence at Stanley Sidgwick without even asking me what I thought about it!'

'But . . . that's insane. Already?'

'Oh, yes! While I was pregnant, she did it. Not a minute to waste! You've got to register them before birth or they don't stand a chance of getting a place. And there's a five-year waiting list, as Vivienne never *ever* stops telling me. Silly me, thinking Florence could just . . . exist for a while, without any pressure to . . . achieve!'

'You should try to calm down.' Simon clears his throat. 'David isn't . . . hitting you or anything, is he?'

'No! Haven't you heard a word I've said?' David would never hit me. I almost say this. Then it strikes me that I have no idea what he is capable of. I don't think he has either. He is not like Vivienne, whose ideas and actions, irrespective of whether one agrees with them or not, are based on rationality. With Vivienne there are rules, guarantees. There is consistency. She is like a dictator in charge of a country, or a Mafia boss. If you love and obey her, you can have every privilege imaginable.

David is knocked over by waves of emotion that he can't deal with, and lashes out in response. I can see now that even his withdrawal into himself after Laura died was a lashing-out of sorts. 'I don't want to talk about David,' I tell Simon.

He pats my arm again. The first time, I was grateful for the gesture. This time it is nowhere near enough. I need proper help.

'Charlie . . . Sergeant Zailer told me what happened to his first wife.'

His comment surprises me so much, I spill a bit of my glass of water.

'What's wrong? I'm sorry if I . . .'

'No. No, it's okay. I just wasn't expecting you to mention it. I . . . please, can we change the subject?'

'Are you okay?'

'I feel a bit faint.' He has caught me off guard. I will not talk about Laura's death, not without time to prepare, to consider what I want to say. I have no doubt that anything I say to Simon will be relayed to Sergeant Zailer. It was a murder case, after all. And Sergeant Zailer does not have my best interests at heart, of that I am convinced.

'Do you want more water? Would some fresh air help? I hope I haven't been too blunt.'

'No, I'm fine now. Really. I should go.'

His mobile phone rings. As he pulls it out of his pocket, I wonder why mine hasn't rung. It is odd that Vivienne has not phoned to check I am all right. I was in such a state before I left. While Simon talks to someone who, it appears from the conversation, is putting pressure on him to see them next Sunday, I reach into my handbag to find my phone, check I haven't missed any calls.

It isn't there. I turn the bag upside down, empty its

contents on to the table, my heartbeat crashing in my chest. I'm right. My phone is gone. It has been taken. Confiscated. I stand up, start to push all the other things back into the bag. I drop my keys on the floor several times, which makes me cry harder. Tears blur my vision until I can't see anything. I fall back into my chair. Simon mutters into his phone that he had better go. 'Here, let me help,' he says. He begins to pack my things away. I am too upset to thank him. All over the restaurant, people are staring at us.

'My phone was in my bag this morning. David's taken it!'

'Maybe you left it . . .'

'No! I didn't leave it anywhere! What's it going to take for you to help me? What has to happen to me? Are you going to wait till I get killed, like Laura?' I pick up my bag and run for the door, colliding with several tables on my way out. Eventually, I make it out on to the street. I don't stop running. I have no idea where I am going.

# 18

Simon had a problem with Colin Sellers. It was well-known among the Ds that Sellers, despite being married to Stacey and having two young kids, had been having an affair with a woman called Suki for three years. It was a stage name. Her real name was Suzannah Kitson. Sellers seemed intent on sharing every detail about his mistress with his colleagues, which is how Simon knew that Suki was a singer, in local restaurants, sometimes on cruise ships. She was only twenty-three and still lived with her parents. Sellers was always in a bad mood when she was cruising, as he called it.

Simon knew nothing about what it would feel like to be married, to go to bed and wake up with the same person day after day, year after year. Perhaps one would get bored. He could see that falling in love with somebody else might be a hazard. Harder to endure was the way Sellers boasted about what he did with Suki to anyone who would listen. 'Not a word to the dragon,' he'd say at the end of each lewd anecdote, knowing that his colleagues sometimes met his wife at parties.

Perhaps he didn't care if Stacey found out. Simon saw no evidence of love, guilt, anguish – any deep emotion at all. Once he had asked Charlie, 'Do you think Sellers is in love with his mistress?'

She'd hooted with laughter. 'His mistress? What century are you living in?'

'What would you call her?'

'I don't know. His bit on the side? His sexual associate? No, I don't think he loves her. I think he fancies her, and she's a singer, so a bit glam, and Sellers is just the sort to need a trophy girlfriend. I bet he's got a tiny knob. And whatever any woman tells you, size does matter!'

As he listened to Sellers telling Proust about the work he and Chris Gibbs had done so far on the Alice and Florence Fancourt case, Simon tried not to wonder about the size of the man's penis. Surely if Charlie was right, Sellers would not have had the nerve to talk about his organ to the extent that he did. 'I've just had a visit from Captain Hardon' he would say, whenever an attractive woman crossed his path.

This morning he was on his best behaviour, under Proust's meticulous eye. The inspector listened attentively, taking the occasional sip from his 'World's Greatest Grandad' mug. Sellers spoke in the sober tone of a man who had taken a vow of chastity and joined the temperance society. The Snowman effect: more powerful than a hundred cold showers.

'The CCTV footage has given us nothing. Same with the search of The Elms. We've been through Alice Fancourt's address book, mostly old friends from London. We've spoken to all of them and none of them could tell us a thing. Nothing from her mobile phone, either, or the home computer, or her computer at work. No leads at all. And so far no luck with finding David Fancourt's father, but we're working on it. He can't have just disappeared.'

Proust blinked and frowned as Sellers raced through his report. The inspector distrusted people who spoke too quickly. Because Sellers' speech wasn't slow and deliberate, Proust feared his work was slapdash. In fact, Sellers was a reasonably thorough if not particularly dynamic detective.

He just didn't have the patience to describe every painstaking step he took in an investigation, preferring instead to offer his conclusions. Simon knew that Charlie often had to show Proust Sellers' pocket book, to prove that no corners had been cut.

Simon tried hard to concentrate on the team meeting, on Proust's stern face, on the sickly colours of the walls and carpet in the CID room, on his own shoes – on anything apart from the large photograph of Alice that was pinned to the board in front of him. It was no use. Even when he wasn't looking at the photograph he could see it in his mind. Alice's hair was up in a ponytail and she was laughing at the camera, her head tilted slightly to one side. Simon thought she was an object of great beauty. Well, not an object, not in that way. And it wasn't her looks, not really. It was the way her character shone out of her eyes. Her soul.

He blushed, shamed by his thoughts. Sometimes he felt as if he were carrying Alice's consciousness around with him. He was afraid that if she reappeared, he'd discover he was wrong about so much. He feared he was getting too used to her being absent, making absence part of her character, in his mind. It was fucked up, he knew. He had to find her, before it got worse. Him; nobody else. If Sellers managed to track her down, if a lead coming from an interview conducted by Gibbs turned out to be the decisive one, Simon didn't know if he would be able to handle it. He had to be the one.

'DC Waterhouse?' Proust's chiselled tone interrupted his thoughts. 'Anything to add?'

Simon told the rest of the team about his interviews at the Spilling Centre for Alternative Medicine. 'So, nothing there either,' Charlie summarised, when he'd finished. There was red lipstick on her teeth.

'Well . . .' Simon wouldn't have said that. Or was he so desperate to be Alice's knight in shining armour that he was seeing potential leads where there were none?

'Well what, Waterhouse?' Proust enquired.

'One thing struck me as odd, sir. Briony Morris – the emotional freedom therapist – she seemed really worried about Florence, but less worried about Alice. That doesn't make sense. She's never met Florence, but Alice has been her friend for a while.'

'Maybe she's one of those stupid twats who goes all gooey over a baby,' Sellers suggested, nodding sagely. 'Plenty of those about. She'd probably care even more if a fluffy kitten went missing.'

Simon shook his head. 'I don't think so. It was strange. I got the impression she'd worried about Alice more *before* she disappeared.'

'She's a woman,' said Chris Gibbs. 'They're all sodding obsessed with babies.' Charlie's eyes, narrow with disgust, blazed in his direction. 'I don't care if that sounds sexist, Sarge. Some generalisations are true.'

'What's your point, Waterhouse?' asked Proust. 'If not that Ms Morris is, as Sellers theorised, overly sentimental and prone to hysteria where babies are concerned?' He glanced pointedly at Sellers, who acknowledged the inspector's wider and more elegant vocabulary by lowering his eyes.

'I'm not sure yet,' said Simon. 'I'm still thinking about it.'

'Well, I'm sorry for interrupting a great mind at work,' Proust said pointedly. There was an alarming gap between one word and the next. Simon refused to be intimidated. 'Do let us know the results of this thought process, won't you?'

'Yes, sir.'

'I've got a theory,' said Charlie. 'Briony Morris knows Alice Fancourt pretty well, knows she's an alternative quack who's been on Prozac for depression and who's had us running round in circles because she invented some mad yarn about her baby not being her baby . . .'

'Briony Morris didn't know anything about that,' Simon reminded her, irritated to have to tell Charlie what she already knew. Was he the only person with a mechanism in his brain that ensured a certain amount of continuity? 'And she's an even more alternative quack.'

'She's worked with Alice for over a year,' Charlie shot back. 'And, quite frankly, sir, you only have to meet the woman once to know she's a flake . . .'

'A flake,' Proust repeated slowly.

'Mad, unreliable, whatever. The point is, anyone who knows Alice Fancourt is going to come to the same conclusion I have . . .'

'Sergeant Zailer, might I remind you that you have not yet come to any conclusion,' said Proust quietly. 'The investigation is ongoing.' The atmosphere in the room seized up. Everyone's normal behaviour became, in an instant, very deliberate.

'Of course, sir. I just mean that, well, that'd explain why Briony Morris would be more worried about Florence. Because she thinks it's most likely that Alice has taken her, and Alice is an unstable freak – not fit to look after a goldfish, let alone a baby!'

Proust turned to face her. 'I see. So we're ruling out the possibility that Alice Fancourt was abducted, along with her daughter, by a third party, are we? Sergeant, we're talking about a woman who vanished in the middle of the night, taking none of her belongings with her. Not so much as a ten pound note, not so much as a shoe. What do your conclusions have to say about that?' Every member of the team took this opportunity to inspect his or her shoes. Time to take cover.

'Answer came there none!' bellowed The Snowman. 'There was no break-in, no one heard any noise. So what I'd like to know is this: why is more attention not being paid to David Fancourt as a suspect? A prime suspect. Why isn't his name up on that board with a circle round it and a big number one next to it? And beneath that, a number two and the name Vivienne Fancourt. It's standard procedure, common sense. If there's no break-in, you look first at the family. I shouldn't have to tell you that, sergeant.'

'Sir, when I interviewed him, my impression was that David Fancourt is genuinely baffled . . .' Charlie began nervously.

'I don't care how baffled he is! This a man whose first wife was murdered, whose second wife last week accused him of lying about the identity of their baby and this week disappeared with that baby. There are so many suspicious circumstances surrounding Fancourt, it would be the utmost negligence not to investigate him from every angle.'

Simon looked up, surprised. He'd made the same point on Friday and Proust had rubbished it. Another one whose mental continuity apparatus had broken down, it seemed. The nerve of the man, plagiarising ideas with no mention of where he'd got them from. Thanks a fucking lot.

'Yes, sir,' said Charlie.

'So get on to it!'

'Yes, sir. I will.'

'Sir.' Simon cleared his throat. 'I was wondering, in the light of what you've just said . . .' In the light of your having stolen my theory and passed it off as your own, you complacent bald shit . . .

'What?'

'Shouldn't we look at the Laura Cryer case again? You know, go over the files, the statements, interview Darryl Beer?'

'I don't believe this!' Charlie muttered. Her eyes shone with indignation. 'Beer *confessed*. David Fancourt was in bloody London on the night his wife was killed. Sir, think about it. Fancourt left Cryer.' She flicked through her notebook in search of facts to support her argument. 'She was too controlling, he said. She wanted to make all the decisions about the baby even before it was born, wouldn't let Fancourt have a say in the name or anything. She was bossy and dominating, tried to stifle him completely, by the sound of it. He hung on for as long as he could, mainly because he was embarrassed to separate so soon after the marriage, but eventually he couldn't take it any more. He was thoroughly sick of Cryer by the time they split up. He found her, and I quote, "physically repellent and tedious", but he didn't hate her. He was just relieved to be rid of her. I doubt he'd have felt passionate enough to stab her with a kitchen knife. He'd found a new woman, Alice, with whom he was happy. Things were going well for him, finally. He didn't have to pay Cryer any maintenance. She earned a stack, much more than him. Why would he kill her?'

'So was Darryl Beer passionate about Cryer, then?' asked Simon. 'Since you're claiming *he* stabbed her.'

'That's different and you fucking well know it,' Charlie snapped.

'Fancourt's son went to live with him after Cryer died.' Proust wrinkled his nose, as if bored or disgusted by the precise details. 'His mother, I gather, was happy to act as an unpaid Mary Poppins, and Fancourt was free to swan off with his new girlfriend. The best of both worlds. It sounds like a viable motive to me.'

Charlie shook her head. 'You haven't met him, sir. All Fancourt wanted, after separating from Laura, was a new start. He wouldn't have risked prison to kill Laura. Alice Fancourt, on the other hand . . . I can imagine her taking a crazy risk like that.'

'You can *imagine*.' Proust sneered at Charlie. 'If I wanted to work with John Lennon, I'd hire a clairvoyant.'

'Sir, if I could just . . .' Simon persisted. The Snowman had asked for the results of his thought processes, so now he could damn well listen to some of them. 'Yesterday I had a look at the Laura Cryer files.'

'I see. So you're asking my permission for something you've already done.' Proust sounded interested, though. The leaden atmosphere had diluted; everyone felt it.

'I noticed some things that didn't seem quite right. There were no cuts on Cryer's arms or hands. If Beer tried to grab her bag and she fought for it, surely there would have been.'

Charlie looked as if she had turned to stone.

'Not necessarily,' said Chris Gibbs. 'It's easy to imagine Beer panicking and plunging the knife straight into her chest. As we know he did.'

'In which case Cryer would have stopped struggling pretty soon after receiving that one fatal blow. So why was there so much of Beer's hair and skin on her body? There were no foreign skin cells found under her nails, nothing at all.'

'Of course there wasn't,' said Charlie. 'Both her hands would have been on the bag, to stop him taking it. As for the hair and skin on her body, Beer probably knelt down and leaned over her after she was dead. He might have checked her pockets, in case there were any valuables he'd missed.'

'Why did he cut the strap off the bag with his knife, then?' said Simon, who'd had this argument with himself already. 'It was cut at both ends. That would take a while to do, with a good quality leather handbag. If Cryer was lying on the ground bleeding to death after the one killer stab wound, Beer could have taken the bag in one piece.'

'Maybe she had the strap diagonally across her chest,' Sellers suggested. 'A lot of women wear their bags like that. When she fell to the ground, it might have been trapped under her body. If Beer wasn't wearing gloves, he wouldn't have wanted to touch the body to move it, would he?'

'The strap was found beside Cryer's body, not under it,' said Simon, amazed to have to tell Sellers such a basic fact, Sellers who had worked on the case. Had none of the team spotted this crucial detail? What the fuck was wrong with them? 'It just doesn't add up. It's almost as if the strap was cut and left by the body to draw attention to the missing bag. To make the stabbing look like a mugging that went too far.'

Proust was looking worried. 'Sergeant, I want you to go over all this again with a fine-toothed comb. Go and see Beer, see what the little toe-rag has to say. It's all going to be in tomorrow's papers anyway, according to the press liaison office. Some pipsqueak has cottoned on to the connection between the names Cryer and Fancourt. If we aren't seen to be going over the Cryer case again, they'll accuse us of negligence, not to mention downright stupidity. And they'll be right!' So that was what had changed the inspector's mind, the threat of censure from the tabloids.

Nothing Simon had said. Might as well be fucking invisible, he thought.

Proust looked pointedly at Charlie. 'All Waterhouse's reservations sound valid to me. You should have been on to this already.'

Charlie blushed and stared at the floor. Simon knew she wouldn't get over this in a hurry. Nobody spoke. Simon waited for Proust to soften the blow, to say, 'It's just a formality, of course. As Sergeant Zailer rightly points out, Beer is as guilty as hell.' But Proust was not a softener of blows. All he said was, 'Sergeant Zailer, can I see you in my office, please? Now.'

Charlie had no choice but to follow him to his cubicle. Simon felt irrationally guilty, like a collaborator. But sod it. All he'd done was inject a bit of rationality into the proceedings. Charlie seemed determined to be dense at the moment. Was she doing it to spite him?

Sellers elbowed Simon in the ribs. 'It's going to take a pretty decent blow-job to get the Sarge out of trouble this time,' he said.

# 19

## Monday September 29, 2003

Feeling worse after seeing Simon, I park the car and prepare myself, once again, to walk into the big, cold, white house that is supposed to be my home. I see Vivienne watching me from the window of Florence's nursery. She does not retreat when she sees me look up at her. Neither does she wave or smile. Her eyes are like two perfectly engineered tracking devices, following my progress along the drive.

When I open the door, she is in the hall, and I do not understand how she could have got there so quickly. Vivienne manages to be everywhere, yet I have never seen her hurry or exert herself. David stands behind her, watching avidly. He doesn't even look at me as I come in. He licks his lower lip nervously, waiting for his mother to speak.

'Where's Little Face?' I ask, hearing no baby noises, only silence vibrating through the house. Hollow, screaming silence. 'Where is she?' There is panic in my voice.

No answer.

'What have you done with her?'

'Alice, where have you been?' says Vivienne. 'I thought you and I had no secrets from one another. I trusted you, and I thought you trusted me.'

'What are you talking about?'

'You lied to me. You said you were going into town to do some shopping.'

'I didn't find anything I wanted.' My lie was pathetic, I can see that now. As if I could even think about shopping in my present distraught state. Vivienne must have seen through my story right from the start.

'You went to the police station, didn't you? That policeman telephoned, Detective Constable Waterhouse. Is it true that you told him your mobile phone had been *stolen*?' She places a disgusted stress on this last word.

'I *was* going to go shopping,' I say, thinking quickly. 'But then my phone wasn't in my bag . . .'

'Detective Constable Waterhouse said you were hysterical. He was extremely worried about you. So am I.'

Defiance rises in me like a fountain. 'My phone was in my bag this morning and I know I didn't take it out! One of you two must have. You've got no right to take my things without permission! I know you both think I'm sick in the head, and so does Simon, but even sick people have got a right not to have their private possessions stolen!'

'*Simon*,' David mutters under his breath. His sole contribution.

'Alice, can you hear how irrational you sound?' says Vivienne gently. 'You misplace an object, and your immediate thought is to involve the *police*. I found your phone in your room, just after you went out. No-one took it anywhere.'

'Where's Little Face?' I ask again.

'One thing at a time.' Vivienne has never believed in the natural ebb and flow of a dialogue. As a child, one of her hobbies was to produce a written agenda for every family dinner. Vivienne, her mother and her father would take it in turn to speak, to deliver their 'daily report', as Vivienne called it. Her turn always came first, and she took the minutes as well, in a notebook.

'All right, then. Where's my phone? Can I have it? Give it to me!'

Vivienne sighs. 'Alice, what's got into you? I've put it in the kitchen. The baby is sleeping. There's no conspiracy against you. David and I are both very concerned about you. Why did you lie to us?' Any impartial observer would see a kind middle-aged woman trying in vain to reason with a dishevelled, shaking maniac in an ill-fitting green dress.

Exhaustion scratches at my brain. The insides of my eyelids feel grainy and the tendons in both my hands ache, as they always do when I am deprived of sleep. I do not want to talk any more. I push past Vivienne and run upstairs.

When I get to the nursery, I throw open the door, more violently than I intended to. It thuds against the wall. I hear footsteps mount the stairs behind me. Little Face is not in the cot. I swing round, hoping to see her in the Moses basket or her bouncy chair, but she is nowhere in the room.

I turn to leave, but as I get to it the door is pulled shut from the outside. A key turns in the lock. 'Where is she?' I scream. 'You said she was sleeping! Let me at least see her, please!' I hear my words crash into each other. I am frighteningly out-of-control.

'Alice.' Vivienne is on the landing, a bodiless voice. 'Please try to calm down. The baby is sleeping in the little lounge. She's perfectly all right. You're behaving like a maniac, Alice. I can't allow you to rampage around the house in your present condition. I'm worried about what you might do to yourself and the baby.'

I sink to my knees and rest my head against the door. 'Let me out,' I groan, knowing it is pointless. An image of Laura appears in my mind. If she could only see me now she would laugh and laugh.

I curl into a ball and cry, not bothering to wipe away my tears. I sob until the top of the vile green dress is sopping wet. It occurs to me that this was what I was wearing the only time I met Laura, and that I cried my eyes out on that occasion as well, once Laura had gone and I realised what a fool she'd made of me. Maybe that's why I hate the dress so much.

It was when I still worked in London, before I moved in with David. Laura booked an appointment with me using an alias, Maggie Royle. I later found out that that was her mother's name before she married Roger Cryer. I met Laura's parents at the funeral, and was naïve and presumptuous enough to feel slighted when they were frosty towards me.

David and I didn't want to go to Laura's funeral. Vivienne insisted. She said something odd: 'You should want to go.' Most people would have said only, 'You should go.' I assumed Vivienne was talking about the importance of doing one's duty willingly rather than grudgingly.

Maggie Royle was my first appointment that day. She insisted on seeing me early in the morning because she had to be at work for a ten o'clock meeting. Over the telephone I asked her, in the way that I would show an interest in any new patient, what she did for a living. She said 'research', which I suppose was true. Laura was a scientist who worked on gene therapy, but she was careful not to mention science.

She arrived at my office in Ealing wearing full but subtle make-up and a navy blue Yves St Laurent suit, the same one in which she was found murdered. Vivienne told me that. 'It was caked in blood,' she said. Then, as an afterthought: 'Blood is quite thick, you know. Like oil paint.' Vivienne makes no secret of how delighted she was when Felix moved into The Elms. 'And he's been *so* happy here,' she says. 'He *adores* me.' I believe Vivienne is genuinely unable to distinguish between the best possible outcome for all concerned and what she personally wants.

Laura was petite, with tiny hands and feet like a child's, but her high-heeled, square-toed suede shoes made her almost as tall as me. I was struck by her colouring. Her skin was olive but her irises were a vivid blue and the whites around them so bright they made her complexion look sallow. Her hair was long, almost black and very curly. She had a wide, full mouth and a slight overbite, but the overall effect was not unattractive. I remember thinking she looked powerful and confident, and feeling flattered that she should have come to me for help. I was eager – more so than I usually am – to know what had brought her to my office. Many of my patients looked shabby and defeated; she looked the opposite.

We shook hands and smiled at one another, and I asked her to take a seat. She arranged herself on the sofa opposite me, crossing her legs twice, at the knees and ankles, and folding her hands in her lap.

I asked her, as I do all my patients at the first meeting, to tell me as much about herself as she could, whatever she felt was most important. It is easier to treat the talkers because they reveal so much more of themselves, and Laura was a talker. As she spoke, I felt sure that I would be able to help her.

I am embarrassed, now, to think that I sat there and nodded and made notes, and all the time she must have been thinking I was a gullible idiot. I didn't even know what David's wife looked like. Laura must have counted on that, must have known David would destroy all photographic evidence of her and of their marriage as soon as things went wrong.

Her voice was deep and serious. I thought I might like her if I knew her better. 'My husband and I have recently split up,' she said. 'We're in the process of getting a divorce.'

'I'm sorry.'

'Don't be. I'm far better off out of it. But divorce isn't good enough for me.' She laughed bitterly. 'I wish there was some way of getting an annulment, some certificate or official document to say that we were never married. Wash off the taint, pretend it never happened. Maybe I should be a Catholic.'

'How long were you together?' I wondered if her husband was violent.

'A pitiful eleven months. We were dating, I got pregnant, he proposed, you can imagine the rest. It seemed like a good idea at the time. I believe we'd been man and wife – or woman and husband, should I say – for two months when I left him.'

'So you have a child together?'

Laura nodded.

'And . . . why did you leave?'

'I discovered that my husband was possessed.'

People say strange things to me all the time in my line of work. My next appointment after Maggie Royle was with a patient who became uncontrollably angry whenever he heard a stranger say his name, even if that person was talking about someone altogether different who happened to have the same name. More than once, he had started fights in pubs as a result of this phobia.

Still, I was surprised to hear Maggie Royle use the word 'possessed'. She looked so rational, so professional, in her smart suit. Not at all the sort of person you'd expect to believe in ghosts.

'I allow him access to our child, the bare minimum, and always supervised by me,' she went on. 'I'd like to deny him access altogether but I'm not sure I can. Don't worry, I know this isn't your speciality; you're a homeopath, not a lawyer. I have a good lawyer.'

'When you say possessed . . .' I began tentatively.

'Yes?'

'Do you mean what I think you mean?'

Laura stared at me expressionlessly. 'I don't know what you think I mean,' she said after a while.

'Can you define possessed?'

'Taken over by the spirit of another.'

'A malign spirit?' I asked.

'Oh, yes.' She flicked her hair out of her eyes. 'The malignest.'

Some of the most disturbed people appear normal until you talk to them at length. I decided to play along, find out as much as I could about Maggie Royle's delusions. If I discovered, as I suspected I would, that she was too severely mentally ill for me to treat her effectively, I would refer her to a psychiatrist. 'Is it the spirit of a dead person?' I asked.

'A dead person?' She laughed. 'You mean, like, a ghost?'

'Yes.'

She sat forward, on the attack now. 'You believe in ghosts?' Her tone was patronising.

'Let's concentrate on what you believe, for the time being.'

'I'm a scientist. I believe in the material world.' I'd like to say that at this point a warning signal started to flash inside my brain, but it didn't. I had no reason to believe that the woman sitting in front of me was anyone other than

Maggie Royle. 'I'm not sure I believe in homeopathy,' she said. 'You're going to give me some sort of remedy at the end of this session, right?'

'Yes, but we don't need to think about that now. Let's just focus on . . .'

'And what will this remedy consist of? What will be in it?'

'That depends on what I decide you need, based on the information you give me.' I smiled sympathetically. 'It's too early to say.'

'I read somewhere that homeopathic remedies are nothing more than pills of sugar dissolved in water. That if you did a chemical analysis of them, there would be no trace of any other substance.' She smiled, pleased with herself. 'As I said, I'm a scientist.'

I wasn't happy that she had diverted our conversation so aggressively, or by the more general anger that emanated from her, but it was her session. She was paying me forty pounds an hour. I had to let her talk about whatever was most important to her. I told myself not to worry; some patients needed to be reassured about the validity of homeopathy before they could relax.

'That's true,' I said. 'The substances that we dissolve in water to make up homeopathic remedies have been diluted so many times that there is no longer any chemical trace of the original substance, whether it's caffeine or snake venom or arsenic . . .'

'Arsenic?' Laura raised two thin arches of immaculately plucked eyebrow. 'Charming.'

'What happens is that the more it's diluted, the stronger the effect becomes. I know it sounds unlikely, but experts are only just now beginning to understand exactly how homeopathy works. It's something to do with the original substance imprinting its molecular structure on the water. It has more to do with quantum physics than with chemistry.'

'Isn't that a load of bollocks?' said Laura, as if she were asking a question that would be sure to enthral me, rather than simply being rude. 'Isn't it true that what's really going on here this morning is that I'm going to hand over my hard-earned cash in exchange for a bottle of water?'

'Maggie . . .' I was about to say something about her hostility, which I thought might make it impossible for me to treat her effectively.

'That's not my name.' She smiled calmly, folding her arms.

'Pardon?' Even then I didn't guess her true identity.

'I'm not Maggie Royle.'

'Are you a journalist?' I asked, fearing I had been set up by one of the tabloids. They never miss an opportunity to attack the alternative health industry.

'I told you, I'm a scientist. The question is, what are you? Do you really believe in this bullshit that you peddle, or are you secretly laughing at all the poor mugs you exploit? Must be a nice little earner. You must be wodged. Go on, tell me. I promise I won't tell anyone. Are you a charlatan?'

I stood up. 'I'm afraid I'm going to have to ask you to leave,' I said, gesturing towards the door.

'No advice for me, then? About how to reconcile myself to the fact that I allowed a passing twinge of lust for David to fuck up my life?'

'David?' I heard myself say. It wasn't the name that put me on my guard. It isn't an unusual name. It was the way Laura said it. As if I knew him.

'Don't marry him, Alice. Save yourself while you still can. And for God's sake, don't have any children with him.'

My eyes must have widened with horror. I felt dizzy. My cosy little world shook.

'You're not a charlatan, are you?' Laura sighed wearily. 'Just a mug. Good news for David, very bad news for you.'

Confrontational behaviour does not come easily to me, but I was determined to demonstrate my loyalty. 'Get out. You've lied to me and taken advantage of my good nature . . .'

'And I see it's easily done. I promise you, the stunt I've just pulled is nothing compared to what David and that creature of a mother of his will do to you.'

'David loves me. So does Vivienne,' I told her, twisting my diamond and ruby engagement ring on my finger, the one that had belonged to Vivienne's mother. When Vivienne gave it to me, I was so touched, I burst into tears. She hadn't wanted to give it to Laura, she said. But she wanted to give it to me. 'I feel sorry for you. I don't even recognise your versions of them . . .'

'Give it time.' She laughed scornfully. 'You will.' We were both standing now, facing one another.

'You make them sound like caricatures from a Victorian melodrama. What have David and Vivienne ever done to deserve the way you're treating them, keeping Felix away from them? Vivienne would be a brilliant grandmother and you're determined not to let her. Is that fair to Felix?'

'Don't dare to bandy my son's name around!' Laura's face contorted with rage.

'Maybe that's what you're scared of, that she'd be closer to your own son than you are.' Awful though this episode with Laura was, I remember thinking that I was glad of the opportunity to defend Vivienne against her chief detractor. She had defended me when one of my patients accused me, in a letter, of giving him false hope of recovery. Vivienne drafted a reply that demolished his case, piece by piece, in language that was both courteous and deadly. The patient wrote to me again a few weeks later, apologising unreservedly.

'Did Vivienne, by any chance, feed you that line?' Laura sneered. 'Let me guess – I'm missing out on being a proper mother and forging a deep bond with Felix because I haven't given up work, and I can't stand the thought of anyone else filling the gaping void that I've left in his life.'

Staphisagria, I thought: the perfect remedy for somebody as bitter as this poor, deluded woman clearly was. 'Do you really think David and Vivienne are such monsters? I mean, why? Have they murdered anybody, tortured anybody? Committed genocide?'

'Alice, wake up.' Laura actually seized me by the shoulders and shook me. I felt the skin on my face wobble and was furious that she'd touched me without permission. 'There *is* no David. The person you know as David Fancourt isn't a human being, he's Vivienne's puppet. Vivienne says no exercise during pregnancy, David agrees. Vivienne says a comprehensive school education is out of the question, David agrees. His personality consists of a few half-formed instincts, compulsions and fears rattling around in a great big vacuum.'

I opened the door of my office, leaning against it for support. 'Please leave,' I said, frightened by the extremity of her description. I didn't believe her, but neither could I flush her words out of my mind.

'I will.' She sighed, straightened her jacket and walked out, her square heels leaving indentations in my office carpet. 'Only, when it's too late, don't come crying to me.'

That was the last thing she ever said to me, the first and only time I saw her alive.

After she died, quite a long time after, I started to have dreams in which I saw her grave. The words 'Don't come crying to me' were chiselled on to the square, grey-green stone. But, in my dreams, night after night, people did go crying to her. Friends, family, colleagues; big, dense, seething crowds of mourners went to the cemetery every day, and wept and wept until their faces were swollen. Not me, though. I never went and I didn't cry. I was the only one who obeyed.

# 20

## *6/10/03, 9.45 am*

Charlie closed Proust's office door behind her, the blood roaring in her ears. She was so angry, she didn't trust herself to speak. Instead, she counted to ten very fast, over and over again, and told herself what she always did at times like these, that it wouldn't always seem as bad as it did now.

'Sit down, Sergeant,' said Proust wearily. 'I don't want to make a meal of this, so I'll get straight to the point. You're allowing your personal feelings to affect your work. I want it to stop.'

Charlie stared at the inspector's tie pin. She did not sit. What Proust described as her personal feelings were, at present, an artillery of white-hot murderous impulses, each one more lethal and explosive than the next. She felt exactly as she had after Sellers' party last year: pure, mind-contorting disbelief at what Simon had done to her. Yet again he had hurt, betrayed and publicly humiliated her. It would have cost him nothing – absolutely nothing – to tell her in private first what he had just told Proust and the rest of the team. Instead, he had gone over her head, put her in the position of having to stand there and gawp like a bemused goldfish while he came out with his impressive theories.

'Sir, you supervised my team's work on the Laura Cryer case. You know as well as I do that Darryl Beer did it.' Charlie paused to breathe. It was important to sound calm, confident. She wanted Proust to understand that she was not pleading with him, merely reminding him of certain historical facts. 'He admitted it.'

'And he's probably guilty.' Proust sighed. 'All the more reason for us to double check. Waterhouse made some good points. The business with the handbag strap, in particular, seems to me to be a discrepancy that requires careful consideration.'

Charlie had never felt like a bigger fool. Of course the matter of the handbag strap was peculiar. She was furious with herself for not having thought of it at the time. She was supposed to be good at her job. Not just good – excellent. That was her strong point, her ego's compensation for an often unsatisfactory personal life. She couldn't bear the prospect of losing her one source of pride.

'Sergeant, I was satisfied at the time, and I still am, that you and your team did everything correctly,' said Proust. 'As you say, I supervised the case myself and it didn't occur to me either. There was the DNA evidence, the guilty plea, the lack of a solid alibi, Darryl Beer's character and record – I know all that, all right?' Charlie nodded, feeling worse rather than better. Proust was being kind to her. For the first time in all the years she had worked for him, there was pity in his voice, which made this exchange all the more mortifying. 'But now that the family's come to our attention again and Waterhouse has raised a few . . . niggles, shall we say, we need to start from scratch, go over every piece of paper, every alibi, even more thoroughly this time. According to Waterhouse, before Alice Fancourt went missing she seemed to be suspicious and afraid of her husband. She believed that he knew his daughter had been swapped for another baby and was deliberately lying about it.'

'But, sir, you *agreed* with me that the story about the baby was bollocks. You agreed we should cuff it.' Charlie was ashamed of the whiny tone in her voice, but she was beginning to lose what little composure she had mustered. And if Proust referred to Simon again as if he were some sort of oracle, she feared she might be sick.

The inspector sat down at his desk and pressed his fingers together at the tips. 'On reflection, I think I might have made a mistake,' he said, trying out humility for the first time at the age of fifty-eight. 'Given that the Fancourt family were already known to us in connection with a serious crime, we should probably have taken the swapped baby story a little more seriously. We could have done a DNA test . . .'

'Yes, we could,' Charlie interrupted angrily, 'and the lab would have taken weeks to get the results back to us, by which time Vivienne Fancourt would have arranged a private test anyway! That was what *you* said.'

Proust glared at her. 'Sergeant Zailer, your determination to be right at all times, at any cost, is unbecoming to say the least. If I can admit I was wrong, so should you be able to.'

Charlie's heart plummeted still lower, right down to her gut. Another insult to add to the list. And this was the first time she had ever, *ever*, heard Proust question his own behaviour or judgement. She wouldn't have been surprised if the bastard had deliberately said that about being wrong in order to set her up, to reveal her as the only truly intransigent person in the room.

She couldn't understand why he was so determined to think the worst of her. She wasn't stubborn and irrational, just terrified of turning out to be the idiot who'd fucked everything up. When she thought about some of the things she'd said earlier in the team meeting, she wanted to groan and pound the floor with her fists. Proust was right: she was losing it. Her feelings for Simon were distorting everything. Charlie needed to be alone, and soon. The furnace of her anger towards Simon had to be stoked, and she could only do that in private.

'I want you to treat David Fancourt as your prime suspect,' said Proust. 'I want you to examine him from every angle, and I want you to assume he's probably guilty of something until you've proved beyond the tiniest doubt that he isn't. What I don't want is this: I don't want you to feel sorry for him because you've decided that he's got a mad wife who's given him a hard time and kidnapped his baby. I don't want to hear you telling your team about the "conclusions" you've reached, when you've got no proof whatsoever to back up your suppositions and when there are still so many unknowns that to conclude anything would be premature to say the least. Clear?'

Charlie nodded jerkily. She had never cried in front of Proust, or any other police officer. If it happened now, she would resign. It was as simple as that.

'Give the Laura Cryer case files to Waterhouse. Let him talk to Beer, and anyone else he wants or needs to. And don't take it personally. Waterhouse hasn't worked on the case before, whereas you, Sellers and Gibbs all have. A fresh perspective and all that.' Proust raised his eyebrows, drumming his fingers on his desk. 'Well?'

'Well, what, sir?'

'Sergeant, I'm not an idiot. I know you're hoping I'll contract an unpleasant disease and die in agony so that you can dance gleefully on my grave, but I assure you, your rage is misplaced. I'm trying to help you to work more effi-

ciently, that's all. You're taking everything too personally
at the moment. Do you deny it?'

'Yes,' said Charlie automatically. It was hard enough to
be a woman in her job; she had no intention of admitting to
an emotional reaction.

'You deny it,' Proust repeated incredulously.

Charlie knew she had pushed it too far. 'No. Maybe . . .'
she began, feeling her face heat up.

It was too late. 'You want Alice Fancourt to be the villain
of the piece because Waterhouse has gone soppy over her.
Ever since she went missing he's been mooning around with
a hazy look on his face, like a thirteen-year-old mourning
the end of a holiday romance. He seems to spend hours just
staring at her photo on the board out there. And you're
jealous, because you want to get into his pants. Oh – I'm
sorry if I've offended your delicate sensibilities. You all
think I'm some out-of-touch grandad when it comes to
personal matters, that I've been married so long I don't
remember any of that stuff, but I know what's what as well
as the next person. I hear the same rumours everyone else
hears. And even a fool can see that you're eaten up with
envy. You won't consider any hypothesis in which Alice
Fancourt is anything other than a hysterical nuisance, a
total and utter waste of time. It's stopping you from seeing
the facts as they are.'

'And what about Simon?' Charlie snapped back at him.
'Is he being objective? If you think I'm biased, you should
talk to him. Alice Fancourt's a saint as far as he's concerned. Why isn't he in here, being hauled over the coals?
He's the one who . . .'

'Enough!' Proust yelled. Charlie gasped involuntarily.
'This is beneath you. Or rather, it should be. I know
Waterhouse is as far from perfect as Land's End is from

John o'Groats, but I've been keeping a close eye on him, and, since you insist on making comparisons, my impression is that his judgement is a great deal less clouded than yours.'

Charlie felt as if she'd been struck by a heavy object. That's because you don't know about his replacement pocket book full of lies, she thought, or the two illicit meetings he had with Alice Fancourt that would undoubtedly have cost Simon his job had Charlie not flown to his rescue. And what the fuck did 'I hear the same rumours everyone else hears' mean? Charlie's blood turned to lead as it occurred to her that Proust might know about what happened at Sellers' party. She had always taken it for granted that Simon wouldn't have told anyone. Now she wasn't so sure.

As if to rub it in, Proust said, 'Waterhouse, you see, is blessed with that important quality that you seem to lack, sergeant: self-doubt.'

'Yes, sir,' said Charlie, who had never felt clumsier, more exposed, less dignified. She wished she were somebody else, almost anybody. Self-doubt? Proust must have been referring to the occasional, brief sabbaticals Simon took from breathtaking arrogance.

'You need to get a grip on yourself, sergeant. Instead of casting about wildly for someone to blame, pull yourself together and do your job properly. Get over this idiotic jealousy and grow up. If Waterhouse doesn't fancy you, there's nothing you can do about it. Now, I've said all I've got to say on the subject, so I won't keep you any longer.' He waved her away with his hand.

Charlie turned to leave, feeling shame of several different varieties swarm through her veins. She knew that Sellers, Gibbs and Simon, who were all still in the CID room, would make sure not to catch her eye as she emerged from Proust's office. She couldn't bear the thought of going over to talk to them about some work-related matter as if nothing had happened, but if she avoided them, they would all imagine she was subdued after receiving the bollocking to end all bollockings from Proust; she didn't know which was worse.

'Oh, and sergeant?'

'Yes?'

'That woman Alice Fancourt mentioned to Waterhouse, from the maternity ward . . .'

'Mandy. I'll track her down.' Let Proust squander the department's resources following up Alice Fancourt's base-less speculations if he wanted to. Let him be the one to end up looking like an idiot for a change.

'It wouldn't do any harm to take DNA samples from her and her baby, would it? Check they match up?'

Charlie nodded. Why not take a sample from every female child born at Culver Valley General Hospital in the past year, just to be on the safe side, King Herod style? It was bloody ridiculous.

She closed Proust's door carefully behind her and marched past her team before any of them had a chance to say anything. Simon looked up. Sellers and Gibbs did not. Charlie speeded up, heading for the ladies' as quickly as possible. It was the only place she could hide, just in case Simon was planning to come after her and ask if she was all right. There was nothing Charlie hated more than to be asked that question.

Inside the toilets, she locked herself in the nearest cubicle, leaned against the door and breathed heavily in and out for a few seconds, releasing some of the tension from her body. Then she sank to the floor and began to sob.

# 21

## *Tuesday September 30, 2003*

I am sitting in the little lounge, fuzzy with sleep, as disorientated as I was yesterday when I'd had none. Opposite me sits a doctor I have never seen before. She tells me her name is Dr Rachel Allen. I don't know whether to believe her. Vivienne could have hired her. She might be an actress, for all I know. She is very young, a tall, pear-shaped woman with short, blonde hair and an excessively pink complexion. She is not wearing any make-up. Her thick calves are bare and blotchy, covered with fine fair hairs. Every time she catches my eye, she beams enthusiastically. I know that Vivienne is listening outside the door, anxious to hear the diagnosis, whatever it might be.

Dr Allen leans forward, takes my hand and squeezes it in both of hers. 'Don't worry about anything, Alice,' she says. I have never heard anything so stupid in my life. Who in my situation wouldn't worry? 'Don't be nervous. We'll soon have you feeling better!' She beams again and hands me a piece of paper. There are questions on it. Do I ever think about harming myself? Often, sometimes, never. Do I feel that I have nothing to look forward to? Often, sometimes, never.

'What's this?' I ask. I need to eat something. I feel weak with hunger, as if there are clawing hands in my stomach, reaching out and finding nothing.

'It's our practice's post-natal depression survey,' says Dr

Allen. 'I know what you're thinking – forms, forms and more forms! I quite agree! Fill the silly old thing in and then we can talk properly.'

'Where's Dr Dhossajee?' I ask. 'I'd rather talk to my own doctor.'

'She's not available. That's why I'm here. Why don't you fill in the form now? Do you need a pen?' She fishes in her pocket and pulls out a blue biro.

I read all the questions. They are too simplistic. 'It's pointless,' I say. 'These questions aren't the right ones for my situation. My answers won't tell us anything useful.'

Dr Allen nods thoughtfully, leaning forward in her chair. 'Have you been crying this morning?' she asks.

'Yes.' I have done practically nothing but cry in recent days. I cried when Vivienne locked me in the nursery. I curled up on the rug and sobbed, clinging to Hector, Florence's big teddy bear, until I fell asleep. When I woke up sixteen hours later, I cried again. I haven't seen Little Face since I went out to meet Simon. I am desperate to see her, just once, even if I am not allowed to touch her.

'You poor thing! How often would you say you cry?' Dr Allen's eagerness to help me is almost tangible.

'A lot. Most of the time. But that's because my daughter's been taken away from me and I don't know where she is, and no-one will believe me.'

'You feel that no-one believes you?' Dr Allen looks as if she too might burst into tears.

'That's right.'

'Do you feel that people and circumstances are conspiring against you?'

'Yes. Because they are. My daughter is missing and I can't prove it, either to my husband or to the police. That's a fact, not a feeling.' I sound cold and heartless. I used to have a heart, but it has been ripped up. It no longer exists.

'Of course!' says Dr Allen vehemently. 'I firmly believe that feelings *are* facts. I take the feelings of patients very seriously indeed. I want to help you. You have every right to feel what you feel. And it's very common for women who've just had babies to suffer the most unbearable feelings of persecution, of alienation . . .'

'Dr Allen, my daughter has been kidnapped.'

She looks flummoxed. 'Well . . . what have the police said?'

'They're not doing anything about it. They say there's no case. They don't believe me.' I feel betrayed by the relief on her face. She is happy to let the opinion of other professionals determine hers.

'You look tired,' she says. 'I'm going to prescribe some sleeping tablets . . .'

'No. I don't need pills. I've just slept for over twelve hours. I'll fill in your form, but I'm not taking anything. There's nothing wrong with me. If I look tired it's because I've slept too much. Give me that pen.' She hands me the biro. I tick a few of the boxes strategically, try to make myself sound as well-balanced as possible.

'How are you feeling physically in general?' she asks.

'A bit dizzy sometimes,' I admit. 'Light-headed.'

'Are you taking Co-codamol?'

'Yes. Is that why I feel dizzy?'

'It's a very strong painkiller. How long ago did you have your Caesarian?'

'I'll stop taking it,' I say. I need a clear head. I was never happy about taking allopathic painkillers, but Vivienne told me I needed them. I believed her. 'I'm also taking two homeopathic remedies, hypericum and gelsemium.'

'That's fine.' Dr Allen smiles tolerantly. 'They might not do you any good, but they won't do you any harm.' Patronising bitch, I think.

I hand my completed quiz back to her. For a bonus of one hundred points: is Alice crazy or not?

'Thank you,' she enthuses, as if I have given her the crown jewels. She sets about reading my answers with great concentration, breathing heavily over them as if trying to get to grips with an impenetrable problem. She reminds me of a horse.

'What if the baby is sick?' I whisper. 'Little Face. What if she's sick?' My head reels with all the fear and excitement of a new idea. 'Maybe that's why someone wanted to swap her, for Florence, who's healthy.' I remember the Guthrie test, blood being taken from Florence's heel. David joked that the test involved singing a selection of Woody Guthrie songs to newborn babies and seeing how many they could identify. Florence's results were fine; there was nothing wrong with her. 'She seems healthy, but . . . perhaps . . . could you arrange for some tests to be done? On the baby? On Little Face?' I begin to hyperventilate. 'That might be it!' I squeeze my hands together. 'And if that *is* the reason why Mandy swapped the babies, or why somebody did, that means Florence is probably safe! Do you see what I mean?'

Dr Allen looks as if she might be a bit scared of me. 'Excuse me a moment, Alice,' she says. 'I'll just nip outside and have a quick word with Vivienne.' If I were at all interested in her opinion, I would object to her sharing it with Vivienne instead of me, but since I know that I am not mad, I don't care what she says, or to whom. I watch her hurry from the room. I wish she would leave. I wish she and Vivienne and David would all leave. I could take Little Face away from The Elms and never come back. David would never be able to torture me again. But I know I cannot do anything so spontaneous. People would see my car. They would see me and Little Face. We would be found and brought back here.

I hear Dr Allen talking to Vivienne outside the door. 'Well?' Vivienne demands. 'What's the verdict?'

'Oh dear! I'm afraid I am quite concerned about her,' says Dr Allen. Neither she nor Vivienne cares that I can hear them. She tells Vivienne most of what I said. I feel terrible when I hear her say that I seem to want Little Face to be sick because that will prove Florence is well. I don't want anything bad to happen to any baby, any child. That should be obvious.

'Look at this,' Dr Allen says to Vivienne. 'For the question "How often do you feel you can't cope?" she's ticked "Never". That's one of our key warning signs. Everybody who's just had a baby sometimes feels that they can't cope. It's natural. So those who deny it . . .'

'. . . are deluding themselves,' Vivienne concludes.

'Yes. And heading for possible trouble. That sort of denial puts too much pressure on a person. Eventually something has to give. I'm *so* sorry,' Dr Allen croons. 'I think perhaps Alice ought to see a therapist or a counsellor.' I would love to. He or she would have to be on my side; that is a therapist's job description. I could cope, if just one person were on my side. But Vivienne would never allow my mind to fall into the hands of a psychiatric professional. She believes such people try to control the thoughts of others.

'. . . seems to be a very firmly embedded delusion,' Dr Allen is saying.

'What makes you so sure it's a delusion?' Vivienne asks.

My heart crashes wildly around my chest. What has happened to my confidence, to make me so grateful for even the smallest sign that not everybody is against me? 'Can I ask you a question, Dr Allen?'

'Of course.'

'Florence has been bottle-fed from birth. She wouldn't breast-feed, you see. The baby upstairs seems quite happy with the same Cow and Gate milk that Florence drank. Does that mean she's likely to be Florence?'

I nod. It's a good question. Vivienne's mind is open. She is trying to apply logic to the problem.

'Well . . .' Dr Allen hesitates. 'A breast-fed baby might protest if she was suddenly switched on to bottles. But if she was bottle-fed in the first place . . .'

'But there are several different brands of formula milk, aren't there?' says Vivienne impatiently. 'Wouldn't a change of brand pose a problem?'

'Maybe, maybe not. Cow and Gate is one of the market leaders. And every baby is different. Some will only take breast milk, some will drink any old thing quite happily. The fact that the baby will drink Florence's usual milk doesn't prove anything either way.' Dr Allen sounds uncomfortable, keen to leave. She is probably wondering if all the residents of The Elms are insane.

I feel encouraged. In the absence of concrete proof, Dr Allen and Vivienne are completely at a loss. I might be miserable, tormented by my husband, desperate for my daughter and without even the hope of help, but at least I know the truth. I have that one thing in my favour.

## 22

## 7/10/03, 2 pm

Going into prisons; Simon had never got used to it. He hated standing in the queue with the other visitors, some of whom he knew for a depressing fact were concealing about their persons – sometimes even inserted into their private parts – lumps of heroin, to be passed to their loved ones under the table at the appropriate time. The screws, mostly corrupt, knew it went on and did nothing about it.

Simon stood with the half-dressed, undernourished girl-friends of this or that nonentity or gangster, depending on your point of view. Their bare legs were mottled, mauve with cold. They teetered on high heels, giggled and whis-pered. Simon heard the word pig. Even without the uni-form, people knew.

After the queue came the frisking, then all prospective visitors were sniffed by police dogs. Finally, approved, Simon headed through the dingy visits hall to HMP Brim-ley's inner courtyard, waiting for the familiar din: 'Fucking pig! Scum! Fucking filth!' Accompanied by the rattle of cages from all directions. The courtyard was surrounded by cells, and the scrotes always chanted enthusiastically. It wasn't as if they had a lot else to look forward to.

Simon stared straight ahead until he'd made it to the secure cell block. The screw who was escorting him led him to a small mustard-coloured room with a brown, ribbed, threadbare carpet. The customary table and two chairs. A camera fixed to the wall, its dark, square glass eye peering down. On the table was a thick plastic ashtray. Any D with sense knew that it was pointless to turn up without tobacco and Rizlas, or a packet of B&H, depending on how generous you were feeling. Scrotes expected it, in the way that waiters expected tips. Optional-compulsory.

Simon felt itchy and uncomfortable. The room stank of stale sweat and staler smoke. Also a salty, sexual smell. Simon didn't want to think about that one. He shuffled on his chair. He'd had a shower that morning, tried to feel clean in spite of his surroundings.

Look where you are, said a voice in his head. Disheartening to think that this was the grubby environment he inhabited, worlds away from Alice Fancourt, from The Elms. He pictured Alice as she was when he first saw her, standing straight-backed at the top of the curved staircase, then sitting on the cream sofa in the living room, her long, blonde hair fanned out against the cushion. People like her shouldn't have to share the planet with the scum that ended up in here. Simon wasn't sure who he had in mind, Beer or himself.

Charlie had instructed him, without eye contact or a smile, to ask Beer about the murder weapon and Laura Cryer's handbag. Whatever Proust had said to her during their head-to-head had done its work. She was making a big production of her new, conscientious approach. There was an unnecessarily large number one on the board in the CID room, with David Fancourt's name beside it, and she had taken to talking in a loud voice about the importance of reviewing all the files on Laura Cryer. Simon wasn't fooled. He doubted Proust was either. Charlie had done this sort of thing before, behaved in a way that was beyond reproach at the same time as making it clear that her head and heart were violently opposed.

Immature, undignified. But what irked Simon most was that he seemed to be the main object of her hostility. He couldn't understand what he had done to offend her. He'd made some good points about the Cryer case. He'd hoped for praise, expected grudging admiration and a heated argument. Instead, Charlie had stopped looking at him. She spoke to him as if she were a zombie reading from an autocue. Sellers and Gibbs didn't seem to have noticed; she was all charm and smiles to them, as if to underline the point.

Simon had heard it said that women were irrational, but he'd thought Charlie was an exception. She had to know that Simon wasn't responsible for the dressing down she'd had from Proust. Her own carelessness had got her into trouble, the stupid things she'd said at the team meeting that sounded more like gossip than police work.

The door of the fetid little room opened, and a youngish man was pushed into the room by an even younger-looking screw. It took Simon a few seconds to recognise Darryl Beer. A crew-cut had replaced his ponytail, and he had put on weight. Beer had been a lanky little shit. He'd had the look and manner of an agitated rodent, scrabbling for scraps. Now his face had fleshed out and he looked more ordinary, like a man who might spend his Saturday afternoon buying garden furniture, power drills, firelighters for the barbecue.

Simon introduced himself. Beer shrugged. He couldn't have cared less who his visitor was, or why he was here. Simon was familiar with the attitude: a pig was a pig, and it was never nice to see one.

'I've got some questions regarding the Laura Cryer murder.'

'Aggravated assault,' Beer corrected him automatically,

folding his hairy arms across his belly. His top was too small. A pouch of pale flesh had escaped, spilling over his belt.

'Stabbing a woman with a kitchen knife. Leaving her to bleed to death. I call that murder.' Beer didn't flinch.

Simon produced a packet of Marlboros and a lighter from his pocket and Beer reached out a hand, one that had 'HATE' tattooed on its knuckles. He lit the cigarette, took a long, slow drag, then another. 'Did you do it?' Simon asked.

Beer looked surprised, then amused. 'You taking the piss?' he said. Simon shook his head. 'I pleaded guilty, didn't I?'

'What did you do with her handbag? What did you do with the knife?'

'Do you know anything about who Laura Cryer was, the work she did?' Beer asked. His tone was conversational. 'If she'd lived, she might have found a cure for cancer. Her research team probably will at some point, thanks to the work she started. Did you know that she was the one who persuaded Morley England to invest forty million dollars in BioDiverse, to fund the work? She could be famous one day. I could be famous.'

'What did you do with the bag and the knife?'

'I don't remember.' Beer grinned, delighted to be of no assistance. He scratched his exposed midriff with the overgrown fingernails of his 'LOVE' hand. 'I was out of it. Why do you want to know that now?'

'Do you remember stabbing Laura Cryer at all?' Beer's attitude had lit the fuse of Simon's temper. Fire crackled in his stomach. All for Beer, or had it been there already, lying dormant? He pictured himself taking an extinguisher and turning it on the flames, as Charlie had once advised him to do. 'Think wet foam,' she told him. 'Even the words sound soggy.' It worked. Could the sensible person who had said that and the overgrown bitchy schoolgirl stomping around the CID room today be one and the same?

'I must have done it, mustn't I?' said Beer. 'There was all that evidence.' The sing-song sarcasm was intended to provoke.

His face belonged in the ashtray. Simon's arms itched to put it there. 'Listen, shit-head. There's a mother and baby missing. The baby's less than a month old. If you tell me the truth, it might help us find them.' As a boy, Simon had had his mouth washed out with soap on the one occasion when he swore in front of his mother. He'd heard the way other cops used profanities – with casual imprecision. His foul language was deliberate and meaningful. Grateful. He savoured each of these words that belonged to a world which excluded his parents.

Beer shrugged. 'You're wasting your time, pig. I reckon your mother and baby are dead.'

Simon took deep breaths. It wasn't true. Was that what Charlie thought too? Why couldn't he bring himself to ask her? Before she disappeared, Alice had made him feel uncomfortable by pointing out his inadequacies as a protector. Her death would confirm everything Simon feared about himself. To think of her as alive and missing was the only way he could banish her disillusionment from his mind, focus on the faith she had once had in him. It still gave him time. The story wasn't over.

'Here's what I think happened,' he said. 'Your brief advised you to cut a deal. After the DNA match, you were stuffed. He told you you'd get life if you pleaded not guilty. No jury'd believe a turd like you.' Simon saw a flicker of discomfort in Beer's eyes. He pressed on. 'Most innocent people would have been furious, insisted on a chance to prove their innocence. But that's the middle classes, isn't it? The sort that society treats well. I know your background. I've been reading up on you, Beer. Deprivation, truancy, broken home, sexual abuse – if you've had that sort of life and then a lawyer tells you you're about to get framed for something you didn't do, you believe them, don't you? Because it's exactly the sort of shit that happens to filth like you every day.'

'It's filth like *you* that makes life what it is for me and mine,' said Beer, roused from his complacency at last. An odd phrase to use, thought Simon, wondering who the 'mine' were. Beer was unmarried and childless. Was he referring to a criminal underclass, as if it were a group identity one might take pride in? A more general under-class?

Simon pulled his chair forward. 'Listen to me,' he said. 'If you didn't kill Laura Cryer, I think I know who did. He's a spoilt rich boy who lives in a big house with his rich mum. He's the one you're helping to get away with murder.'

'I'm not helping anyone.' The sullen mask again.

'You were seen in the garden of The Elms twice in the weeks leading up to Laura Cryer's death. What were you doing there?'

'The what?'

'The Elms. Where you stabbed Cryer.'

'*Dr* Cryer, if you don't mind. She's just a fucking body to you, isn't she?'

'What were you doing at The Elms?'

A shrug. 'I don't remember.'

'If you're worried about getting more jail time for entering a false guilty plea, don't,' said Simon. 'You'd probably be charged, but with time already served taken into account . . . Or is it the prospect of getting out too soon that's bothering you? You made a fair few enemies when you turned Queen's and shopped a load of your old mates, didn't you? Worried you might not last too long outside this place?'

'You're the one who looks worried, piggy.' Beer lit another cigarette from the packet on the table. 'Not me.'

Simon could glean nothing from his expression. 'Whoever's gunning for you will still be around in five, six or seven years' time,' he said. 'You're going to need our protection, whenever you get out. So if I were you . . .' – Simon picked up the Marlboros and put them back in his pocket – 'I'd start thinking about the best way to make us want to help you.'

Behind a cloud of exhaled smoke, Beer's eyes narrowed. 'Next time you come here, make sure you know who Laura Cryer was, what she achieved. You want me to talk because it'll help you with another case, nothing to do with Laura. Or me.'

Laura. Yet he hadn't known her. How long had it been since Simon had thought of Alice as 'Mrs Fancourt'? Significance and familiarity were not the same thing.

'You don't give a fuck about the truth, do you? You just want me to tell you what you want to hear.'

'What are you talking about?'

'All the little piggies lived happily ever after. The end.' And it was. No matter how hard Simon tried, he could not persuade Darryl Beer to say another word.

# 23

## Wednesday October 1, 2003

I open my eyes with a strangled moan. Waking up is the worst part, plunging headlong into the nightmare all over again. David is not in bed. Vivienne stands in the doorway, fully dressed in a smart black trouser suit and grey polo neck. Her face is covered in its usual mask of subtle make-up. I smell her perfume, Madame Rochas. I feel dirty, disgusting. I haven't bathed, or even washed, since Monday. My mouth is thick and dry, my hair matted.

'Do you feel better, after a good night's sleep?' she asks.

I do not reply. I feel groggy. I cannot lift my eyelids, they are too heavy. It is misery. It must be; I stopped taking the Co-codamol tablets after I spoke to Dr Allen.

'Why don't you have a nice bath?' Vivienne suggests, smiling determinedly.

I shake my head. I can't get out of bed with her standing there.

'Alice, this is a struggle for all of us, not just you. Nevertheless, we must behave like civilised people.'

I hear David in the nursery, talking to Little Face in an animated voice. She gurgles in response. I feel exiled, as if I am a million miles away from any possibility of happiness. 'I want to look after the baby,' I say, tears escaping despite my best efforts. 'Why won't David let me? He won't let me go anywhere near her.'

Vivienne sighs. 'The baby is fine. And David's just

worried about you, that's all. Alice, don't you think you ought to concentrate on looking after yourself? You've been through a terrible ordeal.' Her sympathy confuses me. 'That long labour, and then an emergency Caesarian. I think you're putting far too much pressure on yourself.'

She said the same thing when I told her about the trouble I was having coming to terms with the death of my parents. 'Don't fight your grief,' she said. 'Embrace it. Make friends with it. Welcome it into your life. Invite it to stay for as long as it wants to. Eventually it will become manageable.' It was the best advice anyone gave me. It worked, exactly as Vivienne said it would.

'I'm going to take the baby with me today,' she says. 'We'll drop Felix off at school, then go shopping.'

'You don't want to leave her alone with me and David, do you? You don't trust either of us.'

'Babies like a bit of fresh air,' says Vivienne firmly. 'It's good for them. And a bath will be good for you. It really will make a difference, you know, to clean yourself up, put on some nice clothes. It won't make your problems disappear, but it'll make you feel more human. If you feel strong enough, that is. I don't want you to over-exert yourself if you're not ready.'

I believe that Vivienne wants me to love her. More than that, she sees it as her right to be loved by me. At the forefront of her mind is not that she locked me in the nursery or that she is undermining my sense of reality by treating me like an invalid, but all the kind and helpful things she's done for me over the years.

I turn on to my side, away from her. Now that I understand this new sympathy, I feel like a fool. Vivienne wants me to be ill. Of course she does. Her preferred outcome would be for Florence not to be missing, for my mind, rather, to be severely disturbed. I think about well-meaning Dr Allen, who believed I wanted Little Face to be sick.

'Well, you get some rest then.' Vivienne is determined not to let my unresponsive behaviour get to her. She bends down, kisses my cheek. 'Goodbye, dear. I'll see you later.'

I close my eyes, begin to count in my head. Vivienne is taking Little Face out on a shopping trip. Everyone can come and go as they please apart from me. What would happen if I said, as Vivienne just has, 'I'm taking the baby out today'? I would be stopped, of course.

When I hear the front door thud, and, a few seconds later, Vivienne's car engine, I open my eyes and look at the clock. It is quarter to eight. She has gone. I climb out of bed and stumble towards the landing, feeling as if I haven't walked for years. I rub my bare toes against the velvety wool of the stone-coloured carpet and stare down the long corridor, at the rows of white doors on either side. I feel like a person in a dream, the kind in which each door will lead to a room that has a clear purpose, distinct from all the others, and to a radically different outcome. Why is the house so silent? Where is David?

The door to Florence's nursery is open. I weigh my need to go to the toilet against the chance to go into my daughter's room without being watched or monitored. No contest.

I enter cautiously, as if trespassing on forbidden territory, and walk over to the empty cot. I lower my face and inhale the scent of new baby, that lovely, fresh smell. I pull the cord that dangles from the smiling sun on the wall above the cot, and 'Somewhere Over the Rainbow' begins to play. My heart twists. All I can do is hope that Florence is not suffering anywhere near as intensely as I am.

I open the doors of the fitted wardrobe and stroke the piles of her freshly laundered clothes, the ridges of pink and yellow and white, the layers of bobbly wool and fleeces as soft as I imagine clouds would be. Such an optimistic, joyful sight should make me happy, but in the absence of Florence it has the opposite effect.

I close the wardrobe doors, stiff with misery. I should go. Being in here only makes me feel worse, but somehow, despite my growing need to use the bathroom, I cannot bring myself to leave. This room is evidence that I have a precious daughter. It links me to Florence. I sit in the rocking chair in the corner, where I once foolishly imagined I would spend many hours feeding her, holding and stroking Monty, Florence's cuddly rabbit with long, floppy ears. My yearning for my baby tingles in every nerve ending in my skin.

Eventually, physical discomfort forces me to move. I make sure I leave the door ajar at the right angle, exactly as I found it. Then it occurs to me that no-one has explicitly said I am not allowed in here. Am I becoming paranoid? 'Hello!' I call out from the landing. 'David?' There is no reply. Panic grips me. They have all gone for good. I am alone. I have always been alone.

'David?' I call again, louder this time. He is not in the bathroom. I am about to lift the lid of the toilet when I notice that the bath tub is already full. No bubbles or oil, only water. Both Vivienne and I add scented things from bottles to our bathwater, though her additions are considerably more expensive than mine. This bath used to be my favourite in the world. It's a big, old enamel one, a creamy off-white, like the colour of healthy teeth. Two people can fit into it easily. David and I do occasionally, when Vivienne is guaranteed to be out for at least an hour. Did, I correct myself.

I frown, puzzled. I have never known David to have a bath and then fail to empty it and rinse out the tub. Vivienne would regard that as the epitome of bad manners. I touch the water with my hand. It is cold. Then I notice that it is also completely clear. No soap has touched it, I am sure of that. Why would David have a bath, not use soap, then leave the water in?

I hear a loud bang behind me. I gasp and spin round. David grins at me. He has slammed the door and is leaning against it with his hands in his jeans pockets. I see from the expression on his face that I have walked straight into his trap. He must have been waiting behind the door to ambush me for some time. 'Morning, dear,' he says sarcastically. 'I've run you a bath. Nice of me, I think, under the circumstances.'

I am frightened. There is a comic casualness about his cruelty that has replaced the driven bitterness of previous days. Whatever this means, it has to be bad. Either he cares less about me than ever, or he has found, quite by accident, that the desperate sadism born out of his misery and confusion is something he has a taste for.

'Leave me alone,' I say. 'Don't hurt me.'

'*Don't hurt me.*' He mimics me. 'Charming! All I've done is run you a bath, so that you can have a nice, long, relaxing soak.'

'It's freezing cold.'

'Get into the bath, Alice.' His voice is laced with menace.

'No! I need to go to the toilet.' I realise, as I speak, how urgent this need is.

'I'm not stopping you.'

'I'm not going while you're here. Just get out, leave me alone.'

David stays where he is. We stare at one another. My eyes are totally dry, my mind numb and empty.

'Well?' says David. 'Go on, then.'

'Fuck you!' It is all I can think of.

'Oh, very ladylike.'

I have no choice, since I am not strong enough to eject him from the room physically. The contents of my bowels have turned to water. I start to walk towards the lavatory. David moves unexpectedly fast. He leaps in front of me, stopping my progress. 'Sorry,' he says. 'You had your chance.'

'*What*?' I cannot believe that his behaviour is spontaneous. He must have planned every stage of this horror, every word. No-one could improvise such abuse.

'You swore at me. So you can get straight into the bath.'

'No.' I dig my fingernails into my palms. 'I won't! Move out of the way and let me go to the toilet.'

'You know, I could take steps to ensure that you never see Florence again,' he says calmly. 'It wouldn't be hard. Not hard at all.'

'No! Please, you can't. Promise you won't do that!' Dread courses through my veins, spreading to every cell in my body. He sounds as if he means it.

'I can and will do you more harm than you can do me, Alice. A lot more. Remember that. I can and I will.'

'So you admit you know where Florence is, then? Where is she, David? Please, tell me. Is she safe? Where are you hiding her? Who's she with?'

He examines his fingernails in silence. I want to scream and bash my head against the wall. My husband's personality has solidified in this monstrous new incarnation. He has settled into the role of torturer and is enjoying it. Perhaps this is how it happens. I think of all the atrocities in the world and those who perpetrate them. There has to be some sort of explanation. There always is, for everything.

Even now, I cannot stop myself from hoping that things will improve. Maybe I really am crazy. I picture David, looking like the sole survivor of a natural disaster, saying 'I don't know what got into me.' If he put it like that, in terms of an aberration, a temporary possession by some destructive force, I could possibly forgive him. All the love I have ever felt for him is still in me, rippling under the surface, subtly influencing the texture of my thoughts, like bumpy old wallpaper under new paint.

I only have to hold on until Friday. Now that David has made his awful threat, I will take no risks until then. I must sacrifice my pride and dignity if that is the only way to protect Florence. My legs are shaking. Adrenaline rampages through my body. I am in agony from the strain on my bladder and bowels. 'All right,' I say. 'Don't hurt Florence. I'll do anything you want.'

David wrinkles his nose in disgust. 'Hurt her? Are you suggesting I would hurt my own daughter?'

'No. I'm sorry. I'm sorry for everything. Tell me what you want me to do.'

He appears to be mollified for the time being. 'Take off your night clothes and get into the bath,' he says slowly and with deliberate patience, as if I am an imbecile. 'And you'll stay in it for as long as I say.'

I obey his instructions, singing a song in my head to distract me from what is happening: 'Second-Hand Rose', one of the songs my mother used to sing to me when I was a child. My feet, ankles and calves ache with cold as I step into the water. David tells me to sit down. I do, and my heart jolts with the shock. The freezing water has the effect I knew it would – that David must have known it would – on my body. The feelings of pain and humiliation that overwhelm me are so excruciating that for a moment I cannot breathe. For the first time in my life, I understand why people sometimes wish themselves dead.

When I hear David's voice again, it sounds as if it is coming from a great distance. 'You're disgusting,' he says. 'Look at you. Look what you've done. I've never seen anything so foul in my life. What have you got to say for yourself?'

'I'm sorry,' I stammer, my teeth chattering violently.

He stands above me with his arms folded, looking down at me, shaking his head and tutting, revelling in my shame. 'I should never have married you. You were always second best, after Laura. Did you know that?'

'Please let me get out,' I whisper, shaking convulsively. 'I'm freezing. It hurts.'

'I want you to admit that you're lying about Florence,' David orders. 'I want you to tell Mum and the police that you made up the whole story. Will you do that?'

I bury my face in my knees. He is asking me to do the one thing I cannot do, but I am terrified to say no in case he devises worse punishments for me than this, in case he makes good his threat about ensuring that I never see Florence again. I suspect that, for David, all the pleasure is in the threats themselves, in the psychological leverage they afford him, but I can't take any chances.

He sighs and sits down on the closed toilet lid. 'I'm not a violent man, Alice. Have I ever laid a finger on you? Violently, I mean?'

'No.'

'No. And I'm not an unreasonable man. I don't want to have to do this to you, but you've left me with no choice.' He continues in this vein for some time, justifying his actions, interrupting his justifications every now and then to insult me and jeer at me. When I pull my knees up to my chest, he tells me I am not allowed to. I must lay my legs flat against the bottom of the tub. I must not cover my chest with my arms. I do as I am told, but apart from that I try not to listen to him. I hear only the compassionless, hectoring drone of a man who, for years, has been dominated by his mother. In my mind I see the image of a flower tied to a stick, so that it will grow in a prescribed direction. That is David. And now he is overdosing on power, gorging on it, like a starving person who fears this might be his only opportunity to eat.

I do not know how long he makes me sit in the icy, filthy water. Until I can hardly feel any sensation below my waist and my legs are a sort of ghostly blue colour. I feel like an animal, worse than an animal. I am a disgrace. It is my fault that this has happened to me. It doesn't happen to most people, to anybody else. I am the lowest of the low. I can't protect my own daughter.

Eventually David sighs, unlocks the bathroom door and says, 'Well, I hope you've learned something from this experience. You'd better clean yourself up. And the bath. Remember, you're a guest in my mother's house.' He leaves the room, whistling.

# 24

*8/10/03, 2.40 pm*

Simon drove out of Spilling on the Silsford Road, and from Silsford he followed the white, wooden, black-lettered signs and winding lanes all the way to Hamblesford, the village where Laura Cryer's parents lived. He'd left the CID room half an hour earlier than he'd needed to. He preferred to wait outside the Cryers' house, if necessary, rather than spend another minute in Charlie's company.

She'd been trying to bait him all morning. 'I bet she's got huge norks and a nice tight fanny,' she'd speculated about Suki Kitson, Sellers' bit on the side. 'And, let's face it, Stacey's had two kids. Sellers probably flails around inside her like a pickled gherkin in a postman's sack.' Simon recognised the menace in Charlie's voice. When her conversation turned anatomical, it was time to get out of her way. Charlie mentioned parts of the female body as a way of getting at Simon, which made him angry and nervous. He feared it was her way of trying to remind him, obliquely, of his undignified cowardice at Sellers' party.

If she didn't start to behave more normally soon, he would have to have a word with Proust. Charlie was supposed to be his skipper, yet her anger and sarcasm were making it impossible for him to concentrate on his work. He kept having to think of that bloody fire extinguisher and its wet foam to stop himself from giving Charlie a mouthful, or a slap across the face. But it can't have come to this, he thought, can it? And why now? Simon didn't understand what had caused this sudden, rapid deterioration in his relationship with Charlie. Until recently, and in spite of whatever tensions existed between them, they had been good friends. Charlie was pretty much Simon's only real friend, now that he came to think of it. He didn't want to lose her. Who would he have left? Sellers and Gibbs? How bothered would they be if they never saw him again?

Charlie had openly crowed over Simon's inability to get anything out of Darryl Beer. 'Aw, diddums. There you were trying to put right a miscarriage of justice and the nasty scrote ruined it for you. You know how people say "I hate to say I told you so"? Well, not me. I fucking love saying it.'

Simon didn't care that his first visit to Brimley had been unproductive. He hadn't given up hope that Beer would talk eventually, once he'd satisfied himself by exercising what little power he had, making Simon sweat.

David Fancourt's alibi was solid. He and Alice had been in London, watching 'The Mousetrap'. Several witnesses had given statements confirming that both of them were in the theatre all evening. It struck Simon as almost too good an alibi, once he started to think seriously about it. He even caught himself wondering, as he parked in a space beside the war memorial opposite Hamblesford's village-green, whether that play had been specially selected for its symbolic significance. David Fancourt was a clever man. He designed intricate computer games for a living. He could also be vindictive, as Simon had seen with his own eyes. It might have struck him as an ironic touch, to take his fiancée to see a famous murder mystery on the same night that he had arranged for somebody to kill his wife.

Could that somebody have been Darryl Beer? Could both Beer and Fancourt be guilty? He'd have tried the theory out on Charlie if relations between them hadn't been so strained. Instead, he attempted to communicate telepathically with Alice. He didn't believe in all that bollocks, but still . . . Sometimes he was aware of Alice, unseen, quietly watching him, wondering how long it would take him to save her and her daughter. Alice believed Simon was powerful, or at least she had at first. All he had to do was find her, find Florence, and she would see she hadn't underestimated him. The thought of what he might say to her, if and when he found her, made him feel agitated, caught out.

Laura's parents lived in a small white cottage next to a butcher's shop. They had no front garden. Only a narrow pavement separated the front of their house from the main road through the village. The cottage's thatched roof wore something that looked like a hair-net. Simon banged the black wooden knocker against the door and waited. He always felt shy at moments like this, slightly afraid of introducing himself to people he didn't know. His upbringing had not encouraged sociability. Simon had grown up watching his mother stiffen with tension every time the doorbell rang, unless the priest or a close relative was expected. 'Who could that be, now?' she would gasp, eyes wide with fear of the unknown.

Simon had never been allowed, when he lived with his parents, to invite friends back for tea. His mother believed that eating was too personal an activity to engage in while company was present. Too young to think strategically, Simon hadn't thought to keep this information from his classmates, who had taken the piss mercilessly as soon as they found out. Now, as an adult, he understood that

Kathleen had done him a disservice by enforcing this rule, but he couldn't bring himself to be angry. She had always seemed to him to be too frail for censure. As a teenager, Simon had stifled his frustration and made allowances for his mother, though it was a time in his life when an unwelcome look or remark from anyone else turned him rabid with fury, led to breakages and bloodshed, suspension after suspension from school. If he hadn't been the brightest in his year, they'd have booted him out, Simon was sure of it.

Kathleen had phoned him on his mobile again this morning, wanting to know if he was coming for Sunday dinner. That he'd made it last week counted for nothing. There was no respite. The pressure was never off.

After a few seconds the Cryers' front door was opened by a middle-aged man with a barrel chest, wearing bi-focal glasses, a navy jumper with a golfer emblem, navy trousers and slippers. 'Detective Constable Waterhouse? Roger Cryer.'

Simon shook his hand.

'Please come through,' said Cryer. 'My wife's just making some tea. Ah, here she is!' He had a strong Lancashire accent.

Maggie Cryer looked twenty years older than her husband. Simon would have guessed sixty for him, eighty for her. Impossible to ask, of course. Laura's mother was no taller than five foot, thin, with misshapen, arthritic hands in which the tea tray wobbled. She was wearing a green nylon housecoat, tan tights and blue slippers.

'Help yourself to a cup of tea,' she said, lowering the tray unsteadily on to the small table in front of her. She perched beside her husband on a small wicker sofa opposite Simon, whose chair, also made of wicker, was creaky and uncomfortable. 'I hope this won't take long,' she said. 'It's an ordeal for us, even after all this time. A phone call from the police . . .'

'I understand, Mrs Cryer. I'm sorry. But it's necessary, I'm afraid.'

A log fire blazed, making the lounge unbearably hot. Like a lot of cottages, the Cryers' home had small windows and was gloomy even in daylight. The combination of the darkness and the flickering flames made Simon feel as if he were in a cave. There were three framed photographs of Laura on the mantelpiece. None of Felix.

'We saw on the news about his new wife being missing.'

'Roger,' Maggie Cryer cautioned.

'And the little baby. Is that why you're here?'

'Yes. We're going over Laura's case again,' Simon told them.

'But I thought there was no doubt,' said Mrs Cryer. 'That's what they told us at the time, the police. That . . . Beer person definitely did it. That's what they told us.' Her swollen fingers plucked at her sleeves.

'If I could just ask you a couple of questions,' Simon said in an appropriately soothing tone. This was how he would have interviewed his own mother, even though the gentle approach was probably a waste of time. There would be no calming Maggie Cryer, no reassuring her. Simon would have bet any amount of money that Laura's mother existed in a state of permanent agitation. Since the murder or always?

'Don't you want tea?' she asked him.

'I'm fine, thanks.'

'You forgot the milk, love,' said her husband.

'Really, I'm all right,' Simon insisted. 'Don't go to any trouble.'

'I wouldn't mind a spot of milk,' said Cryer.

'It's no trouble.' Maggie leapt up and scurried out of the room.

Once she had gone, her husband leaned forward. 'Just between you, me and the gatepost,' he said to Simon. 'I can't talk about this in front of the wife, she gets upset. It's David Fancourt you want to be looking at. First Laura gets killed and now his second wife and new baby are missing. It's too much of a coincidence, isn't it? And why would Darryl Beer kill our Laura? Why? She'd have just given him her bloody handbag if he'd attacked her, she wouldn't have let it get that far. She's a sensible girl.'

'Did you say any of this to the police at the time?'

'The wife wouldn't let me. She said we could get in trouble, you know, legally, if we said things that weren't true. But nine times out of ten, it's someone known to the victim. Nine times out of ten – I heard an expert say that on television.'

'Why would David Fancourt have wanted to kill Laura?' asked Simon, hoping to hear his own theory repeated back to him.

Roger Cryer stared at him quizzically, as if that question raised several more fundamental ones. Questions about the competence of Culver Valley CID, thought Simon bitterly. Yes, of course the answer was obvious – to everyone but Proust, Charlie, Sellers, Gibbs and the rest.

'Custody of Felix,' said Roger Cryer. 'And revenge, for the hurt she'd caused him. Laura left him. He didn't take it very well. I think he went to pieces a bit.'

Simon wrote this down in his notebook. Not quite the version of events Vivienne and David Fancourt had given Charlie. What had she said at the team meeting? *He found her physically repellent and tedious. He was relieved to be rid of her.* That was it, word for word. Simon's memory was more reliable than Roger Cryer or David Fancourt. A discrepancy, then. 'How do you know he went to pieces?'

'Vivienne Fancourt told us, David's mother. She did everything she could to persuade Laura to give the marriage another go. She even came round here to talk to us, see if we could persuade her. She and Laura didn't like each other, never had. Why would she be so keen to persuade Laura to try again, unless it was for David's sake? She saw how devastated he was and, like any mother, she did what she could to help him. It didn't work, though. Laura's always known her own mind. Once's she's decided, there's nothing anyone can do.'

'Here we are.' Maggie Cryer returned with a small blue jug. She began to pour the tea, three cups, even though Simon had declined.

Her husband looked as if he was fighting the urge to say more. It wasn't long before he lost the fight. 'Revenge.' He nodded. 'David's that way inclined. There was a problem about Maggie and me seeing Felix, after Laura died,' he said.

'Oh, Roger, stop, please. What good will it do?'

'Do you know when we last saw Felix? Two years ago. We don't bother any more. We pretend we haven't got a grandson. Felix is our only one, too. But in the end it was tearing us apart. Everything changed after Laura died, overnight. Literally, overnight. They changed his name from Felix Cryer to Felix Fancourt, took him out of the nursery he loved, where he was really happy, really settled, and plonked him in that bloody ridiculous toffee-nosed grammar school. It was as if David and Vivienne were trying to turn Felix into another person! We were only allowed to see him once every few months, for a couple of hours at a time. And we weren't allowed to see him on our own. Vivienne was always with him, chaperoning. Feeling sorry for us.' His face grew redder as he spoke. His wife had closed her eyes and was waiting for him to finish. Her stiff posture suggested that she was bracing herself against his words.

Simon grew more and more puzzled as he listened. According to Charlie, Vivienne Fancourt had made this very complaint about Laura Cryer, that she had tried to keep Felix away from David's side of the family, that she had not allowed them to see him unsupervised. Was it possible that David had done the same to Laura's parents after his wife's death? Did he see it as a battle between the Cryers and the Fancourts, with Felix as the prize?

'We tried talking to David, even tried begging him,' Roger Cryer went on. 'But he's made of stone, that man. Whatever we asked for, he said no. He wouldn't say why.'

'You said Vivienne Fancourt appeared to feel sorry for you,' said Simon. 'What did you mean?'

Maggie Cryer shook her head, as if to speak on this subject were beyond her.

'She knew we wanted to see more of Felix, that David wouldn't let us,' said Roger. 'It was obvious she pitied us. She kept saying how hard it must be for us, and it was, but her saying that only made it harder. Especially when she couldn't stop talking about all the things she and Felix did together.'

'That was why I gave up,' Maggie whispered. Her hands shook. Simon noticed that the backs of them were covered in brown spots. 'Because seeing Felix meant seeing her and . . .' She shuddered. 'I used to be ill, sometimes for days afterwards. The last straw was when she told me Felix had started to call her Mum. I just couldn't do it any more after that.'

'She was bloody insensitive about it too,' said Roger Cryer, patting his wife's skinny arm. 'Almost in the same breath, she told us she'd had to remind Felix who we were that morning. He'd forgotten, he hadn't seen us in so long. She realised how bad it sounded and apologised, but, I mean, there was no need for her to tell us that, was there?'

Simon was surprised when Maggie Cryer tutted and pushed her husband's hand away as if it were a spider that had crawled into her lap. 'Roger's a terrible judge of character when it comes to women,' she said. 'Insensitive! She said that deliberately. And all the other things. She didn't feel sorry for us at all.'

'What are you talking about?' Her husband looked mystified. 'She damn well did. She said so all the time.'

'Because she knew it was the best way to hurt us. And we could never prove she was being deliberately nasty.'

'But you think she was?' Simon was confused.

'Of course. If you say something hurtful by mistake, you make sure never to do it again, don't you? You don't keep saying the same thing, to the same person, or people. When a clever lady like Vivienne Fancourt makes hurtful remarks again and again, she means them, all right.' Simon looked at Maggie Cryer's hands. They were clenched, two tiny knots of fist in her lap.

# 25

## *Wednesday October 1, 2003*

The bath is spotless. Nobody would ever know. Nobody will ever know. Satisfied that I cannot make the tub shine any brighter, I have a shower, scrubbing every inch of my body, wondering if I will ever feel clean again.

I wrap two large bath-sheets around myself and hurry to the bedroom. My wardrobe is unlocked and the key is in the door. I choose an outfit: baggy trousers and a jumper. These will fit me properly. I hate myself for the pathetic gratitude I feel. Most people take for granted that they will be able to choose their own clothes. There is nothing to stop me walking out of the front door of The Elms and never coming back. Nothing except David's threat: *I could take steps to ensure that you never see Florence again.*

The phone rings, making me jump. I am certain it is Vivienne, ringing to check up on me. I wonder if I should answer it, until I hear David's voice downstairs. At first he speaks too quietly for me to hear anything. When he raises his voice, I can hear that he sounds cross, far more interested in communicating his own opinion than trying to gauge the opinion of whoever he is talking to. It can't be Vivienne.

I hear him say, 'Exactly, to teenage boys, and I guarantee, they'll love it. No. No, because that's not the way we'd market it. No, I can't on Friday. Because I can't, all right? Well, what's wrong with talking about it right now?' Russell. David's business partner.

I have an opportunity. The thought paralyses me. David will be on the phone for at least fifteen minutes. His conversations with Russell are never short, particularly when there is a point of contention. He has never told me what they argue about.

I tiptoe to Vivienne's bedroom and push open the door. The bed is made, as always. There is not a crease on the lilac-coloured duvet. Four photographs of Felix stand on the dressing table, two of him with Vivienne. The room smells of the cream she puts on her face every night. I see her white embroidered Chinese pump-style slippers under the bed, laid out neatly one beside the other, exactly as they would be if she were standing in them. I shudder, half expecting them to start moving towards me.

My phone. That's what I came in here for. I drag myself out of my superstitious reverie, walk over to the bedside cabinet and pull open the single drawer. There it is, exactly where I knew it would be. Switched off. If I am insane, as everyone seems to think I am, how did I know that it would be here? Vivienne said it was in the kitchen.

I turn it on and phone Simon Waterhouse on his mobile. He wrote down the number for me last time we met, reluctant to have me ring him at the police station. I tore up the piece of paper, but I memorised the number. I leave a whispered message for him, saying that he has to meet me again tomorrow, at Chompers, that I need to speak to him urgently. This time our conversation will go well, I tell myself. He will come away from our meeting believing me; we'll be allies, and he will help me. He'll do whatever I ask him to.

I go back out on to the landing and hover for a few seconds, to check that David is still talking to Russell. He is. I can't make out his words any more – he is speaking too quietly – but his voice has the back-and-forth tone I hoped it would. I am as sure as I can be that the conversation is not nearing its conclusion.

I know I ought to put my phone back in Vivienne's cabinet drawer in order to avoid arousing suspicion, but I cannot bring myself to. I need to hold on to it. It is a symbol of my independence. Let Vivienne think that sneaking into her room and stealing it is another symptom of my madness, my illness.

I rack my brains for somewhere I can hide the phone. If I put it back in my handbag, Vivienne will take it out, as I am certain she has once already. There is only one room in the house that Vivienne never goes into: David's study. Nobody goes in there except David, and even he hasn't set foot in it since Florence was born. Vivienne's cleaners, who come for a full day once a week, are strictly banned. As a result, the study is much dustier and messier than the rest of the house. It is full of David's computers, music systems, CD racks offering nothing but classical music and the complete works of Adam and the Ants, his collection of science-fiction novels – row upon row of spines, each one displaying a strange, off-putting title – and several filing cabinets.

After looking around, I decide that behind one of these would probably be the safest hiding place. I am about to investigate this possibility when my eyes come to rest on David's computer. Another means of communication with the outside world, the normal world beyond The Elms.

I lower myself into the swivel chair and turn on the machine, hoping that its faint buzz is not audible. I tell myself I will only have to be nervous for a few moments; if David has heard anything he will be up here in seconds. My heart pounds as I sit and wait. Nothing happens. I hear

David's voice through the floor, angry again, still in the middle of his argument with Russell. I exhale slowly. Safe. This time.

On the computer screen, a small box tells me that, in order to log on, I need to enter a password. I swear under my breath. I had assumed David's computer would be like mine at work, with the password stored in the memory, the logging-on process automatic.

I type in 'Felix', but a sign flashes up to inform me that I am incorrect. I try 'Alice' and 'Florence', but these too are rejected. A shiver of dread makes my skin prickle as I type in 'Vivienne'. This is also unsuccessful. Thank God for that, at least.

Perhaps men are less likely than women to choose the name of a loved one, I think. But what else might mean something to David? He doesn't support a football team. It occurs to me that he might have been clever and chosen a word that no-one would ever associate with him, something totally random: tombola, candelabra. Or the name of a place, perhaps. I try 'Spilling' with no success.

I close my eyes, thinking furiously. What else, what else? I wonder why I am even bothering. There are billions of words, any of which could be the one David has chosen to use as his password. Even if I had time to eliminate all the things he definitely wouldn't have chosen . . . I almost laugh at my next, ludicrous idea. It is worth a try, I suppose. After all, I now know that my husband has an appetite for sick jokes.

I type 'Laura' and press return. The sign-in box disappears and the screen turns blue. In the bottom right-hand corner an hour-glass symbol appears as the computer begins again to whir gently. I am dizzy with shock. David only bought this machine six months ago. As recently as that, he chose the name of his hated ex-wife as his pass-word. Why? *You were always second-best after Laura. Did you know that?* No, it can't be true. I am absolutely positive that David only said that to hurt me.

But I haven't got time to think about it any more, not now. I get in to Hotmail as quickly as I can and set up a new account. The process takes longer than I thought it would, and I begin to sweat as I go through the seemingly endless stages. After what feels like hours, I have a hotmail account and address: AliceFancourt27@hotmail.com.

I hear David's voice again. 'Anyway,' he says. Something about the tone of that one word makes me panic. There is an end-of-conversation edge to his voice, an air of someone who wants to wind things up. Perhaps he is wondering what I am doing up here. I have been left unattended for too long.

I press the 'off' button on the computer and the screen immediately turns black. I run from David's study into our bedroom, leaving the door slightly ajar and standing behind it.

'No, I'll ring you at the weekend,' says David. 'Oh. When will you be back? No, all right, then. Read me their letter, if you've got it there.'

I intended to send an e-mail to Briony thanking her for the cuddly toy she'd sent Florence and saying it would be nice to meet up in a few weeks, once things are on the way to being back to normal. I have to believe things *will* get back to normal. If I'd had time, I could have gone on to describe the awfulness of the past week, told Briony all about Florence vanishing and Little Face appearing. I am desperate to tell her these things – she, I know, would believe me without question – but I decide I can't risk going back to the computer. In my state of heightened tension, I cannot work out how much it matters that I did not succeed in sending this message.

Laura. How many times have I heard Vivienne call her a monster, a despot, a horror, a harpy, both before and after her death? I have lost count. I always assumed David felt the same way, but now, for the first time, it dawns on me that even if he disagreed with his mother, he wouldn't have the courage to say so in public. After everything that he has done to me, I cannot believe that I feel like crying because, six months ago, he chose Laura's name as his computer password instead of mine.

'Hang on, hang on,' I hear him say to Russell. 'They've totally missed the point. We *had* a perfectly adequate supplier, and they offered us terms which . . .'

I stare at my mobile phone. To go back into David's study would be tempting fate, but when I try to think of an alternative hiding place – one in the bedroom, say – my mind is a giant blank. I decide to risk the study, mainly because I know it would never occur to either David or Vivienne that I would go in there, under any circumstances, let alone hide something there.

I insert my hand into the gap between the nearest filing cabinet and the wall. It might be wide enough, but only just. My fingers hit a corner of some kind. It feels like cardboard, but the space is not big enough for me to be able to get a grip on it.

I stand up and, as gently as possible, nudge the filing cabinet forward a little. A navy blue envelope file that was trapped in a vertical position falls on to its side against the wall. I pick it up and open it. It contains three pornographic magazines. I open one and recoil when I see a picture of a naked woman tied to a table. I freeze, my face a cartoon of shock, not knowing what to make of this anomaly. David wouldn't find this sort of thing erotic. What is it doing in his study? It simply isn't possible, and yet here it is, in my hands.

I notice a couple of sheets of paper on the floor that have fallen out of one of the magazines. One is a letter, on watermarked blue notepaper. 'Dear David,' it begins. I look at the bottom of the page. The letter is signed, 'Your loving father, Richard Fancourt'.

My eyes widen. At last, a name. And proof that David's father exists. At least this explains the magazines. They are there to act as a distraction from what David really wants to hide. He must have reasoned that, in the event of me or Vivienne finding the folder and opening it, we would not investigate too closely once we had seen a few of those horrible pictures.

With half my mind standing guard, monitoring David's continuing conversation with Russell, I skim-read the letter, trying to take in the crucial points. David's father is remarried. He is sending this letter to The Elms because he has heard that David still lives there. He is sorry he was not a better father. He is sorry he has not been in touch all these years, but it was probably for the best. The letter is frustratingly long. I try to take in all the words at the same time: *wife pregnant . . . little brother or sister . . . if not for my sake then for his or hers . . . hope we can re-establish contact . . . baby due in September . . . retired from academia . . . taken up bridge . . .*

'Alice! What are you doing?'

'Getting dressed,' I call back, nauseous with sudden terror. I stuff the letters and pornographic magazines back into the file and replace it, pushing the cabinet against the wall. I am so afraid of being caught that I lose my balance and stagger back, crushing something small and hard with my right foot. I grab it, and my phone, and run from the study to the bathroom, locking the door when I get there. David is still talking to Russell. He interrupted his call to check on me. That is how little he trusts me.

Once I am safe, I examine what I am holding. It is a little dictaphone with a tape inside it. There is probably nothing on the tape apart from David's notes about some computer game or other, but I want to listen to it anyway. I glance at the thin wooden bathroom door and decide it isn't safe to do so now. It is all too easy to imagine an immobile presence on the other side. The Elms is a house in which the cracks of light under doors are often interrupted by dark patches the size of feet.

I bury my mobile phone under a pile of clean towels in the bathroom cupboard. It ought to be safe there for a while. Then I slide the dictaphone with the tape inside it into my trouser pocket where it will be completely covered by my baggy jumper, and walk downstairs with forced casualness, like a woman who is concealing nothing.

# 26

## *Entry from DC Simon Waterhouse's Pocket Book*

### (Written 5/10/03, 4 am)

*2/10/03, 11.15 am*

Area: Chompers Café Bar at Waterfront Health Club, 27 Saltney Road, Spilling. I arrived fifteen minutes late and met Alice Fancourt (see index) who was already there. She was standing by the bar when I arrived, with her hand on the pay-phone. I asked her if she wanted to make a call and she said she had been about to telephone me on my mobile phone, to see if I was on my way.

We sat down at a table. We did not order drinks. Mrs Fancourt looked tired. Her eyes were puffy and bloodshot. She was not crying when I arrived, but as soon as she saw me approaching she began to cry. She told me, in a tone of voice that struck me as hysterical, that I needed to get a team of police officers 'out there, right now' to look for her daughter, and that every day I failed to do this made it less likely that Florence (see index) would be found safe and well.

I told Mrs Fancourt that it was not within my power to authorise such activity, but she ignored this and said, 'There must be something you can do, you're the officer in charge of the case. I can't believe you're not helping me when you easily could.'

I asked her about the theft of her mobile phone to which she had referred at our previous meeting (see index). She said the phone had not been stolen. She had misplaced it and her mother-in-law (see index) had found it. I asked her why, in

237

that case, had she been about to use a pay-phone, and she said that she had left her mobile phone in the house. She said she had hidden it, so that it could not be stolen again. When she said this, she had apparently forgotten that, a few moments earlier, she had told me no-one had stolen her phone but that she had misplaced it. I brought up this inconsistency and she became defensive. She said she did not want to discuss this any further.

I then asked her if her husband David Fancourt (see index) was mistreating her in any way. She looked distressed but refused to confirm or deny. My impression was that she was either afraid or embarrassed to answer my question.

Still crying, Mrs Fancourt asked me if I believed an entire family could be jinxed. I replied that I did not. She told me that the Fancourt family has a history of 'severed' (as she put it) parent-child relationships. She listed the following (see index for all): Richard Fancourt abandoning David Fancourt when he was a child, Laura Cryer and Felix Fancourt (separated by Cryer's death), and now, she claimed, herself and her daughter Florence were apart.

She expressed the view that the whole Fancourt family was cursed. She said that she was doomed from the day she married into the Fancourt family, and she further claimed that she had been specifically selected for this unhappy fate because her own parents had died in a car crash.

I asked her by whom had she been selected in the manner she had described, and she replied, 'God, destiny, whatever you want to call it'. I told her that in my opinion this was superstitious and had no basis in fact.

Mrs Fancourt went on to tell me that she had another theory about what might have happened to Florence, or, as she put it, 'an avenue of investigation you could pursue, if you can be bothered, that is.' She said that perhaps David Fancourt had a mistress, whom he had impregnated at roughly the same time that he had impregnated Mrs Fancourt. She suggested that he and his mistress might have swapped the two babies, and that Florence might be in the house of David Fancourt's mistress at the moment. She argued that this would explain why no baby/babies had been reported missing.

I asked her why Mr Fancourt should wish to do this. She said that perhaps he and his mistress wanted her (Alice Fancourt) out of the way so that they could live happily ever after with the two babies, but that David knew that if he divorced his wife, she would probably get custody of Florence, which would be intolerable to him, having previously lost custody of his son Felix to his first wife Laura.

Her theory, she said, was that David and his mistress decided instead to swap the babies, make everybody believe that she, Alice Fancourt, had gone mad, and then either get custody on grounds of madness and/or her rejection of the baby, or, 'worst case scenario', as Mrs Fancourt put it, the plan might have been to murder her and make it look like suicide, which would be plausible if everybody had previously been made to believe that she was suffering from post-natal hysteria.

I told Mrs Fancourt that this hypothesis was extremely unlikely and had no evidential basis. She shrugged and said, 'It's the only thing I can think of.' She added that what had happened was so out of the ordinary that the true explanation was bound to be an unlikely one, rather than the sort of thing that happens every day. I reminded her that she had previously believed that a woman who had been on the same labour ward as her might have swapped her own baby with Florence Fancourt because she feared her boyfriend might harm her child and wanted to give her a better chance in life.

I told Mrs Fancourt that I would pass on both theories to Sergeant Zailer, who could then decide whether or not she wished to take it further, but I said that I thought this would be most unlikely. I added that it would be an improbable coincidence for Mr Fancourt to have impregnated two women who then gave birth at almost exactly the same time. I also said that Mr Fancourt would never imagine he could get away with such a plan, not with DNA tests as readily available as they are today.

Mrs Fancourt told me she had found a letter the previous day, addressed to her husband. The letter was from his father, Richard, and informed David Fancourt that Richard's new wife was expecting a baby, a half-brother or sister for David Fancourt. Mrs Fancourt asked me what I thought about the fact that her husband has a sibling he has never told her, his own wife, about. 'And he's the one you and your sergeant believe over me,' she said, in a tone that I took to convey anger.

She was very concerned by the fact that she had not noticed whether the letter was dated. 'What if Little Face is Richard's child, David's half-sister?' she said. 'I'm sure he said the baby was due in September. Florence was born on the twelfth of September! You have to do something!'

I tried to explain that the case was closed as far as the police were concerned, and that the best thing for Mrs Fancourt to do was wait for the results of the DNA test. I told her that in my opinion it was rash to assume that the baby at The Elms was Richard Fancourt's child; there was no proof to indicate this was the case. 'It would explain why David's so kind to Little Face, so bothered about her, if she's his sister', said Mrs Fancourt. I repeated that there was no reason to assume this, and reminded Mrs Fancourt that only minutes ago she had attempted to persuade me that the baby at The Elms was the child of her husband and his mistress. Mrs Fancourt became angry and said, 'I can't win, can I?'

*During the interview, Mrs Fancourt's manner towards me was intermittently hostile, pleading and apathetic. I made a mental note to mention my concern for her welfare to Sergeant Zailer, with a view perhaps to contacting Mrs Fancourt's GP.*

# 27

## *Thursday October 2, 2003*

Vivienne, David and Little Face are in the garden when I return from my meeting with Simon. It is a chilly, bright day, and their faces are patched with light and shade, the effect of the sun shining through the leaves of the trees overhead. They remain perfectly still as I approach, like three figures in a landscape painting, only ever seen at a distance.

Little Face is in her pram, wrapped in blankets, wearing a yellow woolly hat. I cannot help remembering the day the three of us bought the pram. It was the day after I found out I was pregnant. I didn't want to do anything to tempt fate, but Vivienne insisted we needed to celebrate, so we went to the Mamas and Papas superstore in Rawndesley and spent hours examining pushchairs, prams and travel systems. We were happy then, all of us. Vivienne even allowed David to tease her a little when she insisted that a straightforward old-fashioned pram was the only kind worth considering.

'It's not like you to go for the traditional option, Mum,' he said, and Vivienne smiled. Normally she objects to all teasing, claiming that it is disrespect under another name.

'Where have you been?' Vivienne's hands grip the handles of the pram we eventually chose. As usual, she got her way. 'Why didn't you say you were going out?'

'Just for a drive,' I say, avoiding David's eye, pretending he is dead. Fleetingly, I wish that this were the case. I don't think I will ever get over the indignities he has inflicted upon me, not as long as I know that they exist in his mind as well as in mine.

Vivienne looks dissatisfied. She doesn't believe me. 'I was about to take the baby for a walk round the gardens. Would you like to come?'

'Oh . . . yes, please.' I am thrilled. The grounds of The Elms are vast. I will be able to spend at least half an hour with Little Face, perhaps more.

'Would you like to push the pram?' Vivienne asks.

'I'd love to! Thank you.' I look at David. He is furious. I resist the temptation to smile at him. I am shocked to acknowledge that there is now a small part of me – one that didn't exist until this morning – that relishes his suffering.

'David will take your handbag inside,' says Vivienne.

I unhook the bag from my shoulder. David snatches it from me roughly and retreats indoors.

'Come along then.' Vivienne lets go of the pram and allows me to steer it. My heart nearly bursts as I push Little Face across the grass. I am performing an action that every mother takes for granted, and it makes me want to weep with joy. 'What's wrong?' asks Vivienne. 'You look upset.'

'I was just thinking . . . this is so nice, but . . . much as I'm fond of Little Face, I wish I was pushing my own baby.' I wipe away a tear. Vivienne turns away, and I have the sense that she wishes she hadn't asked.

We walk along the side of the old barn towards the vegetable garden. 'You didn't mind about the handbag, did you? You don't really need the encumbrance, I wouldn't have thought.'

I am surprised. 'No,' I say. 'Not to walk round the garden.'

'It's not as if you're going to need any money for the

foreseeable future, is it? Or your diary or anything. Not while you're recuperating. You need to get a lot of rest, give yourself the best possible chance of a full recovery. Are your car keys in your bag?'

I nod as a new dread takes hold of me.

'Right. Well, I think I'll hold on to it for the time being. I'll put it on the kitchen counter where you can see it, but . . . you're not well enough to be out and about on your own at the moment.'

'You're treating me like a child,' I whisper.

'I hope I am, in the best possible sense,' she says. 'Why are you so protective of your things? I noticed while you were pregnant that you'd taken to walking round the house clutching your possessions, like a commuter on a train who's afraid of being robbed.'

Did Vivienne perceive me as paranoid when I was pregnant, then? It's true, I did often walk around with a notebook and pen in my hand, or my bag, or whatever novel or pregnancy manual I was reading at the time, but only because I wanted to have certain things within easy reach in case I needed them later. The Elms is such a big house, and I was so heavy and uncomfortable towards the end of my pregnancy, I did everything I could to minimise the amount of walking back and forth I had to do.

I know I shouldn't argue. It is so nearly Friday. Friday begins on Thursday night, at midnight. We walk across the paddock towards the river. I lean over to stroke Little Face's soft cheek. I cannot stop myself from saying, petulantly, 'I want to keep my handbag, and my car keys. I don't want them to live in the kitchen.'

Vivienne sighs. 'Alice, I wish I didn't have to bring this up . . .'

'What?' I ask, alarmed. Is there anything else she and

David can take away from me? I have nothing left, apart from David's stupid Dictaphone which is still in my trouser pocket. I have forgotten it until this moment.

'When I arrived home yesterday, I found the upstairs bathroom in what I can only describe as an unacceptable state.' My face heats up as I remember the morning's events, but at the same time I have no idea what she is talking about. I scrubbed that bath on my knees, until it gleamed. 'I can see that you know what I'm referring to,' says Vivienne.

'No. No, I . . .'

She raises a hand to stop me. 'I do not wish to go into the matter in any more detail, I assure you. I've made my point.'

My head swims with disbelief and I feel my perceptions, my whole view of the world, tilt yet again. An urge to be violent seizes me, and I clutch the pram until my knuckles turn white. I do not want to imagine what Vivienne might mean, to reach the obvious conclusion. How could David stoop so low? 'When I left the bathroom, it was clean,' I whisper, mortified.

'Alice, we both know that's simply not true,' says Vivienne patiently, and for a moment I wonder whether I might really be going mad. 'You're clearly more unwell than I thought. You have to admit, you really don't know what you're doing at the moment. You can't seem to control yourself.'

I swallow and nod, my head reeling. If I agree that I am ill, she will trust me. She wants me to be ill.

'I also found your mobile phone in the bathroom cupboard, under all the towels. Were you trying to hide it?'

'No,' I whisper.

'I don't believe you,' says Vivienne. 'Alice, you've got to

face facts. You're sick. You're suffering from an extreme case of post-natal depression.' She pats me on the shoulder. 'It's nothing to be ashamed of. We all need to be looked after once in a while. And you're luckier than most people. You've got me to look after you.'

## 28

## 9/10/03, 12 pm

Charlie and Simon sat side by side on a large green sofa that was covered in milky white and beige stains. They were in the home of Maunagh and Richard Rae, Richard Fancourt as was. The house was a three-storey semi-detached on a wide, tree-lined road in Gillingham, Kent. The drive down from Spilling had been awkward, the conversation stilted and polite, but at least Charlie had not been actively hostile.

Opposite Simon, in an armchair that had a dark, greasy, head-shaped patch in the middle of its back-rest, sat a young boy wearing a maroon school uniform jumper and black trousers. He had messy, sand-coloured hair, a half-eaten sandwich in his hand, and an institutional smell about him that reminded Simon of Gorse Hill, the comprehensive school he had attended in the seventies and eighties.

'Mum and Dad won't be a minute,' said Oliver Rae, whose own school was closed for the afternoon because the central heating had broken down. Simon watched him chew the thick, flecked bread, which looked unappetisingly wholesome. David Fancourt's half-sibling. About thirteen, Simon guessed. Definitely not a baby girl. Not Little Face, as Alice had claimed in desperation.

The lounge door, which did not fit properly in its frame, creaked open, and a large black labrador ran in, barking furiously, plunging its nose straight into Simon's crotch. 'Down, Moriarty! Down, boy!' Oliver shouted. The dog reluctantly obeyed. Maunagh Rae came into the room in a cloud of strong musky perfume. She was a plump woman with straight silver hair cut into a long bob, and a smattering of freckles across her nose and cheeks. Simon could see the resemblance to Oliver. She wore a purple roll-neck sweater, black trousers and court shoes, and small, discreet gold and pearl earrings. A woman of taste, his mother might have called her.

Her smart appearance was a surprise. From the state of the house, he had expected somebody more dishevelled. He was used to seeing houses in worse states of disrepair than this one, but they weren't usually quite so big. They tended to be council-owned and to contain crack heads, dealers, benefit cheats. And much skinnier dogs that were not called Moriarty.

The lounge, where they were sitting, had two large street-facing windows, the tops of which were stained glass. Their frames were rotten. Every time there was a breeze, the panes rattled. The carpet was thin and shiny, more like a maroon sheen on the floor. Yet the six paintings, asymmetrically arranged on the walls, all appeared to be originals, so the Raes must have had a bit of money to play with. Simon couldn't imagine why they'd chosen to spend it on huge canvases spattered with colour blobs. He surmised that Maunagh or Richard must have a friend who was a struggling artist, and they'd bought all this crap from him out of sympathy. All four corners where the walls met the ceiling were blackened, as if they had been singed by flames.

'I gather it took you a while to track Richard down,' said Maunagh.

'Because he'd changed his name,' said Charlie. Colin Sellers, when he'd eventually located David Fancourt's father, had been loudly scathing about men who adopted their wives' surnames after marriage. Charlie had called him a Neanderthal brute, but privately Simon agreed. Traditions were traditions.

'More and more men are doing it,' said Maunagh, as if she sensed some disapproval and felt the need to defend herself.

A small, shambling garden gnome of a man with hunched shoulders and a white beard entered the room. His grey cardigan was buttoned incorrectly and his shoelaces were undone. The state of the house immediately made more sense. Richard Rae hurried over to shake hands with Charlie and Simon. As he clutched each of their hands in turn, he rocked back and forth, nearly head-butting Charlie at one point. 'Richard Rae,' he said. 'It's good of you to come all this way. As I said on the phone, I'm not sure I can help you.'

'Have you seen or heard from Alice Fancourt at all since last Thursday?' asked Charlie. Simon had heard her ask him the same question over the phone. This trip to Kent was probably pointless.

'No.'

'Have you been contacted by anybody out of the ordinary? Can you think of anything that has happened in the past few weeks, something that seemed odd at the time, somebody hanging round outside the house?'

The three Raes all shook their heads. 'No,' said Richard. 'Nothing. As I said, I never met Alice. I didn't know David had married again.'

'You knew about his first marriage, then?'

'Well . . .' Richard paused. He caught his wife's eye and they both looked at their son.

*Sophie Hannah*

'Oliver, love, go and do your homework,' said Maunagh.

David Fancourt's little brother shrugged and ambled out of the room, apparently uninterested in the presence of two detectives in his home. Simon, at his age, would also have done as his mother told him without complaint, but he'd have desperately wanted to know what was going on.

Richard Rae stood in the middle of the room, still rocking back and forth. 'Where were we?' he said.

'We only knew about Laura after she was killed,' said Maunagh, with an exasperated glance at her husband. She sat where her son had been sitting and folded her hands in her lap.

'You're not in touch with David at all, then?' said Simon.

'No.' Richard frowned. 'Sadly, I am not.'

'Do you mind if I ask why?'

'His mother and I separated.'

'Surely you could still have seen your son,' said Charlie. There was no way she'd ever let any man keep her away from her kids. Just let one try.

'Well, yes, but it was, you know, one of those things. One doesn't always know what to do for the best, does one?'

Simon and Charlie exchanged a look. Maunagh Rae was biting her lower lip. Her face was flushed.

'So you decided it was for the best if you didn't have any contact with your son?' Charlie's voice was sharp.

'He had his mother, who was more than enough of a parent. Vivienne was rather like two parents rolled into one. I was always a bit superfluous.'

Maunagh Rae sighed loudly.

'It isn't good for children to be passed back and forth between divorced parents,' Richard said, more to his wife than to Simon and Charlie, it seemed.

'You must have missed David,' Charlie persisted. 'Weren't you ever tempted to write to him? At Christmas, on his birthday? When Oliver was born?'

Richard Rae rocked more vigorously. 'Vivienne and I decided it was best not to confuse him,' he said. Maunagh muttered something inaudible. Simon wondered if she knew her husband was lying. There had been at least one letter, the one Alice had told him about. He wondered why Rae hadn't mentioned it.

Charlie was visibly impatient. She took off her glasses, rubbed the bridge of her nose. It was a signal to Simon. Time for the old trick; the two of them had done it countless times. 'May I use your bathroom?' Simon asked the Raes. They both appeared relieved, as if any other question he might have asked would have been more difficult to answer. Maunagh offered him a choice of three. He chose the nearest one, which turned out to be bigger than his own bedroom, and draughty. It also contained a sculpture of a curvaceous naked woman's torso. Simon couldn't imagine why anyone would want such a thing in their home.

He locked the door, took his phone out and rang Charlie's mobile. 'Charlie Zailer,' she said. Simon said nothing. 'Yes. Excuse me a moment, I'll have to go outside and take this call,' he heard Charlie tell the Raes.

He waited until he'd heard the front door shut, then flushed the toilet for the sake of authenticity. He tiptoed back into the hall, approached the lounge door as quietly as he could, and listened. Maunagh Rae was already in full flow.

'. . . can't bear to sit here and listen to you defend that woman!' she was saying angrily. 'Why did you tell them that you and Vivienne *agreed* it would be better if you kept out of David's life? You didn't agree at all! She drove you out and then poisoned his mind against you!'

'Love, love, calm down. I'm sure it wasn't quite like that.'

'What are you talking about?' Maunagh's voice rose to a higher pitch. 'It bloody well *was* like that.'

'It's all in the past now, anyway. Don't get angry. There's no point in raking over all that unpleasantness.'

'It was clear from David's reply to your letter about Oliver that he's been taught to hate you . . .' Maunagh Rae sounded like a woman for whom raking was still very much on the agenda.

'Love, please, I'll get upset . . .'

'Well, maybe you should be upset. Maybe you should be bloody angry, like I am! David adored you and Vivienne couldn't handle it, that's the truth. She had to be the only one. If a woman like her were having her children now, she'd use donor sperm. She's a megalomaniac, and you know it! So why don't you bloody well say so when you're asked?'

'Love, what good would it do? It's got nothing to do with David's wife and daughter being missing . . .'

'You're a moral jelly, that's what you are!'

'I know, you're right, love. But come on, now, you know that if I knew anything about Alice or the baby, I'd tell them.'

'You know what happened to David's first wife,' said Maunagh. Out in the hall, Simon raised his eyebrows. He froze, waiting. He had an odd feeling of unpreparedness. 'She was murdered, for heaven's sake.'

'Oh, come on, Maunagh.' Richard Rae sounded faintly irritated. From what he'd heard so far, Simon doubted the man could manage full-blown anger. 'One can't accuse people of murder willy-nilly. You're not being fair.'

'Fair! God, it's like talking to a sponge! Why don't you tell them you wrote to David about Oliver?'

'It can't be relevant. They're looking for Alice and the baby. How could my letter be important?'

'You'd do the same again, wouldn't you?' said his wife bitterly. 'If we split up, and I decided to be a bitch and keep you away from Oliver, you'd bloody let me. Is anything worth a fight, as far as you're concerned?'

'You're being silly, Maunagh. There's no need for this. We weren't arguing before the police arrived, were we? And nothing's changed.'

'No. Nothing ever does.

'Come on, now . . .'

'Do you know the name of Oliver's form teacher? Do you know what his favourite subject is?'

'Love, calm down . . .'

'It was only because of me that you wrote to David at all! I wrote the bloody letter for you, word for word. You copied it out! If I'd left it up to you, you wouldn't even have tried, and he's Oliver's only brother, the only one he'll ever have . . .'

Simon wondered what would have happened if his own parents had separated. Kathleen would have wanted her son all to herself. Would his father have fought for equal rights?

He couldn't listen to any more of Maunagh Rae's recriminations. He was about to knock on the door of the lounge when he became aware of a presence behind him. He turned and saw Oliver on the stairs, now dressed in jeans that were too big for him and an Eminem T-shirt. 'I was just . . .' Simon fumbled for an excuse to explain his eavesdropping. How long had the boy been there? Maunagh and Richard Rae had made no attempt to lower their voices.

'Mrs Pickersgill. That's the name of my form tutor,' said Oliver, sounding, for a moment, much older than he looked. 'And my favourite subject's French. You can tell my dad if you like.'

# 29

## *Thursday October 2, 2003*

I am sitting in the rocking chair in the nursery, with Little Face on my lap, giving her a bottle. Vivienne suggested that I should. David's face turned puce with anger, but he didn't dare to object. I was appropriately effusive in showing my gratitude and made sure not to appear at all suspicious. It feels like a long time since I took anybody's kindness at face value.

Vivienne is changing the cot sheet, watching me without looking at me, to check that I am behaving appropriately. Little Face stares up at me every now and then, her expression intent and serious. Experts say newborns are not able to focus until they are about six weeks old, but I don't believe that. I think it depends how clever the baby is. Vivienne would agree. She is fond of telling the story of her own birth, of the midwife who said to her mother, 'Uh-oh, this one's been here before.' I cannot imagine Vivienne ever looking, or being, anything but completely focused, even as a baby.

Little Face keeps turning away from her bottle. She wriggles on my knee. Her mouth twists into a crying shape, though no sound emerges.

Having dealt with the cot, Vivienne throws open the doors of Florence's wardrobe. She starts to empty the piles of clothes into a large carrier bag. I watch the Bear Hug babygro fall in, the sleep suit with the pink hearts on it, the red velvet dress. One by one Vivienne pulls the garments from their hangers. It is the most brutal sight I have ever seen, and I flinch. 'What are you doing?'

'I'm going to put Florence's things in the attic,' says Vivienne. 'I thought I'd save you the job. It'll only upset you to look at them if they stay here.' She smiles sympathetically. A feeling of nausea swells inside me. Not knowing where Florence is or what might have happened to her, Vivienne is willing to empty her wardrobe as if she no longer exists. 'David led me to believe that you didn't want the baby to wear Florence's clothes,' she adds, as an afterthought.

'No. Don't.' I cannot keep the anger out of my voice. 'Little Face has to wear something. I only said that at first because I was upset. It was a shock to see her in Florence's babygro, that's all.'

Vivienne sighs. 'I'll pick up some second-hand things from a charity shop in town. Little Face, as you and David both insist on calling her, can wear those. I'm sorry if I sound cruel, but these clothes belong to my granddaughter.'

I have to press my lips together to hold in the scream that fills my mouth.

Little Face begins to cry, just a whinge at first but it rises to a high-pitched wail. Her face turns red. I have never seen her like this before, and I panic. 'What's wrong with her? What's happening?'

Vivienne looks over at us, unperturbed. 'Babies cry, Alice. That's what they do. If you can't cope with it, you shouldn't have had one.' She turns back to the wardrobe. I lean Little Face over my hand and try to wind her by patting her back, but she only howls louder. Her misery distresses me so much that I begin to cry too.

David appears in the doorway. 'What have you done to

her?' he yells at me. 'Give her to me.' Vivienne allows him to snatch her from my hands. He holds her small body close. Her cheek squashes out against his shoulder, and she is instantly silent, content. Her eyelids slide closed. Together, a perfect image of father and child, they leave the room. I hear David murmuring, 'There, there, little darling. That's better, isn't it, now that Daddy's here?'

I wipe my face with the muslin square in my hand, the one that I tucked under Little Face's chin to catch stray drops of milk. Vivienne stands over me, hands on her hips. 'Crying is the only way babies can communicate. That's why they do so much of it. Because they can't control themselves.' She pauses, to make sure I take in her full meaning. Then she says, 'You know I disapprove of emotional incontinence. This is a difficult time for all of us, but you've got to try to pull yourself together.'

Bit by bit, my soul and ego are being destroyed.

'Whatever you might say, I can see that you are very attached to . . . Little Face.'

'She's a tiny baby. It doesn't mean I'm trying to pretend she's Florence, or to substitute her for Florence. Vivienne, I'm as sane as you are!' She looks doubtful. 'The police have said nothing about any babies being . . . you know. Found. I'm sure we'll get Florence back. You must know that's all I want. And for Little Face to be reunited with her mother, whoever she is.'

'I have to go and pick Felix up from school. Do you think you can manage without me for an hour or so?'

I nod.

'Good. I'll tell David to make you some food. I assume you haven't eaten today. You're starting to look gaunt.'

My throat closes, stopping my breath. I know that my stomach would protest violently against anything apart from water. Silently, I watch Vivienne leave the room. Alone again. I sit and cry for a while, I don't know how long. My tears run out. I feel empty, like a void. I have to remind myself to think, to move, to continue to exist. I would not have imagined, if someone had asked me before all this happened, that I could fall apart so quickly. It has been less than a week.

I know that I must go downstairs, if Vivienne has told David to make me some food. I am about to, and then I remember that David's Dictaphone is still in my trouser pocket. I listened to the tape in the bathroom a while ago, and there was nothing of any significance on it, just a business letter David had dictated.

I cannot bring myself to go into his study. It is inconceivable to me that I was ever brave enough to do so. Instead, I put the Dictaphone in David's wardrobe, in the pocket of a pair of trousers he hasn't worn for ages. I sit down in front of the dressing-table mirror and brush my hair, not because I care how I look but because it is something I used to do every day before my life was ruined.

I walk downstairs, stumbling occasionally on my way down. My brain feels hazy and frayed, as if it is slowly decomposing. My mental fog is broken every so often by a coherent thought. One of these is that it is better to seek David out than to wait to be summoned. If he has some horror in store for me, I would rather face it straight away, get it over with.

I find him in the kitchen with Little Face, who is lying by the door on her Barnaby Bear changing mat, kicking her legs vigorously. Radio Three is on in the background, or maybe it's Classic FM. Those are the only stations David ever listens to. The room is smoky, full of the smell of fried meat. I try not to gag. Tonelessly, David begins to recite,

'Fried eggs, bacon, sausages, beans, mushrooms, tomatoes, fried bread.'

'What?'

'Civilised people say pardon. That's what's on the menu. You didn't have breakfast, so I thought you could have it now. Sorry, would you prefer something else? Smoked salmon? Caviar?'

'I'm not hungry,' I say.

'Mum told me to cook you something, so that's what I'm doing.'

I notice that my handbag, car keys and phone are on the counter under the window; Vivienne said she would put them there. As reliable as ever.

'It's ready,' says David. 'I've even warmed the plate for you.'

I thank him. His face creases in irritation. It is an unpleasant task, to try to imagine the thoughts of a sadist, but I force myself to do so, and wonder if he would prefer me to be defiant, at least initially. That way he can watch my spirit crumble in the face of his cruelty. Perhaps that is what secretly thrills him.

'I don't think I'll be able to eat any of it,' I say. 'I'm sorry. I . . . I don't feel well enough.'

'Try,' says David. 'Have one baked bean, one mushroom, and see how you feel after that. Maybe it'll stimulate your appetite.'

'All right.' I sit at the table and wait for him to put the food down in front of me.

'What are you doing?' he says.

'I thought you wanted me to try to eat.'

'Not *there*, silly.' He laughs. I turn and see that he has put the plate down on the floor, next to the kitchen bin. 'Kneel down and eat it,' he says.

I close my eyes. How can he do this in front of Little Face, a tiny, blameless baby? Her presence, her oblivious background gurgling, makes what is happening so much worse. 'Please, David, don't ask me to do that.' I watch him swell with satisfaction. I'm not sure who I am appealing to, David the tyrant or the reasonable, kind man that I used to be married to.

'You're not housetrained,' he says. 'You can eat on the floor, like an animal.'

My mind shrinks in on itself. If I refuse, David will be only too glad to remind me that it is within his power to separate me from Florence for ever. I don't know if this is true, or if he would really do it, but it would be foolish of me to assume that his bark is worse than his bite. I have been naïve for too long.

I kneel down beside the plate of hot food. Steam rises from it, wetting my face. The smell revolts me and I nearly vomit. 'I can't, I'll be sick,' I whisper. 'Please, don't make me.'

'You're trying my patience, Alice.'

I pick up a mushroom with one hand.

'Put that down!' David shouts. 'Don't use your hands. Put them behind your back. Use your mouth only to eat.'

I am so shaky, I doubt that I can do as he asks without losing my balance. When I tell him this, he says, 'Try,' in a tone of mock-encouragement. I take a deep breath and lower my face, retching at the smell of greasy food. Somehow I manage to stop myself from vomiting up the bile in my stomach, but I cannot control my tears. They drip off my chin and land on the plate.

'Eat,' David orders. I want to do as he says, because I know that I have to and I want it to be over, but I physically cannot put my face in the orangey-yellow mess of beans and eggs. I look around, see Little Face's pink kicking feet, the bristly brown mat next to the kitchen door, chair and table legs, David's brown Italian leather shoes against the white gloss skirting boards. Everything looks so normal and correct. The sound of an orchestra playing something that I know only as the theme tune to the film *Brief Encounter* fills the room.

I look up at David, helpless and desperate, sobbing hard. His face scrunches with anger. He marches across the room towards me, his hand raised. In that instant I am convinced he is going to beat me up, maybe even kill me. I recoil from him and topple over. As I fall on my back, my shoulder catches the side of the plate and it flips up in the air. The cooked breakfast slop lands on my face, neck and chest, its heat burning my skin through my jumper.

'Please don't hurt me!'

'Hurt you? Alice, I have no intention of laying a finger on you.' David looks down at me as I lie on my back, howling. He feigns shock. 'I was just going to swat that fly on the bin, but it's gone now.'

I sit up, brush off as much food as I can.

'I'm not a violent man, Alice. You've tested my patience to the limit with your lies and scheming over the past week, but I've kept my temper. Many husbands wouldn't have been so tolerant. You're lucky to be married to me. Aren't you?'

'Yes,' I say, wishing him dead.

'Look at you, covered in food. You're a dirty pig.' David takes the dustpan and brush out of the cupboard beneath the sink and starts to brush the food off my jumper, but all he does is rub it in. My once cream jumper has a large, wet, orangey-brown patch on the front.

I try to wipe my face but David takes my hand and places

it firmly at my side. 'Oh no,' he says. 'You don't get to make a mess like that and then clean yourself up, as if nothing's happened. I let you do that with the bath, but it's about time you learned that you have to live with the consequences of your actions. You were determined not to eat the nice meal I cooked for you, so you can wear it instead.' He hands me the dustpan and brush. 'Now sweep that mess off the floor, and when you've collected as much as you can, put it back on the plate. You can have it for supper later. Maybe you'll be hungry by then.'

He stares at me. I stare back. In what strange game are we opponents, I wonder. David's harsh expression flickers, as if he might be thinking the same thing, that the two of us are reading out lines from some bizarre script without stopping to question, because that would be too hard, the parts we are playing.

# 30

## *9/10/03, 6.30 pm*

The Brown Cow pub was a short walk from Spilling Police Station in the centre of town, and might as well have been linked to it by a covered walkway, so popular was it with bobbies and Ds alike. It had recently been refurbished in dark, polished wood, with a non-smoking room and an extended menu that offered chicken breast stuffed with Brie and grape mousse as well as the more traditional pub fare that Simon was used to.

Tonight he didn't feel like eating. Alice and the baby had been missing for six days. Not enough was happening, apart from in Simon's head, where his deepening preoccupation with Alice and what, precisely, she meant to him was beginning to starve his brain of oxygen. His mind had become a dark trap. He could no longer block out thoughts of how he had failed her, possibly endangered her life and the lives of two babies.

He felt uncomfortable, sensing that there was a half-formed idea snagging at the back of his mind. What was it? The Cryers? Richard and Maunagh Rae?

He wasn't in the mood for drinking with Charlie, but she'd insisted. They needed to talk, she said, and so here they were, with a pint of lager each and a prickly atmosphere between them. So far they'd discussed bank accounts. While Simon and Charlie had been interviewing the Raes, Sellers and Gibbs had spent the afternoon looking into the Fancourts' finances. They had found nothing amiss, no mysterious sums of money that had vanished without trace. In other words, thought Simon glumly, no evidence to suggest that David Fancourt or any of his nearest and dearest had paid Darryl Beer to do their dirty work.

He stared past Charlie to the picture on the wall behind her. It was of a brown cow, aptly enough. The animal was in profile, standing in a forest clearing. Simon thought the picture was good until he noticed that the natural light that fell around the cow looked quite unnatural, more like rays from a spotlight than beams of sun. For a second, he thought he might be about to grasp that stray idea, the one that was eluding him. But then the moment passed and, irritatingly, he was none the wiser. Was it something to do with money?

'If Fancourt's having an affair, he's keeping it bloody well hidden,' Charlie moved on from matters financial. 'That's what Sellers says and . . . well, he ought to know. He's the expert.' Simon waited for her to say something crude about Sellers' sex life, and was surprised when she didn't. It wasn't like her to miss an opportunity. 'Oh, and this Mandy woman. It appears she and her live-in bloke have taken their baby and gone away. France, a couple of their neighbours said. To buy booze. I'm not sure they'd have been able to get the baby a passport so quickly, though. And the neighbours could be wrong, or lying – this is the Winstanley estate we're talking about, after all. Who goes on a booze cruise two weeks after having a baby?'

'Interesting,' said Simon, feeling his heartbeat quicken. Perhaps more than interesting. Significant, maybe. They were on the verge, he sensed it.

'Yeah, well. The Snowman's certainly in a quandary now.' Charlie allowed herself a small, vindictive smile. 'He has to decide whether to pursue it further, on the basis of Alice Fancourt's say-so alone, or wait a while and hope Mandy and family reappear.'

'What do you reckon?'

'Proust doesn't care what I think.' Charlie sighed. 'I don't know. If it were my decision to make, I reckon I'd follow it up.' She looked at Simon. 'Mandy hadn't even been discharged from midwife care. She didn't tell anyone she was going – the midwife, the health visitor, her doctor. No-one. Not that that means she's got Florence Fancourt, but . . .' She shrugged. 'Simon, I'm sorry I've been a bitch to you.'

'Right.' He was relieved. This surely signalled her intention to revert to her more usual behaviour, which was all he wanted. Then resentment flooded his mind. Now that he knew she was sorry, now that she'd confirmed that she was the one in the wrong, he could withhold his forgiveness with confidence. In private. She'd see no sign of his true feelings.

She smiled at him, and Simon felt immediately guilty. He'd let her down badly, at Sellers' party, and she'd forgiven him. Charlie was hopeless at hiding her feelings. Simon knew she still thought well of him, in spite of everything. Why did he relish the opportunity to hold a grudge against her? Was she right? Was he addicted to the idea that he was hard done by?

'I think we need to have a long, frank talk,' said Charlie. 'Otherwise things are going to become impossible between us.' There was an awkward silence. Simon tensed. What was coming? 'Right, well, I'll start, then,' she said. 'I was really hurt that you said all that stuff in front of Proust and everyone, without telling me first.'

265

'About the Cryer case?' Again Simon felt that unsettling twitch somewhere in the depths of his memory. What was it, for fuck's sake?

'Yeah. Were you deliberately trying to make me look like a dick?'

'No.' Why on earth would she think that? he wondered. 'To be honest, I wasn't sure I was going to tell you, Proust or anyone. I thought you'd all shout me down. I didn't realise Proust was in favour of looking at the case again until he said so, and as soon as he did, I thought: here's my chance.'

Charlie frowned. 'And it didn't occur to you that I might have liked to hear about it first?'

'What does that matter?' said Simon impatiently. 'We're all working together, aren't we?'

'You made me look like an idiot. I should know what's going on, and you made it bloody obvious to everyone that I didn't.'

'Look, normally I'd probably tell you stuff first, but I didn't think you'd be all that receptive. You'd already made it clear you thought there was no doubt Beer was guilty.'

Charlie sighed. 'You made some good points. I still think, on the balance of probabilities, Beer's our man, but I'm not so pig-headed that I wouldn't listen to a new angle. You must think I'm shit at my job if you think I'd do that.'

'I don't think that at all,' said Simon, surprised.

'Maybe I am. Why didn't any of that stuff you said occur to me? I was the officer in charge.' Simon had never heard Charlie express doubts about her own abilities before. It made him feel uncomfortable. 'Well?' she said.

'Well what?'

'Do you think I'm shit at my job?'

'Don't be daft. I think you're brilliant at it. Everyone does.'

'Why don't you sodding well tell me that, then?' said Charlie quietly. 'Why do you make me beg for reassurance?'

'I don't!'

'You just have!'

The conversation was accelerating, becoming more unpredictable. Simon took a deep breath. 'It would never occur to me or any of the team to reassure you,' he said. 'You don't need it. You always seem so confident. Too confident, sometimes.'

Charlie was silent for a few seconds. Her next question, when it came, was an unwelcome one. 'Have you told anyone about . . . what happened at Sellers' party?'

This was exactly why Simon avoided long, frank talks. 'No. Of course not.'

'Nobody? I'm not asking you to name names. I just want to know if everyone's laughing at me behind my back, that's all.'

Simon's mobile phone began to ring in his pocket. He glanced awkwardly at Charlie.

'Forget it.' She lit a cigarette. 'You'd better get that.'

It was PC Robbie Meakin. Saved, Simon thought.

'You lot are looking into the Laura Cryer case again, right?' said Meakin.

'Who is it?' asked Charlie. She hated not knowing who Simon was speaking to, and persistently interrupted every call he took until he told her. One of her many infuriating habits.

'It's Meakin. Sorry, mate, yes, we are. Why?'

'We've just arrested a young lad called Vinny Lowe, friend of Darryl Beer's, for possession of Class A drugs. In with his stash was a bloody great kitchen knife. Lowe swears blind it's Beer's.'

'Where was it found?'

'A health club, of all places. Waterfront, on Saltney Road.'

Vivienne Fancourt's health club. And Alice's. And then, suddenly, Simon had it. He recalled Roger Cryer's exact words, digested their full significance. He nearly turned to Charlie and blurted it out in a jolt of excitement. He stopped himself just in time. He wasn't prepared to risk her assigning this particular lead to Sellers or Gibbs to follow up. When it really mattered, Simon preferred to work alone.

# 31

## Thursday October 2, 2003

'What on earth . . .' Vivienne backs away from me in disgust when she sees the flaking, dried food on my face and neck, the smeary stain on my jumper. I am sitting at the kitchen table. David wouldn't allow me to leave the room. 'I thought you wanted to spend more time with the baby,' he said. 'You can't touch her, obviously, not while you're covered in that mess.'

Vivienne looks angrily at him. 'Was it too much to ask you to keep things under control for one morning?' Felix stands behind her, in his turquoise blazer and trousers, the Stanley Sidgwick uniform. He looks at me in the way people look at road accidents, horrified and fascinated.

'It's not my fault!' David whines like a toddler. 'I cooked her some food, but she refused to eat it. She tried to throw it at me. I caught her arm to stop her and it ended up all over her. As you can see.'

'Why didn't you make her get changed immediately? She's filthy! It's all over her face.'

'She refused! She said she didn't care what she looked like.' He picks up Little Face and leans her against his shoulder. Her turned head slots into the crook of his neck. She is awake, but as David pats her back her eyes start to close.

Vivienne walks slowly towards me. 'Alice, this behaviour is simply not acceptable. I won't have it in my house. Is that clear?'

I nod.

'Stand up! Look at me when I'm speaking to you.'

I do as I am told. Behind her, David is smirking.

'All those clothes must go in the wash. You need to have a shower and get changed. I won't have such . . . slobbishness in my house, I don't care how unwell you are. I thought I'd made my point and you'd understood it, after the bathroom incident, but clearly I was wrong.'

I cannot think of anything to say to this, so I remain silent.

'I see that you haven't even got the decency to apologise.' I know that Vivienne is about to issue a punishment and I am frightened of what it might be. She sounds as if she has reached the end of her tether. If I said sorry it might calm her down, but I can't find the words. I am a block of ice. 'Right. Suit yourself,' she says. 'From now on you won't get dressed at all. I'll take all your clothes and put them in the attic, with Florence's. You can wear a nightie and dressing gown, like a mental patient, until I say different. Is that understood?'

'But . . . the DNA test. I'll have to get dressed for that.' My voice shakes.

Vivienne's cheeks flush. I have enraged her by making a good point. Clearly, in her anger, she forgot about our appointment at the Duffield Hospital, its incompatibility with the penance she's devised for me. 'I don't want to hear another word out of you,' she says, her lips thin and white with fury. 'And I can't bear to look at you in those disgusting, dirty clothes any longer. I won't have it! Take them off and I'll wash them. You should be ashamed of yourself, creating work for other people with your . . . dirty protests!'

She turns to face the window. David grins at me.

I start to count in my head as I remove my jumper. The white bra I am wearing beneath it is also stained orange and yellow, so I take it off. David's smile widens. He nods at the waistband of my trousers, where there is a small patch of brownish grease. I know that Vivienne regards even the smallest mark on one's clothing as unacceptable. With trembling fingers, I begin to take off my trousers, praying that no part of the meal went any further.

Vivienne turns round. When she sees me, her mouth drops open and the skin on her neck wobbles. 'What on *earth* do you think you're doing?' she demands.

I stop, confused.

'Pull up your trousers! How dare you? What do you think this is, a massage parlour? How dare you stand in my kitchen naked?'

'But . . . you told me to take my clothes off so that you could wash them,' I sob. David covers his mouth with his hand, to hide his amusement. Vivienne wouldn't notice anyway. She is incandescent with rage, thinking that I am deliberately trying to provoke her. Tears pour down my face and I fold my arms to cover my bare chest. I cannot bear the injustice or the humiliation for much longer. 'I thought you meant that I should do it straight away,' I try to explain, though I know it will do me no good. Vivienne finds me repulsive.

'I meant that you should go upstairs, wash and change, and bring down your dirty clothes for me to wash. I did not mean that you should strip in broad daylight, in my kitchen. The blind isn't even down! Anyone could see you!'

'I'm sorry.'

'I don't want to hear it, Alice. Go and clean yourself up and put on some nightwear. Now!'

I run from the room, weeping. I keep thinking that I have been through the worst, that nothing more horrible can happen, and I am wrong every time. This particular disgrace wounds me more deeply than any of the others because I did it to myself. Of course Vivienne didn't mean for me to undress in the kitchen. I should have known that – I *would* have known it, were it not for the way David's sick mind has worn me down over the past few days, warped all my perceptions, twisted the way I look at everything. How delighted he must have been to see me subject myself to a degradation he hadn't planned and wasn't expecting, to realise that he has belittled me to the point where I am now so ready to abase myself.

I lock myself in the bathroom and cry until my eyes are slits and my vision blurs. I do not dare to look in the mirror. For so long, I have thought of Friday as the goal. After that, the police will have no choice but to become involved. I will have help, at last. But what sort of person will I have become by then? Will I be in a fit state to be a mother to Florence, even assuming I am lucky enough to have the chance? For the first time, I am not sure.

# 32

## *9/10/03, 8 pm*

'I don't understand you lot!' Vinny Lowe shook his head wearily. 'I can't see why you're making such a big deal of it.'

'Cocaine's a Class A drug,' said Simon. He and Lowe, who resembled a bulldog on tranquilisers, were in an interview room at the station. Lowe's solicitor, a mousy middle-aged woman in a cheap suit, sat beside him. She had said nothing so far, just sighed occasionally.

'Yeah, but it wasn't like I was selling it. There was hardly any there and it was for my own personal use. There's no need to come over all heavy, is there?'

'The manager of Waterfront doesn't see it that way. The stuff was hidden in his establishment, in the crèche, of all places. Inside the baby-changing unit. Nice touch.'

'My girlfriend's the crèche manager,' said Vinny.

Simon frowned. 'And your point is?'

'Well, where else could I have hidden it? The crèche was the only bit I had access to. When I popped in to see Donna. Is she going to lose her job?'

'Of course. She helped you to hide Class A drugs in the crèche,' Simon explained slowly. Lowe shook his head, wide-eyed, as if to suggest that it was a crazy, mixed-up world he lived in if this sort of thing could happen. His solicitor sighed again.

'Look, I've already spoken to the plods that arrested me

273

about this. And then they turned round and said I had to talk to you too. How come?'

'We're interested in the knife that was found with the drugs in the baby-changing unit.'

'I already said, that's nothing to do with me. Must be Daz's.'

'Darryl Beer?'

'Right. It's been there for ages. I just left it where it was.'

'How long exactly is ages?'

'I don't know. Over a year. Two years? I can't really remember. It's just always there.'

Simon tried to catch Lowe's solicitor's eye. No wonder she couldn't be bothered to enter into the spirit, with such a moron for a client. 'Did the knife appear in the baby-changing unit before or after Beer got sent down?'

'Fucked if I can remember that! Must have been before, I guess.'

'Did you see Beer put the knife inside the unit? Did he tell you about it?'

'No, but it must have been him. No-one else knew about our lock-up. That's what we called it.' Lowe grinned.

'Assuming I believe you, how did Beer get access to the Waterfront crèche? Did he also have a girlfriend who worked there?'

'Nah, but he and Donna were mates. We all were, the three of us.'

'Could he have hidden the knife without Donna seeing him?'

'Yeah, course. The changing unit's in a separate room next to the bog, so it's easy to hide stuff without being seen.' Vinny Lowe seemed to inflate with pride. 'That's the beauty of the lock-up,' he said.

Simon stopped, thought hard. Darryl Beer was arrested

at home, mid-morning on a Saturday, the day after Laura
Cryer was killed. The Waterfront crèche opened on Saturday mornings at 9 am, 8.30 on weekdays. Beer could have
gone there first thing, hidden the knife, then gone home.
Why not hide Laura's handbag in the same place, though?
Unless he'd chucked that in a bin somewhere and Charlie's
team had just never found it. All Simon wanted was for
tomorrow to arrive, so that he could make the call he was
desperate to make. Everything would be easier after that;
he'd know so much more.

'Does the crèche take children of all ages?' he said. 'Is
there an upper or a lower age limit?'

Lowe looked baffled. 'Birth to five,' he said. 'Why, you
got nippers?'

Simon didn't answer. He produced from his pocket the
photograph of Vivienne, Alice, David and Felix Fancourt
that had been in Alice's desk drawer at work. 'Do you
recognise any of these people?' he asked Lowe.

'Yeah, that little lad used to go to the crèche. Donna used
to call him Little Lord Font-el-roy, because of his posh
accent. And her, Lady Muck.' He nodded, smiling. He was
behaving like a man without a care in the world. Perhaps he
was too dim to understand that he was about to be done for
possession of Class A drugs. 'So, is she something to do
with that little posh lad, then?'

'Did you see them together, ever?'

'No.'

'Why Lady Muck?'

'That's what me and Daz used to call her. We saw her in
the pool and Jacuzzi all the time.'

'You and Beer were members of the health club?' Simon
didn't try to disguise his disbelief.

'Don't be daft. I wouldn't pay those prices. Nah, we used

Sophie Hannah

to dodge reception and get in through the café bar, Chompers. Any idiot could do it, but not everyone's got the inititative.' Lowe's solicitor flashed him a look of pure loathing, then turned back to the chipped pale pink varnish on her fingernails.

'Lady Muck was in nearly every day, and so were we,' said Vinny. 'Being men of leisure, you know how it is. Well, you probably don't. I swear she used to listen to our conversations. We used to have a laugh, say that she fancied us and that was why she was following us around. She must have known we weren't members, but she never said nothing. We reckoned she got her rocks off listening to us.'

'What did you used to talk about?'

'Business,' said Lowe self-importantly. 'Times we'd been inside. If she was listening, we'd go way over the top, talking about shooters and taking people out. Daz used to say listening to us talking like tough guys made her . . . you know.' Lowe winked. 'We were just talking bollocks. Lady Muck didn't fancy us, she was just a nosey cow.'

'Did you and Beer ever mention your lock-up in front of her?'

'Probably. We used to laugh about it all the time, that all those toffee-nosed parents had no idea their brats' bums were being changed on top of our merchandise.'

'I thought you said the drugs were for your own personal use?'

'Just a turn of phrase.'

Normally Simon would have been furious to have a sleaze like Vinny Lowe in front of him talking shit, but he had too much nervous energy racing around his brain. Anger would have required more attention than he could have mustered. Now that a firm link had been established between the Fancourts and Darryl Beer, Simon had a sense of increasing momentum, and was wrestling with the slight disorientation that always gripped him at this stage in a case. Part of him was afraid to discover the truth. He had no idea why. It was something to do with options narrowing down, the feeling of being pushed into the mouth of a tunnel. He was pretty sure Charlie, Sellers and Gibbs never felt this way.

If only it were tomorrow morning. But that was just a formality, wasn't it? The phone call? He knew the truth, didn't he? Or was there something more? Was he afraid of finding out something else? Simon couldn't shake off a sense of foreboding, of something deeply unpleasant lurking just around the corner, something he couldn't avoid because he couldn't stop walking towards that corner . . .

Alice. That was what really terrified him. What would he find out about Alice? Please let it be nothing bad, he prayed, staring at the photograph in his hand, the family portrait. He shuddered. He didn't want to look at it, didn't want to think about it, but why?

'Just to clarify,' he said to Lowe, mainly to distract himself from the ominous awareness he knew was struggling to reach him. 'Which of the two women in the photograph is the one you and Darryl Beer referred to as Lady Muck?'

Lowe pointed to Vivienne Fancourt. Simon felt a surge of relief.

# 33

## *Thursday October 2, 2003*

I am sitting at the dressing table brushing my hair when David walks in. 'Do you remember our honeymoon?' I say to him, determined to speak before he does. 'Do you remember Mr and Mrs Table, and the Rod Stewart family? The evenings sitting on the balcony drinking retsina? Do you remember how happy we were then?' I know that a few shared nicknames won't bring back those feelings, but I want David to remember, at least, that they once existed. Let him be as tormented as I am.

Scorn contorts his face. 'You might have been,' he says. 'I wasn't. I knew you'd never mean as much to me as Laura did.'

'That's not true. You're just saying that to hurt me.'

'We only went to Greece. Anyone can go to Greece. Laura and I went to Mauritius for our honeymoon. I didn't mind spending that sort of money on her.'

'It doesn't matter how much money you spend, David. It never has. Your mother always gives you more. How many times has Vivienne bailed out your business over the years? More than once, I bet. If it wasn't for her charity you'd probably be working in some grotty factory.'

He clenches his teeth and storms out of the room. I continue to brush my hair, waiting. A few minutes later he is back. 'Put the brush down,' he says. 'I want to talk to you.'

'I've got nothing to say, David. I think it's a bit late for talking, don't you?'

'Put the brush down! Look what I've got.' He shows me a photograph of my parents and me, taken when I was a child. He must have got it from my handbag. It is my favourite picture of the three of us. David knows this. He knows that if anything happens to it, it can never be replaced. 'I think your hair suits you better like it was then,' he says.

In the photograph I am five years old. My hairstyle is an unflattering, masculine short back and sides. My parents were not the most stylish people in the world. They didn't care a damn what anyone looked like.

'I don't like hairy women,' David tells me matter-of-factly. 'The less hair the better.'

'Laura had long hair,' I cannot resist saying.

'Yes, but hers wasn't limp and greasy like yours. And she didn't have hair all over her body. I noticed, when you did your little striptease in the kitchen earlier, that you haven't shaved under your arms for a while.'

'My daughter's been abducted,' I say in a monotone. 'My appearance hasn't been the main thing on my mind.'

'Obviously not. I bet you haven't shaved your legs either.'

'No, I haven't,' I say. I know what is coming, but for once I can see a way out of it. First, though, I have to plunge deeper in. 'Why did you do that, before?' I ask.

'Do what?'

'Pretend I'd refused to get changed, when it was you who wouldn't let me take off that dirty jumper.'

'Because you deserve it,' says David. 'Because you *are* dirty, deep down, and it's about time Mum realised.'

I nod.

David walks over to me. He reaches into his trouser pocket and pulls out Vivienne's white-handled kitchen scissors and a disposable razor. He holds the black and white photograph of me with my parents in front of my face. 'This was a happier time for you, wasn't it?' he says. 'I bet you wish you could turn back the clock.'

'Yes.'

'You weren't a liar then. You weren't all disgusting and hairy.'

I say nothing.

'Well, now's your chance.' He nods at the razor, at the scissors. 'Cut your hair, so it looks like that. And then, when you've done that, I want you to take off your nightie and shave off the rest of your hair.'

'No,' I say. 'Don't make me do that.'

'I'm not making you do anything. You're free to do exactly as you choose. But so am I. Remember that, Alice. So am I.'

'What do you want me to do? Tell me exactly what you want me to do.'

'Take the scissors,' he begins slowly, as if he is talking to a retard. 'Chop off all your thin, straggly, snot-coloured hair. Then take off your nightie and shave your legs and under your arms. And then, when you've done that, you can shave between your legs as well. And when you've done that, you can shave off the hair on your arms and your eyebrows too. When you've done all that, I'll let you go to bed. Big day tomorrow.'

'And if I refuse?'

'Then I'll tear this into tiny pieces.' He waves the photograph in the air. 'It'll be bye-bye Mummy and Daddy. Again.'

An arrow of pain pierces the shield I have built, out of

numb disbelief and necessity, to protect my heart. I wince and David smiles, pleased to have struck home. 'Okay, I'll do it,' I say. 'But not with you in the room.'

'I'm going nowhere. I'm the person you've wronged, so I'm entitled to watch. Just get on with it. I'm tired and I want to go to sleep.'

'And I suppose you're going to tell Vivienne I did it by choice, aren't you? More evidence of my depravity.'

'I had all the evidence I needed last Friday, when you decided to pretend our daughter was a stranger. But some people take a bit more convincing. Mum's not usually as slow as she has been about you. Actually, I think she's beginning to get the message. That business this afternoon . . . and when she sees what you've done to your hair, when she sees you with no eyebrows, and finds a big pile of hair on the bedroom floor . . . because you're too much of a pig to clean up after yourself . . .'

He has said enough for my purposes. I walk over to his wardrobe, open it, and take out the Dictaphone that I put in one of his trouser pockets this morning. I press the 'stop' button, making sure that he sees me, and back away, holding the little silver machine behind me. 'Everything you've said since you came in here is on this tape,' I tell him.

His face turns crimson. He takes a step towards me. 'Don't move,' I say. 'Or I'll scream the place down. You won't be able to get the tape off me and destroy it before Vivienne gets in here. You know how quick she is when she knows something's going on that's not yet under her control. So unless you want her to know what a sick, twisted creep you really are, you'll do what I say.'

David freezes. He tries not to look worried, but I know he is. He has always played the perfect little boy in front of his mother. His ego could not survive exposure as a pervert and a sadist.

'Luckily for you, I'm not as sick as you are,' I say. 'All I want you to do is leave me alone. Don't speak to me or look at me. Stop thinking up new ways to torture me. Pretend I'm not here. I want nothing more to do with you, you sad, pathetic scumbag.' David shrugs, pretending he doesn't care. 'Oh – and one more thing.'

'What?'

'Where's Florence? What have you done with her? Tell me that and I'll destroy the tape.'

'Oh, that's easy,' says David scornfully. 'She's in the nursery. She's here at The Elms where she's always been.'

I shake my head, sadly. 'Good night, David,' I say. I leave the room, holding the Dictaphone tightly in my hand, and close the door quietly behind me.

# 34

## *10/10/03, 9 am*

'Is this a newly discovered eighth circle of hell?' said Charlie, gesturing at the mayhem around her. She and Simon were in Chompers, Waterfront's brash, mock-American diner-style café full of parents in sportswear with fake tans and their snotty, shrieking children. Survivor's 'Eye of the Tiger' was playing at full volume. 'Why's it so packed?'

'They're all waiting for the crèche to open,' said Simon. 'It was supposed to open half an hour ago. I expect they've had trouble finding new staff, after sacking Lowe's girl-friend. Look.' He nodded as a young red-haired girl with a ponytail and freckles came in. She stood at the door and waved. At the sight of her, most of the adults in Chompers leaped out of their seats and began to gather together their bags and toddlers. 'Lisa Feather,' said Simon. 'She was Donna's assistant. Maybe she's in charge now.'

'How come you know so much?' asked Charlie.

'I got here early. I've been in already. I didn't want to do it while the kids were there.' He rubbed his watch strap with the index finger and thumb of his right hand.

'And?' said Charlie.

And after he'd checked out the crèche, while he waited for Charlie, he'd made two phone calls. Yesterday he had thought one would be enough, but in the middle of the night he'd sat bolt upright in bed, knowing exactly why he'd felt apprehensive at the sight of that bloody photograph of Alice, David, Vivienne and Felix in the garden of The Elms. He'd realised that he needed to make two calls, not one.

And now he had, and his hopes were confirmed along with his worst fears. There was no uncomfortable rumbling in his subconscious now; everything had risen to the surface. Simon saw the whole picture as clearly as Charlie's face right in front of him.

'Simon? The crèche?'

'Lowe was right. The baby changing unit's next to the bog. There's a closed door in between it and the main part of the crèche. Hiding anything in the unit would've been a piece of piss.'

Charlie nodded. She felt as if she had embarked upon a long, slow convalescence from a serious illness. She had been torn to pieces and she had only two choices: disintegrate further or fight to rebuild her equilibrium. She chose the latter. Simon didn't love her and he never would. She didn't know why he'd rejected her at Sellers' party, or if he'd told some or all of their colleagues about the incident, and she never would. There was something comforting about accepting, finally, that certain things were beyond her control.

Others weren't. Charlie knew, when she was able to be rational about it, that her value as a person was unrelated to Simon's opinion of her. She had been a confident woman before he came along, and she could be one again. And until she was, however desolate she felt, she would behave well. She would be friendly to Simon, instead of dismissing his suggestions simply because they were his. Charlie hoped she wasn't so much of a pillock that she would let a man who didn't appreciate her fuck up her work, the one thing she'd always known she was good at.

'That's how Beer and Lowe got in.' Simon pointed at the door that led out on to Alder Street. 'It's where I came in when I met Alice Fancourt. Both times.'

'Right. So Beer used the health club without paying, and he hid the knife he used to kill Cryer in the crèche. Is that what we're saying? Is that *all* we're saying?'

Simon hadn't decided yet whether he wanted to tell Charlie some, all or none of what he'd found out. Certainly not all. But if he gave her only a partial account, she might make a phone call herself and find out the rest. Shit. He hated feeling so cornered.

'Beer and Lowe called Vivienne Fancourt Lady Muck,' he said. 'She used to listen to them bragging about their many run-ins with the law. She'd have known Beer's DNA would be on our database, she's not stupid. She wanted Cryer dead because Cryer was restricting her access to her grandson, but she wasn't prepared to take the risk of killing her unless she could be sure she wouldn't get caught. What better way of making sure than framing someone, planting physical evidence of that person at the scene? Especially when that someone's a scrote the police already know.'

'So, what, one day she leaned over in the Jacuzzi and pulled out a clump of Beer's hair?'

'What's the one thing everyone has with them all the time in a place like Waterfront? Come on, swimming, Jacuzzi, sauna – what would you take with you?'

'Fags.'

'A towel,' said Simon. 'All Vivienne would have had to do is swap her towel for Beer's. Or wait until he discarded his and pick it up. It would have had his hair and skin all over it.'

'He could easily have seen her,' said Charlie. 'What if he

left his towel in a locker in the changing rooms and didn't take it to the pool area with him?'

'What if he did take it with him?' Simon persisted. 'What if Vivienne watched him for weeks, months, while she thought up her plan? She'd have known his habits, wouldn't she? She could have worked out the best time to take his towel.' Please let her go for this, he prayed. He couldn't bring himself to reveal the rest, though he knew he'd have to eventually. Unless Vivienne Fancourt were to confess – and why the hell would she?

'This is all speculative.' Charlie sighed.

'I know.' Simon's mouth was a hard, determined line. 'But while we're here, we might as well see what the set-up is with the towels.'

Charlie shrugged, then nodded. It was worth a look, she supposed.

'David and Vivienne Fancourt must have been bloody thrilled when Beer pleaded guilty,' Simon muttered.

'You're assuming they were in it together, then?' He was assuming an awful lot, and Charlie knew she was indulging him. Shit. Would she have gone along with Sellers or Gibbs so readily if they'd wanted to explore a similarly unprovable hunch? Was this the good behaviour she was aiming for with regard to Simon, or special treatment? 'Even if you're right, it's just a guess,' she said. 'There's no evidence.'

Simon's eyes blazed with purpose. He wasn't listening. 'I'm going to find Alice today,' he said.

Charlie thought about the clothes, shoes, car and cash cards Alice had not taken with her. And all Florence's things, left behind at The Elms. She feared the worst. 'You're in love with her, aren't you?' she said. It was all right to say this, she thought. As a friend. 'You might not have been before, but you are now. You fell in love with her after she disappeared. *That* was what made her your perfect woman.' She felt a few missing pieces slot into the jigsaw puzzle in her mind as she spoke.

'We've got work to do,' said Simon curtly. 'It's down in the lift to get to the swimming pool.'

Charlie followed him into a carpeted internal corridor that contained a buzzing sound and the smell of lilies. A brass sign opposite them said 'Main Reception' above a black arrow. They walked side by side in the direction indicated, saying nothing. Charlie's mind was racing, filling in the details of her new theory. Simon, bright red in the face, carefully avoided her eye. She had to be right. He didn't want a woman in his life, not really. He wanted a fantasy, someone imagined and inaccessible. What could be better than a missing woman?

She followed him into the lift, which was mirrored from waist to head height on three of its four sides, and pressed the button marked 'LG'. It was even harder, in here, for Charlie and Simon not to look at one another. The journey from the ground floor to the lower ground floor seemed to take impossibly long. Charlie became aware, at one point, that she was holding her breath. Now she knew what it felt like to be trapped in a lift, and the damn thing wasn't even stuck.

It was a relief to emerge, finally. Another carpeted corridor. This time the sign opposite them said 'Swimming pool', above another helpful black arrow. Charlie heard echoey splashes, a low bubbling, a hum that vibrated under her feet. 'Here we are,' she said.

To their left, there were two doors. One said 'Ladies Changing' and the other 'Gentlemen Changing'. 'Presumably those lead straight through to the pool area,' said

Simon. 'Bloody hell, any idiot could get in. You'd think they'd tighten up their security.'

Charlie shrugged. 'I doubt it'd occur to many people to try and sneak in to a health club without paying the membership fees. I mean, you'd just assume you wouldn't be able to. My sister's health club's like Fort Knox. You need a little card thingy or the barrier won't open.'

'Look.' Simon pointed to a large wooden sideboard directly in front of them. On top of it, white towels were piled high on one side. On the other there was a big, square hole. 'Is that what I think it is?'

'A towel bin.' As Charlie spoke, the door that was labelled 'Ladies Changing' opened, and a woman emerged with wet hair, carrying a crumpled towel in one hand and a pink Nike sports bag in the other. Her head was crooked, trapping a pink mobile phone between her shoulder and her ear. '. . . bloody pool and showers were freezing!' she said, irate. 'One of the boilers is broken. I'm going to ask for a discount on next month's membership if they haven't got it sorted by tomorrow.' She dropped her towel into the square hole. It didn't fall very far; the used towels were piled too high already. The woman tutted and walked towards the stairs, now holding her phone in her hand, still complaining loudly.

'All I'd need to do is reach in and pick up the towel she's just dropped,' said Simon, 'and I could frame her for murder.'

Charlie knew he was right. Right that it was possible; not necessarily that it was what had happened.

'Simon, are you a virgin?' she asked.

# 35

## Thursday October 2, 2003

I am in the kitchen, clutching the tape in my right hand. I cannot believe that my idea, born out of desperation, worked. It did not for a minute occur to David that I was bluffing. My handbag is on the kitchen work surface beneath the back window, next to my keys, mobile phone and watch – all my confiscated possessions. I pick up my watch and put it on, half expecting an alarm to start wailing. I am wondering whether I should put the tape in my bag, hide it somewhere else or destroy it, when I hear breathing behind me.

I curl my hand around the tape and turn. Vivienne is standing about a foot in front of me. I wonder if she was about to touch me. She is wearing her long, navy dressing gown over white silk pyjamas. Her skin is shiny from the night cream she uses, the best that Waterfront's beauty salon has to offer. Her face is greasy, white and spectral. 'What are you doing?' she asks. I don't normally come downstairs after Vivienne has gone to bed. Nobody does. She can't sleep if she thinks anybody else is still up. It is one of the many unwritten rules of life at The Elms. This change in my normal pattern has alerted her to a possible danger.

I decide to use a Vivienne tactic, to answer a question with a question. 'Are you nervous about tomorrow?' She is disconcerted by my prying into her psyche. She is the one who asks, always. 'I mean, it's easier for me,' I continue, my heart leaping up into my mouth with every beat. 'I know what the test result will be. You don't. It must be hard for you. Waiting. Not knowing.' Were it not for my triumph over David, I would not dare to say any of this. It is as if the pilot light of my confidence has suddenly been lit again, though the flame is still a faint, low one.

Her eyes glint. Vivienne is a proud woman. She hates to have it pointed out to her that she is at a disadvantage. 'I'll know soon enough,' she says. Then, as if suddenly aware she has admitted to uncertainty, she adds, 'David is my son. I believe him. You've not been yourself, Alice. You know that.'

'Why do you call her "the baby" if you believe David? You haven't called her Florence once, have you, since you got back from Florida? You don't cuddle her. You supervise her, but you don't touch her.'

Vivienne's tongue flicks out to moisten her lips. She tries to smile again but it is even harder for her this time. 'I was trying to be tactful,' she says. 'I didn't want to upset you.'

'That's not true. Deep down, you can't quite bring yourself to dismiss what I'm saying, can you? I'm Florence's mother. You know what it means to be a mother. And you've always liked and trusted me. You call Little Face "the baby" because, like me, you don't know who she is. And you're terrified of tomorrow morning. Because pretty soon, you'll have to face the truth that I faced last Friday – Florence is missing. The denial you're in at the moment, that's going to end.'

'That's nothing but psychobabble,' she spits, the tendons in her clenched fists sticking out like ropes.

'I'm going to miss Little Face,' I whisper. 'When we have to give her back.'

'Give her back?' Vivienne looks flustered.

'To the police. Well, we won't be allowed to keep her, will we? Not once the police know she's not ours. They'll take her away. We'll have no baby at all.' My voice wobbles.

Vivienne lunges at me and pushes me hard in the chest with both her hands. I cry out in surprise before losing my balance. My shoulder bangs against the top of the oven as I fall to the floor. For a few minutes I cannot move for the pain. I curl up on my side.

Vivienne hovers above me, bending down. I can smell her face cream, its sharp lily of the valley scent. 'This is all your fault!' she screams. The sound of her unrestrained rage is more of a shock than her physical attack on me. I have never heard her shriek like this before. 'What sort of mother goes out on her own and leaves her newborn baby at home to be kidnapped? *What sort of mother does that?*' Her face looms over mine, her mouth a dark cave, wide open. I smell mint-flavoured toothpaste and my own sweat, my fear of her.

And then I am alone in the room, the Dictaphone tape still wrapped in my shaking hand.

# 36

## *10/10/03, 10 am*

'It isn't April the first, is it?' Inspector Giles Proust banged his mug down and picked up his desk diary, examining it in an exaggerated manner for Charlie and Simon's benefit.

Charlie noticed that the diary was another one from the foot-and-mouth charity Proust's wife worked for. Not cattle, Proust had explained years ago, but people who painted with their feet and mouths. 'No, sir,' she said now.

'Right. Didn't think it was. So this isn't a bad joke. You really want me to squander precious funds on a search of The Elms, for the sake of one handbag.'

'Yes, sir.'

'Did the two of you devise this plan in a sauna? You've spent a lot of time in such places recently. Waterhouse?'

Simon shifted in his chair. *Say something, dickhead. Tell them what you know.*

'What exactly goes on in these health club places, anyway?' asked Proust.

'Swimming, sir. And there are gyms and exercise classes. Jacuzzis, saunas, steam rooms. Some have plunge pools.'

'What are they?'

'Pools full of freezing cold water. You go in them after you've come out of the steam room or the sauna,' Charlie explained.

Proust shook his head. 'So you heat yourself up in order to cool yourself down?'

'It's good for the circulation, apparently.'

'And Jacuzzis – that's sitting around in warm, bubbly water, is it?'

Charlie nodded. 'It's very relaxing.'

Proust looked at Simon. 'Do you go in for this sort of thing, Waterhouse?'

Charlie was tempted, as usual, to butt in and answer on Simon's behalf. She stopped herself. He wasn't hers to defend. She must let Simon speak for himself, just as she would Sellers or Gibbs.

'No, sir,' he replied clearly.

'Good.'

He still hadn't answered Charlie's question, the one she'd asked him at the health club. She hadn't repeated it. Was she trying to massage the facts in order to save her ego? She didn't think so. The more she examined her suspicion, the stronger it grew. It made perfect sense. Simon had never had a girlfriend, never mentioned past flings or serious relationships. Gibbs and Sellers were always saying he was probably one of those asexual people, like that comedian Stephen Fry, or was it Morrissey?

He had to be a virgin. He was scared of sex, scared to reveal his inexperience to anyone. That was why he'd run away, at Sellers' party, why he couldn't allow himself to become romantically involved with anybody. The absent Alice Fancourt was ideal for him. Whatever Simon felt for her, it would have to remain theoretical. If I disappeared suddenly, maybe he'd fall in love with me, Charlie thought. Then she remembered another resolution she'd made: don't think about him when you're supposed to be thinking about work.

'Sir, if we had a search warrant . . .' she began.

'Sorry, sergeant. I'm not convinced. It could be a coincidence, Beer sitting in the same warm water as Vivienne Fancourt. Sellers and Gibbs have been back to speak to him again and he's still saying he killed Laura Cryer. Why would he say it if he didn't do it?'

'He's scared of more jail time?' said Charlie. 'It's not going to go down well if he admits he perjured himself to get a reduced sentence. Or he could be scared of what's waiting for him on the Winstanley estate. Same people who used to protect him'll be out for his blood now, won't they?'

'Beer seems to have become attached to the idea of Laura Cryer,' said Simon, playing for time. 'He's got a thing about her. When I talked to him, I got the impression that he imagines there's a sort of . . . bond between them. Maybe to admit he didn't kill her would sever the bond, in his mind.'

Proust snorted. 'Very deep, Waterhouse. Very *psychological*. Look, a knife forensics say could well be the one that killed Cryer has just turned up in a hiding place we know Beer used.' Charlie opened her mouth to speak. Proust raised a hand to silence her. 'Even if you're right, if David and Vivienne Fancourt killed Cryer and framed Beer, the chances of a search of The Elms turning up the handbag after all this time is negligible.'

'Some killers keep souvenirs,' said Charlie. 'Especially if the murder was personal, if their victim meant something to them.'

Proust looked rattled, all of a sudden. 'Why do I have to be bothered with this?' he snapped. 'Interview Vivienne and David Fancourt, get them to talk. Why is the option that first occurs to you the one that involves time and money I can't afford?'

Here we go, thought Simon. Another Proust oratory.

'Do you know how impossible my working life is? Does either of you have a clue? No. I thought not. Well, let me tell you. I come in at the beginning of every shift with a list of things to do, carried over from the previous day. The trouble is, before I have a chance to start doing any of them, more things appear out of nowhere – paperwork, idiots causing problems for no reason, people needing to *see* me and *talk* to me.' He winced, evidently of the view that both these needs were staggering in their depravity. 'That's what it means to be a detective inspector. It's like standing in front of a burst dam and being pushed backwards. Every day I go home with a longer list than the one I came in with. At least I can now put a line through one item: Mandy Buckley.'

Charlie looked up expectantly.

'We'll wait a while and hope she reappears. Sorry, sergeant. I consulted a few people, and the consensus was that we couldn't justify any expense in that direction. It's not as if we've got any reason to suspect her of anything.'

Charlie couldn't bring herself to agree. I'm becoming as hunch-driven as Simon, she thought ruefully.

Simon cleared his throat and leaned forward. 'Sir, Charlie, there's something I haven't told you.'

The Snowman groaned. 'My heart's sinking fast, Water-house. What is it? As for your not having told us, let's save our discussion of that for the disciplinary proceedings. Well?'

Simon could feel Charlie's anxious stare burning into him. 'Felix Fancourt's school, Stanley Sidgwick. Alice told me Vivienne put Florence's name down before she was even born. You have to, apparently, it's so over-subscribed. There's a years-long waiting list, for the boys' grammar and the ladies' college.'

'And?' Proust demanded. 'This is CID, not Offsted. What's your point?'

'When I spoke to Laura's parents, her dad told me that straight after her death, Vivienne took Felix out of the nursery he was at and started him at Stanley Sidgwick. But how could she have, if his name wasn't down already? They wouldn't have had a free place. And if his name *was* down already . . . well, how did Vivienne Fancourt know it would be up to her to decide which school to send Felix to?'

'Fuck!' Charlie muttered. Simon's brain never ceased to amaze her. He missed nothing.

'I figured she *must* have put his name down, and I wondered how long ago. Maybe she'd been planning Laura's murder for years. On the other hand, I thought, maybe she reserved his place before he was born, like she did for Florence, in the hope that Laura would see sense and send him there. But then, if Felix hadn't taken up his place when he reached the appropriate age, the school would have allocated it to someone else.'

'They'd have had to,' said Charlie.

Proust ran his index finger around the rim of his mug, saying nothing.

'I phoned Stanley Sidgwick Grammar this morning,' said Simon. 'Vivienne *did* register Felix before he was born. He was due to start in the lower kindergarten year at the beginning of September 1999, when he was two. They start in the year they turn three.'

'That's far too young,' Proust snapped. 'My children were at home until they were almost five.'

I bet you weren't, though, thought Charlie. Lizzie, Proust's wife, will have been the one stuck at home scraping the squashed Weetabix off the carpet.

Simon ignored the interruption. 'Felix *didn't* start at

Stanley Sidgwick in September 1999. Laura was still alive and had no intention of sending him there. But his place wasn't given to anyone else, despite the long waiting list.'

'What?' Proust frowned.

'Why not?' asked Charlie.

'Because Vivienne Fancourt paid the fees from September 1999, just as if Felix were attending the school. Her argument, apparently, was that if she was willing to pay, they had to keep Felix's place open. And in November 1999, she told the school admissions secretary, Sally Hunt, that Felix *would* start, definitely, in January 2001, at the beginning of the spring term. Laura was murdered in December 2000.' Simon exhaled slowly. That was enough for them to be getting on with. They would think he'd told them everything.

'Fuck!' Charlie shook her head. 'She knew, over a year before, that she was going to kill Laura, and she knew when. Why did she wait so long?'

Simon shrugged. 'Maybe it's no so long, when you're planning a murder. She'd never killed before, she'd have had to get mentally prepared. Also . . . maybe there was some pleasurable anticipation involved. Whenever she saw Laura, during those tense access visits when Laura appeared to have all the power, Vivienne could gloat secretly.'

Proust slapped his palms down on the desk. 'As I said before: interview Vivienne Fancourt. Get her to talk. With everything we've got, we can make her hand over Cryer's handbag, if she's got it. She'll probably confess within minutes.'

'I don't think so,' said Charlie. 'You've not met her.' He never met anyone. She sometimes thought that all The Snowman knew of the world was what she and Lizzie, his agents in the field, told him. 'Vivienne Fancourt isn't scared of me and Simon.' She turned to Simon for support. 'Is she?' He shrugged. They hadn't yet accused her of murder, he was thinking, or of framing an innocent man. 'Oh, come on, you know what she's like. She thinks we're a pair of stupid kids,' said Charlie.

*You know what she's like.* Where had Simon heard that phrase, or something similar? It had seemed odd to him at the time, he remembered, but he couldn't recall the speaker, the subject or the context. He frowned, trying to retrieve the memory.

Charlie tapped her knees impatiently. 'Sir, it occurs to me . . .'

'Does this involve towels?'

'No.'

'I'm glad to hear it.'

'Sir, you're about Vivienne Fancourt's age. You're a senior officer. She thinks she can handle Simon and me, and we're much younger than she is. But if you came along . . . No offence, sir, but you can be pretty bloody scary when you want to be.'

'Me?' Proust was aghast. He gripped the edge of his desk with both hands. 'You're not suggesting that *I* talk to her?'

'I think it's a brilliant idea.' Charlie leaned forward in her chair. 'You could do your dry ice act, it'd really put the wind up her. Sir, you're the only one of the three of us who stands a chance of getting a confession out of her. Your persuasive powers are impossible to resist.'

Proust only noticed and disapproved of flattery when it was directed at people other than himself. 'Well, I'm not sure . . . and I'm also not sure what you mean by "my dry ice act".'

'Please, sir. It might really make a difference. Vivienne Fancourt's used to me by now. If the three of us go . . .'

Charlie stopped. A few days ago, she'd have been too proud and stubborn to ask for Proust's help. She was irritated, briefly, by the thought that she might be becoming more mature. Why should she become a better person when no-one else ever did? Simon didn't. Proust certainly didn't.

'The two of you,' said Simon. 'I won't be coming.' There was somewhere else he needed to go. *You know what Alice is like*. Except that, for the first time since he'd seen her at the top of the stairs, Simon wasn't at all sure he did.

# 37

## *Friday October 3, 2003*

I tiptoe into the nursery, leaving the door slightly ajar. David has not woken up, neither has Vivienne. Nobody has heard me. Yet. I must be quick, as quick as I can be without making any stupid mistakes. The painted eyes of the wooden rocking horse watch me as I cross the room. I approach the cot nervously, half expecting to find Little Face gone, to see nothing but bedding and cuddly toys when I look down. Another of David's cruel jokes.

Thankfully, she is there, where she should be. Her cheeks look warm in the glow of her Winnie-the-Pooh night light. I can tell from her breathing that she is deeply asleep. Now is as good a time as any. And it has to be now.

I pull the Moses basket out from beneath the cot. It already has a sheet and blanket in it. Apart from this I am taking nothing – no clothes, no accessories, not even a bottle of formula milk. I do not want my departure to look planned. All the books I read when I was pregnant said that leaving the house with a small baby feels like a major expedition, because of the amount of luggage you have to take with you. This is not necessarily true, not if one is adequately prepared, and I am. Everything Little Face and I need will be waiting for us in Combingham.

I lift her tiny sleeping body and place her gently in the Moses basket, tucking her in with the yellow blanket. Then, as quietly as possible, I tiptoe out of the nursery and down the stairs, still in my nightie and wearing slippers instead of shoes, so that I make no noise as I walk through the house.

I do not put on my coat. To be outside in the cold for a few minutes in only a cotton nightie will be nothing compared with what I have been through this week. It will be easy. My coat will be found tomorrow morning, on the stand in the hall. I go to the kitchen, pick up my keys that are still on the work surface under the window, and unlock the back door. The front door is too thick and heavy. Opening and closing it would make too much noise.

Once Little Face and I are outside, I lock the kitchen door. I am shivering hard, but I don't know if it's the cold or my nerves. Setting the Moses basket down on the wet grass for a second, I stand on tiptoes and drop my keys in through the open window. They land in exactly the right place, beside my handbag and phone. When Vivienne reports me missing, the police will think it is significant that all my possessions are still at The Elms. It will make them more likely to believe that I did not leave here of my own accord, that some harm must have come to me. I do not feel guilty for misleading them. More harm has come to me than I would have believed possible a few months ago.

There would be no point taking my bag, in any case. If I use my cash or credit card I will be found almost immediately, before the police have a chance to begin their investigation.

I pick up the Moses basket and walk round the house. Wet grass tickles my bare ankles as I cross the lawn to reach the path. I pause for a second in front of the house and look straight ahead of me at the iron gate in the distance. Then I start to walk, accelerating gradually, feeling like an aeroplane on a runway.

I pass my car on the way to the road. I hate to leave it, but cars are too easy to track down. It's only metal and paint, I say to myself, trying not to cry. If my parents are watching me from wherever they are, I know they will understand. I hope they are not. They had a happy life, and I would rather death were the end than have them alive in spirit somewhere, fearing for me in the way that I fear for Florence. When your spirit is consumed by fear and uncertainty, it starts to die.

As soon as I am on the other side of the gate, I feel lighter, as if a rock has been lifted from my back. It is odd to think that most people are asleep now, while Little Face and I are waiting in the shadows by the side of the road. I wonder how many nights I have slept soundly, oblivious, while, not too far away, strangers have tiptoed through the darkness towards an uncertain future.

I wait behind a tree with a sturdy trunk, the Moses basket at my feet. Little Face is still asleep, thank goodness. She always is at this time. Another hour and she will be close to waking up, her body telling her it's time for her next bottle. David doesn't know that most nights I also wake up as soon as she murmurs, that I know the workings of her body clock as well as he does.

I look down the road in the direction of Rawndesley. I can see cars, because the road is lit, but their drivers are unlikely to see me in this dark space between Vivienne's fence and the row of tree trunks. I look at my watch. It is exactly one-thirty am. Any minute now. Not much longer to wait. At that moment, I see the Red Fiat Punto approaching. It slows down as it gets closer.

Our lift has arrived.

# 38

## 10/10/03, 11 am

Charlie hoped she hadn't made a mistake, asking Proust to come with her. He'd done nothing wrong – not yet, they weren't even there yet – but she already resented the inspector's presence. She missed Simon. Purely as a colleague, in this instance. The two of them had interviewed together many times, knew the routine, how to read one another's cues.

She felt nervous as she and Proust drove to The Elms in Proust's Renault Laguna. She couldn't stop sneaking little looks at The Snowman out of the corner of her eye. He was doing fine so far. He seemed calm, undaunted. Still, Charlie felt as if she were in sole charge of an unpredictable toddler. Things could take a turn for the worse at any moment.

She wished he'd put the radio on. She'd suggested it once, on the way to a conference a long time ago, and the inspector had given her a lecture about the foolhardiness of listening to anything when you were driving apart from the engine, in case you missed the sound of impending danger – a faint rumble from under the bonnet auguring an imminent explosion. Proust bought a new car every two years, and subjected his vehicle of the moment to more services than an evangelical church.

They arrived at The Elms, drove in through the open iron gates. Charlie half expected them to snap shut, like metal teeth, behind her. There was something too rigid about the perfectly straight, narrow path that led all the way from the road to the big white cube of house at the end. No turning back, it seemed to say. Too many trees at the front of the house stalked the trim lawn, darkening it with their shadows.

They rang the doorbell and waited. Charlie concealed a smile behind her hand when she noticed Proust adjusting his jacket, trying to look as if he wasn't.

David Fancourt answered the door. He looked thinner, but was as smartly dressed as he had been when Charlie last saw him, in beige trousers and a navy blue shirt. 'I don't suppose you've got any news,' he said sullenly.

'Not yet. I'm sorry. You've met Detective Inspector Proust.' The two men nodded at one another.

'Is it the police?' Charlie heard Vivienne call out. Before David had a chance to answer, his mother appeared beside him. In one smooth, subtle movement, she elbowed him aside, took his place.

David shrugged and stood back. His eyes were dull. He didn't care who stood in front of whom. Charlie had seen this many times before. Relatives of the missing gave up hope after a while, or pretended to. Perhaps they couldn't bear the pity they saw in the eyes of the police officers who came to the door week after week, month after month, with no news. Charlie could imagine how one might decide, in that situation, to present a resigned front to the world. There was nothing more patronising than being let down gently.

She was as sure as she'd ever been that David Fancourt had no idea where his wife and daughter were. His mother, on the other hand . . .

Something about the look on Vivienne Fancourt's face

when she saw Proust made Charlie decide not to say anything, to wait. The inspector looked blank but officious. Charlie tried to imitate his expression, knowing she would hate to have it directed at her. It was a glare that gave nothing to its recipient: no information, no comfort.

'David, could you leave us for a minute, please?' said Vivienne after a few seconds.

'Why? My daughter's missing . . .'

'This isn't about Florence. Is it?' She looked at Charlie.

'No.'

'Then what's it about?'

'David. Please.'

Fancourt sighed, then retreated.

'You know, don't you?' said Vivienne.

Charlie nodded, battling against a sensation of unreality. It couldn't be this easy. It never was. Well, it sometimes was, but not now, for God's sake, not with Proust as a witness. The inspector shuffled his feet, adjusting his position slightly. Charlie knew he was as surprised as she was, could guess what he was thinking. This was the difficult interview he'd been brought along to help with? A woman so keen to confess that she does it on the doorstep? On the way back he would say, 'There's nothing to it, is there?' or something equally maddening.

'You'd better come in.'

Charlie and Proust followed Vivienne to the room she called 'the little lounge', the one that contained the framed photograph of David and Alice's wedding. Charlie hadn't been able to get the picture out of her mind, for some reason. Jealousy, probably.

Nobody sat down.

'If you're going to charge me, I'd rather you got it over with.'

'Charge you with . . . ?' Charlie let the question hang in the air. She didn't like the feel of this at all.

'Abduction,' said Vivienne impatiently.

'You know where Florence is,' said Charlie. Proust listened in silence, his hands behind his back.

'Of course not. What are you talking about?'

'Abduction, you said . . .'

'I didn't abduct *Florence*.' Vivienne was getting angry, as if Charlie was stupidly lagging behind.

'You abducted the . . . other baby?' Charlie still wasn't sure she believed in this mythical 'other' baby. So what was she talking about? Get back in control, she ordered herself. Take the reins.

'You *don't* know, do you?' said Vivienne, a superior sneer on her face.

'Why have you never mentioned to any police officer the fact that you regularly used to see Darryl Beer at your health club?'

No flicker of fear. Damn. Vivienne looked surprised. 'Why would I mention it?'

'So you did see him?'

'Yes. But I didn't think anything of it. I see plenty of people there.'

'What if I were to put it to you that you killed Laura Cryer, that you framed Beer?'

Vivienne turned angrily to Proust. 'Is this some sort of joke, inspector? Me, frame someone for murder? I'm awaiting news of my granddaughter and this is all you've got to say to me?'

'What if I said we could prove it?' Charlie spoke before Proust had a chance to.

'I would say you must be mistaken,' said Vivienne coldly. 'Since the events you are describing did not take place, you can't possibly prove that they did.'

'You took his towel from the swimming area. You removed hair and skin from it, and you scattered that hair and skin over Laura Cryer's body, after you'd killed her.'

Vivienne almost smiled. It turned into an incredulous frown at the last minute. 'You can't honestly believe that,' she said.

Charlie stared at her. Even an innocent person would be nervous by now, surely.

'You told the secretary at Stanley Sidgwick Grammar School, in November 1999, that Felix would be starting in January 2001. How did you know he would? Laura wouldn't have agreed to it. Felix was happily settled in a nursery local to her and she wanted him to stay there. So you must have known she'd be out of the way by then.'

Vivienne laughed. 'You *have* got a vivid imagination, sergeant. Actually, Laura did agree to it. True, she wasn't keen at first, but eventually I succeeded in persuading her. Felix would have enrolled at Stanley Sidgwick in January 2001 whether Laura was alive or dead.'

'You didn't persuade her,' said Charlie. 'What you did was murder her. She hated you, you told me so yourself. Why would she be persuaded by anything you said?'

'Perhaps because I was offering to pay the fees and it's the best school in the country,' said Vivienne patiently. 'Only a fool would turn down an offer like that, and Laura was no fool.'

Charlie wanted to scream. It was just about possible. With Laura dead, Charlie couldn't prove Vivienne was lying. She'd met the type before: people who had such unmitigated contempt for everyone but themselves that

307

they were prepared to stand there and tell the feeblest lies, straight-faced, without even bothering to make them plausible. It's a shitty, pathetic lie, but it's good enough for the likes of you: that was the attitude.

'Shall we go back to the abduction?' said Proust coldly. Charlie wondered what he was thinking.

'Indirectly, I was the cause of Laura's death, that I will concede,' said Vivienne. 'On the night of her murder, I collected Felix from nursery. Without Laura's permission. She would never have given her permission, and I was sick to the back teeth of never seeing my grandson properly or alone. So I kidnapped him. It was breathtakingly easy. The teenagers at his nursery handed him over without a murmur. Wretched place,' she muttered. 'I am aware that what I did is probably against the law, and that if I hadn't done it, Laura wouldn't have come here on the night she was killed. She'd be alive today. She came to recover her son from his wicked grandmother – that was what she thought of me. I wouldn't let her take him, wouldn't let her in. She didn't even come into the house that night, sergeant. So, arrest me for lying to the police, arrest me for taking Felix by all means, but I refuse to accept moral responsibility for Laura's murder. It was her own unreasonable behaviour that drove me to act as I did.' She stuck out her chin in defiance, proud of her speech, the principled stand she had taken.

'Where are Alice and Florence?' asked Proust. 'You know where they are, don't you?'

'No, I don't.'

'May we search your property?' asked Charlie.

'Yes. Am I allowed to ask why you feel the need to?' Her voice hardened into sarcasm. 'I still have Felix, if it's he you're looking for. He lives here now. Legally. Legitimately.' She smoothed down her skirt. 'If that's all, I'll leave you to show yourselves out. I'm due at my health club for a manicure in fifteen minutes. I advise you to stop inventing preposterous theories and get on with finding my granddaughter,' she said quietly on her way out of the room.

Charlie clamped her jaw shut. Why did she always end up feeling like a naughty schoolgirl whenever she spoke to this woman? And she could do without the look Proust was giving her, the one that told her how spectacularly he thought she'd fucked up. 'What now, sergeant?' he said.

It was a bloody good question.

# 39

## *Friday October 10, 2003*

The doorbell rings. Little Face and I are in the kitchen. It is the room in which we are least likely to be seen. There is a door with a frosted glass panel and only one window which is on the side of the house, facing a path, a fence and some trees. I am sitting in an armchair, facing away from the window.

My appearance has changed considerably since I left The Elms. My hair is not long and blonde any more, it is dark brown and short. I now wear glasses I don't need and the sort of obtrusive make-up I haven't worn since I was a teenager. I look a little like Simon's heartless sergeant. It is probably an unnecessary precaution, but it makes me feel safer. There is always a chance that a window-cleaner or passer-by might catch a glimpse of me. By now my picture has been all over the news for days.

Little Face sits in a bouncy chair beside me, asleep. The sound of the bell, so loud and significant to me, doesn't disturb her. She doesn't stir.

Automatically, I get up and close the door between the kitchen and the hall. I listen as footsteps descend the stairs. This routine has been practised many times. We call it our 'fire drill'.

So far, the visitors to the house have been easy to process and send on their way. On Monday, somebody came to read the gas meter. Yesterday the postman delivered a parcel that needed to be signed for. If Little Face and I are in the house alone, I do not answer the door, and, since nobody knows I am here, no-one expects me to. The redecoration ruse has succeeded, so far, in keeping friends and family away.

I press my ear against the door and listen.

'Detective Constable Waterhouse. This is a surprise.'

'Can I come in?'

'Looks like you just have. Don't mind me, will you?'

Simon is here. At the front door, just as he was exactly a fortnight ago, except this is a different house. I am not as frightened as I thought I might be. Of course, I have imagined this situation, exactly as it is happening now, many times. I knew he would find me eventually. When a mother goes missing with a tiny baby, people are interviewed more than once. It is appropriate procedure, no more and no less. I will not panic until I have to. Simon cannot come into the kitchen, not unless he has a search warrant.

I wonder how much time I have left, how long before I will have to leave by the back door and make my way, with Little Face, to the car, which is parked on the next street. The agreed emergency procedure.

I don't want to leave. This house feels more welcoming than The Elms has for a long time. Little Face and I have a bedroom at the back which is not overlooked. The walls are a pale yellow, with jagged white patches here and there where the paint has come off. I suspect it used to be a teenager's bedroom and the white marks on the walls are where posters of favourite bands were torn down before the house's previous owners moved out. The carpet is dark green, and there is a burn mark in one corner, near the window – an illicit cigarette dropped by mistake.

Despite these traces of a previous tenant, I already think of the room as belonging to me and Little Face. It is packed full of everything we need. Bottles, clothes, blankets, nappies, muslin squares, boxes of formula milk, both the powder and the ready-made variety, a steam steriliser, a travel cot – everything on my list was here when we arrived. We don't have much space, certainly not compared with our extravagant accommodation at The Elms, but it's warm and homely. A kind, innocent air pervades the whole house.

I think I was always aware, deep down, that The Elms had a dark, stultifying atmosphere, long before I was personally unhappy there. Perhaps I sensed the presence of unspeakable things, or perhaps it is merely hindsight, but I feel as if I must always have known that it was a house with an ulterior motive. I remember vividly the conversation David and I had when he suggested that we move in to his childhood home, his mother's childhood home. We were in the conservatory. Vivienne had left us alone while she made coffee.

I laughed at first. 'Don't be silly. We can't live with your mum.'

'Silly?' I heard an edge in his voice and saw a look in his eyes that alarmed me, as if in that instant the David I knew and loved had vanished and been replaced by an entirely different person. I wanted that person to go away, and for David to come back, so I quickly backtracked, pretended that he had misunderstood me.

'I just meant, surely she wouldn't want us here. Would she?'

'Of course,' said David. 'She'd love to have us. She's said so lots of times.'

'Oh. Oh, well . . . great!' I said, as enthusiastically as I could. David beamed at me, and I was so happy and relieved that I told myself it didn't matter where we lived, as long as we were together. I never again suggested that anything David said was silly. It's funny, I've never thought about this incident until now. Were there other warning signs that I ignored, ones that will come back to me over time, in flashes of horror?

'Not at work today?'

'I never am, on a Friday.'

The words grow fainter. I tiptoe over to the radio and turn it off.

'So. How can I help you?'

'Don't talk to me as if I'm a fucking idiot. If you'd wanted to help me you could have done so a while ago. Couldn't you?'

My legs go weak, as if my bones have suddenly dissolved. I wrap my arms around myself to stop my body from shaking.

'What? Are you accusing me of withholding some information? What exactly am I supposed to know?'

'Spare me the bullshit. No wonder you didn't seem all that worried about Alice, when I told you she was missing. You know damn well where she is. I should have known last Saturday, as soon as you said, "You know what Alice is like." Fucked up there, didn't you? You had no way of knowing I'd ever met her, unless you'd seen her since last week. You were also the first person who mentioned Vivienne Fancourt to me in a negative context. Very keen to get that point across, weren't you?'

'Vivienne? What's she got to do with this?'

'You know the answer to that as well as I do. Has it occurred to you that we might both be on the same side?'

I should be on my way out of the door with Little Face. I

have heard enough to convince me that Simon knows if not everything then at least enough. Any minute now he might ask to look round the house. I can't understand why I am not sticking to the agreed policy. Just because Simon says that we are all on the same side does not make it true. Haven't I learned, even now, that words can be used to create illusions, to set traps?

'What do you mean?'

'You want to protect Alice from Vivienne. So do I. And Florence. You didn't seem worried about Alice on Saturday, but you were certainly worried about Florence, weren't you? Because when Alice ran away, she came here. She told you Florence was missing, that someone had taken her and left another baby in her place. She probably also told you the police didn't believe her, weren't making any attempt to find her daughter. Did Alice bring the other baby with her, when she came here?'

'I don't know what you're talking about.'

'Yeah, you do. Why do you think she brought her, this baby who wasn't her daughter? Why didn't she leave her at The Elms?'

'You're barking up the wrong tree.'

'Because she was scared of what David or Vivienne would do to her? Would either of them harm a defenceless baby? I don't think so. Do you? Or perhaps it was because, once that baby was missing, we'd have to look for Florence. Why do you think it was?'

There is silence. She doesn't know. Neither does Simon. I am the only person who knows the answer to that question. I am taut, rigid with apprehension, barely able to believe this conversation is taking place.

'Where are Alice and the baby?'

'I've no idea.'

'I'll be back with a search warrant. Sure, they can sneak off in the meantime, but where will they go? It's been all over the news, this case. Everyone's on the lookout for a woman with a young baby.'

He is right. It has also been suggested on the news that my appearance might have changed.

'Stubborn, aren't you? Look, I'm pissed off that you lied to me, but like I said, we're on the same side. So here's what I'm going to do. I'll tell you what I know, even though by doing so I'll be risking my job.'

Oh, thank you, thank you!

'Not for the first time, I suspect.'

'What the fuck's that supposed to mean?'

'I can imagine you always thinking you know best, no matter what anyone else says.'

'Yeah, well. What everyone else says is overrated.'

'So you're going to tell me what you know? Even though it's against the rules? I'm honoured.'

'Don't fuck with me, all right?'

No, don't, I agree silently. Now is the time to co-operate. It's my only hope, mine and Florence's. That is becoming increasingly apparent.

'In return, I hope – I really fucking hope – that you'll start making my life easier instead of harder. Think about what Alice would want you to do at this point. She's needed my help for a while, and yours, to nail Vivienne Fancourt.'

'Nail? Sorry?'

'Fuck it! We think . . . I think Vivienne Fancourt killed Laura Cryer. Darryl Beer – he's the one who's in prison, who confessed to the murder – he used to spend time in a health club called Waterfront. Vivienne Fancourt's a member. We think she framed Beer by planting physical evidence at the scene, evidence she got from a towel Beer had used at the club.'

'Right. Right.'

I nod, although no-one can see me. The words, the details, are new to me, but I recognise this as the story I have wanted Simon to tell, ever since I first saw him. I couldn't tell it on my own.

'Since Alice went missing, we've found what we believe to be the murder weapon, a kitchen knife. It was in the crèche at Waterfront, in the baby changing unit. Beer and a mate of his, Vinny Lowe, used the unit as a store, mainly for drugs. We have good reason to suspect that Vivienne Fancourt knew this. Lowe admitted he and Beer had talked about it in front of her several times. They deliberately boasted about their shitty exploits when she was listening. Beer could have put the knife in the changing unit, but so could Vivienne Fancourt, to make it look like Beer had done it. We can't prove anything. Beer's still claiming he did it.'

My eyes widen. Felix spent nearly as much time in the Cheeky Chimps crèche as he did at home, before he got too old to go there. I shudder, imagining him and all the other children playing in the same room as a knife that had been used for what was effectively an execution.

'If Alice has got anything else, any concrete proof that Vivienne killed Laura, we could do with knowing what it is. Urgently. Like, now.'

'Proof? What sort of proof?'

'Laura's handbag. Has Alice seen it, at The Elms? It's a long shot, but . . . maybe she found it somewhere she shouldn't have been looking. Was that what first made her suspect Vivienne? I need to know. The bag was never found. We could search The Elms but I wouldn't hold out much hope. People as clever as Vivienne Fancourt don't keep incriminating evidence lying around.'

'I don't understand. Sorry, I'm playing detective now. Whoever killed Laura, why didn't they hide the handbag with the knife, in the crèche? Or throw both away?'

'Vivienne wanted the knife to be found, eventually, in a place that was linked to Beer. A knife can be wiped clean and used again. Why would Beer keep the handbag, once he'd nicked the cash from it? He wouldn't. And so neither would anyone who wanted to make it look like Beer was guilty.'

I shake my head. No, that's not it. But I can't think and listen at the same time.

'So . . . are you going to search The Elms?'

'No. The boss has said no. Anyway, there's no point. I'm fairly certain Cryer's bag's long gone. We'll never find it.'

Again, I shake my head. I think of my own handbag, on the kitchen work-surface at The Elms. I picture everything inside it: my notebook full of lists of baby names, my coconut lip balm, the photograph of me with my parents, the one David threatened to tear up. If you take a woman's handbag away from her, you have power over her. What better trophy, what better symbol of an execution success-fully and justly carried out, than the victim's handbag?

Vivienne would have kept it, and not only for senti-mental reasons. She wouldn't allow a piece of evidence linking her to a murder to escape from her domain. She would keep it somewhere where she could check on it regularly to make sure it was still there, that no-one had found it or disturbed it in any way. She only feels secure if everything that matters to her is well within reach. Where, how, could she have disposed of the bag and been totally certain, as certain as she would need to be, that no trace of it would fall into somebody else's hands, that no-one had seen her?

In that instant, I know. I know where it is. I open my mouth, then close it again before any loud exclamations have a chance to escape. I would love to push open the door, run to Simon and tell him everything, but I can't. The first thing he will do, if I reveal myself, is take Little Face away. He believes me now, and I'm not yet ready to let go of her. I have to prepare myself, mentally.

I tiptoe over to the kitchen table, pick up a biro and write a short note on the dog-eared pad. Then I take the car keys that are dangling from a hook on the wall and put them in my pocket. I lift Little Face out of her bouncy chair as gently as I can, taking care not to wake her. It occurs to me that I will need to take some milk with me and there is none made up. I can't make any without washing up a bottle, which will involve turning on the hot tap. I can't risk it. The boiler here is so noisy, Simon would hear me.

I lower Little Face into the Moses basket on the floor. She is still sleeping soundly. I cannot take her with me. She's better off here. Even if Simon were to leave now, or soon, it would surely take him hours to get a search warrant, and he won't come back until he's got one. I can be back before him with the proof he needs, with Laura's bag. And I'll have had time to think, by then, of what I am going to say to him, how I am going to explain my actions.

'So why don't you tell me about the detective work you've been doing? Or should I say the acting? Pretending to be a detective.'

It is nearly impossible to drag myself away, but I must. I have to know if I am right about the handbag.

I kiss Little Face on the cheek and she rubs her lips together in her sleep, as if she is having a leisurely chew on something tasty. I hate to leave her. 'I'll be back very soon,'

I whisper in her ear. Then I unlock the back door, slip out, and lock it again behind me. I walk down the path at the side of the house and out on to the road. The wind and light assault my senses. So this is what outside smells and tastes like. I do not hurry. I know I should, but I want to savour the experience of walking down a normal residential street like an ordinary person. I feel giddy, unreal.

No-one watches me climb into the black VW Golf and pull away from the kerb. My whole body buzzes with fear, impatience, adrenaline. It is my turn to do a bit of detective work.

# 40

*10/10/03, 11.10 am*

'What's that?' Simon grimaced as a shrill, mechanical, juddering noise assaulted his ears. The whole room seemed to vibrate.

'The sodding boiler!' Briony Morris raised her eyebrows and sighed heavily. 'Apparently there's some sludge trapped in the pipes somewhere. Every time the heating comes on, this is what happens. It's never been as bad as this before, though. I'll have to get on to British Gas again. Anyway. You were saying. About me playing detective.' She crossed and uncrossed her legs.

'You admit it?'

'No point denying it, if you know.'

'Detective Sergeant Briony Morris.'

'All right, don't embarrass me. Who told you? The school secretary, presumably.'

'Sally Hunt. She was surprised I was asking, said she'd had the exact same conversation with a detective sergeant who'd phoned in early July. She remembered your name. It's not every day they get a call from CID. Or people impersonating CID.' Simon paused. 'She was surprised, but I wasn't. To find out that you'd been in touch.'

'You weren't?' Briony looked puzzled, perhaps even a little disappointed.

'I knew Alice knew. About Vivienne. At first I didn't. At first I thought I was ahead of the game, the only one who'd worked it out.' Simon's voice was full of scorn for himself. 'I just put together something Laura Cryer's father said about Vivienne starting Felix at Stanley Sidgwick as soon as Laura had died with something Alice had let slip about long waiting lists. Let slip deliberately, as it turned out.'

It had come to Simon, eventually, why he'd felt uneasy, in that interview with Vinny Lowe, staring at the photograph of Alice, David, Vivienne and Felix in the garden at The Elms. It wasn't the photo itself that had bothered him, it was where he'd first seen it: in Alice's desk at work. As soon as he remembered what else had been in the desk, everything clicked; the picture was complete.

'There was a Stanley Sidgwick brochure in Alice's desk drawer, in her office,' he told Briony. 'It had a post-it stuck to it. Alice had written on it, "Find out about F – when name down? How long waiting list?" When I first read that, I assumed F stood for Florence, dickhead that I am. Alice had told me exactly what she thought of Stanley Sidgwick Ladies' College. It was Vivienne who wanted Florence to go there, not Alice. No, F stood for Felix. Alice and David only chose the name Florence once she was born, anyway. I checked with Cheryl Dixon, Alice's midwife. And Alice hadn't been back into work since the birth, so F had to be Felix. That's when I realised: that note was a message for me, for the police. Alice knew Vivienne had killed Laura, and she wanted us to know too.'

Simon had expected resistance, but Briony nodded. 'It was Alice's idea to ring the school,' she said. 'I just did the acting because she was too shy. During her pregnancy – seeing the way Vivienne's behaviour changed towards her, her obsession with getting control over the grandchild – she became convinced that Vivienne had murdered Laura. I thought she was just being hormonal at first, even though

I'd always hated Vivienne. And Alice had always loved her – what an irony! Anyway, I just took the piss. And then one day Alice said, "Vivienne's always talking about the years-long waiting lists at Stanley Sidgwick. How come Felix was able to start the minute Laura died?" That's when I rang up, and . . .' Briony shook her head. 'It's pretty scary to realise someone you've met is a cold-blooded murderer. I tried to persuade Alice to go to the police, but she wouldn't. She said Vivienne'd just lie her way out of it, say she'd put Felix's name down to start when he started with Laura's full knowledge and permission. And with Laura dead, who could prove otherwise?'

Simon nodded miserably. 'The case against Vivienne Fancourt is going to be almost impossible to prove. Darryl Beer's still saying he did it, and there's the DNA evidence. We can't prove Vivienne Fancourt framed him. It's all circumstantial.'

'Alice was terrified of Vivienne knowing she knew. She said Vivienne'd kill her. Otherwise I think she'd have risked going to the police. But she didn't dare, in case Vivienne was questioned and someone revealed where this suspicion had come from.'

'Where's Alice?' Simon said suddenly. 'She's somewhere in this house, right? Persuade her to come and talk to me. I won't let Vivienne Fancourt touch her.'

Briony looked away. 'What about Florence?' she said. 'Alice said you didn't believe her, that you refused to look for Florence. Vivienne's obviously behind all that, you must realise that now.'

'Where did Vivienne get the other baby from?'

'I don't know! Honestly. Neither does Alice.' They stared at one another in silence. Then Briony sighed and said, 'Look, please just find Florence, okay? This is all a bit too weird for me. Alice and I had planned everything. We knew there wasn't a snowball's chance in hell of Vivienne being locked up for Laura's murder, so Alice and Florence were going to escape. I was going to hide them for a while, until they found somewhere more secure. I'm not a bad actor – as you know. I could have convinced David, Vivienne, anyone that I had no idea where they were. And then, middle of last week, I get a frantic phone call from Alice saying Florence is missing, that someone's swapped her with another baby! I feel as if I'm living in some kind of surreal parallel universe. What's going on?'

'But you still helped them escape, didn't you? Alice and the baby?'

'Any baby – any adult, for that matter – is better off out of that house of horrors.' Briony shuddered. 'Answer my question. You seem to know everything. Do you know where Florence is?'

Simon considered it. Did he? Just because he was often right didn't mean he was incapable of being wrong. *You're hardly the most objective judge, are you?* 'I think so.'

'Is she safe?'

'If I'm right, then yes. She's safe.'

A loud series of clanking noises came from down the hall. It sounded as if someone was playing dominoes with sheets of metal. Then there was a whooshing sound that stopped as suddenly as it had started. 'Fuck!' said Briony. 'Sorry. Sounds like my boiler's exploded.'

A faint mewing began, growing steadily louder until it was a plaintive wail. At first Simon took it to be a cat. But not for long, not once he saw the trapped look on Briony Morris's face.

He stood up and walked in the direction that the crying was coming from, ignoring Briony's shouts for him to wait.

He pushed open the white wooden door at the end of the hall and found himself in the kitchen. In front of him was the malfunctioning boiler. In front of him, also, was a Moses basket with a baby in it. The baby from The Elms. She stopped crying when she saw him looking down at her. Simon had never held or spoken to a baby, so he turned away. There was a note on the kitchen table. It was short, but it told him enough.

Briony ran into the room after him. 'Well,' she said. 'Here we all are, then. Fuck!'

Simon pulled his mobile out of his pocket and phoned Charlie. 'I've found them,' he said, as soon as she answered. 'The baby's right here in front of me. Send some uniforms to collect her. And then meet me at Waterfront as soon as you can. Sooner.'

# 41

## *Friday October 10, 2003*

A numb calm descends on me as I enter the ladies' changing room. The swimming pool is closed today because one of the boilers has broken and the water is too cold. In here it is also colder than usual, and quieter because the televisions are off. So are the lights, apart from the dim, square emergency lights in the corners.

I hold the key to locker 131 in my hand. Ross, the man with the South African accent who showed me round a fortnight ago, gave it to me. He remembered me, from my first visit, remembered I was Vivienne's daughter-in-law. He believed my lie about being sent by her. I noticed he was wearing a manager's badge. Last time I saw him he was a membership adviser. At some point during my two weeks of torture, Ross has been promoted. It strikes me that we are more separate from our fellow human beings than we like to think. We all must walk past people every day whose outer skins hide raw, churning agonies that nobody could imagine.

I am nervous, excited, almost giggly, knowing how close I am to finding something, finally, that I can use to prove what I have known for some time. But as I cross the room, my euphoria dissolves and I have a sense of my brain drifting out of and above my physical self. I feel detached as I open Vivienne's locker, as if someone is pulling unseen strings to make me move. Seconds later, I find myself staring at a big white holdall, so bulky it barely fits the space.

I pull it out, throw it down on one of the wooden benches and unzip it. A strong citrusy smell emerges, probably washing powder, and a faint trace of Vivienne's favourite perfume, Madame Rochas. One by one, I remove from the bag a pair of trousers, a shirt, a pair of tights. Underwear, brilliant white. Beneath these I find a dry swimming costume and a make-up bag. Slowly, disappointment seeps into my mind, starting at the edges of my consciousness and moving inward. I cannot accept that I might be wrong. I turn the bag upside down and shake it out, more vigorously than I need to. I shake and shake, panting, beginning to panic. Nothing falls out.

I hear a groan and realise it has come from my own mouth. My movements are out of control. I am crying. I hurl the eviscerated bag down on to the bench and collapse in a defeated heap on top of it. I feel a jab of sharp pain in my upper thigh, as if I have sat on something with a hard corner. And yet Vivienne's holdall is empty. It is not possible that I missed anything.

I stand up and examine the bag again, less hysterically this time. I notice, as I turn it over in my hands, that there is a large pocket along one side. Beneath the zip, there is a small, rectangular bulge. My heart begins to race. I cannot bear this for much longer. For the past two weeks, my spirit has been killed and brought back to life, killed and brought back to life. I have been jolted back and forth between hope and despair so often that it is hard to cling to any sense of reality.

With fingers that feel floppy and useless, I unzip the side pocket of the holdall and pull out a small, fawn-coloured handbag, the strap of which has been cut away. There is a

Gucci logo on the side of the bag. It's Laura's; I recognise it from her visit to my Ealing office. It is strange to see it in this context, years after Laura's death, and stranger still to realise that I am shocked. Every time I prove to myself what I know, I can hardly believe it. Some small naïve part of me still thinks, 'Surely not'.

I unzip the bag and pull out a plastic wallet full of photos of Felix as a baby, then a beige lipstick called 'crème caramel' and a small red leather purse. A set of keys with a 'Silsford Balti House' key-ring. The small accessories of a life cut cruelly short. A wave of pain hits me and I have to sit down.

'Hello, Alice,' says a voice behind me.

I spring to my feet, adrenaline piping through my body. Vivienne. 'Get away from me!' I shout. Mortal fear. I've heard the expression often, but I have never realised what it means. It is what I am feeling now. It's worse than any other kind of fear. It is the paralysing terror that grips you in the seconds before you are killed. I want to disintegrate, give up, lie down on the floor and allow it to happen, because then at least the terror would stop.

It is only the thought of Florence that pushes me back, back, towards the blue door at the far end of the changing room as Vivienne advances on me, smiling. I am holding Laura's bag in my right hand, gripping it tight. Vivienne is holding nothing. I wonder where she is hiding whatever it is that she intends to use to kill me.

'Where is my granddaughter? Where is Florence?' she asks.

'I don't know!'

'Who's the other baby? Who is Little Face? You were the one that swapped them, weren't you? You wanted to keep Florence away from me. Just as Laura kept Felix away from me.'

'You killed Laura!'

'Where's Florence, Alice?'

'I don't know. Ask David, he knows.'

Vivienne shakes her head. She holds out a hand towards me. 'Let's go home,' she says. 'We'll ask him together.' I stagger backwards until I meet resistance. I have reached the door to the pool area. As quickly as I can, I push it open with my back. Vivienne's eyes widen with shock and anger as she works out what I intend to do, only seconds after I've worked it out myself. She isn't quick enough. Once I'm on the other side, I slam the door shut behind me and lean against it, praying that this is the only way to get from the ladies' changing room to the pool.

I hear Vivienne's palms, the same ones she takes to the beauty salon along the corridor once a week to have expensive creams rubbed into them, slap against the wood of the door. 'Let me in, Alice. We need to talk. I'm not going to hurt you.' I don't answer. It would be a waste of energy. I need to use all my strength to keep the door between us closed. I feel pressure on the other side, and picture Vivienne pushing, using all her weight to shift me. Vivienne is lighter than me, but more powerful, thanks to the weights and machines on the floor above our heads. Her body has been put through hours of training, like the body of a soldier. The door inches open, bangs shut – tiny movements back and forth.

All of a sudden there is no resistance. I am pushing against nothing. Vivienne has stopped. I hear her sigh. 'If you won't let me through, I'll just have to talk to you like this. And I'd rather we were face to face.'

'No!'

'Very well. Alice, I'm not the devil incarnate that you seem to think I am. What choice did I have? Laura wouldn't let me see my own grandson. Do you honestly believe I'd have harmed Felix? I adore that boy. Have I harmed him since she died, since he's lived in my house? No. I dote on him. He has everything he could possibly want, and more love than any other child in the world. You know that, Alice.'

I try not to hear her words, the reasoning of the dangerously, psychotically unreasonable. Her justification is horrific to listen to, like poison dripping into my ear. I press my body hard against the door. Vivienne could make a sudden lunge at any time. 'Does David know you killed Laura?'

'Of course not. I didn't want you to know either. I've always tried to protect you and David from unpleasantness, you know that. And believe me, it was deeply unpleasant. Even that is an understatement. You've never stabbed another human being, so you can't possibly know how horrible it is.'

'You framed an innocent man!'

A contemptuous snort. 'You wouldn't say that if you'd met him. I'd hardly call him innocent. *You're* an innocent, Alice. You have no idea what people are capable of.' She is pushing again. All my muscles ache with the effort of leaning. Opposite me is another blue door identical to this one. I could try to run through the men's changing rooms and up to reception, but Vivienne would run faster. She would catch me. 'The sensation of stabbing someone,' she says, her tone wistful. 'I wish I could forget what it felt like. You imagine it's going to be easy, like slicing a chicken breast, but it isn't. You can feel the texture of everything you're cutting through – the bone, the skin, the muscle. Layers of resistance. And then the softness, once you get through all that. The pulp.'

'Shut up!'

'In retrospect, I think a gun might have been preferable, but where on earth was a person like me going to get a gun? I don't exactly mix in those circles, do I? And I don't know how to aim. No, a knife was the only option.'

'You hid it in the crèche. Felix played there. How could you do that?' Sweat pours off me. I can feel rivulets of make-up running down my face.

'He knew nothing about it!' Vivienne sounds indignant. 'It didn't affect him. A person in my position can't afford to be sentimental.'

'You're a monster.'

She sighs. 'Alice, you of all people should know how pointless it is to be judgemental about these things. You have no idea how much pain that woman put me through. She paid for it, that's all. I didn't enjoy killing her. It was simply something that had to be done. And I'm the one who's suffered since. Not her. Me! Wondering what I did wrong, why she disliked me so much. Now there can be no satisfactory resolution. Do you think I'm *happy* about that?'

I move my feet slightly so that I am at a better angle. I close my eyes and try to visualise the straight line of my back and the straight line of the door, pressed together so tightly that not even a grain of sand could fit in between.

'Laura didn't die immediately,' says Vivienne. Her voice sounds as if it is coming from much further away. I picture her sitting on one of the wooden benches. 'She begged me not to let her die, to take her to the hospital.'

'Stop it! I don't want to know!'

'It's a bit late for that, dear. I tried to protect you from the truth, and you wouldn't let me. You can't hide from it now.'

'You're sick!'

'I told her I couldn't, of course. She promised she'd let me see Felix as often as I wanted to. She even offered to give him to me altogether. Anything, she said, if I didn't let her die.' A pause. 'Don't think I wasn't tempted. No-one likes to watch another human being bleed to death. But I knew she couldn't be trusted, you see. And she was a selfish woman. In her final moments, she didn't call out Felix's name, not once. All she said was "Please don't let me die, please don't let me die", over and over. It was always me, me, me with Laura.'

I am shaking, nauseous. I gag, and bile fills my throat. I cover my ears with my hands. I have to find a way to stop her, before she puts any more images in my head that, if I live through this, will make me frightened to be alone with my thoughts.

I become aware that I have lost sensation in one of my feet from pushing it against the floor too hard. I need to adjust my position. As I shift my body slightly, pressing my hands against my ears so hard that both sides of my jaw ache, I feel something slam into me. I cry out as I am thrown to the floor.

When I look up, Vivienne is standing over me. She must have launched herself at the door from a distance. She has always had a talent for being able to guess the precise moment at which you are likely to weaken. She knew I wouldn't be able to endure her gloating commentary on Laura's death.

I scramble to my feet and run, oblivious to where I am going. Too late, I realise I am heading for the pool. If I'd gone in the opposite direction, I might have had a chance of making it through the men's changing rooms and up the stairs before Vivienne. 'Give me Laura's bag, Alice,' she says. 'Give it to me, pretend you never saw it, and we'll say no more about this whole business.'

She marches towards me, holding out her left hand. I cannot back away because the pool is right behind me, so I dart to one side. Vivienne grabs my arm. I try to wrench it free, but her grip is too strong. I am on the ground again. My arms flail above my head. I cannot hold on to the handbag. There is a small splash as it drops into the pool. I think of the photos of Felix, probably Laura's favourites, the ones she wanted with her all the time. They will be ruined now.

I try to roll away from Vivienne so that I can stand up, but she pushes me down on to my front and hauls me forward. I feel a sharp pain in my lower abdomen. My scar. I wince, imagining the wound opening, blood seeping out. The top half of my body dangles over the pool. I grip the stone surround with both hands. 'Please! No!' I sob, but my body has gone limp. I cannot hope or fight any more. I know I will lose. Nobody can win when Vivienne Fancourt is the opponent.

'You're a joke!' I gasp. If I'm going to die, I might as well tell her what I really think of her. 'You must know you'll never get what you want. You're desperate to be surrounded by a loving family, and you never will be!'

'I already am. David and Felix adore me. So will Florence.'

'You'll never know who loves you and who's only pretending to because they're afraid of what you'll do to them if they don't. Or because you throw money and presents at them, and they're too shallow and greedy to resist. Like David. He *hates* you! He told me, he really, really hates you! He wishes you were the one who'd left, not his dad!'

Vivienne growls like an animal, hauls me forward again and pushes my head down into the water. I feel myself plunging down into the bright blue cold. The water envelops my head, shoulders, chest. I feel as if my heart is going to burst out of my body. I try to pull my head up, but Vivienne forces it down again. Water fills my mouth, my lungs. I try to punch and kick, but I am jelly, I am liquid. I want it to be over, know it won't be long.

Now my whole body is in the pool. Vivienne's hand is on my neck, keeping my head submerged. I see lots of colours, then darkness. Everything is slipping away. I will never see Florence again. I will never see my Little Face again – and she *has* been mine, if only fleetingly. Everything is shrinking: thoughts, words, regrets, even love. It's over. It has all evaporated, is all evaporating even now.

No more pressure. I am released, drifting. Is this what it feels like to be dead? I feel lots of hands on my legs and arms. How is Vivienne doing this? I open my eyes and cough. There are blurred figures above me. I am not in the water any more. A searing pain rips through my chest and throat and I cough up water.

Someone is patting me on the back. I look up. It is Simon. I see other things too: Sergeant Zailer, putting handcuffs on Vivienne. A bald man watching, water dripping from the cuffs of his shirt and suit jacket. And Briony. 'Florence,' I whisper.

'It's okay,' says Simon. 'We've got her. She's fine.'

Somewhere in my mind, I feel a letting-go, something tight unravelling. I slump in his arms.

# 42

## *13/10/03, 9.30 am*

Simon stood in front of The Elms and stared at its façade. He couldn't believe this was only the second time he'd been here. The place had been so significant in his thoughts over the past few weeks. But here it was, a symbol of nothing, just stone and wood and paint. Anyone might live here.

Today the house looked neutral and impassive in its whiteness. All the curtains were closed. Heavy, thick folds of material hung at every window. Simon imagined the dozens – he didn't think that was an exaggeration – of dark, mainly empty rooms that he couldn't see. Outside there was bright sunshine. The one remaining inhabitant of The Elms had chosen to refuse admission to the brightness of the day.

Simon had volunteered to talk to David Fancourt. He'd said he thought Fancourt might find it easier to deal with a man. Charlie had agreed, after some persuasion. If she was aware of Simon's ulterior motive, she gave no indication of it. The truth was, he wanted – more than wanted – to go back to The Elms one more time before he spoke to Alice. He needed to see the house she'd come to regard as her prison, to feel that grand, suffocating stillness that he'd had only an inkling of on his first visit. Maybe then he'd understand why Alice had done what she'd done. Maybe then he wouldn't be quite so angry with her.

It had been such a shock, seeing her alive. And her

appearance . . . she looked as if she had deliberately dressed up as Charlie. Simon had been so repulsed both by the idea and the reality of this that he had been unable to move at first. Only when he heard Charlie yell did he rouse himself to drag Vivienne off Alice, and he only managed it with The Snowman's help. He could easily have been too late.

Simon knew he ought to be relieved that Alice was alive, but all he felt was a biting fear. He had imagined, in her absence, that he wanted some sort of relationship with her. The old Alice, the one who looked nothing like his sergeant. But perhaps that person, the one he thought he had seen that day at the top of the stairs, no longer existed. Maybe she never had. And even if Simon could somehow find her, he knew his insecurities and hang-ups would ruin everything.

That and what he now knew about her. There was only one way in which you could know a person, Simon decided. Observe his or her actions, and make inferences accordingly. Instead of focusing on the sort of person he believed Alice was and trying to predict how she would behave, he should have worked backwards from the facts. What must she have done? Therefore what sort of person is she?

Perhaps it would be better never to get close to anyone. Other people intruded too far into one's psyche. They asked too many difficult questions. *Simon, are you a virgin?*

He was aware of feeling angry, but it wasn't the boiling rage he was used to. This was a cold, stodgy disillusionment that had settled like a lump of lead in his stomach. For once, he didn't want to hit and punch and spit until he got it out of his system. He didn't want to rush into action of any kind. This new feeling had to be hidden, nurtured. It was proud, and complicated, and wouldn't be hurried. It required dwelling on. Simon didn't know if it was Alice or

Charlie or both who had made him feel like this. All he knew was that he wanted to be left alone with his thoughts for the time being.

David Fancourt opened the door, just as Simon was about to press the bell for the third time. 'You,' he said. He was wearing maroon paisley pyjamas and a brown towelling robe. Stubble darkened his face, and his eyes were red and watery.

'Is now a good time?'

Fancourt laughed bitterly. 'I don't think there's much point waiting for one of those. You might as well come in now.' Simon followed him through to the kitchen and sat down. This was the chair I sat in last time, he thought, the same chair. Fancourt sat across from him.

The inside of the house was very different now. Dirty plates and cups littered every surface. Rubbish had spilled out of the overflowing bin on to the floor. In the hall Simon had spotted a scuffed pile of newspapers that looked as if they had been kicked around by someone in muddy boots. 'You don't seem to be coping very well on your own,' he said. He felt sorry for the man. Fancourt couldn't handle the knowledge that his mother was a murderer. When Charlie had told him, he'd not said a word, apparently. He'd just stared at her. 'You shouldn't be alone at a time like this. Wouldn't you rather be with your son?'

Fancourt scowled. 'Felix is better off without me,' he said.

'Why? I don't understand.'

'It's better that way.'

Simon lowered his head, trying to make eye contact. 'Mr Fancourt, you've done nothing wrong. You shouldn't feel guilty for something your mother did.'

'I should have known. The night Laura was killed, I should have known that story was nonsense.'

'What story?'

'About Laura asking Mum to have Felix overnight so that she could go to a club. She'd never have done that. She couldn't stand Mum. I always thought it was a bit strange, but . . . I was too stupid to work out the truth.'

'You weren't stupid. No son would suspect his mother of murder. In your shoes, I wouldn't have done.'

'I'm sure you would. *Simon*.' Fancourt flashed an exaggerated mock-smile at him.

'About Felix coming home . . . maybe you'll feel differently in a few days.'

'I won't.'

Simon sighed. Now was perhaps not the best time to assail the poor man with new information, but he needed to know. The test results were back. There was no excuse for not telling him. And, depressed and apathetic as Fancourt seemed, there was no indication that he was delusional or in any way unstable. Anyone would be depressed in his situation. Simon thought his reaction was entirely normal. Maybe he was even right about leaving Felix with Maggie and Roger Cryer. It was better for the boy to be in a stable family environment while his father recuperated.

Simon felt guilty for having thought so badly of Fancourt, whose only crime, as far as he could see, was abrasiveness, irritability under pressure. And for that, and because of his own jealousy, Simon had hated him, slandered him. He owed it to him now to tell him the truth. If anything would jolt Fancourt out of his torpor, this news would.

'We've found your daughter,' Simon said gently. 'We've found Florence.'

Fancourt looked at him, finally. The expression on his face was unmistakable: boredom. 'I don't want her here either. Give her to Alice.'

'But . . .'

'Alice is a good mother. I'm not a good anything. I won't change my mind.'

'I feel as if I owe you an apology, Mr Fancourt.'

'I've got what I'm owed. What goes around comes around, as they say.'

Simon couldn't understand the man. Wasn't he going to fight for his wife and daughter, for the chance to be happy? Whether Fancourt was interested or not, Simon had to say what he'd come to say. He decided to proceed with his planned speech. 'We found Alice and the baby in the home of Briony Morris, Alice's friend from work. After the . . . business at the health club, we arranged for tests to be done on both of them.'

No reaction from Fancourt.

'There was a match,' Simon continued. 'The baby Alice took from here on Friday 3 October was her daughter.' He sighed, shaking his head. He wished he could feel even a fraction of Fancourt's indifference, assuming it was genuine. 'There was only ever one baby, Mr Fancourt. Mr Fancourt? David? Do you understand what I'm saying? There has only ever been one baby. There has only ever been Florence.'

David Fancourt yawned. 'You don't need to tell me that,' he said. 'I've known it all along.'

# 43

## *Tuesday October 14, 2003*

Simon sits across the room from me in Briony's long, narrow lounge. Briony sits beside him on the sofa. I'm glad she's here. The redecoration process is still far from complete, so the furniture is all covered in white sheets. I feel as if our surroundings are a stage set, not a real place.

And the combination of the three of us is odd, jarring. Though I am grateful for Briony's presence – and I sense Simon is too, because this exchange might otherwise be too awkward – there is a connection between me and Simon, a connection of understanding, from which Briony is excluded. Her company will force us both to play roles for a little while longer.

I can see that he knows. When he arrived, the three of us moved hesitantly, suspiciously, around the room like nervous lions who could not see their prey clearly enough to pounce on it. Briony didn't ask Simon to sit down; she forgot her manners in her eagerness to discover Florence's whereabouts. It was Simon who suggested sitting down. I was glad he did. He had news, he said. I needed to be still before he spoke. No amount of preparation for a moment like this can ever be adequate. But then, there aren't many moments like this in the average lifetime. For most people, there are none.

Simon waited until I had settled myself in a chair. Then he told us. There was – is – only one baby. The baby I took from The Elms on Friday 3 October is my daughter. Little Face is Florence. He expressed himself in all these different ways, one after the other, as if he were making three separate points. Briony might have wondered why he was repeating himself, but I knew what he was trying to say: that there is no way of looking at this situation, no way of phrasing it, that allows for the existence of an alternative perspective. For my benefit and Briony's, Simon was determined to round up all the ambiguity at the margins and drag it out into the open, where it could be illuminated by the cold spotlight of his factual approach.

And now we're all sitting here in silence, as if someone has cut out our tongues. It won't last for ever. Someone will break the silence. Not me. Maybe that's part of Briony's role: to speak when Simon and I can't.

'What are you saying?' she asks eventually. 'The baby upstairs is Florence? Little Face is Florence?'

They let her come back to us, straight after the DNA test. I was still recovering in hospital from Vivienne's attack, and they brought Little Face back here, to Briony. I was amazed. I'd assumed they would take her straight to David. 'No.' I shake my head. 'That's not true.'

'Yes,' says Simon with equal force. 'The DNA test proved it beyond doubt.'

'A DNA test proved beyond doubt that Darryl Beer murdered Laura. And now we know he didn't.'

'I'm not wasting my time answering that. You know the difference.'

'It must be a mistake,' I say. 'I'd know. She's my daughter. I'd know.' I slump in my chair. My lower lip is trembling. I try to still it by clamping it in place with my teeth. I must look like a truly mad person. There would be a certain amount of relief in being truly mad. No-one could hold you accountable for anything.

Briony has crossed the room and is leaning over me. 'Alice, are you okay? Don't worry, all right? We'll sort out this . . . misunderstanding. Of *course* those tests can be wrong. And the police – no offence . . .' – she glanced at Simon – '. . . but they've got pretty much *everything* wrong so far . . .'

'I don't know which police you're talking about, but it's not me,' says Simon, with a voice like stone. 'Me, I only got one thing wrong. Pretty seriously wrong, as it turns out.'

I do not like the sound of that – his voice, his words. I can imagine him being unforgiving. Because he tried so hard, in his own hesitant way, to save me. Haven't I learned from living with David that sadism can be the flip side of chivalry, when the object of one's attention slides off her pedestal somehow?

'Little Face is my daughter. I swear she is,' I whisper. I need water. My throat is so dry that soon it will be sore.

'That's what *he's* saying,' Briony murmurs, her hand on my shoulder.

'No, I mean Florence. *Florence* is my daughter.'

'I need to talk to Alice on her own,' says Simon.

'I need a glass of water,' I say, but nobody hears me.

'I'm not sure now's . . .' Briony starts to protest. She doesn't want Simon to put any pressure on me. She's afraid my mind won't be able to take it.

'Now,' he insists.

'It's okay,' I say. 'I'm all right. Honestly, Briony. I'll be fine. You go upstairs and check on the baby.'

She looks unconvinced but she leaves the room. Slowly. She is a good friend.

Once she's gone, I look at Simon. He stares back at me

with blank eyes. His fierce determination seems to have left the room with Briony. A few moments ago I was slightly afraid of his anger. Now I feel as if we will never reach one another, either in rage or in understanding. I am as cut off from him as if there were a glass screen between us. It's funny: when Briony was here, I imagined that she was the only thing standing in the way. Obviously not.

'Good performance,' says Simon. 'Excellent, in fact.'

'What? What do you mean?'

'How are you feeling? After . . . you know. Actually . . . that's none of my business. We should talk about Laura Cryer. I need a statement from you.'

'Simon, what do you mean? What performance?'

He makes a point of not hearing me. I can't say I blame him. I should try to talk to him properly, as I've imagined doing many times. But in my fantasies it has never been like this, with Simon so stony and remote. I am hurt. I suppose this is a good sign. After everything I have been through, I can still feel normal emotions. My heart has not shut down completely.

'You knew Vivienne had killed Laura. Let's start there,' Simon says dispassionately, writing in his notebook. 'When did you know?'

He isn't ready to talk about Little Face. I'm not sure I am either.

'The business with the school: when did you think of that?'

'When I was pregnant. I didn't exactly know, not at first. I had a sense of it. I felt it. Haven't you ever felt the presence of danger?'

But Simon is determined to tell the story his way. 'You were happy to be under Vivienne's wing until you got pregnant. Then her attitude to you changed.' He looks up, acknowledging for the first time that we are partners in this dialogue. 'Didn't it?' he says.

Something inside me wilts. His manner is so matter-of-fact. It suggests that whatever I might have suffered is pretty much irrelevant. Yes, Vivienne's behaviour towards me changed. Suddenly she was no longer my fierce, benevolent protector. I had something she wanted more, far more, than she had ever wanted me. I was just the carrier. She started to monitor what I ate. She stopped me going out. I wasn't allowed in pubs, or to drink a glass of wine with a meal.

'I saw that she was determined to control every aspect of Florence's life. I guessed that it must have been the same for Laura. Until then, I'd always believed David, that Laura was an unreasonable dictator who wouldn't let anyone near Felix.' I shake my head. 'I was stupid and naïve. Vivienne wanted to own Felix, and Laura wouldn't stand for it. Once I'd worked that out, I couldn't believe that Laura dying had nothing to do with it. And my pregnancy . . . When you're pregnant, all your perceptions are sharper, more extreme. Sometimes irrational. At first I wondered if perhaps I was magnifying the feeling I had that Florence and I were in danger, but . . . my instinct, it was so strong. It wouldn't go away.'

Simon frowns. I get the impression that subtleties make him impatient, unless they are his own.

'Vivienne made a mistake,' I tell him. 'When she put Florence's name down for Stanley Sidgwick, when I was five months pregnant. She never should have told me about the long waiting list. She must have thought I was too stupid to wonder about Felix. Not that she'd ever have imagined I'd have turned against her. I was her devoted disciple.'

'Vivienne's proud of what she did,' says Simon. 'She's trying to turn her guilt to her advantage. She seems determined to use her situation as some sort of platform, championing grandparents' rights.'

'She's not sane. Isn't she, technically, a psychopath?' A woman like Vivienne Fancourt is beyond my psychological training and experience. That Florence and I inhabit the world alongside her is a truth I find difficult to absorb.

'She'll probably get lots of media attention.'

He is trying to get at me. When he talks about Vivienne's hypothetical future publicity, he sounds almost boastful. I want to ask him if he is certain that Vivienne will stay in prison until she dies, but I am afraid he would use such an enquiry as another opportunity to hurt me. 'You're annoyed with me. For wasting police time.'

'Annoyed?' He laughs without a trace of warmth. 'No. I'm *annoyed* when I get stuck in a traffic jam. I'm annoyed when I spill coffee on a clean shirt.'

'How could I have told you, Simon? I couldn't risk it. What if you'd alerted her to the fact that I was suspicious? I'd have ended up like Laura.' I shiver, remembering Waterfront, the water sealing shut above my head, pressing down on me.

I was desperate to tell Simon, from the second I met him. By then I'd given up on the idea that I would ever be able to tell my own husband. How I wished I could talk honestly to David, after Briony had phoned the school. But he would never have listened. In his eyes, Vivienne could do no wrong. He thought she was supportive while I was pregnant. He kept saying how grateful we both should be, and all the time I was feeling more and more used, more and more incarcerated.

Poor David. I know how shattered he must be. I feel

sorry for the person he might have been, had things turned out differently, for the potential he once had, the six-year-old boy abandoned by his father, who had to love his mother, whoever she was, because she was the only parent he had. David needed to believe in his version of Vivienne, and I can't really blame him for that.

I must try not to think about him. I want to have a boiling hot bath, to wash his taint off me, but I know that the damage he has done cannot be so easily erased. I don't even care that he's ruined any faith I had in the idea of permanent love between a husband and a wife. I have no desire to marry again. The tragedy is that David has destroyed my faith in myself. It turns out that I was stupid to love him, stupid to marry him. In the past week, I have had my nose rubbed in that stupidity so often that part of me believes I deserved what I got.

My patients do this all the time, blame themselves for the suffering inflicted upon them by others. I tell them it isn't their fault, that no-one asks or deserves to be a victim. Sometimes I am irked when I see no sign of their self-confidence springing back to life as a result of my wise, encouraging words. Now I know that wisdom and insight only go so far. They can help you to understand why you have contempt for yourself, but they cannot take that contempt away. I don't know if anything can.

'So. Because you were scared of coming to us, you abducted your own daughter,' says Simon woodenly. 'You knew that if you and Florence went missing, the police would look carefully at your close family, discover that there was already a connection to a serious crime and investigate further. Which we did.'

'I took Little Face and ran away,' I say carefully. 'Some-one else abducted my daughter.'

He ignores me. I don't know why I am still bothering, at this stage. Is it habit? Fear of his ridicule?

'You took Florence and ran away, knowing we'd look into Laura's murder again. Correct?'

'No! I took Little Face and ran away, so that then, by anybody's definition, even your sergeant's, Florence would be recognised as missing. I wanted you to look for *Florence*.'

'That's shit and you know it. You probably heard me saying that to Briony, when you were hiding in the kitchen. Now you're rehashing it, thinking I'll be stupid enough to believe it because it was my theory.'

He is far from stupid. He's cleverer than I realised.

'Trouble is, it never *was* my theory. I'd worked out the truth by then, all of it. I just wanted to make Briony think, about why you might have run off with a baby who supposedly wasn't yours. Don't you feel guilty for lying to her, treating her like an idiot? After everything she's done for you?'

Tears well in my eyes. Briony, unlike Simon, understands that I have to do whatever I feel it takes to protect my daughter.

'You wanted us to know Vivienne had killed Laura,' he continues compassionlessly. 'You left that brochure, with the Post-it note, hoping we'd pick up on it. What was the original plan? You and Florence run away to Briony's and we look into your disappearance, get suspicious about Laura's death, start to suspect Vivienne? Then we find the brochure . . . If we put Vivienne away for Laura's murder, you and Florence would be safe, wouldn't you? How were we supposed to prove it, though? Did you think about that?'

I shrug helplessly. 'You're the police. You were more likely to find a way of proving it than I was.'

'Smart move, leaving that note on the school brochure. You're pretty good at indirect communication, aren't you? At manipulating people. You worked out that we'd only get the message we were supposed to get from that Post-it note if we *already* suspected Vivienne. Otherwise we'd have assumed F stood for Florence and seen it as irrelevant – just a harmless note to yourself, about the practicalities of getting your daughter into the school. We'd never have known you suspected Vivienne unless *we* suspected her, unless we were beginning to realise how dangerous she was – and if we realised that, we'd know not to let her get a whiff of your suspicions and make you her next target.'

I am thrown by his accuracy. It is as if he has been living inside my head. And yet he still resents me. 'I had to be so careful,' I say. 'I hoped that you'd speak to Darryl Beer again and he'd tell you he didn't do it. Then, since David and I were in London on the night Laura died, you'd have to think of Vivienne. So I made sure to be disparaging about Stanley Sidgwick in front of you whenever I could. I hoped that, once I'd disappeared and you'd found the brochure, you'd wonder why I was so keen to put Florence's name down for a school I hated.'

'Well, I did think that. Like a trained fucking seal, I thought everything you wanted me to think . . .'

'Simon, don't . . .'

'. . . until now.'

My heart stops. 'What do you mean?'

'I'm intrigued. Why the change of plan? You and Florence were going to run away to Briony's, then on from Briony's to somewhere more secure – it was all arranged, it's all in Briony's statement. So what changed?'

'Someone took Florence . . .' I begin.

'Lie, tell the truth, it doesn't matter any more. I know

347

what happened. Florence happened, didn't she? Florence was born, and suddenly, unexpectedly, the plan wasn't enough, was it? You needed a deeper cover. You didn't feel protected any more by the idea that in due course you and Florence would run away. What you felt was sheer terror. Vivienne was on her way to the hospital, she was about to meet her granddaughter for the first time. You couldn't stand the thought of it, could you? A murderer, touching your daughter, bonding with her.'

'What are you saying?' I feel raw and exposed, as if my brain and heart have been cut open.

'Vivienne – the killer in your family – was on her way to meet your baby. You wanted to run away *then*, to hide *then*, prevent that meeting from ever taking place, that contamination of your child – the loving attention of a monstrously evil woman.' I begin to cry as he describes my feelings to me. I wish he were less articulate, less precise. 'But you couldn't hide, could you? You couldn't hide Florence. David was there, looking forward to showing her off to his mother. You had to stay put, endure it. So you started to think about other ways to hide. About how to hide from somebody *even when you're right in front of them*.' Simon looks up. 'Feel free to take over the story at any point,' he says.

'I don't know what you're talking about.'

'Yes, you do,' he says quietly. 'You know, I haven't told Charlie . . . Sergeant Zailer that you and Briony knew about Vivienne. I've said nothing about your call to Stanley Sidgwick. I've protected you both from a variety of possible charges. I could lose my job, if anyone ever finds out.'

'Thank you.' I wipe my eyes. I still cannot work out what Simon feels about me. A lot of things, probably, but I would feel more comfortable if I could identify a dominant emotion.

'If you want to pretend you've been suffering from post-natal depression and that's why you went temporarily mad, that's why you failed to recognise your own daughter and wasted a load of police time . . . well, I might even let that pass. I might not tell Sergeant Zailer – or even Briony – the truth. I'll carry on protecting you, if you ask me to.' He sighs heavily. 'But in return, I want the truth. I need to hear you say it. And if that's too much to ask, you can go fuck yourself.'

The walls of Briony's lounge close in on us. Something, right from the start, has been pushing us together, towards this moment. 'What do you want me to say?'

'I want the full story, the truth. Am I right?'

Towards this moment.

'Yes,' I say. 'Everything you've said is true.'

Simon closes his eyes, leans his head back against the chair. 'Tell me,' he says.

'I was scared.' In many ways, this is the only thing that needs to be said. It's certainly the main thing, the factor that dominated all other considerations. 'I realised, once Florence was born, that if Vivienne knew I'd taken her and run away, she'd have looked for us. Even if she'd never found us, I'd have been nervous, always looking over my shoulder. I suppose I sort of knew all this before Florence was born, but at that point it didn't occur to me that there might be anything more I could do to protect us.'

'And then?' Simon prompts. His voice sounds faint, as if he's lost all energy.

'You put it better than I could have. I needed a deeper cover, and I had this . . . this thought. It seemed so crazy, but . . .' I shrug. 'I hoped it might be crazy enough to work. If I could make *Vivienne* believe that the baby in her house was

349

not her granddaughter, even before she disappeared . . .' I falter. I've never put any of this into words before. I feel as if I'm learning a new language, one that can only just describe the primal, instinctive thoughts and feelings I had after Florence was born.

'Vivienne trusted me. I was counting on her believing me. Not only to make things easier.' How can I explain to Simon that, even knowing Vivienne was a murderer, I still needed her support? I was not free of her, emotionally. I don't even know if I am now. 'I hoped she wouldn't just assume I was mad. She's too scared of losing her grandchildren, after the battle over Felix. However impartial she pretended to be while she waited for the DNA test, I knew that part of her believed me. What I was saying had the horrible ring of truth, because it chimed in with all her worst fears. It's human nature. We find it all too easy to believe in our most dreaded nightmares come to life. What I was saying about Florence struck a chord with Vivienne because it mirrored her own anxieties.'

'If Sergeant Zailer had believed you, there would have been a DNA test straight away,' says Simon. 'What would you have done then?'

'I'd have had to move quicker, stall for as long as I could to give myself a chance to escape. I knew Vivienne'd arrange a DNA test, if the police didn't. I knew I'd have to take Florence and go to Briony's before the test. As it turned out, I had nearly a week to prepare. Do you remember our second meeting at Chompers?'

Simon doesn't respond. Of course he remembers it.

'When you arrived, I was on the pay-phone. I'd just phoned Briony. I was in such a state, it was hard to think strategically, but I had to. I even tried to send Briony a friendly but distant e-mail, saying something about getting together soon, to make you think I couldn't possibly be with her. I knew you'd look at David's computer.'

'We didn't find any e-mail.' Simon frowns.

'I was interrupted.'

'When did you tell Briony about Florence's fictional abduction, then? On the phone?'

'I wanted to put that in the e-mail too,' I remember this as I say it. 'No. I told her when she came to pick us up. On the night we . . . left The Elms.'

'Why not tell Briony the truth? You trust her completely, don't you?'

I nod.

'So why?'

'I don't know,' I mutter, staring at my lap. I really don't know. I could have told Briony everything – about my sudden desperate need for a deeper cover. She'd have understood. I could have told her. I chose not to.

'You didn't want her to think you were crazy,' says Simon. 'Oh, you don't mind her thinking you're crazy now – post-natal depression crazy, ordinary crazy, imagining your baby is a stranger. You were happy for us all to think that. And then, no doubt, you'd have made a brave and relatively quick recovery, and suddenly recognised Florence again – a happy reunion, though you'd never really been apart. Was that the idea?'

Again, I nod.

'That sort of delusional madness is easy to own up to, isn't it? Because there's no responsibility attached to it. It's helpless, not deliberate. You've lost your grip on reality and you're just flailing around, hallucinating. No-one could blame you for that, could they? Whereas a carefully-thought-out plan to pretend your daughter isn't your daughter. It may be mad, but it's knowing, it's precise. Some might say it's just plain wrong.'

'I wasn't afraid of blame,' I tell him. 'You've just made me realise what I was scared of, though. I was scared of explaining something that made perfect sense to me, something I *had* to do, that felt so logical and inevitable, so *right* – I was scared of sharing that with someone else, even Briony, and having them tell me I'd lost my mind. Because I *knew*, you see. I knew that however freakish it sounded at first, it was the only thing I could do. I had to do it.'

'I can see the logic in it. Maybe Briony would have too. Crazy enough to work, you said. I can understand that. You wanted Vivienne to think that David was the one who was keeping her grandchild from her, not you. When you and Florence disappeared, she was supposed to think David had disposed of you and the so-called other baby just before the DNA test, so that it couldn't be proved that he'd been lying about Florence's identity.' Simon sounds as if he is reading out a list of charges against me. Perhaps, in his head, there exists such a document.

I wonder if Vivienne could ever have believed her own son to be capable of such ruthlessness, or whether she would always have made excuses for him. 'I didn't only want Vivienne to believe me,' I say. 'I hoped I could convince David, if I seemed sure enough. It was like . . .' I finish the explanation in my head: I was trying to make Florence mine and mine alone by influencing David and Vivienne's thoughts, their most fundamental perceptions, so that when they looked at her they saw not a daughter, not a granddaughter, but a stranger's child. Florence would have been right in front of them, yet at the same time hidden. The incongruity appealed to me. It was how I would protect my daughter, until we managed to escape.

'I didn't really want to tell Briony the whole truth,' I say. 'Somehow it felt . . . too personal. There was only one person I wanted to tell everything to, and that was you, Simon. There was no evidence to support my insistence that Florence wasn't Florence, but you almost believed me, didn't you?'

'I did believe you,' he corrects me.

'You never said so. You never said, unequivocally, "I believe you, Alice". If you had, I'd have told you everything. Laura, everything. I was just waiting for that sign, to let me know I could trust you, that you trusted me no matter what . . .'

'Please.' A look of disgust warps his face. 'That's a bit hard to take, from someone who's done nothing but lie to me from the moment we met.'

'I'm not lying now, am I?'

'I gave you no choice.' He coughs, sits up straight in his chair. 'Missing people, unless they're experienced at eluding the police, are usually found. You and Florence would have been.' I realise that he is trying to put me back in my place, to put a suitable professional distance between us. 'Vivienne would have insisted on her DNA test then, and the game would have been up. And if we hadn't looked into Laura's death again, or if we'd reached the same conclusion we reached originally, you'd have been back at square one.'

'Maybe I could have stayed hidden. The case would have stopped being such a high priority. You'd have had other, more urgent cases. You'd have scaled down your efforts.'

'You were staying at the home of a friend and colleague. We'd have found you.'

'I'd have moved on. Sooner rather than later. But you're probably right. I'm not the sort of person who knows how to disappear and start a new life abroad, like people do in films. I had to try, though. And I know the police give up eventually. They have to, because they're needed elsewhere, on other cases, new missing people. Whereas Vivienne would never have given up, never. *That's* why I lied, about Florence being . . . swapped. I couldn't have lived happily or easily, knowing that Vivienne knew I had her grand-daughter, that she knew exactly what I'd done to her. I'd have spent Florence's whole childhood waiting for my punishment to find me. I know it sounds insane, I know she's not some all-knowing, all-seeing God-like figure, but . . . well, I just couldn't help feeling she'd find a way of getting to me, somehow.'

Simon nods. 'So you tried to make sure she wouldn't care enough to look for you. And there was only one way that was going to happen – if she didn't believe the baby you had with you was Florence. But that part of the plan was shaky as well. Vivienne wanted to find you, all right. She wanted to get her DNA test and her proof.'

I sigh. 'I underestimated her. I didn't take into account how much she would want Little Face to be Florence. I thought that by the time we disappeared, she'd believe me, wholeheartedly. She'd still want the DNA test, just to be certain, but I was pretty sure she'd make up her mind in my favour long before the test. And then, I guessed, she would be almost relieved when the "other" baby disappeared. Vivienne would hate to have a child in her house who she perceived as an impostor. She *did* hate it. And I thought, when she looked for Florence – as I knew she would, she'd never *stop* looking – she'd look for just Florence. She wouldn't look for me and the other baby.'

'Alice, there is no other baby.'

I shake my head. Simon mustn't misunderstand me, not now. 'I also wanted Little Face to be Florence,' I say quietly. 'But only with Vivienne out of the way, only if I could be sure she wouldn't hurt us.'

'You knew she was Florence.'

'Yes, but . . . in my heart, I didn't feel I was lying. Everything I said felt true. Florence was *my* baby, definitely mine. Little Face was quite different. Little Face was the baby who might have been stolen from me at any moment. Or I might have been stolen from her. I didn't know whose she would turn out to be. Do you understand?'

'You disowned your own daughter. You're the best liar I've ever seen in action.'

'Because it didn't feel like a lie! It was agony,' I say, my eyes filling with tears. 'Do you know what the worst part was, the absolute worst? Destroying all the photographs, the only photographs of Florence.' That awful moment, when I opened the back of the camera, feeling as if what I was letting in was not light but the worst sort of darkness. 'I did it, though. I had to, Simon. It was like I was being driven by this . . . this force, and I had to do everything I did.'

'You lied to me. I trusted you.'

I do not ask: then why did I never feel I had your trust? Why did you never once say, 'I believe you'?

'You have to try to understand what I did,' I tell him.

'What the fuck do you think I've been doing? I think I've done well, all things considered. I think I've done pretty fucking well. Not perfect, though, not by a long shot. There are still some things I can't get my head round.'

'Simon, the details don't matter . . .'

'The details are *all* that matter. Why all that bollocks about Mandy Buckley, from the labour ward? Why ask me to look for David's father?'

'Because he was married to Vivienne, and they split up!

Something made him so desperate to get away that he didn't even keep in touch with his son. Contact with David would have meant contact with Vivienne. I guessed – maybe wrongly – that he was bound to know what she was really like, and maybe he'd even wondered, when he read about Laura's death in the papers . . .'

'So we were supposed to find him so that he could tell us all this?'

'Yes.'

'Right.' Simon seems to deflate. 'I should have known that, I suppose. And Mandy?'

I shrug, embarrassed. 'If I was going to insist someone had swapped my baby for another baby, I had to produce a few possible theories, didn't I? I panicked. Things got a bit . . . cluttered in my mind at that point.'

'You made yourself appear less plausible, coming out with all that shit. It's part of the reason . . .' He stops, colours slightly.

'Part of why you didn't wholly believe me?' I feel vindicated. 'Simon, will you try not to be angry with me? Will you try to understand?'

I am still trying to understand myself. It is going to be difficult, to produce a coherent narrative out of all this. All I know is that for a while there was a baby called Little Face. She had a perfectly round head, blue eyes, milk spots on her nose. Nobody was sure who she belonged to.

Simon stands up. 'I can protect you from some things, but not from everything,' he says. 'Even with the extenuating circumstances taken into account, you abducted David's daughter and wasted a lot of police time. Postnatal depression might be considered a mitigating factor, but . . . I can't guarantee it won't be taken further.' He is hiding behind an official vocabulary. Not Simon Water-house but a representative of the police force.

'What about our friendship?' I ask, wondering even as I say it whether we have one. Perhaps this connection between us will evaporate as soon as our shared business is concluded. But Simon got inside my head in a way that no-one else ever has. It will be hard, I think, to get him out. 'Will our friendship be taken further?'

He doesn't reply. We look at one another. I don't know what he is thinking. I am thinking that the time will never come, for any of us, when the last question is answered. There will always be loose ends, threads dangling from all our lives – the unresolved, the unsatisfactory. Florence has been born into an untidy world, and a time will come when I'll have to explain to her that I won't always be able to give her an explanation, that she won't always be able to find one for herself. But we'll stumble on, she and I, into our messy future. And we'll have each other.

# Acknowledgements

I would like to thank the following people, all of whom helped significantly: Carolyn Mays, Kate Howard, Karen Geary, Peter Straus, Rowan Routh, Lisanne Radice, Nat Jansz, Chris Gribble, Hilary Johnson, Rachel Hoare, Adele Geras, Jenny Geras, Norman Geras, Dan Jones, Kate Jones, Michael Schmidt, Katie Fforde, Morag Joss, Alan Parker, Marcella Edwards, Anne Grey, Wendy Wootton, Lisa Newman, Debbie Copland, Lindsey Robinson, Susan Richardson, Suzie Crookes.

MARGARET MURPHY

NOW YOU SEE ME

'This is crime for the computer age . . . The truly exciting ending is a triumph of inventiveness' *Guardian*

When Megan Ward goes missing, suspicion falls on the stalker seen outside her house. The police would love it to be so simple, but the closer they look the more mysterious Megan herself becomes. They find no photos, no passport, no family or friends from an earlier life. Only the corrupted computer files in Megan's strangely impersonal room.

Meanwhile Patrick Doran, owner of Safe Hands Security, is living his own nightmare. A hacker has breached his computer network, where he thought he had safely buried his past.

Then her landlady is murdered – and the shadowy Megan re-emerges. The woman who doesn't exist becomes very real, very elusive and very dangerous.

'A skilfully plotted story with strongly drawn characters.'
*Sunday Telegraph* on *Darkness Falls*

HODDER &
STOUGHTON

ANDREW TAYLOR

NAKED TO THE HANGMAN

'Crime at its best, perfect for a cold winter night in front of
a roaring fire'                    Joan Smith, *The Sunday Times*

As a young police officer in Palestine during the closing
months of the Mandate – the cradle of Middle Eastern
terrorism – Richard Thornhill saw and did things which
still haunts his dreams and make him fear for his sanity. Is
he himself a killer? Now, when a retired colleague is found
dead in the ruins of Lydmouth Castle, the past comes back
to claim him – and Detective Chief Inspector Thornhill
finds himself under suspicion of another murder.

His wife Edith and his former lover Jill Francis join forces
in an uneasy alliance to try to help him. But there are many
complications – scandalous allegations have been made
about Miss Awre's School of Dancing; the Ruispidge
Charity's annual dance for young people is under threat;
teenagers haunt the newly opened Italian coffee bar and
yearn for fumbled intimacies in the sheltering darkness of
the Rex Cinema; an Oxford don is looking for love; the
Angel of Death wears khaki shorts and drives a Ford van.

And the Spring floods are rising higher than they have in
living memory, drowning a multitude of secrets . . .

**Publishing in October 2006**

**H**

**HODDER &
STOUGHTON**

# PETER ROBINSON

## PIECE OF MY HEART

'The Alan Banks mystery-suspense novels are, simply put, the best series now on the market'        Stephen King

As the organisers clear up after the party, they find an abandoned sleeping bag containing the body of a young woman, brutally murdered. Detective Chief Inspector Chadwick, a hard-headed WWII veteran, is assigned to the case. Chadwick has no time for the youth of the day, disrespectful and caring nothing for the sacrifices of an older generation. But the victim was related to a local band, the up-and-coming Mad Hatters, and Chadwick finds himself drawn unwillingly into the psychedelic Sixties pop scene.

After a difficult summer, DCI Alan Banks is back home in the Yorkshire Dales. When he is called to investigate the murder of a journalist writing an article on the Mad Hatters, he discovers it is not the first time the ageing rock superstars have been brushed by tragedy. And Banks will have to go back a generation to discover exactly what kind of hornets' nest has been stirred up.

'Demonstrates how the crime novel, when done right, can reach parts that other books can't . . . A considerable achievement'        *Guardian*

HODDER &
STOUGHTON